HIGH PIQUE
The Sixth Buxton Spa Mystery

CELIA HARWOOD

NEUF NEZNOIRS LIMITED

Published by Neuf Neznoirs Limited
Unit 20, 91-93 Liverpool Road, Castlefield, Manchester, M3 4JN.
e-mail: gemggirg@gmail.com

ISBN 978-0-9933261-5-8

© 2021 Margaret Fowler

The rights of Margaret Fowler as author of this work have
been asserted by her in accordance with the
Copyright, Designs and Patents Act 1993.

All rights reserved. No part of this publication may be reproduced,
stored in a retrieval system, or transmitted, in any way or form, or by
any means, electronic, mechanical, photocopying, or otherwise,
without the prior permission of the author and publisher.

British Library Cataloguing in Publication Data.
A catalogue record for this book is available from the British Library.

Printed and bound in England by 4edge Ltd. Hockley, Essex
Tel: 01702 200243

For
Tim Brooke-Taylor, OBE
1940-2020

When I grew up in Buxton,
I thought I was living in Enid Blyton.
Now I realize I was living in Agatha Christie

Burbage-on-the Wye

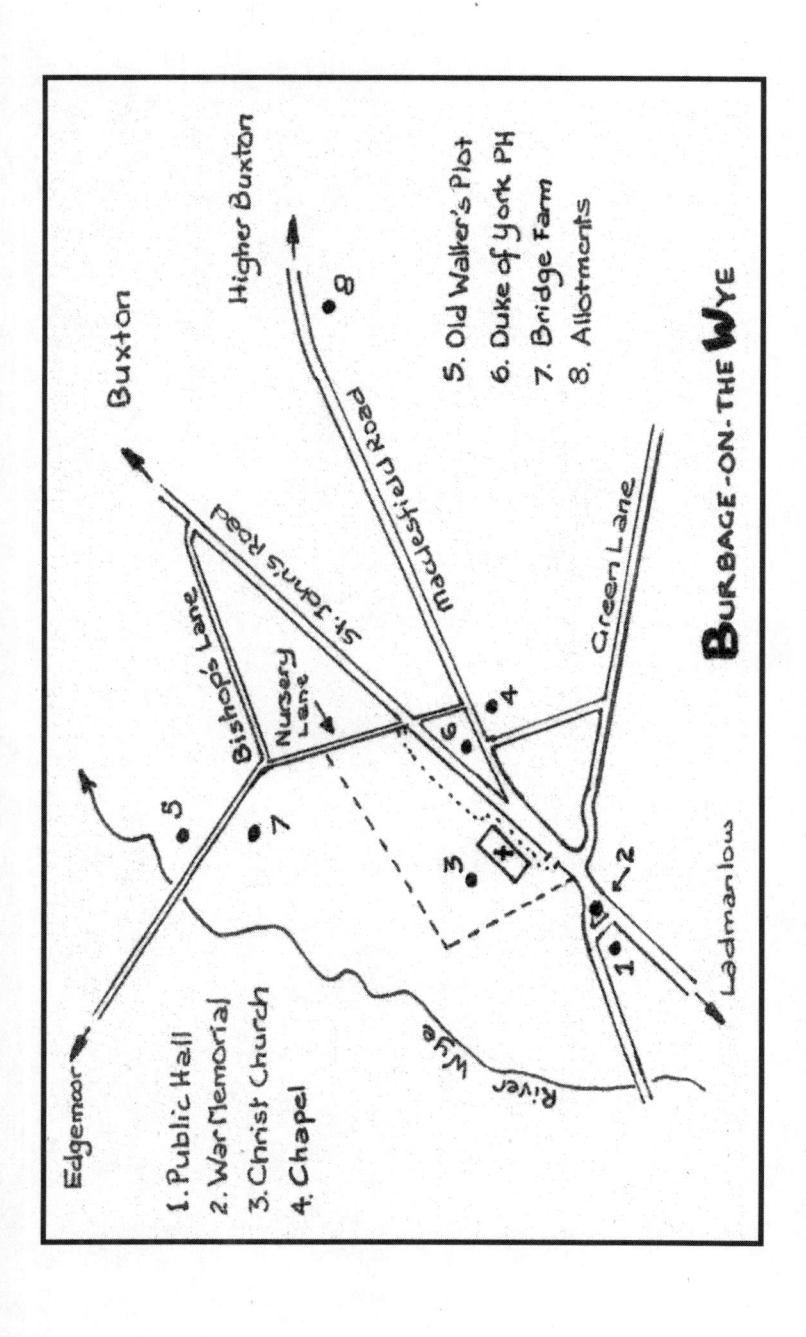

Roads/Places:
- Edgemoor
- Buxton
- Higher Buxton
- Ladmanlow
- Bishop's Lane
- St John's Road
- Nursery Lane
- Macclesfield Road
- Green Lane
- River Wye

Key:
1. Public Hall
2. War Memorial
3. Christ Church
4. Chapel
5. Old Walker's Plot
6. Duke of York PH
7. Bridge Farm
8. Allotments

CHAPTER ONE

At half past twelve on the twenty-first of June, 1924, Eleanor Harriman, a solicitor in her father's firm of Harriman & Talbot, Solicitors, Notaries, and Commissioners for Oaths, was in her office on the first floor of their Hall Bank premises. She was drafting a document and her Boxer dog, Napoleon, was sitting at the bay window supervising the world. His attention was divided between two groups of people: one group, mostly going to or away from the Saturday market on the Market Place, was passing up and down Hall Bank; and the other, mostly visitors, was meandering about on The Slopes opposite. At the sound of footsteps on the stairs leading up from the ground floor, Napoleon turned to look expectantly at the door of Eleanor's office.

James Wildgoose, Mr Harriman's confidential clerk of many years standing, entered and Napoleon moved forward to acknowledge his arrival.

James turned to pat Napoleon and then, putting a sheaf of papers onto Eleanor's desk, said:

'Here are the three letters in the Murchison matter, Miss Eleanor.'

'Ah, yes, thank you,' said Eleanor, glancing at her watch.

Eleanor picked up each letter in turn, quickly scanned the pages, and then handed the papers back to James.

'Thank you, James. My father particularly wanted them to go out in today's post. Would you tell him that I have checked them and ask him to sign them, please.'

'I'll do my best, Miss Eleanor. They'll have to go out

shortly if they're to catch the next post, but Mr Brittain is with Mr Harriman at the moment and I don't know how long he will be engaged.'

'Oh, I see. I didn't think Father had any appointments today.'

'He didn't. Mr Brittain telephoned this morning and asked to see Mr Harriman immediately. He arrived about fifteen minutes ago.'

'Is that Mr Brittain, the farmer, or Mr Brittain, the land agent?' asked Eleanor.

This was crucial information. Mr Brittain, the farmer, was a jovial man with an opinion on every subject which he was willing to share with anyone who would listen. He rarely needed advice from Mr Harriman but when he did, a long appointment was necessary, even for the simplest matter.

'Mr Brittain, the land agent,' said James, smiling.

'Ah, that's all right then,' said Eleanor, returning James' smile. 'Time means money to him so he won't stay long.'

James laughed. 'I shall have the letters signed immediately Mr Brittain leaves.'

'Thank you, James. If Mr Brittain hasn't left in time, perhaps you could have Mr Talbot sign them.'

'Mr Talbot hasn't returned from Court yet,' said James. 'He is a little later than usual.'

'Oh,' said Eleanor, surprised. 'Then, if necessary, I think you had better interrupt my father. I am sure he won't mind.'

'Yes,' agreed James. 'That will be the best plan.'

Eleanor returned to her work and Napoleon resumed his surveillance from the window.

The office was open on Saturdays but only until one o'clock and, at five minutes to one, Mr Harriman came upstairs to see his daughter. After patting Napoleon, he sat down and said:

'I've signed those letters, Eleanor, and James is seeing to them now and then he will close up. I was with Mr Brittain unexpectedly.'

'Yes, James explained what had happened.'

'Mr Brittain has given me instructions regarding a boundary dispute which needs to be resolved as quickly as possible and I wonder if you have capacity to take carriage of the matter and give it your attention straightaway.'

'Yes, of course,' agreed Eleanor.

'Mr Brittain acts for the vendor on the sale of a parcel of land. The parties have agreed a price but the sale is conditional on the boundary of the property being clearly established. Apparently, at some time in the past, it was the subject of a dispute which may or may not have been fully resolved. I believe there is no urgency as far as the prospective purchaser is concerned but Mr Brittain would like the boundary issue resolved as quickly as possible. As Mr Brittain sends us quite a bit of work, I should like to accommodate him and provide an answer as soon as possible, despite his rather unreasonable request for haste.'

'I suppose he is anxious not to lose his commission on a sale,' said Eleanor, laughing. 'Of course, I completely understand his need for haste. I can finish off what I need to do on my other files now and begin straightaway if you like.'

'No, no! Thank you for the offer, Eleanor, but it is not that urgent. First thing on Monday will be quite sufficient. There is no need to forgo your usual round of golf with Philip.'

'Ah no, no golf today. Philip's gone to collect his new motor car, so I have to confess that my offer to work this afternoon was not quite as altruistic as it might have seemed.'

'Ah,' said Mr Harriman, 'the much-anticipated new Bentley.'

Eleanor's friend, Philip Danebridge, was the cousin of her former fiancé, Alistair Danebridge, who had been killed in France. Philip had survived the War but had returned with lungs damaged in a gas attack. He had bought his first

Bentley in 1920 and thoroughly enjoyed driving it. Almost twelve months previously, the Bentley had been severely tested during a chase along rough country roads in pursuit of a killer and, although the motor car was still perfectly serviceable, Philip decided to use the chase as justification for ordering the newest model.

There had been quite a long waiting period because each Bentley motor car was produced individually. After the chassis had been completed by Bentley, the coachwork had to be built to the specifications of the buyer. Philip had engaged Vanden Plas, in Hendon, and there had been decisions to be made as to the choice of colour for the coachwork and the leather interior and the style of various fittings and pieces of equipment. All of the occupants of the Hall Bank office had contributed their opinion regarding these decisions, except Mr Harriman. Mr Harriman was not a motoring enthusiast and he found it all very amusing and teased Philip regularly.

On the previous Saturday and Sunday, the twenty-four hour motor car race held at Le Mans had taken place. The only British motor car which competed was the latest model Bentley, a 3 litre Sport. Philip together with Richard, Eleanor's young nephew, had waited anxiously for the news of the race. The previous year, they had been disappointed when the Bentley, competing for the first time and within sight of success, had suffered a punctured petrol tank and narrowly missed victory. It was a gruelling race, three relatively straight stretches and three very tight corners on a dusty surface of gravel and dirt mixed with tar. This year only twelve out of the forty-one competitors had managed to finish. Although a French motor car had the fastest lap time, completing the 10·7 mile circuit in just over nine minutes, the Bentley had won first place, successfully completing 120 laps and covering the greatest distance. Richard had been promised the first ride in the new Bentley.

'So,' said Mr Harriman, 'it's finally ready then? Richard will be pleased.'

Eleanor said: 'The coachbuilders telephoned earlier this week to say that the motor car was finished, which was quite fortuitous. Philip was going down south anyway because he had arranged to drive his parents to Harwich so that they could take the train ferry to Zeebrugge. They are going on a three month tour of the Continent. Philip decided to combine the two trips and they left early this morning. Vanden Plas offered to deliver the new Bentley, of course, but Philip wanted to collect it himself. He said he knew it would look odd but he couldn't bear the idea of someone else driving it. You know what he's like.'

'Yes, I do,' said Mr Harriman, laughing.

'So, what is this boundary dispute about? Do we have very much information?'

'Not so far,' said Mr Harriman. 'The owner of the land died about four months ago and the land was offered for sale. The executor is an accountant in Derby, a distant cousin of the deceased's mother, and he knows very little about the land, although he was aware that there had been a dispute about the boundary, a long standing one, apparently. He instructed Mr Brittain to sort out the boundary and find a purchaser. The prospective purchaser is not from Buxton and intends to settle here and wants to build a house on the land. Mr Brittain has left a substantial bundle of documents with me and, first thing on Monday morning, James will sort them into date order. Your task may not be very straightforward. I suspect it will require your flair for assembling facts, tracing connections, retrieving missing information, exercising your imagination, filling in gaps, and reaching a conclusion.'

'Hmmm,' said Eleanor, rolling her eyes, 'and he wants the correct answer immediately.'

'Of course,' said Mr Harriman, smiling. 'I am sure you

will enjoy the challenge.'

Before Eleanor could comment further, Mr Harriman's partner, Edwin Talbot, arrived back from Court and was greeted by Napoleon as he came into Eleanor's office.

'Ah, Harriman, there you are,' said Edwin. 'I looked in at your office on the way in and wondered where you were. I'm a bit late because it was Superintendent Johnson's last day in Court today and, at the end of the list, there were speeches from the Bench and the Bar. All the usual flattering things were said, of course, but the expressions of appreciation were genuine and heartfelt nevertheless.'

'Superintendent Johnson hasn't always been easy to deal with and sometimes we have found him to be over-cautious but he's certainly been very conscientious,' said Eleanor.

'Someone reminded me this morning that he's been in Buxton for ten years,' said Edwin.

'That must be right,' said Mr Harriman, nodding, 'because he was here during the War and, if you remember, he was in charge of the Special Constables during the railway strike in 1919.'

'Yes, apparently the Special Constables are giving him a dinner at the Hydro Hotel next week and they've organised the presentation of a retirement gift.'

'Is he retiring? Not being transferred?' asked Mr Harriman. 'I would consider him still a young man.'

'Perhaps he's just retiring from the police force and has something else he wants to do,' said Eleanor.

'I'm not sure what he intends to do,' said Edwin, 'but it's true, he does look quite young. In fact, he doesn't look much older than the new chap, Ferguson, who's replacing him. He was in Court today as well, being introduced.'

'Where is he from?' asked Mr Harriman.

'Matlock,' said Edwin, 'and, apparently, the position of Inspector is being re-instated which means that Buxton police station will revert to its former status and, as well as a replacement Superintendent, we shall have a new Inspector.'

'Two incomers at the same time and one a revived role at that. It sounds like a recipe for confusion and muddle until they sort themselves out and get into a routine,' said Mr Harriman.

'It does rather,' said Edwin.

'Superintendent Johnson must be rather gratified at the thought that to fill his shoes and carry out his role it requires both a new superintendent and an inspector,' said Eleanor.

'On the contrary,' said Edwin, smiling and teasing Eleanor, 'we all know how heavily Superintendent Johnson depended on your services in the past. However, apparently the new Superintendent has made a speciality of detective work. So, Eleanor, it will be safe for you to follow Superintendent Johnson's example and retire.'

'That's excellent news,' said Mr Harriman, laughing. 'Perhaps this office will now be able to stick to routine legal work instead of dealing in red herrings.'

Eleanor glared at them both, pretending to be offended. 'I'm too busy for detection at the moment, anyway. I have a boundary dispute to resolve.'

'And I'm off home,' said Edwin, laughing. 'Helen and I have promised to take the boys on a walk to Deep Dale this afternoon. Oh, and I'll bring in some redcurrants on Monday.' Edwin's house on Spencer Road had a large, productive garden from which he often supplied fruit or vegetables. As he turned to go to his own office and put away his files, he said: 'James has already closed up.'

CHAPTER TWO

The Buxton weather was notoriously changeable and this year it had been disappointingly wet and cool during the first few weeks of the Season, causing some outdoor events to be cancelled. On this Saturday afternoon, things looked a little more promising. The sky had been clear since the early morning and, although there was quite a strong breeze, the air was warm. Visitors to Buxton were occupied in their usual pursuits: promenading up and down Broad Walk and nodding to acquaintance or stopping to chat with friends; strolling in the Pavilion Gardens, where they relaxed in deckchairs and listened to the band, played tennis, croquet, or bowls, or watched others doing so. In their usual numbers, they trooped into Mr Nall's showroom to examine his exquisite pieces of furniture, vases, and souvenirs made from Ashford black marble, inlaid with intricate patterns of coloured stone. In the windows of Mr Bright's shop in the Crescent arcade, they studied items of jewellery and silver trinkets to buy as keepsakes.

They dawdled along the Devonshire Arcade to look in at the shops or to borrow books from the subscription library, or they ventured further afield to the shops and refreshment rooms along Spring Gardens. Some exerted themselves to walk up Temple Lane to view the wonders of Poole's Cavern and its museum, then listened to the band and took tea at the café in the gardens there. Others took tea at their hotels or their favourite tea shops, according to their tastes and budgets, or sampled the renowned pastries at Collinson's café. At the baths, either the newly refurbished Natural Baths or the Hot Baths, they bathed, withstood therapeutic douches, had themselves immersed in peat, or underwent other treatments for the benefit of their health or purely for pleasure. The Well Women at the Pump Room welcomed them as usual and offered them spring water to drink, which was ostensibly their reason for coming to Buxton.

While sipping their spring water, they glanced as usual at the list of visitors published in the latest edition of the *Buxton Advertiser* hoping to see the names of friends or acquaintances from previous years whom they could contact. And if Lady X and her daughters, or the Honourable So and So were staying at the Hydro or the Crescent, there was a name to be dropped in letters or postcards sent to friends at home.

Away from all of this activity, in the seclusion of the affluent residential area known as The Park, Lady Carleton-West, self-appointed doyenne of Buxton society, was sitting at a writing desk in the smaller of the two drawing rooms at her home, Top Trees, the town's largest mansion. Lady Carleton-West had a well-endowed figure, large hands and feet, and had not been blessed with particularly good looks. Nevertheless, under the expert, and staggeringly expensive, guidance of Monsieur Raymond at Maison Christophe, she had contrived a wardrobe of gowns which flattered the curves of her ample figure and defied the current fashion for flatness. She had a commanding presence. Her belief in her own importance and indispensability to the good taste of Buxton society often caused her, unwittingly, to give offence to others, but her self-confidence prevented her from noticing. It would never have occurred to her to question her own motives or suffer from self- doubt.

In front of Lady Carleton-West, on the writing desk, was a copy of that day's edition of the *Buxton Advertiser* and she was engaged in scanning the list of visitors, but only those at the most fashionable hotels. She was reading out the names and making a note of those she recognised and any new names of interest.

'Sir Gerald Hilton-Smythe and family,' said Lady Carleton-West. She made a note of the name on her writing pad. 'Mrs Albright. That's General Horatio Albright's widow, she must be out of mourning.' She made another note and continued scanning the list. 'Mrs Julian Astley-Cove, no, I don't know her . . . although I'm sure I've heard that name . . . I must look it up . . . Major and Mrs Roger Summerson . . . Yes, they were here last Season, quite acceptable.' Lady Carleton-West made a note of the name and the hotel. 'Lady Amelia Anneresley? No, I don't think I know that name . . . I wonder if that is the Northumberland Anneresleys. Oh, but the next name is very interesting. The Honourable Hugo Berkeley-Trent is staying at the Hydro. He's the Earl of Milborough's youngest son. I simply must have him on my guest list. I shall invite him to dinner. You must call on him immediately, Marmaduke. Before someone else notices his arrival. You must . . .'

She turned and looked across at her husband who was slumped in an armchair drawn up, as usual, in front of the fireplace although no fire burned there. As it was now the height of summer, the empty grate was filled with a "tasteful" arrangement of crumpled coloured paper and pine-cones, in front of which was a large vase of flowers. Sir Marmaduke was busy digesting his luncheon and had dozed off. He gave a little snort at the sound of his name but did not stir.

'Marmaduke!' said Lady Carleton-West, loudly and sternly.

Sir Marmaduke woke with a start and looked around him, confused. 'Eh, what!'

'Do pay attention, Marmaduke. Please!'

'Yes, my dear. What is it?' asked Sir Marmaduke, mildly, squinting and trying to focus his eyes on his wife.

'The Honourable Hugo Berkeley-Trent. The Earl of Milborough's youngest son. The Earl was here for the Season the last year before the War.' Lady Carleton-West waved her list impatiently at her husband. 'I simply must have him. There's no time to waste.'

Sir Marmaduke hauled himself up and sat to attention, like a gun dog waiting for the command to retrieve.

'What a piece of luck my having time to browse through the list of visitors this afternoon,' said Lady Carleton-West, 'instead of leaving it until tomorrow as I usually do. I'm certain to be the first to see his name. And how fortunate that he has arrived now and not later in the Season. There will be time to establish a proper acquaintance before we leave for the Highlands.'

Sir Marmaduke was intending to travel to Scotland in August for the opening of the grouse season and Lady Carleton-West was already anticipating being able to mention to her fellow guests at the shooting party the fact of her acquaintance with the Earl's son. She imagined herself saying casually: "Of course, in Buxton, we have a very wide circle of friends and acquaintance. Hugo Berkeley-Trent was our guest at dinner recently. He's the Earl of Milborough's youngest. A charming gentleman."

Lady Carleton-West returned her attention to the task in hand.

'A dinner invitation will be frightfully short notice but that can't be helped. I must have him and I don't know how long he will be in town.' She looked at her watch and then rose majestically from her chair and rang the bell for Ash, the Top Trees butler. Her thoughts were already racing ahead to the gracious welcome she would give to the Earl's youngest son.

'Marmaduke, you must call on him immediately.'

Sir Marmaduke frowned. He was now fully awake and absorbing the details of this command.

'But, my dear,' he began, mildly. 'On whom am I to call?'

The question remained unanswered because at that moment Ash silently opened the door and entered the drawing room.

'Ah, Ash,' said Lady Carleton-West. 'Have the motor car brought around immediately. Sir Marmaduke is going to the Hydro Hotel.'

'Very good, m'lady,' said Ash, solemnly, quite accustomed to receiving orders from the lady of the house, even when they concerned his master. Sir Marmaduke rarely gave orders; he was destined only to obey them.

'But first, bring me the copy of *Burke's Peerage* from the library.'

'Yes, m'lady.'

Ash disappeared and Lady Carleton-West continued to read the list of visitors. Sir Marmaduke slumped back in his chair again and closed his eyes. Ash returned, placed the book on the writing desk, bowed and retreated, closing the door silently behind him.

'Now, whom shall I invite to dinner? I need people of a similar age to the guest of honour,' said Lady Carleton-West.

She thumbed through *Burke's Peerage* to find the correct page. Then she ran her finger down the list of names to find the entry for the Earl of Milborough.

'Ah, here we are. Hugo, born in '89.' Lady Carleton-West scribbled the dates on the sheet of blotting paper on her desk. 'That makes him thirty-five. Now, the Hilton-Smythes. How old is Gerald?'

Lady Carleton-West did not bother with the rest of the entry in *Burke's Peerage* for the Earl of Milborough and instead flicked the pages back to find the entry for Hilton-Smythe. Sir Gerald proved to be young enough and he and his wife were added to the guest list. Lady Carleton-West then summoned up a picture of the younger local people of her acquaintance, naming them in turn, rejecting some, and noting the names of others on the blotting paper. Then, she sat back and looked at the list. She frowned and then sighed. She began talking to the somnolent Sir Marmaduke, without bothering to turn around to look at him:

'Most of the presentable younger people are out of Buxton at present. Mr Harriman's youngest daughter, Cecily, is the right age and respectable enough. Quite charming, in fact. Unfortunately, her elder sister, Eleanor, is quite unsuitable. Far too independent and strong willed to be a comfortable dinner guest. Fortunately, Cecily takes after her mother. She was a lady and very generous with her time and support for our causes. Of course, being a member of the aristocracy herself she was fully aware, as I am, of how important it is to engage in charity work on behalf of those less fortunate. Eleanor Harriman always seems a little grudging with her time. Yes, I shall certainly invite Cecily.' She paused. 'But would it be proper?'

Lady Carleton-West was always very particular about etiquette. She tapped her finger up and down rapidly on the desk as she considered the question.

'Can I invite the younger sister and not the elder sister as well?' She swivelled round in her chair so as to look at Sir Marmaduke: ' What do you think?'

Lady Carleton-West waited for her husband's response but Sir Marmaduke, having no opinion on the matter, merely grunted.

Taking that for support for her plan, Lady Carleton-West continued: 'Yes, I think that will be possible without bending the rules. Although Cecily is a widow, she was a married woman, and a married woman does take precedence over an elder unmarried sister. That is perfectly correct. Miss Eleanor Harriman can have no objection to that.' She nodded, decisively. 'I'm glad that is settled. Besides, too many members of the same family at one table is quite fatal to good conversation.' She paused. 'Although, if I need to make up the numbers, their father would be acceptable.'

If Eleanor Harriman had known of her rejection during this selection process, she would not have considered her omission from the guest list a hardship.

'What are you waiting for, Marmaduke? You heard me tell Ash to have the motor car brought round.'

Sir Marmaduke hauled himself out of his armchair and said, resignedly: 'I shall go and change. What did you say this chap's name is?'

'The Honourable Hugo Berkeley-Trent.' Lady Carleton-West pronounced the name slowly and clearly.

'Confound the fellow!' said Sir Marmaduke, as he turned to leave.

Lady Carleton-West glared at her husband's departing back and returned to compiling the guest list for her dinner party. In her haste to secure her titled dinner guest, Lady Carleton-West had overlooked another name on the list of visitors to Buxton that week, an oversight which was later to cause her both embarrassment and regret.

0 0 0

DIARY Saturday 21st June

Hydro Hotel very well-appointed, surprising for such a small town, but clearly very popular. Must tell Rupert his recommendation was well-founded. My suite of rooms comfortable and will do very nicely until I get settled. Mr Lomas, the owner, is a gentleman, very outgoing and with a great sense of both occasion and humour. Perfectly suited to his role in life.

Amelia and I went to inspect my new rooms at The Square. Very convenient for the hospital but will need redecoration. Amelia advises against green – says although known to be restful, north facing rooms need more colour. Will have to discuss further.

CHAPTER THREE

The following morning, when Eleanor and Napoleon went for their first walk of the day, the early morning clouds were dispersing and there was the promise of a beautiful summer's day ahead. On Sunday afternoons, if the weather was fine, Eleanor and Napoleon generally went walking with three of Eleanor's friends. Two of those friends were currently on holiday and the third, Doctor Catherine Balderstone, had telephoned the day before to say that she would not be able to spare the time to go walking. Her surgery was being re-painted and on Sunday she needed to check that everything had been put back and made ready for Monday. The two friends had agreed to meet in the Gardens at lunchtime for a picnic lunch instead.

Just before one o'clock, Eleanor and Napoleon left Hall Bank, with their picnic basket, and walked to the main entrance to the Gardens. Catherine had just arrived and they showed their season's tickets at the entrance and walked along the crowded promenade. They passed the Winter Garden and the Central Hall and then they stopped. The fine weather had brought many of the visitors out of doors and the Gardens were busy.

'Where shall we sit?' asked Eleanor.

'Let's go down to the river away from the crowd,' said Catherine. 'Sitting and watching the water flow calmly will be just what I need at the moment.'

As they took the winding path that descended the side of the valley and walked down towards the river Wye, Eleanor postponed asking any questions. When they had spread out the picnic rug and Napoleon had settled down beside it, Eleanor opened the picnic basket which contained various choices of sandwiches and cakes.

Eleanor said: 'Why the need for soothing? Do you have some particularly difficult cases at the moment?'

'No, not at all. In fact, that is partly what has made me feel cross. Not real cases at all. Just women with too little meaning to their lives. There has been an outbreak of "nerves" all of a sudden and women wanting something to calm them.'

Catherine laughed and then took a bite of a cheese sandwich.

'Perhaps it's the poor weather we've been having lately,' suggested Eleanor.

'Probably,' agreed Catherine, 'but, really, it is too trying and such a waste of my time when I could be treating people who are seriously ill. I had to do a home visit yesterday to a house in The Park and this morning when I was trying to get my surgery straight, I was called out to one of the hotels, the Claremont. The Park visit was to a mother who insisted that I prescribe a tonic for her sixteen year old daughter. She wouldn't let the daughter speak for herself and I had to spend half an hour listening to the mother describing the symptoms which she considered to be signs of illness. All I could detect was that the daughter is growing up and forming her own opinions and, because the daughter's opinions don't coincide with those of her mother, the daughter must be ill.'

'Of course,' laughed Eleanor. 'Any reasonable person would see that and agree with the mother. I suppose she thought you lacked sympathy.'

'Worse! I was ignorant. She informed me that, if I had a daughter of my own, I would understand. When I explained that the daughter had no medical condition that I could diagnose, the mother was still not satisfied. There really was nothing I could treat. Then the mother insisted that the daughter must be suffering from nerves and needed a tonic to calm them. I suggested a patent nerve tonic that she could buy ready-made but, no, that wasn't good enough. She wanted something specially made up.'

'So what did you do?'

'I gave her a prescription and the chemist will make up a bottle of mixture which is exactly the same as the patent one. It won't do the daughter any good but it won't do her any harm either.' Catherine sighed. 'I spent quite a long time there, listening to all of the nonsense just to make sure I hadn't missed any physical signs that something was wrong. My bill will reflect the length of time I spent there but, as the mother was not completely satisfied, I expect that I shall have difficulty getting my fee paid.'

'What about the other one, at the Claremont, was she a visitor?'

'Yes, describing vague and imaginary symptoms but convinced that she was not long for this world. In reality, suffering from nothing more than boredom. She complained that she couldn't sleep from nervous anxiety and wanted me to prescribe *Veronal*. She assured me her own physician prescribes it for her without hesitation but she had forgotten to bring the tablets with her.'

'And did you prescribe the *Veronal*?' asked Eleanor.

'Absolutely not. She was trying a well-known trick, pretending to have a prescription from her own doctor in order to get me to supply the tablets she wanted. As you know, since the law changed, *Veronal* can now only be supplied on prescription. The new regime is sensible because these drugs were much too readily available. They are prone to accidental or deliberate overdose and are addictive. But, this new control over them has caused problems because they were often sought by people who had no proper need of them and they can no longer obtain a supply.'

'I believe our grandmothers' generation was awash with

over the counter medicines for what they called susceptible nerves.'

'But dangerously addictive. And most likely their condition had nothing at all to do with nerves. It was simply a case of boredom from the restrictions society placed on them,' said Catherine.

'Frustration at having their behaviour constantly monitored and being told that ladies don't do this or that or whatever it was they wanted to do. Like your young Saturday patient, probably. I remember how frustrated my grandmother's rules made me feel.'

'Thank goodness we don't have to cope with that sort of restriction anymore,' said Catherine, 'but there are plenty of physicians who are prepared to prescribe these potions and plenty of ladies like the one I visited today who insist that they need them. It is an unsatisfactory situation.'

'Yes, I imagine that many households still have a bottle or two of *Veronal* tucked away at the back of a cupboard.'

'I'm sure they do. And one can always get around legislation, even laws supposedly passed for the good of society. As you lawyers well know,' said Catherine, smiling.

'I shall ignore that,' said Eleanor. 'Now, help yourself to more sandwiches and let me distract you with this.'

She pulled out that day's edition of the *Buxton Advertiser* from the picnic basket and flicked through to find the page she wanted.

'This is the offering at the Opera House next week. It's a new play and has obviously been written especially to attract and inspire doctors. It is just the tonic that you need at the moment.'

'Oh, dear,' said Catherine, pulling a face.

'It's called *The Outsider* and it's billed as being novel and arresting, a medical drama and romance intertwined. Are you ready?'

'Probably not, but go on,' said Catherine, laughing.

'Right, the heroine is unable to walk and desperately in love with a man whose attention is straying to women who can walk, dance, play golf and enjoy life generally.'

'Obviously this man is the villain of the piece,' interrupted Catherine.

'Undoubtedly. And the hero is a doctor, a foreigner, shunned by the rest of the medical profession but offering a miraculous cure. This cure involves the use of some kind of rack, as in mediaeval torture, in order to cure his patients. It's very risky though, so there is no certainty of a cure and the girl, desperate to get her man back, just has to trust him.'

'Good grief! Why would anyone be gullible enough to fall for that?'

'Oh, but women are supposed to fall for that "just trust me" line. That's what these pieces of theatre rely on. Anyway, back to the play. The hero incurs the wrath of the whole of the medical profession.'

'I'm not surprised. With a torture rack as a centre piece. That sounds like a wonderful evening's entertainment,' said Catherine, shaking her head in disbelief. 'Really, where do these modern writers get their ideas from?'

'So, of course, the hero doctor wants to use the heroine to prove that his method works.'

'Give me patience!'

'But according to the review, the cure is a triumph and the play comes to a wonderful climax and, I'm quoting here, the play deals frankly, almost brutally, with a certain aspect of sex, but always cleanly.'

'Always cleanly? Well, that's a relief!' said Catherine. 'I think I can guess at the certain aspect of sex which, of course, is troubling the villain but not specifically mentioned in that list of things that the girl cannot do.'

Eleanor looked back at the list: 'I suppose it comes under the "enjoy life generally" category. One cannot be too explicit for fear of offending the Lord Chamberlain, who is remarkably sensitive in these modern times.'

'Of course,' agreed Catherine, 'I wonder how many letters the editor of *The Times* received when the play was first performed in London.'

'It might be the sort of play that London audiences like.'

'Possibly, but I can't see it being a great success here. Can you honestly see the matrons of The Park trotting along to see that sort of play?' asked Catherine.

'No, the mere mention of the word sex sends them rushing for the smelling salts.'

'The cure I'd prescribe for the heroine is just to get rid of the villain she's in love with, the one with the roving eye. He sounds like a complete cad. What a superbly silly play. I'm glad you've given me the summary. I certainly won't need to waste my money on a ticket.'

'Neither shall I,' said Eleanor.

'You know, the medical bit of that play is pure nonsense but there are plenty of women like the heroine who are in love with the wrong man. Or worse, marry the wrong one.'

'Yes, they're the ones in the murder mysteries who end up killing their husbands in a novel way,' laughed Eleanor.

'I see plenty of them in real life but fortunately they don't take to murder.'

'No, just a bottle of nerve tonic,' said Eleanor, laughing.

'True,' said Catherine, joining in the laughter. 'News of that play was just the tonic I needed. Thank you, Eleanor, you have succeeded in cheering me up. I can always rely on you to do that. Now, tell me about the new Bentley that Philip has bought.'

They chatted happily, enjoying their picnic, and watching the passing parade of visitors and local people. When it was time for Catherine to return to her surgery, Catherine thanked Eleanor for the picnic and for helping to restore her to good humour. Eleanor had intended to remain in the Gardens and read a book but clouds were now starting to gather and the wind was increasing in strength. Instead, she decided to go back to Hall Bank to read and then take Napoleon for his afternoon walk later on.

CHAPTER FOUR

At four thirty, Napoleon reminded Eleanor that it was time for his walk and they strolled along Broad Walk until they reached the corner of Fountain Street and the side entrance to the Gardens. After they had passed the ticket booth, they wandered their way down a path which led towards the wide flat plain beside the river. The wind, which had now become quite strong, was cool and unpleasant and there were not many people left in the Gardens now. It was ideal kite flying weather and Eleanor noticed, some distance away, two boys struggling to launch one.

Eleanor recognised the two boys but she decided not to interrupt them. One of them was her nine year old nephew, Richard, and the other was his best friend, Thomas. Eleanor was amused to see that Thomas was dressed as a cowboy. The previous year, Richard and Thomas had been dedicated pirates for several months. Then, after the prize giving at a fancy dress parade at the St Mary's Garden Fête, they had both flirted briefly with being an aviator and then Zorro. Soon afterwards, Richard had lost interest in dressing up but not Thomas. He had a vivid imagination and he was a clever mimic. His mother was convinced that he was a born entertainer. He became completely absorbed in whichever role he chose to play and recently, as a result of several trips to the picture theatre, he had been a cowboy, a Mexican bandit, and a musketeer. The roles alternated according to his mood and Eleanor was never sure which character she was likely to meet. Today, he was wearing a check shirt, chaps, a waistcoat made of some brown material intended to imitate leather, and a heavy belt which was serving as a holster.

Thomas was holding the kite and Richard was holding the string. Richard moved forward a little way and then started to run. The kite trailed behind him, made a few desultory feints and bounces along the ground, but refused to lift, and then flopped onto the grass. The two boys decided on a second attempt to launch the kite but this time they reversed their roles so that Thomas was holding the string and Richard was holding the kite. The boys were so absorbed with the kite that they had not noticed Eleanor. Napoleon had now lost interest in a scent he had been pursuing and he sat down on his haunches beside Eleanor. Then, he slowly slid his front paws forward and made himself comfortable while he watched the action.

Eleanor's attention was momentarily distracted by the approach of a very elegantly dressed couple, sauntering slowly along a path a little distance away. The lady, carrying a parasol, stopped to admire a flowering shrub. Then, a sudden gust of wind caught the parasol and it would have been blown away, but for the quick reflexes and agility of her companion. He was very tall and so had the advantage of height. They both laughed at the incident. The lady stopped to close the parasol and remained looking at the garden and the gentleman moved on a few paces towards a park bench. He was about to sit down when he noticed the two kite flyers, remained standing on the path, and watched them instead.

Eleanor turned her attention back to the two boys. By this time, they had retraced their steps to their starting point and as soon as the wind was favourable, Thomas began to run. Richard tossed the kite into the air so that it would catch the wind. As soon as Thomas felt the kite lifting, he turned his head back, twisting as he ran, so that he could watch the kite rise. The kite lifted a little way off the ground but then a gust of wind tossed it to one side and, instead of continuing to lift, the kite dipped suddenly and then started spinning. To accommodate the shift in the wind, Thomas changed direction slightly but kept running at top speed, his head still turned back towards the kite. Without realizing it, he was now heading towards the path where the tall gentleman was standing. This change of direction happened very quickly and Eleanor, too far away to intervene, started moving forward ready to deal with the aftermath of the accident which she could see was about to happen.

Fortunately, the gentleman, who had now been joined by his companion, had been watching the whole operation with interest and, like Eleanor, he was now anticipating its inevitable conclusion. He moved in front of the lady to shield her, and stood ready to rescue Thomas. Thomas's attention was still totally absorbed by the kite but then, at the very last moment, as though sensing an obstacle, he turned his head, pulled up, and came to an abrupt halt only inches in front of the tall gentleman. The gentleman had put out a restraining hand to steady Thomas in case he stumbled and fell. The lady gave a startled: 'Oh!'

Thomas froze, his head level with the tall gentleman's watch chain, and then he slowly raised his head and looked up, wide-eyed, at the gentleman's face. He took a small step backwards and, after a sharp intake of breath, said:

'Gosh! Sorry, sir.'

He flapped his arms up and down at his sides like an agitated penguin and hopped from one foot to the other.

'It was the kite, you see. It wouldn't lift.'

'So I observed,' said the gentleman, smiling. 'Apology accepted. No harm done. May one enquire your name, young man?'

'Thomas, sir.'

'How do you do, Thomas,' said the gentleman, bowing slightly.

At this point, Richard arrived, slightly breathless, having run towards Thomas to provide moral support.

'And this is .. ?' said the gentleman, looking at Richard.

'Richard, sir,' said Thomas. 'He's my best friend.'

'How do you do, Richard,' said the gentleman.

Thomas was energetic and had a zest for life which frequently caused him to act before thinking. As a consequence, he was prone to mishaps. For self-preservation, and as a way of extricating himself from difficult situations, he had perfected the art of distraction, rather like a magician who, by inviting the audience to focus intently on something completely irrelevant, draws their attention away from the essential step which is required to launch a trick. So, as a diversion from this current mishap, Thomas immediately introduced a new topic.

'Richard's father got a medal,' announced Thomas.

'Oh, and may one enquire what medal that was?' asked the gentleman.

'It's a DSO,' said Richard, proudly.

'Oh, I say!' said the gentleman.

'I've seen it,' said Thomas firmly, scotching any doubt as to the medal's existence.

'I'm allowed to take it out and look at it sometimes,' Richard explained.

'It's a very important medal,' added Thomas, folding his arms across his chest to emphasise his point.

'It is indeed,' said the gentleman, gravely. 'Very important.'

'Have you ever seen one?' asked Thomas, unfolding his arms and twirling around on one foot.

The gentleman paused. 'Er, yes. I have actually.' He turned to Richard and said: 'You must be very proud of your father.'

'Yes, sir,' said Richard, nodding vigorously.

Thomas, continuing with his distraction ploy, said: 'But

he's not here anymore. Because of the War, you know.'

'I see,' said the gentleman, gravely, slowly nodding his head. 'I am very sorry to hear that.' He paused. 'Perhaps, then, in the absence of someone to guide you, you would allow me to suggest a few corrections to your technique with the kite.'

'Oh, wizard!' said Thomas delightedly, bouncing up and down on the spot.

'Yes, please, sir,' added Richard.

'Excellent. This way then, young gentlemen.' He turned to his companion and said: 'With your permission, of course, Amelia. It will only be a short diversion.'

He took off his hat and gave it to the lady, who laughed and nodded. Richard retrieved the kite and handed it to the gentleman.

Eleanor had stopped walking forward when the tall gentleman had stood ready to save Thomas from injury. She was too far away to hear the conversation but she could see that Thomas had talked his way out of a scrape, as usual, and she decided that there was no need for her to get involved. She watched as the trio, deep in conversation, walked away from the path and back towards the starting point, completely unaware of her presence. The gentleman made some minor adjustments to the tail of the kite and then demonstrated how to catch the wind and how to let the line out to stop the kite from dropping. Then, the gentleman handed the string to Thomas and, carrying the kite, walked away from the two boys. He waited for the wind, called instructions to Thomas, and then launched the kite into the air. He then ran forward to help Thomas.

As the kite ducked and dived, the gentleman helped to adjust the string and control the kite. When the kite was flying successfully, he shook hands with Richard and patted Thomas on the shoulder, Thomas's hands being fully occupied with the kite string. He returned to his companion, retrieved his hat, and the two of them, smiling, resumed their walk, leaving Eleanor greatly impressed by the gentleman's kindness to the two boys. She had not seen either of these people in the gardens before and she assumed that they were visitors. On the way back to Hall Bank, she wondered about the identity of the tall and handsome stranger with such charming manners.

0 0 0

DIARY Sunday 22nd June

Amelia and I attended St John's church for service this morning. The Vicar preached an extraordinary sermon. Talked about Well-Dressings. No idea what they are. Must find out. Something about the revival of pagan customs associated with wells and emphasised that the purpose of the modern ceremony is to bless the water in accordance with Christian tradition and not to make offerings to the spirits. What have I got myself mixed up with? Also learnt that a sermon is preached each year to raise funds in support of the work of the Devonshire Hospital and Buxton Bath Charity.

Met two charming young rascals in the Gardens later today. Kite flying. One of them very proud of his father. Another casualty of that wretched War. Haven't flown a kite for years. Thoroughly enjoyed the exercise. Amelia thought it very amusing and undignified. Said it reminded her of the contests that the boys have over whose kite has gone the highest. As kites are only for windy weather have agreed to meet the two rascals at the cricket nets later this week.

CHAPTER FIVE

The modern custom of dressing the wells which took place in the summer months, mainly in Derbyshire and Staffordshire, was linked indirectly to an ancient Celtic tradition. For the Celts, natural springs were sacred places, a portal through which people in the temporal world could contact the spiritual world. These springs were often surrounded by a grove of trees which shielded the water source from the secular world. It was customary to leave votive offerings at a sacred spring and ask for help or healing. The Romans had also followed this practice, re-dedicating the Celtic springs to their own deities. They tossed objects into the water: coins, or tablets inscribed with curses or requests for help. This pagan practice of visiting springs for spiritual support did not completely die out even after Christianity became the official religion. Even now, people toss coins into wells or fountains, for luck or to make a wish, without realising the origin of the practice.

The cluster of springs at Buxton, now located under The Crescent, had been sacred to the Celts. The Romans had re-dedicated them to their goddess, Arnemetiae. After the Normans arrived, the springs were re-dedicated yet again, this time to St Anne. The Christian pilgrims began arriving and a chapel dedicated to her was also built. With the Reformation and later Puritan reforms, the springs officially lost their spiritual significance. Scientists began analysing the chemical properties of the water ascribing a secular reason to their curative powers and the practice of drinking or bathing in the water became purely medicinal.

The old beliefs had remained, however, and in the hamlets and villages the water still had a spiritual power. Many years ago, in the village of Tissington, seventeen miles south of Buxton, the villagers had attributed their miraculous escape from an outbreak of disease, which had killed many people in nearby villages, to the power of the water from the wells in their village. They gathered around the wells to bless them and give thanks for their deliverance. This blessing evolved to become an annual event and spread to other villages with wells fed by spring water.

In 1840, the Duke of Devonshire had a fountain installed in the Market Place to provide clean, fresh water pumped from a reservoir fed by a spring. This water supply was a great boon to the residents of Higher Buxton who previously had to trudge down the steep hill each day and in all weathers to fetch buckets of water from the well at the lower part of the town. In celebration of this gift, a dedication ceremony and blessing of the water was proposed and the Buxton residents decided to revive the old custom of dressing the fountain with flowers. This proposal generated a great deal of debate and alarm at the prospect of reviving a pagan custom based on the superstitions associated with water. To allay these fears it was emphasised that the ceremony, then called the Well-Flowering, was merely one of thanksgiving for the benefit of the water.

The ceremony became an annual event involving both of the wells. The Vicar and other clergy, the Mayor and Town Councillors, the official guests, and the town's residents all assembled at the fountain on the Market Place for the blessing of that water and then, accompanied by brass bands and followed by the crowd, the official party processed down the hill to St Anne's Well to bless the water there. Each year, before the ceremony, large colourful panels illustrating a text from the Bible, were erected in front of both the Market Place fountain and St Anne's well. The panels consisted of a layer of moist clay into which flower petals, seeds, and other natural objects had been pressed in an intricate pattern to form the letters of the text itself and the picture illustrating it.

Over the years, the ceremony evolved to become the Well-Dressings festival and it had become one of the highlights of the summer in Buxton. The streets, shops, and houses were decorated with flowers and flags. The mayoral procession had become a general parade and, without the strictly Protestant Victorians noticing it, a pagan element from the old May day celebrations had crept in. Now, school children danced around a Maypole, and instead of a May Queen, a young girl was crowned as the Rose Queen and, with her retinue of train bearers and pages led the parade. The Morris Men danced and the bands played. Naturally, the festival attracted those who provided other forms of entertainment, particularly at fairs, and seeing an opportunity for profit, added themselves to the event: Punch & Judy, a greased pole challenge, and foot races. Large numbers of visitors arrived in gigs, carts, carriages, omnibuses and, in later years, excursion trains run by the two railway companies.

Although the wells were still blessed at a religious ceremony and dressed with a picture illustrating a text from the Bible, the festival had become a form of popular entertainment. Some residents were concerned that the festival was losing its religious significance and becoming a purely secular event. There had been criticism of the quality and respectability of some aspects of the entertainment provided and also the behaviour of some elements of the crowd it attracted. Factions had developed and opinion was divided. The many letters to the editor of the *Buxton Advertiser* left no doubt as to the strong feelings of the partisans.

The Well-Dressings themselves required elaborate preparation and many months of work and were organised by the local people providing their time and resources freely, but the Festival needed the co-operation and the resources of the local authorities. Roads had to be closed, traffic had to be controlled, the behaviour of the crowd had to be monitored, and the safety of the visiting dignitaries and officials had to be guarded. All of this cost public money.

In 1915, with the absence of so many of the men who helped organised the Well-Dressings, the Festival was cancelled and it had not yet been revived. In the first summer after the War, Buxton was still mourning its dead and was not in the mood to celebrate. As the town began to recover, reasons were put forward, usually lack of funds or lack of interest, in justification for postponing the event's revival for yet another year. Every year, the proposal to revive the festival had been the subject of deliberation, argument, procrastination, and its cancellation a source of disappointment to its supporters.

In 1924, when, yet again, the question of revival arose, money of any kind, public or private, was in short supply. The Council had spent significant amounts of money on the development of the new park, Ashwood Park, on the banks of the River Wye at the northern end of the town, which, unlike the Pavilion Gardens would be a public park. Recently, in an attempt to promote the park and justify the expense, the Council had expended yet more public money organising band concerts there.

The Council had made the controversial decision to engage for these concerts, and for a considerable fee, a Lancashire band, the Irwell Bank Band, whose players came from and were supported by the Irwell Bank Cotton Mills, near Bolton. There were several local bands of very high calibre which could have performed just as well and for much less expense. The Burbage Silver Prize Band was well-established and competent enough to organise its own band contests in the Concert Hall and offer valuable prizes.

There were other bands of equal quality at Fairfield and Tideswell. Even if these bands had been paid the same fee as the imported band, the cost would have been less because the Council would not have had the expense of providing accommodation for the band members. The Council had further offended the local bands and their supporters by refusing to disclose the fee they had paid to the imported band.

The bad weather at the beginning of the Season had caused the Council to take out costly insurance against the cancellation of these outdoor events and their fears as to the likelihood of poor weather had been well-founded. The concerts were poorly attended and questions were currently being asked and unfavourable opinions strongly expressed at Council meetings. The Council managed to offend the local bands even further by refusing to respond to requests for information about the fee paid to the imported band. Other people questioned the expense incurred in arranging the band concerts and this dissatisfaction led to accusations that the Council was furthering its own political interests instead of supporting the local community.

This was the atmosphere in which the question of revival of the Well-Dressings was currently being considered. At the beginning of the year, a Special Committee had been appointed to consider the question. The Committee's awareness of the Council's lack of funds provided a strong incentive for it to find reasons which would justify not reviving the Festival. Those who did not approve of the Festival had voiced their opposition forcefully, which encouraged the Committee to believe that their decision would be accepted with approval.

Eleanor's experience of the decision-making process of committees did not fill her with confidence. In fact, she was convinced that the appointment of a committee was a signal that the quest for revival was doomed again this year. She hoped, for the sake of the many people who would benefit from the event, that her fears would prove to be unfounded. She had been discussing the revival with Mrs Clayton, their housekeeper, the previous week and they were expecting some news to be published in that Saturday's edition of the *Buxton Advertiser*.

On Monday morning, on her way to the dining room, Eleanor stopped to talk to Mrs Clayton. Napoleon sat down in the hallway to supervise the preparation of breakfast.

'Good morning, Mrs Clayton.'

'Ah, good morning, Miss Harriman. I didn't see anything about the Well-Dressings in the *Advertiser* on Saturday. Have you heard anything?'

'No, nothing further, I'm afraid. I know how anxious the local tradespeople are to have the Festival revived. It does bring in a lot of visitors to the town.'

Mrs Clayton said: 'The committee meeting was last Wednesday so I was expecting to hear soon.'

'Let's just hope, for the sake of the town, that no news is good news,' said Eleanor. 'There is a Council meeting next week I think so perhaps the Committee's decision will be announced then.'

'It's getting a bit late though, isn't it? Lots of my neighbours have flowers ready to provide to make the pictures and some are quite willing to help with the petalling, but it takes a lot of work to organise the Festival. It can't be done in just a few days.'

'No, and delaying the announcement of the decision in this way is not helpful,' said Eleanor. 'I know there has been opposition to the revival and I don't know how influential those opponents are, but one could be forgiven for thinking that the decision, even if it is in favour of the revival, is being deliberately delayed until it is too late for anyone to recover the situation.'

'You are probably right,' said Mrs Clayton. She sighed.

'It is a shame though. It used to be such an important event, something to really look forward to, especially for the children. And there are children now who have never seen the Well-Dressings, it's been such a long time since we had one. But it's not just for the children's benefit. It brings the townspeople together.'

'Yes, it does,' said Eleanor. 'I have some very happy memories of participating in the Well-Dressings, although I doubt whether the same could be said for some of my teachers when I was in the Infants Class. I recall making them very cross because I could not remember which way to go in the Maypole dance. My ribbon always seemed to get into the wrong place or get tangled with someone else's and I could never understand why. All of my sisters and Edgar were always much better at it than I was.'

'My boys were much too young for the Maypole dance before the War and now they consider themselves too grown up for it. They were looking forward to taking part in the parade though. We'll just have to wait and see what the Council decides,' said Mrs Clayton, with a shrug. 'Now, will Mr Danebridge be here for lunch?'

'Oh, thank you, Mrs Clayton, I'm glad you reminded me. No, he's not able to come today.'

'I expect he will be too busy with his new motor.'

Eleanor laughed. 'No, I think he has to see a client. He will be here for lunch tomorrow though.'

'Right you are, Miss Harriman. Mr Danebridge is very kind. He's promised my two boys a ride in the new motor and you wouldn't believe how excited they are.'

CHAPTER SIX

Eleanor and Mr Harriman had just finished breakfast. Mr Harriman was still reading the newspaper and Eleanor was leaving the dining room when she heard clattering on the stairs. Napoleon went to the top of the stairs ready to deal with intruders. Mrs Clayton, still holding a knife she had been using, appeared at the kitchen door.

'Aunt Lella! Aunt Lella! Come and see!'

Richard came bounding up the stairs, face flushed with excitement, arms propelling him upwards. Eleanor had a fair idea what all the fuss was about but decided to feign ignorance.

'Whatever can the matter be, at this hour in the morning!' she said, pretending to look alarmed.

'We've been in the motor and we went really, really fast! Come and see! Mr Danebridge is waiting to show you!'

Richard turned abruptly and raced back downstairs, confident that Eleanor would follow.

'Good morning, Richard,' said Eleanor to her nephew's retreating back.

Mrs Clayton, satisfied that the house was not under attack, returned to the kitchen.

Eleanor smiled and went calmly downstairs, followed by Napoleon. She assumed that "we" referred to Richard and Thomas. She knew that Richard had asked if his friend could share the first ride in the new Bentley.

'Come and look, Mr Wildgoose!' called Richard, as he reached the foot of the stairs and rushed through the entrance hall.

The motor car was parked outside in Hall Bank and, by the time that Eleanor reached the front door, Richard had resumed his place next to Thomas on the back seat. Philip was waiting on the pavement.

'Good morning, Lella,' he said, smiling broadly. He turned and, with a sweep of his arm, said: 'May I present the new Bentley. I've just taken the boys for their ride, as promised.'

'Good morning, Philip,' said Eleanor, laughing. 'Yes, I gathered as much from Richard's garbled message. Good morning, Thomas.'

'Good morning, Miss Harriman,' said Thomas, politely.

James stood in the doorway for a few moments, said good morning to Philip and the boys, admired the motor car, smiled indulgently, and returned to his desk.

Mr Harriman had put aside his newspaper and now arrived to join the admirers.

'Good morning, Philip. So, this is what all the fuss is about. Is this the same model as the one that won at Le Mans last week?'

'No, that was the Sport,' said Richard.

'This is much better,' asserted Thomas.

'I see,' said Mr Harriman. 'And you two chaps have tested it, have you?'

'Rather!' said Richard.

'Mmmm,' nodded Thomas.

Mr Harriman walked forward to admire the Bentley parked neatly alongside the kerb, a 3 litre Tourer, long, sleek, and serene: dark green bodywork and mudguards contrasting with the brilliant chrome of the radiator and the huge headlamps, wide running boards, and the large, long bonnet hinting at the power of the engine it concealed. The hood was down and the windshield lowered forward over the bonnet revealing the pair of small racing windshields, the large steering wheel, the polished woodwork of the dashboard housing a variety of dials, and the smooth burgundy coloured leather upholstery of the interior.

'That is indeed a splendid vehicle,' said Mr Harriman, nodding appreciatively. 'Certainly worthy of all the fuss.'

'It's a Green Label,' said Richard.

'That means it can go a hundred miles an hour,' added Thomas.

Meanwhile, Eleanor, followed by Napoleon, had made a slow circuit of the motor car viewing it from all angles and taking in its beauty and all its features.

Philip looked at Eleanor. 'What do you think, old thing? Will it do?'

Eleanor smiled and nodded. 'It certainly will. I agree with Father. It is splendid. In fact, it is a beautiful piece of work. Congratulations on your choice. I think it is perfect and I can see why you wanted it. Oh, here's Cecily come to admire.'

Eleanor turned as her sister, having walked up Hall Bank, stopped to greet Mr Harriman.

Philip said: 'When I collected the boys earlier on, Cecily agreed to come and fetch them so that I could go straight home. I've got to be at the showroom shortly.' Turning to the motor car, he said: 'Right, you chaps. Show's over for today. Hop down now.'

Cecily watched as the two boys clambered out and said: 'Well, boys, did you enjoy your ride?'

'We went on the Ashbourne Road,' said Richard, nodding enthusiastically, 'and we went really, really fast,'

'A hundred miles an hour, I should think,' said Thomas, nodding confidently.

'Goodness!' said Cecily, looking alarmed. 'I hope not!'

'Probably,' added Thomas, quickly down-playing the speed.

Dealing with grown-ups, particularly mothers, could be so very tricky. They were always emphasising the importance of honesty but then when you were honest, they got alarmed. He could foresee trips in the motor car being banned by his mother in future. He looked at Cecily anxiously and held his breath.

'Was it really that fast?' asked Cecily. She looked at Philip with concern.

Philip was standing behind the two boys and they could not see his face. He smiled at Cecily and slowly shook his head but, not wanting to spoil their story, he said:

'This Bentley can certainly do that speed. I'm sure we came pretty close.'

'Oh,' said Cecily, nodding. 'Then I am pleased I was not with you. I am sure I should not have enjoyed it half as much as you two seem to have.'

Thomas breathed again. Disaster averted. 'It was wizard!' he said, flapping his arms up and down by his sides.

Eleanor had listened to this exchange with amusement. A short distance out of Buxton, the Ashbourne Road followed the line of the old Roman road. Instead of winding gently around the contours of the landscape as the old pack-horse routes did, this road ran for miles in an almost straight line, surging ahead in a sequence of rises and dips, contemptuous of the local topography. It was a road on which speed was possible and Eleanor was certain that, earlier that morning while there was no traffic and before taking the boys for their ride, Philip would have tested the performance of the Bentley along that stretch of road.

'Thomas,' said Eleanor, 'we are all planning to go in the Bentley with Mr Danebridge for an excursion next Saturday, provided that the weather is fine.'

Philip added: 'We would be very pleased if you would join us. If you are free, that is. Would you like to come?'

Thomas hopped up and down on one leg, arms flapping. 'Oh. yes please. Very much.'

'Excellent,' said Cecily, 'I shall telephone to your mother and ask her permission.'

'Oh,' said Thomas, frowning. 'You won't tell her how fast the Bentley can go, will you?'

'No, not at all,' said Cecily. 'I shouldn't think she'll be interested in that.'

'And in any event,' added Philip, 'on Saturday, we shall be going at a much more sedate pace than today.'

The two boys turned to look at Philip, their disappointment obvious on their faces.

'We can go at a hundred miles an hour again on another day,' said Philip. 'Without the ladies.'

Richard and Thomas looked at each other, understood the pact, and then nodded.

'Can Napoleon come with us for the picnic, Aunt Lella?' asked Richard.

Napoleon was standing beside Eleanor and hearing his name looked up in anticipation of action.

Eleanor laughed: 'Oh, I think we know what he would prefer, Richard, but it's for Mr Danebridge to decide. It's his motor car.'

'Of course he can come,' said Philip. 'In the meantime, we all have work to do this morning and it's getting late so I'd better get along.' He stepped on the running board and climbed into the driver's seat. He turned to the two boys. 'Right, you two, between now and Saturday, I need you to help me. We had thought of going to Matlock Bath, so you can decide which roads we should take.'

'We've got a map,' said Richard.

'Excellent,' said Philip. He started the engine, waved, and, as the motor car moved slowly forward, he called to the boys: 'But don't think this trip will be all pleasure. I shall need you two to navigate for me and to look out for potholes in the road. Some of the roads hereabouts are not fit for motor cars like this.'

0 0 0

Just after eleven o'clock that morning, Eleanor was at her desk frowning. The bundle of documents brought in by Mr Brittain on Saturday morning had been sorted by James into date order: conveyances, mortgages, wills, and grants of probate created over the last one hundred and fifty years as the ownership of a farm had passed down between several generations of the same family. Eleanor was working her way through the documents and they now formed two piles on the corners of the desk: one pile read, one pile still unread. One of these documents was spread out on her desk and was the cause of her frown.

The parcel of land that Eleanor was considering was on the lower part of Bishop's Lane in Burbage, officially Burbage-on-the-Wye, once a separate hamlet but now part of Buxton. Nevertheless, Burbage was a separate parish and had its own church, Christ Church, constructed in 1861, in the centre of the village. It was an imposing stone building with a square tower and a ring of six bells. The church itself was on a ridge high above the river Wye and the churchyard, which included a graveyard was on two levels. There was a smaller area on the same level as the church and a larger area at a much lower level on a wide, flat terrace which had been formed by the river thousands of years ago. Despite its more recent origins, Christ Church followed the ancient custom of clypping, a ceremony which took place on the last Sunday in July, and required the congregation to gather outside and, holding hands, encircle the church. The name was derived from the old Anglo-Saxon word for "embrace" and provided an accurate enough description of the ceremony itself but its purpose had been lost in time. Various explanations were put forward and, ironically given the opposition to the Well-Dressings, some parishioners believed that it was performed in order to bring luck for the coming year.

Bishop's Lane led west from St John's Road past a few houses and then through fields up to a large house called

Edgemoor, which nestled below the high ridge known as Burbage Edge. The Bishop in question was the Right Reverend George John Trevor Spencer, a relative of the Duke of Devonshire, who had been the Bishop of Madras between 1837 and 1849. Since then, he and his extended family had lived at Edgemoor, where he ended his days in 1866. In 1861, his son had been appointed as the first incumbent of Christ Church. The connection with the Bishop's family had now been lost but the name of the lane remained unchanged.

The piece of land being sold was part of a much larger farm, acquired by the Clough family in the last years of the eighteenth century, well before the arrival of the Bishop, when the land in that area was being parcelled out in compliance with the recent Enclosure Acts. The farm had passed from one generation to the next and, at some time in the past, the river Wye flowing along its lower boundary had flooded and then changed its channel. This had left a small area, the ownership of which had been claimed by the Clough family but the boundary between this piece of land and a neighbouring farm had been the subject of a dispute. The latest Clough claimant to the parcel of land had died suddenly earlier in the year and, in order to raise the money to pay death duties, the executor had chosen to sell this parcel of land as it was conveniently located on the edge of the farm.

The document which Eleanor was currently reading was spread out over the desk. It was a very large piece of stiff parchment with an impressive wax seal affixed near the bottom right-hand corner. The cause of her frown was the difficulty of deciphering words, written over a hundred years ago by a clerk using a quill pen and a style of hand-writing and a form of spelling no longer current.

James Wildgoose came into Eleanor's office as he usually did every morning at about that time bringing the day's post that related to Eleanor's files. Napoleon, who had been snoozing beside the desk, got up to greet James and received his usual pat.

'The post, Miss Eleanor,' said James.

Normally he placed the post on the edge of the desk closest to him but today there was no clear space. He hesitated.

'Oh,' said Eleanor, looking up. 'I'm sorry, James.'

She held out her hand and took the letters.

'Thank you. I'm struggling with the handwriting on this old deed. It's more in your line than mine, I think.'

'Perhaps I can assist,' said James.

James had been the confidential clerk for over thirty years, serving Eleanor's grandfather and now her father. The current Mr Harriman had not seen the need to introduce typewriters or secretaries as some solicitors had and all of the office's documents were still drawn up by James in his beautiful copperplate handwriting.

'It's this word here,' said Eleanor. 'I can't make it out. It's one of a list of noxious trades prohibited on this piece of land. Have you any idea what the word is?'

Eleanor turned the document around so that James could see it and pointed at the offending word.

James looked at the document and said, immediately: 'Catgut. Catgut spinner.'

'Goodness, were there ever any such persons in Buxton?'

'I have not heard of any,' said James, smiling wryly. 'I believe catgut spinning is a particularly unpleasant trade but it has nothing to do with cats. It concerns sheep, of which there are plenty in Burbage, so perhaps it was thought necessary to ward off any temptation to engage in that particular industry.'

'Then it certainly shall be banned from this plot of land,' said Eleanor, laughing. 'What is catgut spinning, anyway? In case I am ever asked.'

'It utilises the intestines of sheep to produce the strings used in musical instruments, such as the violin.'

'Heavens! I shall never be able to enjoy a violin solo in the same way again, but thank you, James, you have resolved my dilemma with this deed.'

James nodded and departed. Napoleon sat down ready to resume his snooze and Eleanor turned the document back towards her, ready to return to her task. At that moment, Mrs Clayton entered Eleanor's office carrying a tray with Eleanor's morning cup of tea.

'Oops,' said Mrs Clayton, seeing the documents spread over the desk. 'Best not get this anywhere near those papers. Where would you like me to put your tea, Miss Harriman?'

'Ah, thank you, Mrs Clayton. Tea is a welcome sight after these dusty documents. I think it will be best if I take it standing up.'

Eleanor stood up and moved away from her desk. She took the cup and saucer from the tray that Mrs Clayton offered.

'I'm trying to resolve a boundary dispute on some land on Bishop's Lane. It's an odd-shaped piece of land near the river.'

'Oh, that'll be Old Walter, I expect.' said Mrs Clayton.

'Walter Clough?' said Eleanor, surprised.

Mrs Clayton nodded.

'How did you know?'

'Oh well, practically everyone in Burbage knows that story, and a good few in Buxton as well. It's been told often enough,' said Mrs Clayton, smiling.

'What story is that?'

'Old Walter used to come into town on market day and complain about it to anyone who'd listen. He always said it would be the death of him and it was. He died of apoplexy after he had a violent dispute with his neighbour about that boundary. Although some said the apoplexy was brought on by the shock of the death of his grandson, he being expected to inherit.'

'Mrs Clayton, the extent of your knowledge about the goings on in this town never ceases to amaze me. Please tell me more.'

'I don't rightly know all the details, only what I've heard. I gather it goes back, oh, it must be fifty or more years ago now, to the time when there was a set-to about a boundary. Mr Ward, he had Gutter Farm then and it was just after his son drowned himself in the Watford Reservoir. One of his fields down the bottom end of the farm was next to one of Old Walter's fields. He was a relation of some sort of Mr Ward. Only a distant one, mind, and Old Walter had somehow got the right to this field, or that's what he claimed. Mr Ward said it was part of his farm, always had been.'

Mrs Clayton paused for moment, frowning, and then continued:

'Both of those farms have been there for hundreds of years so you'd think they'd know where their boundaries started and finished, wouldn't you?'

'Yes,' agreed Eleanor, 'the boundary of this particular piece of land seems to be on the river, which would be easy enough to spot.'

'Ah, well, I think that was the trouble. I seem to recall that the dispute might have had something to do with the river shifting. It used to flood something terrible there in the old days until they put the drain in and built up the lane where the bridge is now. Alf would know more than I do. He's come across Old Walter often enough in his time.'

Alf was Mrs Clayton's brother, a joiner, coffin maker, and undertaker who, because of his trade, knew a great deal about the residents of both the town and the surrounding district. He met his clients in the unguarded moments that follow the death of a relative, visiting their houses to collect the dead body. He kept many secrets. Known for his discretion, he was trusted and well-respected. Mrs Clayton, who heard a lot of conversations concerning the clients of the Hall Bank office, was similarly discreet and trusted.

'Perhaps you would ask Alf if he recalls anything about the dispute,' said Eleanor. 'I know I can count on you to be discreet. The parcel of land is for sale but only if the boundary has been clearly defined. I gather the purchaser wants to build a house there.'

'I see,' said Mrs Clayton. 'Old Walter was saving that land for his grandson. He won't need it now so I suppose that's why it's being sold.'

'What happened to the grandson?' asked Eleanor.

'Died, a few months back. Only nineteen.'

'Oh, that is sad. And you think that is what caused Mr Clough's death.'

'That's what people said at the time but Old Walter was getting on, so who's to know? At least if the boundary is settled, the new people will be able to live in peace.' Mrs Clayton laughed. 'Although, only if whatever is decided about the boundary suits Old Walter, otherwise, knowing him, he'll be back to have his say. And I hope whoever buys it builds something decent. It's lovely, that lane and we don't want something ugly spoiling it.'

'I agree with you there. I always enjoy that walk, especially in the early morning.'

'I'll ask Alf what he knows about the dispute if that will help.'

'Thank you, Mrs Clayton. Every piece of information is useful.'

With that Mrs Clayton took her tea-tray and headed back to the kitchen, followed by Napoleon who was always convinced that Mrs Clayton, whilst preparing food, needed a second opinion on any proposed ingredient.

After Mrs Clayton and Napoleon had left, Eleanor turned her attention back to the documents on her desk so as to make the most of the time remaining before lunch. Although Philip had had to cancel lunch, he had arranged to be back at Hall Bank later that afternoon with the new Bentley so that, when Eleanor had finished work for the day, he could take her for a drive.

0   0   0

DIARY Monday 23rd June

Visited my new rooms again this morning. Suggested colours for paint and paper. Amelia gave them her approval. Amelia chose fabric for curtains and gave directions to a local firm for them to be made up. I appreciate her assistance. Beyond my capacity. Afternoon tea at hotel. Amelia has now returned home.

Received a dinner invitation from a Lady Carleton-West. No idea who she is, asked someone at dinner – raises funds for the Devonshire Hospital. Therefore, assume the invitation is to welcome me to Buxton. Must say everyone is amazingly friendly.

CHAPTER SEVEN

On Tuesday, Philip arrived for lunch promptly at one o'clock and joined Eleanor in the dining room.

'Hello, old thing. How was your morning?' asked Philip.

'Dusty,' said Eleanor. 'Full of old documents. How was yours?'

Before Philip could reply, Mr Harriman arrived and said: 'Ah, Philip. Glad you could join us. How's the antiques trade? Had a good morning?'

'Yes, a very good morning, as a matter of fact. I was just about to tell Lella. I've got a new commission.'

'Excellent,' said Mr Harriman. 'Before you begin telling us about it, please help yourself to this chicken salad Mrs Clayton has prepared for us. It looks delicious.'

At this point, Edwin Talbot arrived in the dining room, greeted Philip, and took his seat. The conversation paused until the serving dishes had been passed around and everyone had settled.

'Now,' said Mr Harriman, 'what were you about to tell us, Philip? What's this commission?'

Philip said: 'One of the auction houses that I buy from contacted me a week ago to ask if I was interested in looking at a piece of eighteenth century furniture on behalf of a customer. He wanted an opinion as to its authenticity. This is strictly confidential, of course. The customer is a collector and he is a regular client of the auction house, but he bought the piece in question from a different source. When he showed the piece to one of his friends, who is also a collector, the friend cast doubt on its authenticity. He agreed that it seemed to be genuine, but there was something about the piece that wasn't quite right. He wasn't able to point to anything specific but it left him puzzled.'

'I imagine that conversation caused a slight dampening of his friend's enthusiasm for the piece,' said Edwin.

'Oh, absolutely. Spoilt the whole experience,' said Philip. 'I know exactly how he would feel. So this customer asked my usual auction house to recommend someone who could give him an opinion. The manager telephoned me this morning to say that their client wanted to engage me to examine the piece and write a report.'

'That's wonderful news,' said Eleanor.

'Yes, it is, isn't it. The collector is willing to pay for a report, whatever the finding, because he feels he must know one way or the other but, if the piece proves not to be genuine, he intends to commence Court proceedings, in which case I might be called as an expert witness.'

'And what does this piece of furniture purport to be?' asked Edwin.

'It's a Hepplewhite dressing table.'

'And, if it is genuine, how valuable?' asked Eleanor.

'On the basis that it was genuine, the client paid £290, which is a considerable sum.'

'Good grief!' said Mr Harriman. 'One could buy a modest house for that price not just one piece of furniture.'

'Yes,' agreed Philip. 'Some collectors do tend to get things out of proportion. This collector is very wealthy so perhaps he can afford to have a different perspective. And, of course, he may be merely thinking of investment. Victorian furniture is going out of fashion at the moment. It's considered too large and ponderous for modern taste and Georgian furniture fits the current preference for finer, less solid looking items. There is a growing demand for it and that means prices will increase.'

'And an increase in demand and, therefore, profit will lead

to an increase in temptation to produce seemingly genuine items?' said Mr Harriman.

'Inevitably,' said Philip, 'although reproductions are usually quite easy for the professional to spot.'

'So, if the Hepplewhite isn't genuine, why has no-one spotted that already?' asked Edwin.

'Because most of it may be genuine. If a piece of furniture has had some part of it repaired or replaced at a later date, that repair can sometimes be difficult to detect. The introduced material might only be a very small proportion of the whole. A repair might have been made using material taken from another piece of furniture from the same period or the same maker even. The repaired item is a perfectly good piece of furniture in itself but is not completely original. For the purists, it is less valuable.'

'So, for example,' said Edwin, smiling as he teased Philip, 'if the spare wheel on your new Bentley was damaged and had to be replaced with one from another model Bentley, you would not feel the same about your motor car and might even consider it less valuable.'

'Ah, Talbot,' said Mr Harriman, 'that is not a fair question to put to the proud new owner.'

Philip laughed and shook his head. 'I couldn't even consider such an eventuality.'

'So how do you tell if the furniture has been repaired or altered?' asked Eleanor.

'Well, it's a skill one picks up with experience. You have to be able to recognise the materials and the construction methods used at the relevant time, and the habits of the famous makers. If something just does not look right, you have to analyse all the component parts until you find the bit that caused you to doubt the origin of the piece. It's like a piece in a puzzle that doesn't fit. In fact, the process is very similar to the method you use, Lella, when you are solving a case. You know how things should look, how people should behave, and when they don't look or behave as expected, something nags at you until you can identify what is out of place.'

'Well, Philip,' said Mr Harriman, 'you have spent enough time helping Eleanor with her cases to have learnt all her methods. Should you enjoy doing more of that sort of investigation?'

'Yes, very much so, and I am hoping that if I get it right this time, I shall be asked for my opinion again.'

'I'm sure you will carry out a thorough investigation,' said Mr Harriman, 'that is the important part, after all. Whatever your conclusion, genuine piece or fake, the client needs to feel confident that you have been thorough and that your report is soundly based. As I am sure it will be. If I hear of anyone wanting anything similar, I shall certainly recommend you.'

'Thank you,' said Philip, 'that is very kind of you.'

Edwin said: 'And, Philip, if you are writing a report that might be used in litigation and you need some pointers as to the formalities and so on, let me know. I'm quite happy to discuss the report with you.'

'Oh, yes please. I do want to make a success of this and I would very much appreciate your guidance.'

'I've been thinking about what you said before about the value of a fake piece,' said Eleanor, frowning. 'Surely, in the case of a really competent imitation, it is hard not to admire the crooked craftsman. After all, he must be applying as much skill and dexterity as the maker of the genuine article.'

'I agree,' said Philip, 'but people trading in antiques would prefer it if he stuck to using his skills legitimately.'

'But then,' said Eleanor, 'he would not make as much profit, would he? He doesn't have the famous name. A piece of furniture known to be a reproduction would not fetch as high a price as an article supposed to be a genuine Chippendale or Hepplewhite, would it?'

'Absolutely not,' agreed Philip.

'So now we come to the heart of the matter. The piece of genuine furniture looks exactly like the fake. How do you put a value on each? Why is one more valuable and, therefore, more expensive than the other? In fact, is one actually more valuable than the other?'

Philip frowned. He said: 'No, you don't understand . . .'

Before he could finish, Mr Harriman laughed and, turning to his daughter, said: 'Eleanor, I suggest that you stop your cross-examination of Philip and let him eat his lunch.'

Eleanor also laughed. 'Sorry, Philip. You are quite right, Father. I get carried away following a train of thought.'

'I hope that if I am ever in the witness box, I don't have someone like you putting the questions,' said Philip.

'Well,' said Mr Harriman, 'if it ever seems likely that you are going to be called as an expert witness, perhaps Eleanor can give you some practice beforehand.'

'That's an idea,' said Philip.

Edwin said: 'Yes, as an expert witness, you must be prepared to get questions that make you cross. You will find that the other party's counsel will not allow you to explain a point you have made, or finish a sentence you have started, especially if your answer seems to be against his client.'

'Oh, I'm quite used to that,' said Philip. He grinned at Eleanor. 'After Lella, nothing could be as daunting.'

0 0 0

By half past three that afternoon, all of the deeds belonging to Old Walter's parcel of land at Bishop's Lane had been scrutinised and they were now stacked on the corner of Eleanor's desk in the "read" pile. Eleanor had worked her way methodically through them and, on a large sheet of butcher's paper, she had compiled a timeline regarding the disputed boundary. She was satisfied that she now had an answer and was double checking the relevant dates, when James came in with the afternoon's post.

Eleanor looked up and then looked at her watch.

'Goodness, is that the time!'

'Yes, Miss Eleanor. Unfortunately. Time for Lady Carleton-West's committee meeting.' James, knowing how much Eleanor detested these meetings, smiled wryly. He added: 'I was just going to mention it in case it had slipped your mind.'

'Never!' said Eleanor, with feeling. 'On the contrary, the thought of it haunts me from one meeting to the next.' She groaned as she put down her pen and stood up. 'I was just getting to an important point with this wretched boundary.'

'I've had the motor car brought round from the garage as I anticipated that today you would probably not have time to walk.'

'Oh, thank you, James. You are a lifesaver.'

'I feared you would lose all track of time puzzling your way through those deeds. I'm sure they present an irresistible challenge for you.'

'You know me too well,' said Eleanor, laughing.

0   0   0

Eleanor turned the motor car into the carriageway at the front of Top Trees and pulled up at the bottom of the front steps. Lady Carleton-West did not allow motor cars to park at the front of the mansion. She complained that they "spoiled the line of the house" but what she really meant was that they detracted from its grandeur. So, guests had to leave their motor cars at the front steps for Lady Carleton-West's chauffeur to move them to the rear of the house, out of sight.

Eleanor found these committee meetings a trial and only attended because Lady Carleton-West had thought it appropriate for her to take her late mother's place and, the

Harriman family having now left The Park, it was a way of keeping the Hall Bank practice in touch with their former neighbours and potential clients.

Eleanor sighed, picked up her bag, alighted from the motor car, and walked up the steps to the front door. Ash, Lady Carleton-West's long-standing, long-suffering butler, had opened the door before Eleanor could ring the bell.

Ash had a wicked sense of humour which he kept well-hidden from his employer. She was not known to have a frivolous nature. However, some favoured guests, including Eleanor, occasionally caught a glimpse of Ash's wit.

'Good afternoon, Ash.'

'Good afternoon, Miss Harriman,' said Ash, inclining the top half of his body forward in the very dignified movement he had perfected over the years. It amused him to make the bend deeper or slighter according to his assessment of the person being received. Eleanor, a known ally, got almost a full bow.

'Here I am again for more deliberations over fundraising,' said Eleanor. 'I hope you are keeping well.'

'Very well, thank you, Miss Harriman,' replied Ash, as he stood aside to allow Eleanor to enter. Then he added slowly, his words heavy with meaning. 'Her ladyship is in the Oak drawing room.'

They understood each other perfectly. It was Lady Carleton-West's habit not to appear in the drawing room until Ash had informed her that all of the committee members had arrived and were waiting for her.

Eleanor noticed that several tables had been placed along the walls of the entrance hall. An assortment of carboard boxes was stacked on top of each table.

Ash, seeing her glance, sighed and said: 'For the Hospital Bazaar. Items waiting to be sorted.'

'Oh, bother!' said Eleanor.

'Indeed, Miss Harriman,' said Ash, with just the hint of a

smile.

'I think I know what lies ahead,' said Eleanor.

'Yes, Miss Harriman. But I shall greatly appreciate having the entrance hall restored to order.'

'Then we shall do our very best to accommodate you.'

'I am much obliged, Miss Harriman.'

'Am I very late?' said Eleanor, without sounding at all contrite.

Ash smiled. 'Everyone has arrived, Miss Harriman,' he said, without sounding at all reproachful.

'Oh, dear,' said Eleanor, her tone indicating unrepentance.

Ash smiled and, as he turned and began to walk across the large entrance hall, he added, with a slight emphasis: 'Including the new Mrs Wilks.'

'Ah,' said Eleanor, with equal emphasis and an upward inflection.

Mr James Wilks was a prosperous Huddersfield cloth manufacturer, a "self-made" man who had postponed marriage for the sake of building his empire. At the age of forty, he was ready to produce a son and heir and, for the first time, considered the question of marriage. Unknown to Mr Wilks before his proposal of marriage, the first Mrs Wilks had been an active campaigner for women's rights, including the vote, and after her marriage continued to attend rallies with an enthusiasm strongly disapproved of by Mr Wilks.

After nine years of marriage, there was still no son and heir, for which Mr Wilks blamed Mrs Pankhurst, and he decided to remove his wife to a quieter, more conservative location, out of temptation's way. Not wishing to admit to his motives, however, he told his friends and acquaintances that for the benefit of his health he needed to spend time in the clean air of Buxton. For the maintenance of his social position, he installed the first Mrs Wilks in a large mansion in The Park. Unfortunately, after only six months, the first

Mrs Wilks was on her way to London to attend a rally when she was killed in a railway accident.

Mr Wilks let the mansion in The Park temporarily, returned to Huddersfield and, after a suitable period of mourning, set about finding a more docile wife. That had proven to be a longer process than he expected but he had eventually found a candidate for the position of the second Mrs Wilks. His business interests in Huddersfield still required his attention for some of the time but, on their return from the honeymoon three months ago, he had installed the second Mrs Wilks in his mansion in Buxton. She was destined to be referred to by everyone as "the new Mrs Wilks."

Lady Carleton-West, having satisfied herself that the new Mrs Wilks had the right credentials, left her visiting card and, after the correct interval, paid a formal call. The new Mrs Wilks was pronounced to be "acceptable" although "very young and inexperienced." On her first visit, Lady Carleton-West had noted various irregularities and it was obvious to her that the new Mrs Wilks was completely ignorant when it came to managing a household and dealing with servants. She formed the view that her own advice and guidance were indispensable to the new Mrs Wilks and resolved to reform her.

The first Mrs Wilks had been far too independently minded for Lady Carleton-West's taste and had not been invited to join her committee. However, the new Mrs Wilks, having been judged useful, had been invited to join. For Lady Carleton-West, "useful" meant possessing two attributes: the first, sufficient personal resources and enough wealthy social contacts to draw on when gathering funds in support of Lady Carleton-West's many charitable causes; the second, insufficient social ambition to be a threat to Lady Carleton-West's own position. Lady Carleton-West was still recovering from the challenge and threat of deposition which had been posed some time ago by Mrs Preece-Mortimer, whose effrontery had left her almost speechless. As a result, Lady Carleton-West was wary of newcomers, even useful ones.

CHAPTER EIGHT

Ash opened the drawing room door and announced: 'Miss Harriman, your Ladyship.'

Lady Carleton-West was seated at a table surrounded by her committee.

'Miss Harriman,' she said, 'at last. I was afraid we should have to begin without you.'

'I'm very sorry, Lady Carleton-West,' said Eleanor, trying to sound more apologetic than she felt. 'I was . . .'

With a sweep of her hand, Lady Carleton-West indicated that Eleanor should take a seat immediately and that her excuse was of no interest.

'Let us begin, ladies,' said Lady Carleton-West. 'Shall I take the chair as usual?'

The ladies were silent. Eleanor wondered whether, in Lady Carleton-West's long career of forming and bullying committees, anyone had ever dared to respond to that question in the negative.

'Thank you, ladies. Miss Harriman will take the minutes as usual,' continued Lady Carleton-West.

Eleanor sighed inwardly. She had already taken her notepad and pencil out of her handbag in anticipation of this decree.

'Now, ladies, first of all I should like to welcome Mrs Wilks to our committee. Mrs Wilks has kindly agreed to join us and I am sure she will be a great asset.'

Mrs Wilks smiled shyly. Eleanor had heard of the arrival of "the new Mrs Wilks" but had not yet met her.

'Now, ladies,' said Lady Carleton-West, 'as you know,

Doctor Apthorp has resigned from his role at the Devonshire Hospital and he and Mrs Apthorp have left Buxton. I believe that a new doctor has been appointed to replace him and is expected to take up the post quite soon. Accordingly, I propose to call on the new doctor's wife and ask her to join this committee in place of Mrs Apthorp. I hope I have everyone's approval.'

Again there was silence. Eleanor made a note of this proposal and hoped that the new doctor's wife was fond of committees because it did not seem that she would be given any choice in the matter.

'So, shall we turn to the main item on the agenda,' said Lady Carleton-West. 'This year's Top Trees Charity Bazaar.'

'Before we begin, Lady Carleton-West,' said Miss Pymble, hesitantly, 'may I ask if anyone else has heard the news about a baby being found abandoned in the Pavilion Gardens.'

'It's dreadful to think that such a thing could happen here in Buxton, is it not?' added her twin, Miss Felicity, her junior by five minutes.

The other ladies looked concerned, more for the Pymble twins who had dared to interrupt the agenda, than for the abandoned baby. They waited for someone to respond. The Pymble twins were elderly spinsters, daughters of a clergyman, who had arrived in Buxton many years ago. They ran a lodging house and still found time for a multitude of activities connected with the church and with charitable works.

'Yes, I did hear something about that,' said the new Mrs Wilks, hesitantly. Everyone's attention was now on her and she blushed. She added: 'I heard that the baby was quite new and there were flowers scattered all over it.'

The new Mrs Wilks did not reveal her source. She had not yet made any friends in Buxton and, living in splendid isolation, she had only her servants as a source of contact with the outside world. In fact, she had heard the news from her parlour maid, who had heard it from the cook, who had heard it from the butcher's boy when he delivered an order earlier in the day.

The new Mrs Wilks added: 'I believe the baby was found at somewhere called the Temple Mound but, being a new resident, I'm not sure where that is.'

'It's somewhere in the Pavilion Gardens,' said Lady Carleton-West, dismissively. 'People call it the Temple Mound but that's just popular nonsense.'

'Apparently,' said Miss Pymble, 'there is talk of pagan sacrifice.'

'Because of where the baby was found,' added Miss Felicity.

'Fiddlesticks!' said Lady Carleton-West, impatiently. 'Miss Harriman, I'm sure you know the truth about this so-called temple.'

The committee usually relied on Eleanor when facts were needed. She was the first to admit that she had a tendency to get carried away with facts, especially when they concerned history, but having been given permission to speak and being in a slightly rebellious mood, Eleanor decided to give a full explanation and risk contradicting Lady Carleton-West.

Eleanor turned towards the new Mrs Wilks and said: 'The Temple Mound is at the northern end of the Gardens towards the edge of the bowling green, Mrs Wilks. It is a slightly raised area which has been left between the two channels of the River Wye. That is the river which flows through the Gardens.' Then, turning to the meeting in general, Eleanor continued: 'The site was investigated by a gentleman in the mid-eighteenth century and he found what he believed to be the base of a Celtic temple. That is how the mound got its name.'

'No doubt the gentleman was one of those ignorant amateur enthusiasts. He probably found nothing more than a few rocks,' said Lady Carleton-West, scornfully.

'I believe,' said Eleanor, quietly, 'that the foundations that the gentleman saw were re-discovered when the Gardens were remodelled by Mr Milner fifty or so years ago. The stones were removed but the mound was left untouched. Also, a stone was found on the site bearing the name of a Celtic goddess, probably *Aeona*, the goddess of nature. Springs, such as ours, were sacred to the Celts so it is possible that the temple was dedicated to that goddess. The Temple Mound was at one end of an ancient grove of trees which surrounded the springs and extended as far as the Grove Hotel at the other end. The trees were removed when The Crescent was built over the springs.'

There was silence followed by a slight rustling of garments as the ladies turned to look at Lady Carleton-West. They were ever watchful of her signals as to what was to be approved and what was to be condemned.

'Nevertheless,' said Lady Carleton-West, 'this story of a baby on this mound in the Gardens cannot possibly have anything to do with pagan sacrifice. Not in this day and age. Not in Buxton.'

'Then, do you suppose it has something to do with midsummer?' ventured Miss Pymble.

'The baby was scattered with flowers,' added Miss Felicity.

'I don't see the connection,' said Lady Carleton-West, coldly.

'Well, midsummer used to be celebrated in the villages by the young people staying up all night and then, in the morning, collecting flowers and bringing them into the village,' said Miss Pymble.

'It's still celebrated by some people,' added Miss Felicity.

'By farmhands, perhaps, but certainly not in the towns,' said Lady Carleton-West. 'I think that in Buxton we have moved to a level of sophistication beyond the superstitions of those in the surrounding country-side.'

'Well, there are some people working in Buxton who come from the local farms,' said Miss Pymble, in defence of her suggestion. 'They may still be aware of the old customs.'

'And the baby has been found on midsummer's day, which is today,' said Miss Felicity.

'And our Vicar did preach a sermon on Sunday on the danger of reviving pagan customs. That was because of the talk of resuming the Well-Dressings,' explained Miss Pymble, 'and some people are opposed to the idea. The Vicar referred to the fact that the dressing of the wells using flowers to create a picture was not very far removed from the pagan custom of bringing flowers as offerings to the spirits of streams and wells.'

'Now I see your point, Miss Pymble,' said Lady Carleton-West. 'I too heard that sermon. But surely you are not suggesting that this baby was left as part of some pagan midsummer rite.'

'Oh, not at all, Lady Carleton-West, I know very little about pagan rites,' said Miss Pymble, quietly.

'We merely wondered, that was all,' added Miss Felicity.

Eleanor thought she detected an undertone of defiance, like a child who disagrees with a parent and expects to be sent to her room to reflect and repent.

'Very well,' said Lady Carleton-West. 'I shall send a letter to the Well-Dressings committee reminding them that the true purpose of the ceremony is to bless the water in the wells and has nothing to do with this superstitious nonsense.'

The ladies all nodded dutifully and Eleanor refrained from smiling. Lady Carleton-West's solution to every difficulty was a letter to the offending party or committee advising as to the correct way of thinking and the appropriate remedial action to be taken. Eleanor was sure that the Council's Special Committee appointed to consider the Well-Dressings would make its own decision. In fact, she feared that it had already decided that there would be no festival again this year.

'Now,' said Lady Carleton-West, impatiently, 'perhaps we can return to the item which is on the agenda. At our last meeting, we agreed that, at usual, we shall hold the Top Trees Charity Bazaar and that the funds raised will be donated to the Devonshire Hospital Fund. I have the final list of the stalls for the bazaar and the names of those in charge of each stall. I shall hand the list around. Our task today is to sort all the items we have received to date and identify which items are relevant for each stall. I am sure that you all noticed the tables in the entrance hall as you arrived. They represent each stall and they are labelled with the name of the stall and the person in charge. Once the items have been sorted, Miss Harriman will assess any deficiencies of stock and note any items which still need to be gathered.'

The ladies remained silent but nodded in agreement. Eleanor sighed inwardly.

'Before we begin work,' resumed Lady Carleton-West, 'at our last meeting, I asked you all to consider other means by which we could raise funds during the Bazaar. Does anyone have any suggestions.'

'I believe the members of the Burbage Institute organised an afternoon tea last week for the Hospital,' said Mrs Hampson. 'A china tea service was donated by Hargreaves China Shop and that was raffled to raise a donation to the hospital funds. Perhaps we could have a similar raffle.'

'I see,' said Lady Carleton-West, 'I shall see what can be done about offering a raffle prize.'

'Lady Carleton-West, I should like to draw your attention to an advertisement in the *Buxton Advertiser* that you may not have seen,' said Mrs Wentworth-Streate. 'On the day planned for the Top Trees Bazaar, there is to be a garden fête and American tea at The Grange. I wondered if perhaps the date for the Top Trees Bazaar ought to be reconsidered. The Grange is not so very far from here.'

'What, pray, is an American tea?' asked Lady Carleton-West.

'I am not quite certain,' said Mrs Wentworth-Streate.

'I believe,' said Mrs Hampson, 'the idea is to bring an item of food which is shared with those attending, or to bring an item for a stall and then buy something in return.'

'Yes, that is what we have heard,' agreed Miss Pymble.

'Do you mean that refreshments are not provided?' asked Lady Carleton-West, her eyebrows raised to their maximum height.

'We haven't actually been to one,' said Miss Felicity, defensively.

'I only know what I have been told,' said Mrs Hampson.

'I have seen them advertised before,' said Mrs Wentworth-Streate. 'They seem to be the latest fashion.'

'How extra-ordinary!' said Lady Carleton-West, lowering her eyebrows into a frown. 'They seem to be a fearfully haphazard arrangement. Americans do have such very different ideas as to what constitutes entertainment. To be successful, a bazaar cannot just be left to chance and the whim of those who attend. It must be carefully planned. The precision that goes into organising the Top Trees Bazaar is the secret of its success. Let us hope that this American event will prove too unpopular to be repeated. We shall proceed with our chosen date. There being no other items on the agenda for today, I declare the meeting closed. Now, ladies, we can begin work. Please follow me.'

The committee members dutifully filed out to the entrance hall and took up their positions. The abandoned baby was forgotten as they enthusiastically sorted and commented on the stock of crocheted d'oyleys, drawn-thread work, painted plates, embroidered handkerchiefs, knitted socks, leatherwork spectacle cases, and other such essentials of a successful bazaar.

Eleanor's thoughts drifted to the flower-covered baby on the Celtic temple site: that was the beginning of a story which she was certain needed a middle and an ending.

CHAPTER NINE

When Eleanor returned to Hall Bank from Top Trees, she went in search of Mrs Clayton. The housekeeper was preparing dinner and Napoleon was in the hall sitting attentively like a Trafalgar Square lion with his front legs stretched out and his paws just across the doorway into the kitchen. Entry into the kitchen was forbidden but he knew if he abided by the rules Mrs Clayton would offer him titbits of his favourite food. She knew exactly what his preferences were. It was a partnership of several years' standing. Napoleon gave Eleanor a quick sideways glance to acknowledge her arrival and returned to his task of watchdog.

Mrs Clayton looked up from what she was doing and said: 'Ah, Miss Harriman. How was the meeting? The kettle's just boiled. Would you like a cup of tea?'

'I am greatly in need of tea, Mrs Clayton, but don't let me disturb you. I can make it.'

Napoleon moved to one side to let Eleanor into the kitchen.

'You carry on with what you were doing,' said Eleanor. 'I came to ask you about a rumour I heard at the meeting. I was sure that, if there was any truth in it, you would be bound to know. One of the ladies said that a baby had been found abandoned in the Pavilion Gardens. On the Temple Mound.'

'Oh, yes, Miss Harriman, that's quite true. I haven't had a chance to tell you. Alf was on his way past here at lunchtime and he called in and told me. He wondered if Mr Harriman had heard anything. He was called out early this morning to do the collection. Fair put out about it he was, too. When he got to the Pavilion Gardens, that new Inspector was holding forth. He hasn't been in the town five minutes but he was giving it as his opinion that it was something to do with the Well-Dressings. He said what else could you expect in a town where they had such old-fashioned notions. Primitive customs he called them. I heard he was from Sheffield but Alf says judging by his accent he's from down south. Either way, I don't suppose he understands about things like the dressing of the wells.'

Eleanor said: 'I don't know where he has come from.'

'Well, wherever he's from, he wasn't a bit sorry about the bairn, poor little mite. Just shrugged and told his sergeant to deal with it and went back to the station.'

'But, the baby, was it found on the Temple Mound?'

'Yes, a boy, only tiny. No clothes on, just wrapped in a cloth. Alf said he couldn't be sure but he thought the baby might have been already dead when it was left there. So that's a mercy, at least.'

'Did Alf say what made him think that?'

'He said the cloth had been wrapped round very tightly and it hadn't been disturbed as you might expect it would have been if the baby'd been alive. Moving his arms, kicking his legs about, which they do if they cry, and he would be bound to be crying, wouldn't he? Left there all by himself and probably hungry.'

'And he had been scattered with flowers which sounds rather odd. Is that true?'

Mrs Clayton nodded. 'Just a few flowers and some leaves as well. From an ash tree.'

'Oh dear, a pagan symbol. I hope that detail doesn't become public knowledge otherwise people will be convinced that the abandonment of the baby on the mound really is associated with some pagan rite.'

'And, of course, it is midsummer today,' added Mrs Clayton. 'That could just be co-incidence, I suppose.'

'Yes, but we've had enough discussion about the supposed practices of the Celts already from the opponents of the revival of the Well-Dressings without this baby providing further fuel to their fire. I can already imagine the use that some people will make of this incident.'

'I shouldn't worry. It'll turn out to be nothing to do with the pagans. Like as not he was somebody's chance child they couldn't afford to keep. There's been a bit of that lately, according to the papers.'

'Yes, that's true. It is rather disturbing to think that someone would be callous enough to abandon a baby in that way but I suppose with unemployment and inflation the way they are, people are finding it impossible to make ends meet. But, it is a life, after all, and it shouldn't be cut short like that.'

'There's a lot of folks struggling to feed themselves, even those who have employment. An unplanned child and an extra mouth to feed is the final straw for some families. And women can't get any help from their doctors, of course, although it's not for want of asking.' Mrs Clayton sighed. 'We all thought that if only the War would end, things would be all right again but it wasn't to be, was it?'

'No, unfortunately, and all we can do is make the best of it. I hope the Well-Dressings do go ahead. It would be good for everybody. It would buck people up.'

'I agree but I'm not very hopeful,' said Mrs Clayton, as she turned back to the kitchen bench intending to finish preparing the dinner. Then she turned back to Eleanor. 'Oh, now, I almost forgot. Mr Harriman asked me while you were at the meeting if we had anything for Lady Carleton-West's bazaar because, if not, he would send a donation. He asked me to speak to you about it. I've checked the store cupboard and there's still six pots of the Seville marmalade I made in January, and four pots of gooseberry Jam from the fruit James gave me from his garden, and three pots of red currant

Jelly I made yesterday with the fruit from Mr Talbot's garden. That should do, I think. Or I could make some cakes as well.'

'No, that will do splendidly, Mrs Clayton. I don't think there is any need for cakes. We are such martyrs to her ladyship. I shall let it be known that you made the jam and it will all be snapped up in the first ten minutes. It is a shame that you never knew my mother. She loved doing this sort of thing and together you would have made a formidable team.'

'I'm sorry too,' said Mrs Clayton, 'I have heard several people speak very highly of her and of her charity work.'

'I'm no good at it at all,' said Eleanor. 'I'm afraid I'm a disappointment to the ladies of The Park. They all expected me to follow in my mother's footsteps.'

'Well, we all have our talents, Miss Harriman, and it seems you have followed in your father's footsteps instead.'

Eleanor laughed. 'And I think it is probably just as well that my mother is not here to see that particular development. Perhaps when Richard goes away to school and Cecily has more time to spare she will step in and save the family's reputation. Now, Leon, we have work to do. Come on.'

Napoleon did not move.

'He's not in the way, Miss Harriman. He's good company.'

Eleanor looked at Napoleon and said: 'Oh, I understand. You have work to do here. I shall see you later then.'

'Dear me,' said Mrs Clayton, 'I was that busy thinking about the baby and the Bazaar I forgot about Alf's message. When he dropped by this afternoon, I asked him what he could remember about Old Walter and he said Old Walter was a bit tiresome with his story and he didn't really pay much attention. He does remember Old Walter saying that if it ever came to Court he would be proved right because he had the papers to prove it. Alf said he's sorry he couldn't help.'

'Thank you, Mrs Clayton. Please tell Alf not to worry. I think I found the solution and I think Old Walter was right. It's a shame he didn't go to Court.'

'Knowing Old Walter, I think he probably preferred having something to be cantankerous about.'

0   0   0

Just before the office closed that afternoon, Eleanor's friend, Doctor Catherine Balderstone, called in at Hall Bank to ask Eleanor to witness her signature on a document.

'I suppose you've heard about the baby found on the Temple Mound,' said Catherine.

'Yes, I was at a committee meeting at Lady Carleton-West's this afternoon.'

'I assume the police will be looking for the mother. At least if she killed it, the new *Infanticide Act* will save her from hanging.'

'Only if she can prove that the balance of her mind was disturbed not having fully recovered from the effect of giving birth,' said Eleanor. 'I do have my doubts about the wisdom of that new defence. It makes childbirth sound like temporary madness.'

'It is rather Scylla and Charybdis, isn't it? Murder or madness. Which would you be prepared to admit to?'

'Could childbirth deprive one of one's reason to that extent?'

'I haven't witnessed it in any of my patients,' said Catherine. 'When I read the parliamentary debates, I couldn't see any medical basis for the amendment to the law. I suspected that the honourable members were not really interested in understanding childbirth and were more concerned in finding a way to deal with the current high rate of mortality in illegitimate children. I suppose they thought it was understandable that a mother who has no means of feeding or caring for the child might, out of desperation, resort to causing its death and, therefore, should not be punished.'

'And that's a social problem not a medical one,' said Eleanor. 'It would have been better if the honourable members had addressed that instead.'

'Exactly, but we are still stuck with the legislation.'

'The Pymble twins have suggested that leaving the baby on the Temple Mound is associated with it being midsummer. I think they were hinting at infant sacrifice and pagan rites. Apparently, the Vicar preached a sermon on the subject on Sunday. Something to do with deterring people from reviving the Well-Dressings.'

'Yes,' said Catherine, 'I have heard rumblings of opposition to that. It's all such a muddle in some people's minds.'

'The fact that today is midsummer is probably irrelevant but the choice of the site is curious.'

'Yes,' said Catherine. 'One would expect the mother to hide the body so as to escape detection for as long as possible, not leave it in a busy location at the height of the Season where someone was bound to see it.'

'It does seem as though someone wanted to make a point,' agreed Eleanor. She sighed. 'I suppose we shall just have to wait and see whether the police are able to find the mother. Now, on another topic altogether, I heard from Lady Carleton-West at the committee meeting that the new doctor had been appointed to replace Doctor Apthorp at the Devonshire Hospital.'

'No, as usual, Lady Carleton-West has got it wrong,' said Catherine.

'And?' said Eleanor. 'The correct version?'

'Replacements for Doctor Apthorp are still being interviewed so there has been no new appointment as yet.'

'But Lady C is certain that the new Mrs Doctor is going

to join her committee.'

'Well, perhaps she is confused. There is a new consultant who has just been appointed to the Hospital but I have no idea whether he is married or not. He specialises in conditions affecting the chest, so he will be a real asset to the work of the Hospital. He doesn't take up his post until the beginning of July, but I believe he has now arrived in Buxton.'

'Where has he come from?'

'No idea. He was recommended by the Duke of Devonshire but I don't know what the connection is. The War possibly. He was a Major and a decorated war hero as well.'

'Have you met him?'

'No, but some people have. He came as a guest of the Duke of Devonshire to the official opening of the extension to the Cottage Hospital in April. I'm told that he is very personable. Excellent manners. Handsome as well, has a good tailor.' Catherine laughed. 'I fully expect some of my female patients to develop chest complaints and desert me, especially the unmarried ones.'

0 0 0

DIARY Tuesday 24th June

Brocklehurst arrived to begin work on my rooms. Gave him directions.

Heard a rumour this afternoon that a baby had been found on a place known at Temple Mound. Mr Lomas explained where this is but was unable to enlighten me further. Everyone else had a theory, some wilder than others. Several mentioned the Well-Dressings festival.

CHAPTER TEN

On Wednesday morning, when Edwin Talbot arrived at Hall Bank, Eleanor was in Mr Harriman's office discussing the wording of one of the deeds for Old Walter's plot of land.

'Morning, James,' said Edwin, as he hung his hat on the peg in the hall. He paused at the door of Mr Harriman's office and, as Napoleon greeted him, he bent to tickle him behind one ear.'

'Good morning, Eleanor. Good morning, Harriman.'

'Ah, Talbot. Good morning. Before you go up, just cast your eye over this deed, would you? Eleanor has found the solution to that boundary dispute on Bishop's Lane. The last three lines are the relevant ones.'

Edwin took the document held out by Mr Harriman, and sat down to read it.

'Yes, James?' said Mr Harriman, as James appeared in the doorway of his office.

'I'm sorry to interrupt, Mr Harriman, but Mr Wilde has telephoned and wonders if he might speak to you. He says it is of the utmost urgency but prefers not to tell me what it concerns. He would appreciate it if you would speak to him immediately. That's Mr John Wilde, the sexton. Not Mr Wilde, the butcher.'

'All right, James. You can put the call through.'

Edwin prepared to leave but Mr Harriman raised his hand and shook his head and Edwin returned to considering the deed.

Mr Harriman picked up the telephone stand, put the

earpiece to his ear, and spoke into the mouthpiece.

'Good morning, Mr Wilde. This is Mr Harriman speaking. How can I be of help?'

Eleanor watched as Mr Harriman listened, began to frown, and at intervals said: 'Of course' and 'Certainly,' and 'And how old is Joshua?' and then 'Just one moment, please, Mr Wilde.'

Mr Harriman removed the earpiece, and turning to Edwin, said: 'Would you be free at some time today? To see Mr Wilde and his grandson?'

Edwin raised his eyebrows and said: 'I'm due in Court in half an hour. This afternoon, perhaps?'

'It's early closing,' said Eleanor.

'Oh, of course. Shall we say, twelve. I should be back by then.'

Mr Harriman resumed the call: 'Mr Wilde, you will appreciate, I'm sure, that although I should like to help you, this is not my area of expertise. However, Mr Talbot will see you and your grandson at twelve o'clock today.' He listened again and nodded. 'Bail, yes, I see.' Then, after another pause, added: 'Not at all, Mr Wilde. We shall see you at twelve then. Goodbye.'

Eleanor and Edwin looked expectantly at Mr Harriman.

'Well, in all the years of this practice, I don't think we have ever had such a case. Mr Wilde's grandson has been charged with preventing the lawful and decent burial of a dead body.'

'Goodness,' said Eleanor. 'That sounds a bit grim.'

'And it is also a little ironic, don't you think?' said Edwin. 'Given that Mr Wilde is the sexton at Christ Church and responsible for seeing that everyone has a decent burial.'

'It is rather,' agreed Mr Harriman. 'Many years ago, in my father's time, there was someone charged with disposal of a corpse with the intent to obstruct or prevent the Coroner's inquest but I'm sure we have never had a client charged with this particular offence. It is rather an obscure one.'

'Whose body has been denied burial?' asked Edwin.

'From what I can gather, the offence with which the grandson has been charged relates to the body of the baby that was found on the Temple Mound in the Pavilion Gardens.'

'Ah, yes,' said Edwin, 'I read the report in the *Sheffield Daily Telegraph* this morning. I assumed that the baby had been abandoned. The more usual charge is attempting to conceal the birth of a child and usually it is the mother who is charged not a third party.'

'Well, whoever did this and whoever is charged, it is all very unsatisfactory,' said Mr Harriman.

'At least this charge against Mr Wilde's grandson will put paid to any rumours of pagan sacrifice on the Temple Mound,' said Eleanor.

Mr Harriman said: 'Let us hope so. The Wesleyan Methodist minister was telling me only yesterday that he has had letters from members of his congregation opposing the revival of the Well-Dressings and raising fears of the return of superstitious practices. That sort of bigotry is never far below the surface. Mr Wilde is well known around the town, an upright citizen and pillar of the church, and always concerned to do the right thing. And, naturally, Mr Wilde wants us to defend his grandson.'

'He assumes that there is such a defence,' said Edwin.

'Yes,' said Mr Harriman. 'I thought it better not to comment to Mr Wilde on that point. I'll leave that to your good judgment, Talbot. The grandson has yet to be bailed so Mr Wilde will bring him in at twelve o'clock.'

'I heard you ask Mr Wilde. How old is the grandson?'

'Fourteen.'

'Hmm,' said Edwin. 'that makes it even more interesting.' He turned to Eleanor. 'As we are not likely to get another such case in the next fifty years, would you like to sit in on this one? I can explain that you are there to take notes.'

'Yes, please.'

'Excellent,' said Edwin. 'That will leave me free to concentrate on assessing the demeanour of the accused. It is always critical at that first interview. This could be a jolly interesting case. Perhaps while I'm in Court you could check the case law and see what you can whip up in the way of a defence. It's a common law offence, by the way, not a statutory one.'

'If you are going to defend young Wilde, that rules me out as Coroner, but that's all right. I haven't received notification about the baby from the police yet,' said Mr Harriman.

'Oh, yes, of course. I wasn't thinking. You won't be able to sit. You don't mind awfully, do you, Harriman?'

'No, not at all. I had better let the new Superintendent know though and he can arrange for someone else to sit. I shouldn't think there will be much in it. The inquest, that is. The more interesting issue is how the body got where it was found. I shall be intrigued to know what young Wilde has got to say on that subject.'

Edwin stood up and handed back to Mr Harriman the deed he had been holding. 'I see what you mean about those last three lines. That description certainly fits the piece of land that was created when the river changed course and it should be enough to satisfy the prospective purchaser. Mr Brittain will be pleased. Well done, Eleanor.'

'Yes, well done,' said Mr Harriman. 'I shall telephone Mr Brittain immediately and give him the good news.'

CHAPTER ELEVEN

At twelve o'clock, Mr Harriman had a brief word with Mr John Wilde before James ushered him and his grandson upstairs to Edwin's office and announced them. Eleanor was already seated in the corner armed with a notebook.

The accused, Joshua Wilde, was a gangly youth, wearing a well-worn tweed jacket over dusty overalls. The jacket was slightly too small and his bare wrists protruded beyond the ends of the frayed cuffs. He shuffled in, eyes cast down. He was almost six feet tall and very thin. His body seemed to have concentrated on growing upwards without bothering to fill out. He towered over his grandfather who was almost a foot shorter and bent over, either from age or the kind of manual work he performed. By contrast with his grandson, Mr Wilde senior, was dressed in his best suit.

When the formalities of introduction were over, Mr Wilde said:

'I'm sorry the lad's in his working clothes, Mr Talbot. I brought him straight here from the police station and he hasn't had time to change.'

Edwin said: 'I understand, Mr Wilde. Please don't worry about that. I shall, of course, do my best to help your grandson, but you must appreciate that this is a very serious offence and a rather unusual one at that. The level of assistance I can give will depend entirely on the facts.'

'Oh, I understand, Mr Talbot. I don't know what the lad said to the police but he's all but admitted it to me.'

In order to deflect Mr Wilde from putting words into his

grandson's mouth, Edwin said:

'I understand that you are the sexton at Christ Church so you have experience of these matters.'

'Aye, thirty years I've been sexton and I don't know what the vicar's going to say when he finds out about this. We've never had a criminal in our family, Mr Talbot. I don't know what the lad were thinking. I'm only glad his father's not here to witness it. Killed in the War, of course.'

'Yes,' said Edwin, 'I believe he died trying to save his commanding officer.'

'That he did,' agreed Mr Wilde, 'and left a wife and four children. Joshua here is the eldest. I managed to get him a job with George Beresford, as a favour like, because his mother could never afford to get him apprenticed. But I don't want you to think we're here for charity, Mr Talbot. I'll see to it that your bill is paid. Have no fear.'

'Thank you, Mr Wilde. I appreciate that but before we talk about fees, let's just hear what Joshua has to say and then I can decide how best to proceed.'

'He's a good lad, Mr Talbot, and he's never been in any bother before.'

'That will certainly count in his favour. All right, Mr Wilde, let's see what can be done.'

During this conversation, Joshua had sat with his head bowed and his face expressionless. Edwin studied the paper which Mr Wilde had given him on which was written the charge against Joshua.

Edwin looked up and said: 'Joshua, you've been charged with preventing the lawful and decent burial of a dead body. Was that explained to you at the police station?'

Edwin waited for a response but Joshua said nothing.

'Do you understand what it means?'

Joshua nodded but still did not look up.

'Joshua, I want you to tell me exactly what happened. You must understand that, if I am going to help you, I need to know all the details, even if there are things which you think might count against you or that you think your grandfather might not approve of. Do you understand?'

Joshua did not reply. He began to pull at the threads on one of the frayed cuffs of his jacket.

'Is it all right if your grandfather stays?'

Joshua nodded.

Edwin decided to start with familiar and neutral territory in order to get Joshua talking.

'Right, then,' he said, 'first of all, tell me who you were working for.'

'Mr Beresford.'

'And what is his trade?'

'Builder.'

'When did you start working for Mr Beresford?'

'T'other day.'

' Monday?'

'Aye.'

'So, you have only just finished school?'

Joshua nodded. 'Last week.'

'And on Monday where were you working?'

'The Shakespeare Hotel.'

'Was anyone else working there with you, apart from Mr Beresford?'

'Will Fiddler.'

'What time did you arrive at the hotel?'

'Eight o'clock.'

'And what work were you doing?'

'Clearing out the old stables.'

'Do you mean that they were to be demolished?'

Joshua shook his head. 'Clearing 'em to make more room for motors.'

'Oh, I see. Isn't it a bit late in the year to be doing that sort of work? It's the middle of the Season when most of the visitors arrive.'

Joshua nodded.

'And did Mr Beresford only begin that work on the Monday, the day you started working for him?'

'Aye.'

'Which would have been the twenty-third?'

Joshua frowned and then nodded.

'And can you describe for me the work you were doing at the Shakespeare's stables?'

'Ripping out the 'orse boxes.'

'And what time did you finish work?'

'When it were dark.'

'That seems like a long day.'

'We did extra time to get the job done. To please Mrs Erskine.'

'Is that the owner of the hotel?'

Joshua nodded.

'Right. Now, I'd like you to tell me about the baby.'

'I found it.'

'And where was that?'

'In one of th' 'orse boxes.'

'Which one?'

'Last one.'

'How many horseboxes are there or, rather, were there before you started work?

'Six.'

'So you had cleared all but one of the horse boxes? And the baby was in the last one?'

Joshua nodded.

'And where was the baby exactly?'

'Up in the far corner.'

'Can you describe for me what you saw?'

'I didn't rightly know what it were.'

'What did you think, at first?'

'Just an old blanket, or clothes, or summut left behind.'

'So, when you got closer what did you see?'

'A bairn. It were wrapped up, like.'
'And was the baby alive?'
'I thought it were dead.'
'What made you think that?'
'It weren't crying nor moving nor anything.'
'And then what did you do?'
'Waited for Mr Beresford to come back.'
'So Mr Beresford wasn't there when you found the baby?'
Joshua shook his head.
'And where was he?'
'Off talking to Mrs Erskine.'
'And what about Will Fiddler?'
'He'd gone off wi' a load of the old timber.'
'Gone off where?'
'Loading the cart.'
'Where was the cart?'
'In the lane at the back.'
'And what did Mr Beresford say when you showed him the baby?'
'He were right vexed. Swore a lot.'
'Why was that, do you think?'
'He said the police 'ud stop us getting on wi' the job.'
'Anything else?'
'Mrs Erskine would likely give him the sack if the work got held up.'
'Anything else?'
'I were a meddlin' fool and I weren't to say nowt about the bairn to anyone.'
'And what about when Will Fiddler returned from loading the cart?'
'Him and Mr Beresford went away to have a talk.'
'And what happened then?'
'He told me to take the rest of the old timber to the cart.'
'Mr Beresford?'
Joshua nodded.

'And when you had finished doing that, what did you do?'

'Will and me took out the last 'orse box.'

'And the baby had been moved while you were away?'

'I spose so.'

'Can you remember roughly what time it was when you found the baby?'

Joshua frowned and shook his head. 'Towards sixish.'

'You said earlier that you worked late to get the job done. What time did you finish that night?'

'Just after eight.'

'And did you go home then?'

'No, I were going to, but Mr Beresford said not to.'

'Why was that?'

'He were going to the White Lion with Will for a drink. He said I had to go too.'

This was the longest sentence Joshua had spoken and Edwin wondered if Joshua was starting to trust him.

'Can you recall exactly what Mr Beresford said to you?'

'If I wanted to work for him, I had to learn to drink with him as well.'

Mr Wilde, senior, who had remained admirably silent until this point, made an explosive noise of disapproval.

'And how did you respond to that?'

'I couldn't say nowt.'

'So, you went with them to the White Lion?'

Mr Wilde could no longer contain his indignation. He leaned forward and said: 'Joshua doesn't drink, Mr Talbot, not at his age.'

Joshua turned to his grandfather. 'But I had to, grandad, didn't I? I didn't want to lose the job.'

Edwin glanced at Mr Wilde.

'Sorry,' said Mr Wilde, contritely, as he subsided back into his chair.

'How old are you, Joshua.'

Joshua hesitated. 'Fourteen.'

'I want you to tell me the truth because it is important, even if you think your grandfather will disapprove. Did you have anything to drink at the White Lion?'

Joshua nodded.

'A half? Or a pint?'

'A pint.'

'All right,' said Edwin. 'Tell me about the baby. How did it get onto the Temple Mound?'

'I put it there.'

'Whose idea was that?'

'Mr Beresford and Will.'

'Tell me what they said about it.'

'It were a bit of a lark they said. To give those as didn't want the Well-Dressings summut to think on.'

'And what did you say to that?'

'I said I didn't want to.'

'So why did you do it?'

'Mr Beresford said I had to. He tried to make out as I knew summut about it'

'Was he suggesting that you had left the baby there?'

Joshua nodded.

Edwin was aware that Mr Wilde was fidgeting and finding it hard to remain silent and he sympathised.

'He said he'd tell the police I knew all about it,' mumbled Joshua.

'Do you have any idea whose baby it was?'

Joshua shook his head energetically.

'Or how it came to be in the horsebox?'

Joshua frowned. 'How would a'? It weren't nothing to do wi' me.'

'And had you ever been in those stables before? Or in the Shakespeare Hotel?'

'Course not. I don't go to hotels.'

'So, let me just see if I have understood correctly. While you were loading the cart with timber, somebody, Mr

Beresford or Will, moved the baby out of the stables. Then you and Will went in and removed the last horsebox.' Joshua nodded. 'So when you left to go to the White Lion, the baby was no longer in the stables.'

Joshua said: 'No. It were gone.'

Edwin did not comment but he was thinking that someone, Mr Beresford or Will, had moved the baby during the afternoon and might also be guilty of an offence. He thought that he could probably make use of that information but decided to put it to one side for the moment.

'So when Mr Beresford told you to go and get rid of the baby, what did you say?'

'I asked him where it were?'

'And he said what?'

'I'd to go back to the Shakespeare. It were in the cart in the lane.'

'And you went back to the cart and took the baby. What time was this?'

'I don't know but it were almost dark by then.'

'So you don't own a watch?'

Joshua shook his head vigorously. 'Can't afford one.'

'And what about the flowers?' asked Edwin. 'There were flowers and leaves scattered around the body. Did you do that?'

Joshua looked down at his hands and nodded.

Edwin waited and then said: 'And what was the reason for the flowers?'

Joshua glanced at his grandfather and then said: 'I help grandad sometimes. I know people throw flowers into the grave after the coffin 'as been lowered in. So I put some on the baby. I felt sorry for it.'

'And how did you come to the attention of the police?'

'I felt funny in the 'ead. I went to sit down on a bench and I must've fallen asleep.'

'Was the bench near the Temple Mound?'

'Aye.'

'And I suppose the park keeper found you?'

'When he were locking up. He said sleeping in the Gardens weren't allowed.'

'I see, so that must have been at some time after ten o'clock.' said Edwin. 'Did the park keeper mention the baby?'

'No.'

'It was the park keeper who reported you to the police. Did you know him?'

Joshua shook his head.

'Then, how did he know who you were?'

'Took my name and address. He said I had to prove I weren't a homeless person or he'd have me charged as a vagrant. 'Cos he'd found me sleeping on the bench.'

'Well, I think that is all for the moment. Thank you, Joshua. Now, if you don't mind going downstairs and sitting in the hall for a bit, I'd like to talk to your grandfather.'

Joshua stood up slowly and shuffled to the door.

When he had gone, Mr Wilde said: 'Can ye do anything for the lad, Mr Talbot?'

'Not in relation to the charge itself, I'm afraid. As you have just heard, Joshua admits that he put the baby on the Mound. It seems that he did break the law and what he did is an offence, whether he realised that or not.'

'He understood it were not right, though. You heard him say so,' said Mr Wilde. 'He's a bright boy and he's also honest.'

'There is just one point I need to clear up, Mr Wilde. Joshua said that he is fourteen, but I notice from the date of birth on the charge sheet that that is not quite right.'

Mr Wilde sighed. 'Is that important?'

'Very important.'

'He's not far off and George Beresford wouldn't have waited. He wanted someone who could start straightaway and he said if anyone asked Joshua's age, he'd to say he were fourteen.'

'So, Joshua wasn't quite fourteen when he left school, either.'

'No, a couple of weeks off. Joshua has to have some form of employment to help his mother. She gets a widow's pension, of course, but it's not enough and she takes in washing but lately she's been too poorly to work.'

'I see.'

'I thought leaving school a couple of weeks early wouldn't make a deal of difference.'

'It may not make a difference as far as the school is concerned but it does make a big difference as far as the law is concerned. In Joshua's favour.'

'That's something, I suppose.'

'It's very clear that Joshua was taken advantage of by Mr Beresford and, in relation to the baby, acted at his direction. Mr Beresford's part in this is another matter which will have to be dealt with by the police. I don't want to get your hopes up but, if we can put the right evidence before the court, it just might be possible to save Joshua from having a criminal record. Would you let me have the names of people you think would be willing to give him a character reference. His school-teacher, perhaps. Someone who has known him for a long time.'

'Oh, I can certainly do that, Mr Talbot. There's any number of people as knows what a good lad Joshua is. He takes after his father. But George Beresford, now. Always on the wild side, larking about without minding what trouble he causes for other people, and that young Will Fiddler is no better. But George is old enough to have more sense. And as for taking advantage of the lad in that way, well, I don't know what to say. I had my reservations about placing Joshua with him but times are hard, Mr Talbot, and I thought it better than nothing at all. I'm right pleased you're willing to help Joshua and, as I said, I don't expect charity. I can pay your fees whatever they are.'

'Thank you, Mr Wilde. Joshua has been very badly served and I'd like to help him. I'm sure Mr Harriman will agree with me.'

'It's kind of you to take an interest, Mr Talbot. I'm right disappointed in George Beresford, getting Joshua into this. I shall have something to say to him next time I see him.'

'Joshua's only just out of school and he's been taken advantage of. It's a poor introduction to working life.'

'Aye, it is that.'

CHAPTER TWELVE

As it was early closing, Eleanor and Edwin met in Mr Harriman's office for their usual chat before Edwin left to go home and the office closed. Edwin explained to Mr Harriman how the baby had been found in the hotel stables and why it was placed on the Temple Mound.

Mr Harriman said: 'Erskine. That name is familiar to me. That was the name of the landlord at the Shakespeare Hotel. There was an accident there a few months ago. Mr Erskine died after falling down some stairs. I suppose his widow owns the hotel now.' He paused. 'Well, now, what did you make of Joshua Wilde?'

Edwin said: 'I think he has been honest with us and told us all he knows. What was your impression, Eleanor?'

'I agree,' said Eleanor. 'He wasn't exactly talkative but he didn't seem to me to be hiding anything. It is an extraordinary story.'

'I did get the impression that Beresford thought Joshua knew more about the baby than he was admitting to,' said Edwin, 'that he was somehow involved in the baby being left in the stables.'

'Surely Mr Beresford was not suggesting that Joshua was the father,' said Eleanor.

'It's unlikely, given his age,' said Edwin. 'But it's possible that he thought Joshua had hidden the baby, or that he knew who had, and only pretended to find it. It's understandable, I suppose, because Joshua, very conveniently, was alone at the time he found the baby. Joshua said that Beresford was cross at the thought of being held up with the job he was doing.'

'There is another explanation, of course,' said Mr Harriman. 'If Beresford had something to do with leaving the baby in the stables in the first place, he may have made sure that Joshua, very conveniently, was the one to find it. Beresford wasn't there at the time, remember.'

'I think the facts suggest that Beresford himself can be ruled out,' said Edwin.

'What do you mean?' asked Mr Harriman.

'Well, surely, if Beresford had been involved in any way, he would not have left the baby in the stables. He must have known that if it was discovered that would prevent him from getting on with the job. No, I think we can probably rule Beresford out on those grounds.'

'I see what you mean,' said Mr Harriman.

'That leaves Will Fiddler,' said Eleanor. 'He might be involved. We need to keep him in mind. He wasn't there when Joshua found the baby but he might have abandoned it or helped whoever did. From what Joshua said, Beresford seems to accept that Fiddler hadn't been involved but can we trust Beresford?'

'It's hard to understand Beresford's actions otherwise,' said Edwin. 'It was a very callous way to treat an employee especially one so young and trusting as Joshua. I doubt whether Joshua has had much to do with people like George Beresford. He comes from a respectable family. He's not quite fourteen and only just left school.'

Mr Harriman said: 'Not quite fourteen? When Mr Wilde telephoned, I'm sure he said that Joshua was fourteen.'

'Yes,' said Edwin. 'He probably did but Joshua won't turn fourteen for another couple of weeks. Joshua left school last week because that is what suited Mr Beresford. Joshua is very tall and he certainly looks old enough to have left school. I just hope he didn't lie to the police when he was asked his age at first.'

'So, when he left the baby on the Temple Mound, he wasn't yet fourteen,' said Mr Harriman. 'That changes things somewhat, does it not?'

Edwin said: 'Just a little. If and when it goes to trial, he will have turned fourteen. But that won't change the fact that, when he committed the offence, he was under fourteen. The onus will be on the prosecution to prove that, at the time, he knew this action was seriously wrong.'

'And,' said Eleanor, 'according to Joshua, when Mr Beresford sent him to put the baby on the Temple Mound, both Mr Beresford and Will Fiddler were treating it as nothing more than a harmless prank. That certainly would not have given Joshua the impression that what he was doing was a crime or even that there was anything seriously wrong.'

'And there is still that element of obeying the directions of one's employer,' said Mr Harriman. 'An employee of Joshua's age is not going to question his employer, particularly as he had only begun work that day.'

'And he shouldn't really have been employed at all,' said Eleanor. 'Mr Beresford was in the wrong there as well.'

'There is also the issue of drinking at the White Lion. Mr Beresford knew that Joshua was under age, even if he was not aware of the changes made last year by Lady Astor's bill. When Joshua left the baby he was definitely affected by what he had been drinking.'

'This case is proving to be even more interesting than I originally thought,' said Mr Harriman. 'Is there anything known about the identity of the mother?'

'Not so far,' said Edwin.

'And until the *post mortem* report we won't know whether the baby was alive at the time it was abandoned,' said Mr Harriman.

'No, and that's another possible charge,' added Edwin, 'although so far it has not been brought against Joshua.'

'Or the mother,' said Mr Harriman. 'That's something else to bear in mind. If the baby was stillborn or died shortly afterwards, the mother may have hidden it hoping that it would not be discovered for some time.'

'Whoever left the baby must have known that the old stables were there and that they were not being used,' said Eleanor. 'I wonder if there is a connection between the mother and the hotel. Someone who works there perhaps?'

'But someone who works at the hotel would surely know that the stables were about to be renovated.'

'A guest at the hotel?' suggested Eleanor.

'A bit far-fetched, don't you think?' said Edwin.

'Clutching at straws,' said Eleanor, smiling.

'But, if the police do think Joshua was involved in the abandonment of the baby and, possibly involved in the baby's death, it is important to find the mother. If the baby was still born, the mother's evidence is vital,' said Mr Harriman. 'It would be useful if we could find her.'

'That may not be easy,' said Eleanor. 'She may have left town. People who knew her and knew of her condition would naturally ask questions about the baby the next time they saw her. She might not want to explain what happened.'

'It is not easy to put oneself in the position of the mother,' said Edwin, 'but wouldn't you think that, if the baby had been born alive and the mother, for whatever reason, could not keep it, she would have left it somewhere more public than the stables, in the hope that it would be found and taken in by someone.'

'One would think so,' said Mr Harriman, 'and with that motive in mind the Temple Mound would be a more obvious place to leave the baby. But this is all speculation and we have very few facts to go on. A lot will depend on whether or not Joshua's account of events is accepted. Did he strike you as a good witness.'

'No. He seems truthful enough but he would be a

suggestible witness,' said Edwin. 'He would be easily intimidated by a forceful prosecuting counsel.'

'I agree,' said Eleanor. 'He was clearly intimidated by Beresford. That's why he got himself into this mess.' Eleanor paused, then added: 'We really need to find the mother, don't we? She may be the only one who knows the truth.'

'How do we find her?' said Edwin. 'We know nothing about her.'

'Well,' said Eleanor, 'as we said earlier, whoever it was who abandoned the baby must have known about the stables. It is a rather obscure place to leave a baby, certainly not the sort of place one would normally think of, or come across by chance. We also concluded that it must have been someone who did not know that the stables were about to be renovated.'

'Such as?' asked Edwin.

'Someone who previously worked at the hotel, perhaps,' suggested Eleanor.

Edwin said: 'That's possible, I suppose. I can see by your expression that you have a suggestion to make.'

'As far as I know the only information about the baby that is public knowledge at the moment is the fact that it was found in the Gardens. There hasn't been anything to connect it with the Shakespeare Hotel or even any mention of that hotel.'

'That's true,' said Edwin.

'So the people at the Shakespeare Hotel will not yet have been hounded by newspaper reporters. They may still be willing to answer questions. I could just go to the hotel and see what I can find out.'

'It might be worth trying, I suppose,' agreed Mr Harriman. 'I don't see any reason why you should not say that you are a solicitor asking for information on behalf of a client. That should reassure them that you are not linked to the newspapers.'

'Philip is going to inspect the Hepplewhite furniture this afternoon so we've abandoned golf for today. If I go to the hotel now, I should still be able to get there before the newshounds.'

0   0   0

The original Shakespeare Inn had been built in Spring Gardens at the beginning of the nineteenth century, when improvements to country roads had made travel less arduous and the number of travellers requiring accommodation in Buxton had increased. An early sketch of the Shakespeare Inn shows an elegant three storey Georgian building in front of which stand some fashionably dressed visitors, who could easily have stepped out of a Jane Austen novel. Inns were often named by reference to some local feature and the Shakespeare Inn is thought to have been so named because it was close to a small, rather primitive, building a little further down Spring Gardens grandly known as The Theatre. A letter written from lodgings in Hall Bank by a young lady visiting Buxton in 1810 described the theatre as "a mean building" noting that "but for the words Pit and Boxes over the door, it would be mistaken for a barn." The Inn had been added to over the following hundred or so years and was now known as the Shakespeare Hotel. It was also now somewhat shabbier in appearance. Although some of the guests who stayed there were on holiday, it now catered mainly for commercial travellers.

When Eleanor entered the hotel, the reception area was empty. She rang the bell on the desk and waited. After some minutes, a young woman dressed in black and wearing a white apron appeared behind the reception desk.

'I'd like to speak to Mrs Erskine, please.'

'Yes, ma'am.'

The young woman nodded and went away. A few minutes

later, an older woman appeared and took up the position behind the reception desk.

'Mrs Erskine?' asked Eleanor, smiling.

The woman behind the desk did not return the smile. Eleanor found it difficult to judge Mrs Erskine's age. She was wearing a fashionably cut low-waisted frock made of black crêpe de chine, patterned with bright red and yellow roses, and featuring various drapes, flounces, and bows. The frock would not have been out of place at an afternoon tea party for bright, young debutantes but it seemed rather frivolous behind the heavy, dark wood Victorian reception desk and served to emphasise the lady's mature years rather than disguise them. Mrs Erskine's hair had been cut in a style which was fashionable but did not flatter the shape of her face. The several rows of Marcel waves which lavishly adorned each side of her head drew attention to her rather prominent jaw. She was wearing make-up, or "face paint" as Lady Carleton-West called it disapprovingly. Powder, lipstick, rouge, and eye make-up had all been applied with skill and in imitation of the current Hollywood stars of the picture theatre.

Mrs Erskine was, in fact, a devotee of the cinema. In Mrs Erskine's imagination, the director had cued "action" and the cameras were rolling. As she looked at Eleanor, she adopted a pose: chin down, lips pouted, head tilted slightly to one side, eyes wide open.

'To whom am I speaking?' she drawled.

'My name is Eleanor Harriman. I believe you are the landlady of this hotel.'

Mrs Erskine changed her pose to express indignation. Her eyes narrowed: 'I am the *proprietor* of this establishment, yes.'

She emphasised the word *proprietor* to indicate that in her view her status was above that of a mere landlady.

'Oh, I am sorry.' Eleanor paused. 'I wonder if I could ask

you a few questions. I am enquiring about the baby who was found on the Temple Mound in the Gardens yesterday. You have probably heard about that.'

'I have and I've had the police here as well.' The pose for the film director was temporarily abandoned. Mrs Erskine raised her chin, looked straight at Eleanor, and added, sharply: 'What do you want? Are you from the newspapers?'

'No, not at all,' said Eleanor, calmly. 'I am a solicitor and I represent someone who is connected with this incident. Here is my card.'

Mrs Erskine took the card without looking at it and placed it face down on the counter.

Resuming her pose for the camera, Mrs Erskine smoothed down the flounces on the skirt of her dress, patted the back of her hair, and said, in condescending tones: 'I'm afraid I can't help you.'

Mrs Erskine paused for effect, tilted her chin, and gave a little pout. She took a deep breath and delivered her next lines, languidly:

'I don't know anything about it and I don't want to, either. The less people know about that horrid little affair the better as far as I'm concerned. It's bad for business.'

Mrs Erskine looked down at the counter, then up again at Eleanor from under her lashes, and then began rearranging the items on the counter. She slid the register to the right and lined it up against the edge of the counter. The inkstand and the pen used by clients to sign the register were now too far away from the register. Sensing that Mrs Erskine was getting bored, Eleanor adopted a conciliatory tone.

'Yes, I quite understand your position, Mrs Erskine. This incident must have made things unnecessarily difficult for you, particularly as you are not implicated in any way. I don't want to ask you any questions about the baby or about your hotel. I am simply trying to find the mother of the baby because I believe she may have information that will help my client.'

Eleanor thought that, just for a moment, a flicker of anxiety had passed across Mrs Erskine's face. But then, Mrs Erskine posed for the imaginary camera again. She took a deep breath. She had her lines word perfect.

'I don't know anything about that either,' she said, indignantly. 'Anyone could have gone into the stables. It's got nothing to do with this hotel.'

Mrs Erskine looked down at the inkstand and then slowly moved the register back to its original position. Then she raised her eyes slightly and looked up at Eleanor from under thick lashes, her face slightly at an angle to the camera.

'That's what I told the policeman who came here asking questions.'

The imaginary camera continued to roll and Mrs Erskine raised her chin, tossed back her Marcel waves and, focussing on a point slightly above and to the right of Eleanor's head, spoke her next lines with conviction.

'As I said to him: "I'll have you know this is a respectable establishment. Unlike some as I could name. That teashop a few doors down, for instance." I said: "You should be ashamed of yourself, trying to suggest it was one of my waitresses or one of my chambermaids that left that baby here." And then I told him to leave my hotel.'

Mrs Erskine then glared at Eleanor, challenging her to criticise her performance in the starring role of wronged hotel keeper, or rather proprietor of the establishment. Eleanor suddenly realised that, in her indignation, Mrs Erskine may have given away more than she intended. Eleanor decided to end the interview and pursue her enquiries elsewhere.

'I'm very sorry to have troubled you, Mrs Erskine,' said Eleanor, turning away from the reception desk. 'Thank you for your time.'

Eleanor walked out of the hotel, turned right, walked a

little way along the row of shops and stopped outside "the teashop a few doors down" which was The Cosy Corner. As it was early closing, it was not possible to pursue the enquiry further. Eleanor resolved to return the following morning. She knew something of the history of this tea shop and its owner and thought that it was very likely that Mrs Erskine's waitress or chambermaid had been employed here.

The Cosy Corner was owned by Miss Henrietta Swinscoe, an elderly but still feisty and independent minded spinster or, to use the term she preferred, *femme sole*. At the age of eighteen, she had refused several very good offers of marriage, declaring that she had no intention of becoming a piece of property owned by a husband or of confining herself to "polite" drawing room conversation. She intended to support herself and to have her own opinions. Progressive ones at that. Her family was well-off, upper-middle class, conventional, and profoundly shocked.

Miss Swinscoe's ambition was to provide a place where women could meet and exchange information about subjects generally regarded as unsuitable or unnecessary for women. Her teashop had provided the venue for those campaigning for better education and better working conditions for women, and also for women to be given the vote. The teashop had been the venue for many meetings of the Women's Tax Resistance League and other such organisations. Eleanor was familiar with the history of the tea shop and smiled at the thought that its owner and Mrs Erskine were chalk and cheese. An unmarried mother might easily have found a refuge here.

CHAPTER THIRTEEN

Eleanor returned to Hall Bank. The office was now closed and Mr Harriman was in the sitting room, writing a letter. As Eleanor entered, she was greeted enthusiastically by Napoleon.

Mr Harriman put down his pen and said: 'Any luck?'

'Very definitely.'

When Eleanor had finished describing her investigations, Mr Harriman said: 'You know, Eleanor, I have often said that Cecily reminds me of *your* mother, but you remind me of my mother. Your grandmother. Absolutely no detail escaped her attention and her intuition was remarkable. My brothers and I would get into the most awful scrapes, make all sorts of elaborate excuses to try to hide the truth, but she would always find us out. I think you have inherited her skill of extracting information without people realising that they are giving themselves away.'

Eleanor laughed but before she could respond, the doorbell rang. Napoleon got up from the hearth rug and listened attentively. They were not expecting visitors and Mrs Clayton had the half day off. Eleanor went downstairs and found her sister, Cecily, on the doorstep.

They went back upstairs and Eleanor said: 'It's Cecily.'

'Come in, come in,' said Mr Harriman.

Cecily, seeing Mr Harriman sitting at the writing desk, said: 'I'm sorry to disturb you, Father, if you're working. I came to see Eleanor.'

'No, no, it's quite all right. I'm not working. In any event, you are always a welcome distraction, Cecily, never a disturbance. In fact, we were just talking about you and Grandmother Harriman.'

'I was always terribly frightened of her,' said Cecily, laughing. 'I mustn't stay too long. Richard's bringing Thomas home to tea today. They've been out at the cricket nets with a new friend who helped them with their kite. He seems to be taking an interest in them.'

Mr Harriman frowned. 'Do we know anything about this new friend? What is his name?'

'The boys call him Mr Kite. I haven't met him but some of Richard's schoolfriends are there and some of the cricket club members as well.'

Mr Harriman said: 'Ah, so that's all right then.'

'Actually, I think I saw your Mr Kite in the Gardens the other afternoon. I was taking Napoleon for his walk but Richard and Thomas didn't notice us. They were too busy trying to fly their kite and I watched from the side lines.'

'That is the latest enthusiasm,' said Cecily. 'At least, when it is windy. Otherwise, it is cricket. They told me all about the gentleman who helped them with the kite. Apparently, Thomas nearly knocked him over. He must be a very patient and forgiving sort of person to have then gone on and helped them with the kite.'

'That's true, but he did appear to be enjoying himself as well, to the extent of removing his hat and running about like a boy. I noticed that Thomas is a cowboy at the moment.'

'Yes,' said Cecily. 'Previously he and Richard were the three musketeers. I mentioned to Thomas that they were only two, not three. Thomas, very solemnly and without even having to pause for thought, informed me that the other musketeer was away on a dangerous mission to save the King of France. I do not know where he gets his ideas from.'

'He certainly has a vivid imagination,' said Mr Harriman. 'And a way with words.'

'Far too vivid, unfortunately, and it is getting him into

trouble,' said Cecily. 'His mother came to tea last week and told me that the headmaster at Thomas's school had written to her regretting that he was unable to accept Thomas at the start of the next school year and suggesting that Thomas might be happier at a school, as he put it, where discipline was not considered so important. He's going to join Richard at Homeleigh instead.'

'Oh, how very rude,' said Eleanor, indignantly.

'I thought so,' said Cecily. 'Thomas is very lively but he is also very well-mannered and considerate of others. I certainly do not regard him as ill-disciplined. His mother was very cross too, although she hasn't told Thomas why he is changing schools. She said that sometimes she wonders why she bothers with school though because she is convinced he won't ever want a proper job and will end up on the stage.'

'He certainly has charm,' said Eleanor. 'I watched him talk himself out of a scrape when he nearly bowled the kite gentleman over in the Gardens.'

'Yes, he is very good at that. Talking his way out of a scrape,' said Mr Harriman. 'I've seen him in action.'

'It is impossible to be cross with him,' said Cecily. 'He can be very entertaining. That is his problem. His mother says that when she is trying to be strict with him, he always makes her see the funny side and manages to distract her from the issue in hand.'

'Well, I hope Holmleigh is more to his taste,' said Mr Harriman, 'because, as you say, he is good natured. Now, do you want Eleanor to yourself? Is it something private?'

'Oh, no,' said Cecily, 'and, in fact, it involves you as well, Father, as you will see when I explain. I have received an invitation from Lady Carleton-West to a dinner party.'

Mr Harriman's and Eleanor's surprise at this news was evident from their faces.

'I know,' continued Cecily, 'it is rather a surprise. The

invitation specified no reason for the dinner party and it is quite short notice. I have no idea why I am being honoured in this way.'

'I think the word "used" might be more appropriate than "honoured" because that is all Lady Carleton-West knows,' said Eleanor, laughing. 'I'm only invited to committee meetings because Lady C finds me useful.'

Mr Harriman, adopting a theatrical pose, frowned and with mock disapproval, said: 'Should I be offended at not also being asked to dine, I wonder? Am I not to be similarly honoured?'

Cecily and Eleanor laughed at this suggestion.

Cecily said: 'You know very well that, if you did receive such an invitation, Father, you would plead at least six prior engagements and have nothing to do with it.'

'You are perfectly correct, Cecily,' said Mr Harriman. 'So, what have you decided to do?'

'Well, I thought at first I would decline, which is why I didn't mention the invitation sooner but it is a little difficult to find a convincing reason for not going. Besides, I thought that it might do me good to go,' said Cecily, tentatively. 'I am getting to be rather a hermit.'

'Then, of course, you must go,' said Mr Harriman. 'Don't let this pair of cynics deter you.'

'Yes,' agreed Eleanor. 'As far as Lady C is concerned, you are the only socially presentable representative of the Harriman family left in Buxton, so you must go and keep up appearances for the sake of the rest of us.'

'You are a pair of old cynics,' said Cecily, 'but, thank you, I knew I could count on you. Yes, I did wonder if you would have Richard. But the other reason for my being here is that I went shopping this morning because I thought I might treat myself to a new frock. There's not enough time to have something made so I went to Milligans. I found several lovely frocks that suited me very well but everything is so expensive nowadays. I do have some money put away but I felt I couldn't justify the expense of a new frock, not just for one dinner party.'

'Very sensible,' said Mr Harriman, nodding his approval. 'I am sure that you will look charming whatever you wear, Cecily, but why not let me buy the frock for you? I should be very pleased to do so.'

'Thank you, Father, that's very thoughtful of you and most generous, but really I couldn't ask you to.'

'You're welcome to have one of mine,' said Eleanor, 'if you think there is anything suitable.'

'That's exactly what I came to ask, Eleanor. When I walked out of Milligans, I was considering where else to go and I remembered the blue and gold cocktail frock you wore to Miss Roston's engagement party and I was wondering if I could borrow that.'

'Yes, of course, you can. I've only worn it that once and the people who were at that party are certainly not part of Lady C's set so no-one will know.'

'Thank you, Eleanor. It is a beautiful frock and I shall feel much more confident wearing it.'

'And, of course, we shall mind Richard for you. It is always a pleasure to see him,' said Mr Harriman.

'Thank you. Now, I must go. I promised I would be back in time for tea.'

'I'll ask Mrs Clayton to parcel up the frock for you,' said Eleanor, 'and Susan can come and collect it.'

'No, there's no need. I'll bring Richard a little earlier on Friday and change here, if I may. I shall need you to boost my morale.'

'Yes, that's an excellent idea,' said Eleanor. 'Remember how we used to do that before Lady C's parties when we first came out.'

'Oh, don't remind me,' groaned Cecily. 'It is not long enough ago for me to have forgotten the terror.'

0 0 0

DIARY Wednesday 25th June

School holidays have begun – at least for some. Met my two kite flying friends at the Cricket Club nets this morning as promised. Very active club. Everyone very welcoming. One gentleman kind enough to remember my batting average at Oxford. Richard shows great promise. Thomas is a delightful character. Extraordinarily skilled at being able to distract the bowler from his designs on the wicket. Could become a successful magician, I think. Very intelligent, but prefers to play the fool. Must be a challenge to his parents. His father is a solicitor apparently – probably has no sense of humour. Look forward to meeting the pair again.

CHAPTER FOURTEEN

The following morning, on her way to the dining room for breakfast, Eleanor stopped to say good morning to Mrs Clayton. Napoleon was already keeping Mrs Clayton company from his usual spot in the hall.

'Good morning, Miss Harriman.'

'Good morning, Mrs Clayton. As I said the other day, you know a lot about the tradespeople in this town. Do you know anything about Mrs Erskine at the Shakespeare Hotel. She's the landlady or, I should say "the proprietor of the establishment." I was corrected by her when I referred to her as the landlady.'

Mrs Clayton shook her head. 'No, not really. Alf did the funeral for Mr Erskine. I suppose Mrs Erskine must have taken over from him. I do remember Alf remarking on how Mr Erskine was a good bit older than her. They weren't local and I don't think there are any children. Alf said not many people came to the funeral.'

'Had Mr Erskine been at the Shakespeare Hotel very long?'

'Let me see now, he took over from Mrs Barson. I don't recollect exactly when that was but it would have been not long after the start of the War.'

'Mrs Erskine apparently has plans for the hotel. She is having the stables converted into garages.'

'Well, I hope she won't stop there. It's been looking rather run down over the last year or so.'

0   0   0

Just after ten forty-five, Eleanor continued her mission to find the mother of the abandoned baby. She arrived at The Cosy Corner and saw that it was almost full and all the customers were female. Eleanor's friend, Doctor Catherine Balderstone, had once jokingly told her that more personal information about symptoms was exchanged between women over tea and cakes in tea shops than was ever imparted by them in the consulting room of their own doctor.

Eleanor had decided that the indirect approach would be best so she went in and sat down at a vacant table. She picked up the menu, decided on a pot of tea and a buttered scone, and then looked around. She counted ten tables, nearly all occupied, and there was a sign at the foot of the staircase indicating that there were more tables upstairs. After a minute or two, a waitress came to Eleanor's table, took her order, and disappeared. Eleanor planned her strategy. The waitress who had taken her order was clearly in a rush and that suggested a shortage of staff. There seemed to be only two waitresses and a person at the cash desk. Both waitresses were well past middle-age so Eleanor eliminated them as the potential mother of the baby. She decided that the staff shortage was the ideal conversation opener. Eventually, the waitress came back with Eleanor's order on a tray. She looked flustered and, apologising for the delay, set out the tea things on the table.

Eleanor said: 'The young lady who served me two weeks ago doesn't seem to be here today?'

'Oh, no, Miss. She left last week, sudden like. No notice or anything. Just didn't turn up for work.'

'Oh, how annoying for you. That must have been such a nuisance when the café is so popular. She did seem to know what she was doing,' said Eleanor, hoping that she was expressing the right level of sympathy.

'Yes, Miss, it were a nuisance. Very unfortunate. And she'd hardly been here five minutes. Me and Elsie 've had to do extra until Miss Swinscoe can get someone to replace her.'

'Oh, dear. That is unfortunate. Well, I mustn't keep you when you're so very busy.' Eleanor smiled at the waitress. 'I do hope the young waitress is all right. Perhaps she will be back soon. What was her name again? She did tell me and I've forgotten.'

'Molly, Molly Brandon.'

'Oh, yes of course. Now I remember. And I think she told me she lives on South Avenue.'

The waitress frowned. Someone at a neighbouring table waved to catch her attention and, as she turned away, she said: 'I thought it were Fairfield.'

'You're probably right,' said Eleanor, to the departing waitress.

She poured her tea and settled down to enjoy her scone. She smiled as she considered her next move.

0 0 0

Eleanor returned to Hall Bank and was greeted by Napoleon.

James said: 'Ah, Miss Eleanor. You're back. Mr Harriman asked me to let you know that he would like to speak to you about the Wilde matter.'

'Thank you, James,' said Eleanor as she and Napoleon went into her father's office.

'Eleanor, I'm glad you're back. While you were out, Mr Wilde telephoned to say that Superintendent Ferguson has had Joshua brought in for further questioning. I don't know anything more.'

'I don't like the sound of that,' said Eleanor, taking a seat, 'but I do have some good news. I think I may be able to find the baby's mother.'

Napoleon settled down beside Eleanor and she described for her father the strategy that she had used to try and trace the mother.

'So, I now have a name and she lives somewhere in Fairfield. That's a good starting point.'

'That was very clever of you,' said Mr Harriman.

'I'm not sure about clever,' said Eleanor, smiling. 'Philip describes my talent as dogged determination and a refusal to give in.'

'Well, whatever it is, it works.'

At this point, Edwin arrived back from the police station, flicked his hat onto the peg in the hall, gestured towards the door of Mr Harriman's office and, after a nod from James, turned the doorknob and stuck his head around the door.

'Ah, Eleanor. You're here too. Good.'

Edwin came in and, as he sat down, ran his hands through his hair in a gesture of despair. Napoleon sat up and looked at him with concern.

'That new Superintendent is making himself unpopular already and, really, I think he has gone too far. He had Joshua Wilde brought in for further questioning. Apparently, during the first interview, Joshua didn't answer all the questions put to him and the Superintendent is convinced that Joshua is hiding something.'

Mr Harriman frowned and said: 'I know we had our differences with Superintendent Johnson, but at least we never had occasion to think that he was acting unfairly. Ferguson has only just been promoted to Superintendent. He's new both to the job and to the town. I suppose he is just trying to establish his authority.'

'Well, he's not going about things the right way if he wants to win the town's respect,' said Edwin, fiercely. 'His whole demeanour is inappropriate.'

'Dear me Talbot, he has got on the wrong side of you, hasn't he? It's not like you to get your feathers ruffled.'

'Your feathers would have been ruffled too by this fiasco, Harriman. I sat in on the interview and if the same method of questioning was used the first time, I am not at all surprised that Joshua remained silent. I would have done the same in his position. It was the new Inspector who questioned him both the first time and this second time. His approach was so intimidating, Joshua was probably afraid to say anything. And, as we found the other day, Joshua is a young man of few words even in less hostile company. The questions put to him today were so absurd it was impossible to answer them. The Inspector accused Joshua of being the father and helping the mother put the baby in the stables. He's now proposing to charge Joshua with concealing a birth.'

'Well, Eleanor has some news that might help with that issue,' said Mr Harriman.

Before Eleanor could respond, there was a knock on the door and Mrs Clayton appeared with a tea tray.

'Mr Wildgoose thought you might be in need of a cup of tea, Mr Talbot.'

'He was right, Mrs Clayton. That is exactly what I need. Thank you,' said Edwin, taking a cup and saucer from Mrs Clayton. 'And some of your special biscuits too. Excellent.'

'I'm sorry to interrupt but I know you've been to the police station for young Joshua, Mr Talbot, and I didn't have chance to talk to you before you went out. Alf asked me to let you know that he's offered to take Joshua on as an apprentice joiner and Mr Wilde has agreed.'

'Ah, that is very welcome news,' said Edwin.

'That will be a great relief to Mr Wilde and to Joshua's mother,' said Eleanor.

'Mr Wilde is going to ask you to draw up the papers so that Joshua can start next Friday. When he turns fourteen,' said Mrs Clayton, with emphasis.

'All square and above board,' said Edwin, smiling at Mrs Clayton.

She had brought tea for everyone and when she had

finished serving it, she left, closing the door quietly behind her.

'Now, what was the news you were going to give me, Eleanor?'

Eleanor told Edwin the story of tracing the baby's mother.

Edwin said: 'That information is extremely helpful, Eleanor. Joshua should be very thankful to you. I don't think Superintendent Ferguson has even begun looking for the mother.'

'And if we can get this young woman's side of the story it might put Joshua's part in this whole affair into better perspective,' said Mr Harriman.

'Yes,' agreed Edwin, 'and I am quite hopeful of getting a good result despite the threat of this new charge.'

0 0 0

That evening, after dinner, Eleanor and Philip had taken Napoleon for a walk and were sitting in the Gardens watching the tennis. It had been a perfect summer's day and now, above the trees that surrounded the gardens, the sky was a clear blue gradually turning golden and the warm air was occasionally stirred by a very gentle breeze. At first, Napoleon had looked at the tennis court, watching the movement of the ball, but he quickly tired of that. Other dogs chased balls. Boxers were more interested in people. So he changed his focus and began contemplating the spectators and the players as they milled about. It would still be light for at least another two hours, so there was plenty of time for the crowd to provide entertainment for him. He wandered about greeting the people he knew, introducing himself to those he did not. A new match had just started.

Philip had now inspected the suspect piece of Hepplewhite furniture and as he watched the tennis, he was mulling over his conclusions.

'Philip?'

'Yes, old thing.'

'Do you think you could pretend to be a long lost cousin?' asked Eleanor.

'Of whom?'

'Of a waitress in a café?'

'What are you thinking!' said Philip, pretending to be shocked. 'There has never been a waitress in our family.'

Philip sat forward to concentrate on a volley between the players.

'Oh, well played!' he called, as one of the players lobbed the ball to land just inside the line and out of reach of the opposing player.

Eleanor said: 'I need information.'

'You always need information,' said Philip, gloomily. 'Have you forgotten that because of your passion for information a year ago, I ruined my reputation at the Club. A reputation, I might add, which was impeccable. I was famous for my neatness of dress, my sophistication, and my intellectual agility. Now, most of the members think of me as a drunken, dishevelled idiot smelling of whisky.'

Eleanor laughed. 'You're exaggerating.'

'I assure you I am not. And along with my reputation, I ruined a perfectly good suit as well. Anyway, what is so interesting about this waitress and her long-lost cousin?'

'She may be the mother of the baby on the Temple Mound.'

'The waitress or the cousin?'

'The waitress. She's left her job. Suddenly and without giving notice.'

'Then, I'm sorry to quibble but she's no longer a waitress. How did she lose the cousin?

'She doesn't have a cousin.'

'Then he or she is not lost, long or otherwise.'

They sat in silence for a while watching the tennis.

'What makes you think that?' asked Philip.

'What?'

'That this ex-waitress is the mother of the baby.'

'The police haven't identified her yet but I think I may know who she is.'

'Then you don't need information,' said Philip.

'Yes I do, because what I have at the moment is a name and a lurking suspicion. That is all.'

'I've always been wary of lurking suspicions,' said Philip. 'My mother warned me against them when I was young. No good can come of them. I advise you to give them up.'

'You're not taking things seriously.'

'Yes, I am. I'm watching the tennis.'

Eleanor remained silent.

Eventually, Philip frowned and said: 'Why are you interested in this maternal person anyway?'

'It might help one of Edwin's clients.'

'Ah, so that means you can't explain further. Client confidentiality and all that. Good. No explanation means that I can go back to watching the tennis in peace.'

There was another prolonged silence and then the match was over. The four players on the court shook hands at the net and vacated the court for the next four. Philip got up to talk to someone he knew, Napoleon milled about the crowd, and then they both returned to Eleanor.

Once play recommenced, Philip said: 'About this long-lost cousin. If this person is solely a figment of your imagination, you are at liberty to make the cousin a "he" or a "she" according to your whim. Therefore, there is no reason why you can't take on the role yourself.'

'No, I can't.'

'Why?'

'Because I've already been to the café where she worked. I was in a different role then.'

'I see,' said Philip, 'then it serves you right for meddling.'

There was now a longer silence between them as they watched the tennis. Napoleon wandered off to greet a red setter who had arrived with another tennis player and the two dogs sat down, companionably, to watch the action.

'Couldn't you just wear a wig or something? Women are clever at changing their appearance.'

Eleanor refrained from commenting, sensing that, for all his objections, Philip might be about to relent.

'Does it have to be a long-lost cousin?'

'What do you mean?' asked Eleanor.

'Well, even a cousin who hasn't seen her for some time might be expected to know something about this waitress. One could easily be caught out with the wrong details while pretending to be a relative.'

'Who then?'

Philip did not reply, still reluctant to be drawn into the hunt.

Eventually, he asked: 'How much do you actually know about this waitress?'

'Only her name and the fact that she lived or lives in Fairfield.'

'A wide choice there, then. What makes you think that she has anything to do with the baby? Or can't you tell me?'

'I can't give you the details and they wouldn't help anyway. Something that was said to me led me to wonder if the mother of the baby worked as a waitress in this teashop. The only girl of the right age employed there left suddenly last week.'

'It's a bit of a leap of faith, isn't it?' said Philip. 'I don't mean to question your undoubted and, I acknowledge, previously proven ability to search out relevant facts by unusual means and join them to form a conviction, but this link you have drawn does appear a little tenuous.'

'Well,' said Eleanor. 'I agree that it sounds a bit thin. There may be no connection at all between these two events.

I accept that it may just be co-incidence but, all the same, the baby must have had a mother and, if she is not the waitress, who was she and where is she?'

'She could be anywhere,' said Philip. 'She could have left town. If she has any sense, she will have done so just to avoid being pestered with questions.'

One of their friends from the Tennis Club was now on the court.

'I say,' said Philip, 'Roger's backhand is improving, just look at the way he is returning the ball. His serve isn't too bad either. We will have to watch out; we're up against him next week. Right, I am going to take careful note of his play and see if I can spot any weak points.'

They watched their friend for a while, appreciating the display on the court. When the match was over, Philip said:

'Instead of a long-lost cousin, who might be expected to know *something* about this waitress, couldn't someone who is not expected to know anything about her go to the teashop instead? Perhaps someone with a parcel to deliver or some such excuse and, on being told she no longer works there, ask for her address?'

'Yes, that's a much better idea than the cousin. You could say she bought something at your showroom and asked for it to be delivered.'

'Whoa! I said someone could go to the teashop, I didn't say I would go. Besides,' said Philip, pretending to be offended. 'I am not a delivery boy; my business is successful enough to employ someone else in that capacity.'

Eleanor continued regardless: 'You could say that she purchased a man's watch and that would allow you to extend the enquiry to the father.'

Philip groaned. 'I said "could go" not "will go" and I'm still considering my position. Besides, I've got an important report to write, if you remember. It could be the turning point in my career.'

Eleanor remained silent until the tennis finished and people started packing up and drifting away. Napoleon, sensing an imminent departure, stood up and shook himself energetically and the trio began walking back towards the entrance of the Gardens.

Philip said: 'This is my first and final offer. I shall go to your teashop with a parcel and enquire for your waitress. There is to be no mention of watches, babies, fathers, or cousins. Those are my terms.'

'Thank you, Philip. I accept.'

'What is the name of the teashop?'

'The Cosy Corner, in Spring Gardens. Just down from the Shakespeare Hotel.'

'Just one further point. Why would they give me the address? What if they just offer to take the package instead so they can keep it for her to collect?'

'They won't. She left under a cloud so they are unlikely to want to do her any favours.'

'I must be mad,' said Philip, shaking his head vigorously.

Napoleon looked at him and, seeing the shaking head, nudged Philip's hand with his nose in sympathy.

0 0 0

DIARY Thursday 26th June

Note from Charlesworth. Difficulty over boundary resolved to his satisfaction. Purchase of land can now proceed. Excellent news. Must get Grosvenor down to look at possibilities. This town is certainly to my liking. Think I have made the right choice in coming here.

Went to the Opera House this evening to see a play "Plus Fours." Magnificent building. Very silly play. Difficult to find a plot.

CHAPTER FIFTEEN

The next morning, Philip went, as agreed, to The Cosy Corner teashop, carrying a small package, an empty box wrapped in brown paper and tied with string. He enquired for Molly Brandon and, as Eleanor had predicted, he was told that the waitress no longer worked there. There was no offer to take the package and pass it on and no questions were asked. He was given the address without any trouble. He returned to his showroom, telephoned to Hall Bank and gave the address to James to pass on to Eleanor.

James had the motor car brought around from the garage and Eleanor set off for Fairfield. As she drove, she thought about the coming interview with the waitress and realised that she had been so focussed on finding her that she had given little thought as to how to begin. It didn't seem appropriate to begin by asking a complete stranger is she was the mother of a baby left at the Shakespeare Hotel but there seemed to be no alternative. Eleanor had no idea how the waitress would react to this intrusion so, on reflection, she decided that it was best not to have a plan or any preconceived ideas and to wait and see what sort of response she got.

At the top of Fairfield Road, she turned right into the main street of the town and then, a little further along, turned right again along a lane which led past a scattering of houses and then open fields. A short distance further on, there was a pair of single storey cottages on the left hand side of the lane and opposite them, a row of two storey cottages, built at right angles to the lane. The cottages were surrounded by fields.

She stopped the motor car in the lane. There were no motor cars in this part of Fairfield and Eleanor was conscious that it was rather conspicuous. She was surprised that the sound of its engine had not attracted attention and brought a curious neighbour out to investigate. Then, Eleanor realised that the occupants of the cottages were probably at work or out in the fields because, at that time of the year, labour for hay-making was much in demand.

Molly lived in one of the cottages in the row. They were freshly whitewashed and in good repair. At the back, each cottage had its own, well-tended vegetable patch closed off by fences from the open farmland beyond. There was a path leading along the front of the cottages and Eleanor walked along it to reach the right front door. She knocked. There was no reply and she waited, trying to detect any noise within which would suggest that the cottage was occupied.

Eleanor stepped back slightly so as to be able to see any movement at the windows, one next to the front door and one above it on the upper floor. Any movement of a curtain, however slight, would indicate a presence within. There was no sign. Eleanor knocked again, harder this time and a little more urgently. The harsh metallic sound of the door knocker was amplified by the absence of background noise and when Eleanor stopped knocking, there was a rather unnerving silence. There seemed no point in trying any adjoining cottage. If there had been anyone at home, the noise of Eleanor's knocking would have brought them out to see what the fuss was about.

Eleanor was beginning to wonder about the wisdom of this idea and she was tempted to just return to Hall Bank. Then she recalled how she had badgered Philip into obtaining the address for her and she told herself sternly that this was no time to give up. She stepped back from the cottage door and looked around. At the far end of the row, there was a path which led to the rear of the cottages. She followed the path and then counted back from the end of the row to reach the back door of the cottage where the waitress lived. She knocked on the door and stood close to it trying to detect any sound from within. She stood, perfectly still, for about a minute, imagining someone within the cottage doing the same thing, standing perfectly still and hoping that the intruder would go away.

Eleanor was just about to give up when she heard a sound. There was a clatter. The noise reverberated. Some inadvertent movement had caused something metal, a pot, or a saucepan lid perhaps, to fall onto a stone floor. There was no further sound. Eleanor knocked on the door again, insistently. Then, there was a noise on the other side of the door. A bolt was being slid back stealthily. The door opened just enough to reveal a slither of head and a wary eye.

'What do you want?' asked a female, rather hoarse, voice.

'I should like to speak to Molly Brandon, please. Are you Molly?'

'What do you want?' repeated the voice.

'Miss Brandon, I should like to talk to you about the baby found in the Pavilion Gardens on Tuesday morning. I think I can help you.'

'Who are you?'

'My name is Miss Eleanor Harriman. Here is my card.'

Eleanor held out a card and a hand came cautiously around the door to take it. To Eleanor's disappointment, the door was closed and she feared that that was the end of the interview. After a moment or two, the slither of head and the eye reappeared.

'Why are you here? No-one can help me.'

All of a sudden, Eleanor saw a way forward. 'Miss Brandon, I know that you left your baby in the old stables at the Shakespeare Hotel and I imagine that you are wondering how it came to be in the Gardens. I know what happened to your baby and I can put your mind at rest.'

Eleanor waited, hoping that the bait would be taken.

'Where is he?'

Eleanor assumed that the baby was still in the morgue and she had no idea whether or not the *post mortem* examination had taken place but it would be necessary. This information would not be helpful to the mother.

'He was found in the Gardens by one of the park keepers and was taken to a doctor.'

'I want him back. Can you help me?'

Eleanor did not want to lie or provide false hope. She was sure that her father would do whatever he could to make the arrangement but, as there would have to be an inquest, it was the Coroner who decided when a body could be released to the relatives, and Mr Harriman had had to arrange for another person to act as Coroner.

'I'm not sure whether that is possible just at the moment,' she said. 'That's not something over which I have any control but my father knows the Coroner and I can ask him to try to arrange for you to see your baby.'

The girl said: 'How do I know you haven't come just to make trouble for me? Why would you care about me?'

'Because I think you may need help and because I am also trying to help the young man who moved your baby from the stables at the hotel. He was tricked into it and now he is in trouble. He didn't harm your baby in any way.'

There was a long period of silence. Eleanor hoped that was a good sign.

'You'd best come in.'

The door swung open and Eleanor went through into a small kitchen. The girl motioned for Eleanor to sit down at the kitchen table. She then picked up a saucepan lid which had fallen onto the floor, the source of the noise which had given away her presence. She sat down opposite Eleanor and there was an air of total despair in the way she slumped into the chair. Eleanor guessed that she was about seventeen or eighteen. Her hair was dishevelled and her clothes were creased. She looked like someone who had remained in the same clothes for days and probably had not slept or eaten recently. Her face was drawn and her cheeks hollow but Eleanor could see that, better groomed, she would certainly be considered very pretty.

The girl said: 'How did you find me?'

'I went to The Cosy Corner and they gave me your address. Do you live here alone?'

Molly shook her head. 'With my friend and her husband.'

'And your mother? What about her?'

'Mam passed away five years ago. She had the consumption.'

'I'm sorry to hear that. You must have still been at school then.'

Molly nodded. 'But Dad said I had to leave and earn me keep.'

'So you went to work at the Shakespeare Hotel?'

Molly nodded.

Eleanor waited a moment and then continued: 'And you were working at The Cosy Corner until a few days ago.'

'Look, what's this got to do with my baby. You said you could help me get him back.'

'Yes, I have promised to do that and I shall keep my promise but, before I can do anything to help you, I need to understand what happened, how your baby came to be in the stables. You see, before I can ask my father to arrange for you to see your baby, I need to be sure that the baby found in the Gardens is your baby and not someone else's.'

'But he *is* mine!'

'I believe you but we need to provide proof and you are the only one who can do that. That is why I need to ask you questions.'

Eleanor waited.

Molly nodded and sighed.

'All right,' she said softly.

'One of the waitresses at The Cosy Corner told me that you left work there without giving any notice. Was that because of the baby?'

Molly nodded. 'He weren't supposed to come this early. I thought I still had a couple of months before I had to give notice.'

'So when was he born?'

'Sunday night, well, early hours of Monday morning.'

Molly was fighting back tears and Eleanor waited for a few moments before her next question.

'Tell me what happened. How did he come to be in the stables.'

Molly took a deep breath and then said: 'I were took bad just as I were leaving work. The café opens on Sunday afternoons in the Season. I thought I wouldn't be able to get home and I didn't know what to do so I hid in the old stables. I thought I'd be safe there.'

'How long did you stay in the stables?'

'All night. He didn't come for a long time and then when he did come he weren't moving or making any noise so I knew summut were wrong. I sat with him 'til it were getting light and but I couldn't see him breathing. I sat for a while looking at him and thinking what it were best to do but I didn't know. I went to tell his father and I were only away a couple of hours.'

'So you left the baby in the stables and then came back again a little while later and you were not to know that Mrs Erskine had decided to have the stables converted into garages. You must have got a shock when you went back to collect your baby.'

'It were awful. I went in through the lane at the back, not past the hotel, and there were men there and I didn't know why. I thought they must have found him and I didn't know what to do. I should never have left him.'

Molly looked down at her hands and began to cry and Eleanor suspected that the relief of being able to tell someone what had happened to the baby had released all the pent up emotion of the last few days. She waited, knowing that there was nothing she could say that would help.

When the crying had begun to subside, Eleanor said: 'I'm sure you were only doing what you thought best and it might help you to know that the person who moved your baby and left him on the Temple Mound in the Gardens did so very respectfully and with great care. It is unfortunate that the builders working for Mrs Erskine arrived that morning.'

Molly looked up, her face tear-stained, black circles under her eyes.

She said: 'Why did it have to be that morning? She'd wanted it done for a long time and Mr Erskine wouldn't agree. Didn't want to spend the money. He wanted to sell the hotel.'

'I believe Mr Erskine died recently.'

'Yes, and good riddance to him.'

'Mrs Erskine seems to be in charge of the hotel now. I spoke to her recently. I didn't like her very much.'

'She were a right cow!' said Molly and then put her hand over her mouth. 'Sorry. Bad language, but it's true. And he couldn't keep his hands to hisself. Although that's not surprising, married to her.'

Eleanor wondered if the man with the roving hands was the baby's father, but if he had died, that did not make sense because Molly had just said that she had been to see him. She decided to postpone that line of enquiry for the moment. Molly seemed to be calmer when not talking about the baby so Eleanor decided to ask her about the hotel instead.

'How long did you work for Mrs Erskine?'

'Since I left school.' Molly paused while she counted. 'Three years, a bit more.'

'And what sort of work did you do?'

'We was supposed to be chambermaids but she had us waiting at table as well.'

'Was she difficult to work for?'

'Yes, and then she got the wrong end of the stick about me, thanks to Mr Erskine.'

'How was that?'

'Like I said, he couldn't keep his hands off. Saying are you all right and putting his arm round. Saying we was working too hard. Wanting to talk. Smelling of drink. Mary said it were just that he were lonely but I didn't buy it.'

'Who is Mary?'

'One of the chambermaids. We all tried our best to keep out o' his way but he was cunning. He'd corner you if he found you were alone.'

'And Mrs Erskine, did she know about it?'

'Oh, she knew about it all right but she wouldn't do anything nor say summut to him. It were Mr Erskine as owned the hotel and had the money, so I suppose she just had to put up with it.'

'And is that why you left the hotel?'

Molly shook her head. 'No. It were worse than that. Mrs Erskine found him with his hands on me one day when I were doing out their room, not with my say-so I might add, and it weren't the first time she had caught him out.'

'With you?'

'No, with the other girls not me, but with me it were different.'

'Why was that?'

'Because I had to rush out of the dining room serving at breakfast. The smell of bacon, that's what set me off. I hadn't told anyone I were in the family way 'cos I knew I'd lose the job and before that I'd managed not to let on.'

'And what happened?'

'Mr Erskine, he were standing in the corridor and when I got back, he wanted to know if I were all right. Tried to put his arm round me.'

'And Mrs Erskine got the wrong idea?'

'She put two and two together and got four, or thought she had. I suppose she convinced herself that the baby were his. Ugh!' Molly gave a long drawn-out shudder. 'As if I could ever have been interested in him. He were 'orrible.'

'So, Mrs Erskine may have thought that Mr Erskine was the father of your child?'

'Aye. And then he went and died so he weren't there to speak up for me.'

'When did Mr Erskine die?'

'A couple of weeks after that. St Patrick's Day. Mr Erskine, he were Irish and he'd been out celebrating. He fell down the stairs to the cellar. They took him to the hospital but he died the next day.'

'And when did you leave the Shakespeare?'

'Mrs Erskine gave me notice the day after Mr Erskine died.'

'And why was that? Did she give any reasons?'

'She didn't say much. She just said I were to leave at the end of the week.'

'Did you ask why?'

Molly nodded. 'She said she didn't think I were the sort of person she wanted to have in the hotel.'

'Do you think it was because she really did think the baby was Mr Erskine's?'

Molly nodded. 'It were the only reason I could think of. I said if she were giving me notice because of that, she had no right. And I said if Mr Erskine hadn't died, he'd be there to tell the truth and now it were too late. I said it were very convenient for her that Mr Erskine were dead. All I meant were that now she could give me notice without him sticking up for me but she must have took it the wrong way.'

'Why? What did she say?'

'She just looked at me. Cold, like. She said what were I

123

suggesting. And she hoped I were not implying that there were anything amiss about Mr Erskine's death. Mr Erskine fell and there is a witness to that.'

'And what did you say to that?'

'I just spoke without thinking. I know I were speaking out of turn but I were that cross. I said we all knew she would be happier without him. Then she called me all sorts of names that I won't repeat. Said I were to get out straightaway. No notice, no character. She'd see to it that I'd never work in the town again and if I ever mentioned anything to anyone about Mr Erskine or about the hotel, she'd go to the police and make a complaint against me.'

'What sort of complaint?'

'She'd say I knew something about Mr Erskine's death.

'But were you anywhere near when Mr Erskine fell?'

'No, but she were.'

'Tell me what happened?'

'I'd come down the back stairs to get some guest soap from the store cupboard and when I were going back up to finish turning down the beds, she were in the corridor. I heard a bit of a commotion as I were going back up.'

'So you didn't see what happened?'

'No. When I came back down Mrs Erskine were in the corridor still. She said I weren't needed any more that night and to go up to my room. I thought it were a bit rum when there were still work to do, but us girls knew not to question what we were told.'

'Then Mr Erskine died and you were dismissed without a reference. And with nowhere to live either. Is that when you came here?'

Molly nodded.

'But you managed to get the job in the teashop without a reference?'

'Yes, my friend as lives here worked for Miss Swinscoe. She were leaving to be married and Miss Swinscoe took me on straightaway.'

'That must have made Mrs Erskine very cross,' said Eleanor.

'It did. She told Miss Swinscoe a heap of lies and tried to get her to sack me but Miss Swinscoe said she didn't believe any of it and she weren't going to be bossed about by the likes of Mrs Erskine.'

'You said before that Mrs Erskine was judging the behaviour of others by that of herself. What did you mean by that?'

'She were very friendly with the men guests, one in particular, a commercial traveller. Too friendly if you know what I mean.'

'Oh dear, that is no way to run a hotel. I think you did very well to leave, Molly, and I think that you have been very brave. I admire your determination and the way you have managed to cope with all of this. And on your own too. I suppose the father of your baby was not willing to marry you.'

Molly took a deep breath and then said: 'He can't. And anyway his mother didn't think I were good enough for him.'

Molly closed her eyes and then leaned forward, her elbows on the table and her head in her hands. She was shaking and sobbing, taking in great gulps of air. Eleanor looked on helplessly and waited. This was not the moment to express sympathy or ask questions.

When Molly seemed a little calmer, Eleanor said quietly: 'Tell me about the father. You said that on Monday morning you went to tell him about the baby.'

'To the churchyard. That's where he is.'

'The father of your baby has died?'

Molly was fighting for control again. Eleanor could see that more tears were not far away. She nodded encouragement and waited.

'When did he die?' she asked, eventually.

'February.'

'This year?'

Molly nodded. 'The fifteenth.'

Eleanor waited.

'It were an accident and it were my fault.'

'But if it was an accident, how could it have been your fault?'

Molly frowned. As she began speaking, she looked down at the table but her mind's eye was somewhere altogether different.

'I went to see him. When I found out about the baby. I daren't tell anyone and I didn't know what to do. I were desperate. I went to tell him because I knew he'd help me.'

Eleanor said: 'And what happened?'

Molly didn't respond at first, then, still frowning, she said:

'It were just after the midday whistle when they stop for dinner. I went to find him at his work. I couldn't go to his house because his mother didn't like it. I went up the hill to the kiln where he worked and I called to him. He didn't expect to see me, not at his work. It weren't allowed and he were looking at me and didn't see the railway wagon. I can still see him looking at me. Surprised like, when he were hit. Next minute he were gone.'

Molly put her hands over her eyes to shut out her vision of the accident. She rested her elbows on the table and another bout of sobbing began, this time even more intense. After a while, Molly quietened down.

Eleanor said: 'I know what it is like to lose someone you love. My fiancé and my brother were both killed in the War, so I do know something of what you are feeling.'

Molly looked up, shaking her head. 'But it weren't your fault that they died.'

'I understand what you mean and I cannot imagine what it must be like for you.'

'People always say give it time, it'll get better but that's not true.'

'No,' agreed Eleanor.

'I thought at least if I had the baby, his baby, I could make it up to him. I sometimes visit his grave and I told him, if it were a boy, I'd call him Arthur.'

'After his father?' asked Eleanor.

Molly nodded: 'But I couldn't even do that properly and now I've lost them both.'

Molly stared at the wall behind Eleanor, her eyes a blank.

'When you went back to the stables to find your baby, what did you intend to do?'

'I were going to take him to his father's grave so they could be together.' She sighed. 'I just want my baby back,' she whispered.

Eleanor felt such compassion for Molly that she was struggling to remain objective. She wanted to help Molly but realised that there was very little she could do. Then she thought of her friend, Catherine, and was sure that she would be able to help.

Eleanor said: 'Will you let me help you?'

Molly did not respond. She continued to stare at the wall.

'It wasn't your fault that your baby was not strong enough to live and no-one can blame you for that. I have a friend who is a doctor and I think you would like her. Will you let me arrange for you to see her? You do need someone to check that you are all right, at the very least, and she will do that for you but she will also be able to help you.'

'I can't afford a doctor.'

'She is a very good friend of mine and if I ask her to see you, I know she will do so without charging you anything. Shall I arrange for you to see her?'

Molly nodded.

'Good. I'll telephone her as soon as I get back to my office. And I shall ask my father to try to arrange for you to see your baby. I'll leave you now. Will you be all right?

When will your friend be back?'

'Sunday. She's gone to stay with her mother,' said Molly. 'Her husband's away fruit picking.'

'I don't think you should be on your own. Are you friends with your neighbours?'

Molly nodded.

Eleanor said good-bye and walked back to her motor car reflecting on how difficult life could be for some people. As she was driving back to Hall Bank, she decided not to telephone Catherine at her surgery but to call in there instead. She didn't want to risk the conversation being overheard by someone at the telephone exchange.

CHAPTER SIXTEEN

When the office closed that afternoon, Eleanor took Napoleon for a walk and then, leaving him with Mrs Clayton, walked up to Catherine's surgery at Hardwick Mount. Catherine's receptionist knew Eleanor very well and as Catherine was with a patient made an appointment for Molly for Monday morning. Eleanor wrote a short letter to Molly giving her the necessary details and the receptionist assured Eleanor that it would go into the post that evening. Molly would receive it in plenty of time to keep the appointment. Eleanor wrote a note to Catherine explaining the appointment.

On leaving Catherine's surgery, Eleanor realised that she was not far from the lane which led from Hardwick Mount down to the rear of the Shakespeare Hotel. She decided to see how easy it would have been for Molly to get to the stables without anyone in the hotel noticing. She walked a little way down the lane, and then stood for a minute considering the scene. She could see the back of the hotel and the stables. From the stables, the lane led to an archway, through which the horses, and now motor cars, could pass in order to reach Spring Gardens.

Eleanor was wondering what further useful enquiry she could make when she noticed a door at the rear of the hotel open and a girl leave the hotel. She was wearing a summer frock and carrying a bag. Eleanor thought this was probably the staff entrance to the hotel. She looked at her watch and wondered if the girl, perhaps one of the chambermaids, was going off duty. Eleanor watched as the girl walked through the archway, turned left into Spring Gardens, and disappeared out of sight. Even though Eleanor was standing in the lane, the girl leaving the hotel had not noticed her. Eleanor waited a little longer and then walked the rest of the way down the lane and through the archway into Spring Gardens. She was satisfied that it would have been possible to get from the teashop to the stables within a matter of minutes and without being seen or challenged, just as Molly had described.

0 0 0

That evening, Mr Harriman and Philip were in the sitting room enjoying a pre-dinner sherry, with Napoleon stretched out on the hearthrug. When Cecily and Richard arrived, Cecily and Eleanor disappeared into Eleanor's bedroom so that Cecily could get ready for the dinner party. Richard joined the menfolk but with a glass of Mrs Clayton's elderflower cordial. He and Thomas had taken seriously Philip's request that they plan the route to Matlock Bath for their picnic excursion the following day. Richard had brought with him a road map and a notepad on which he and Thomas had written down some directions. He held it up to show Philip.

'Excellent,' said Philip. 'Come and sit at the table and we'll have a look at what you've decided.'

Richard unfolded the map and spread it out on the table. 'When we get to here,' he said, putting his finger on the map. 'you can stop at Brierlow Bar to make sure you have enough petrol and water.'

'Hold on,' said Philip, 'that's on the Ashbourne Road. We're going to Matlock Bath. Shouldn't we be on the Bakewell Road?'

'Well, you could,' said Richard, slowly, emphasising the could. 'But we thought it would be better to go on the

Roman road again so we can go really fast.'

'We'll see about that,' said Philip. 'How are we going to get from Brierlow Bar to Matlock Bath?'

'That's easy,' said Richard, as he traced the route. 'You go along here to the Newhaven Inn and then you turn left.'

'I see,' said Philip. 'We're going the long way round, then?'

'Yes,' said Richard.

'So, it could be quite a while before we get to the picnic?'

'The picnic is only for my mother and Aunt Lella,' said Richard, as if stating the obvious. 'You want to try out your new motor, don't you?'

Philip looked across at Mr Harriman who was supressing a smile and shaking his head at the reasoning of his grandson.

'Indeed,' said Philip, trying not to laugh. 'So, where do we go after the Newhaven Inn?'

'Like this,' said Richard, tracing the route again, 'and we get to Grangemill, see where it says Holly Bush. Thomas's mother says this was where the coach and horses used to stop in the old days.'

'She's quite right,' said Mr Harriman. 'That was an old coach road once and you could get all the way from Derby to Chesterfield. And before that the packhorses used to go along that way and long before them, thousands of years ago, there was a trackway which we now call the Portway. Perhaps, Philip, you could take a short detour before turning at Newhaven and visit the stone circle at Arbor Low.'

'That's an excellent idea,' said Philip.

'If you're going to take the long way and a detour, perhaps you should have lunch before you leave,' said Mr Harriman.

'Oh, no,' said Richard, 'that would take ages. We need to go as soon as Mr Wildgoose has closed the office.'

'Right,' said Philip. 'But what about my new motor car on that road, though. There is a cross-roads at Grangemill and there have been a few accidents there. A couple of years ago it was described as one of the most dangerous crossroads in the country.'

'Don't worry, Mr Danebridge. When we get there, we'll keep a lookout for other motor cars for you.'

'Thank you,' said Philip. 'That will be reassuring. Now, where are we going from there?'

'The Jelly road,' said Richard. 'I can't remember exactly what it's called properly.'

'Ah, the Via Gellia,' said Mr Harriman. 'It was made for a man who knew Latin. He thought he was important enough to have a road named after him so he named it himself.'

'It's a very steep, winding road but at least it has quite a decent surface,' said Philip. 'And then when we reach the main road, we turn left to get to Matlock Bath. Well done! That all looks very satisfactory, Richard. Ah, here's your mother. Are you ready?' Philip stood up. 'You look very elegant, Cecily. May we escort you to your carriage.'

Philip had arranged to play the role of chauffeur, accompanied by Richard, and, after everyone had agreed that Cecily looked lovely and that the borrowed dress suited her, Philip and Richard escorted her out to the Bentley parked outside in Hall Bank.

'Thank you for taking me to Top Trees, Philip. It is very kind of you and I really do appreciate it.'

'Think nothing of it, Cecily. Like everyone else, I am pleased that you are going.'

'I am pleased too, although it's ages since I went to one of Lady C's dinner parties. I've only been to her drawing rooms recently. They are much less formal and I've always been there with my family. I have to confess to being just a little nervous.'

'A bit like coming out, but for the second time round.'

'Yes,' said Cecily, laughing. 'And almost as terrifying.'

'It will be good for you to be back in The Park again.

You're very different from Lella. You fit in there.'

'I know. Eleanor is far too Bohemian for The Park. Far too independent.'

'Yes,' laughed Philip, 'she is in a class of her own. That's part of her charm.'

'Lady C doesn't see it that way.'

'No, she likes all her guests to be docile and biddable. Lella could never be described that way, thank goodness. Right, here we are.'

Philip stopped the motor car at the foot of the front steps of Top Trees, got out, and opened the door for Cecily.

'Make sure you enjoy yourself,' he said, handing her out of the motor car.

Philip waited while Cecily went up to the front door where Ash, the butler, was standing and he watched her go inside. Then Ash came down the steps towards Philip.

'Good evening, Mr Danebridge,' he said.

'Good evening, Ash. No need to move the motor car. I'm playing chauffeur this evening.'

Ash bowed, and failing to hide his smile, said very solemnly: 'Very good, Mr Danebridge. Carriages at 11.30 p.m. then.'

'Jolly good,' said Philip, as he got back into the Bentley, laughing. Richard waved regally to Ash and Ash saluted as they drove off.

0 0 0

After dinner, while Eleanor and Philip took Napoleon for his walk, Mr Harriman and Richard read *William Again*, the latest *William* book which Mr Harriman did not altogether approve of. He had agreed to read it with Richard but reserved the right to insert caveats every now and again about William's behaviour, noting what was acceptable and what was not. When Eleanor, Philip, and Napoleon returned there was a lively debate going on about some prank William had carried out which Mr Harriman considered could not be allowed to go unpunished.

Eleanor got out the playing cards and they played *Old Maid* and *Fish* until it was time for Richard to go to bed. Philip told Richard about a new game, called *Touring*, which he had heard about. It took players on an imaginary journey by motor car and, as Richard was now old enough for such a game and was passionate about motor cars, Philip promised to get it for him in time for his birthday in September.

After Richard had gone to sleep, Mr Harriman, Eleanor and Philip discussed Philip's report regarding the suspect piece of furniture and then moved on to the subject of the baby found on the Temple Mound. Mr Harriman and Eleanor had just begun a debate on the legal position of the mother and the merits or otherwise of the *Infanticide Act* which had recently come into force, when Philip suddenly noticed the time and left for Top Trees to bring Cecily home. After he had escorted Cecily upstairs, he said goodnight to everyone and arranged to arrive back at Hall Bank the next day ready to leave for the picnic at a quarter past one.

'Well,' said Mr Harriman to Cecily, 'come and entertain us. Have you managed to redeem the Harriman name and reputation with the people of The Park?'

Cecily laughed. 'I don't know about that. There were certainly plenty of Park people present, all the usual ones dining at Lady C's expense.'

'Was it a big party?' asked Mr Harriman.

'Sixteen at table and then a few more guests arrived later. Lady C wanted to introduce two of her latest musical "discoveries" and they entertained us with a recital.'

'Was that the reason for the dinner party?' asked Eleanor.

'No. It quickly became apparent that the reason was the presence in town of The Honourable Hugo Berkeley-Trent.

Lady C has somehow managed to capture him and presented him as her prize. He appeared to be as puzzled by his invitation as I was by mine. He was on Lady C's right, as guest of honour, and I was surprised to find myself on his other side. He's in his mid-thirties, I would guess, and I think that may have been why I was seated next to him. There were not many people of our age there.'

'And what was the Honourable Hugo like?' asked Eleanor.

'Very elegantly dressed and quite good looking. I didn't have very much opportunity to talk to him. Until the table turned, I had to pay attention to my neighbour and then, after that, Lady C continued to monopolise her prize. Mr Buckley, as Mayor, had precedence on Lady C's left but he was largely ignored and must have felt somewhat neglected. I did hear enough of her conversation with the guest of honour to know that he is very gracious and has impeccable manners. I suspect that he was thoroughly bored but managed to hide it very well. At one point, Lady C was telling him about the Devonshire Hospital and how important it was to the town and how vital her role is in supporting it and raising funds. Her acquaintance with the Devonshires was referred to, of course. Then I had to pay attention to my neighbour and when I next looked back at Lady C she must have made one of her outrageous statements, you know that insensitive way she has. I didn't hear what she had said but Mr Berkeley-Trent put his table napkin to his lips and I am certain it was to stifle a laugh.'

'Perhaps she was trying to extract a donation from him for the Hospital,' said Eleanor. 'She wouldn't think that sort of conversation out of place at a dinner party and with a person she barely knew.'

'I don't know. I think he was trying so hard not to laugh out loud that he almost choked. He glanced around quickly to see if anyone had noticed his reaction but fortunately no-one else seemed to have been paying attention. He took a sip of wine and then gave me the most charming of conspiratorial smiles as he put his wine glass down. I'm afraid I had to smile back, however disloyal that may have been to Lady C. He really did behave beautifully towards his hostess all evening and she didn't deserve it.'

'Lady Carleton-West is a fearful old trout,' said Mr Harriman. 'And I rely on you girls not to repeat that opinion,' he added, sternly. 'Nevertheless, I do acknowledge that, despite her blunders, she does do a lot of good for the town, and especially for the Devonshire Hospital.'

'We all know that Lady C wants one of those new O.B.E awards.' said Eleanor. 'Or an invitation to the garden party at Buckingham Palace. Lady C was green with envy when she heard that Miss Dodd, the headmistress at The Grange School had been invited to next week's garden party.'

'I am sure that Lady C is not the only one who is devoting time to charity work in the hope of receiving official recognition. And we must give Lady C her due,' said Mr Harriman. 'This town has certainly benefitted greatly from the funds she raises and she has always been very active.'

'Oh dear, that makes her sound like a volcano,' said Eleanor, laughing. 'Although there certainly are some similarities.'

'Yes, indefatigable is probably the word I want,' agreed Mr Harriman.

'She is certainly that. But we are digressing from the main topic of conversation,' said Eleanor. 'Tell me more about this paragon of etiquette.'

Cecily frowned. 'I only had chance to speak to him again for a few minutes while coffee was being served in the drawing room. Then, unfortunately he had to leave. Lady C announced that two of her protégés were going to sing for us and while we were all rearranging ourselves, he seemed to take that opportunity to escape. I don't think Lady C noticed.

He was very apologetic and said that he had an invitation for tomorrow that required him to get up very early, before dawn, and asked to be excused. Lady C was obviously disappointed. She rang for Ash and then walked with the guest towards the drawing room door. I only heard part of their conversation because people were moving about and those close to me were talking. Lady C thanked him for coming and then said something to him to which he replied: "Oh, please, there is nothing to apologise for. You were not to know. I am sure it was mere inadvertence." Then Ash arrived and the guest left. But, by the look on Lady C's face when she came back into the room, something had definitely troubled her.'

'What sort of look?' asked Eleanor.

'I can't quite describe it. In books sometimes a person is described as looking mortified and I'm not sure exactly how that looks but I think that might have been the sentiment that Lady C was expressing.'

'How very odd,' said Eleanor. 'It is hard to imagine Lady C being mortified. She usually just charges on oblivious to the effect she is having on anyone else's feelings.'

'Yes, it was odd. She was definitely put out. I have never seen her look like that before.'

'And is the Honourable Hugo just visiting Buxton?'

'I believe so,' said Cecily. 'He's staying at the Hydro. After dinner, when the gentlemen had joined us in the drawing room, I heard him asking a lot of questions about Buxton, as though he was genuinely interested and I think he must be staying for at least two weeks because when Lady C told him about the charity bazaar for the hospital, he said he would make every effort to be there.'

'Well,' said Eleanor, 'then perhaps the bazaar will be a little more interesting than usual. I shall make a point of attending.'

'I wasn't aware that there was a choice,' said Cecily, dryly.

CHAPTER SEVENTEEN

'The question now is how do we get the mother to tell her story in support of Joshua without leaving her at the mercy of Superintendent Ferguson and his determination to charge somebody with concealing the birth?' asked Edwin.

On Saturday morning, Eleanor and Edwin were in Mr Harriman's office and Eleanor had recounted the details of her interview with Molly Brandon.

Edwin continued: 'Based on the facts we have I don't think the charge would stick but it would be unfair to put the girl through the ordeal of a trial.'

'I agree,' said Eleanor. 'I have asked Catherine to see her because I think Molly does need help and perhaps it would be better to do nothing further for the moment. However, she does want to see the baby and I wasn't sure whether that would be possible or even whether it would be appropriate given the state she is in, but I did promise to ask if it could be arranged.'

Mr Harriman said: 'I shall have a word with Doctor McKenzie and see what his view is.'

'Good,' said Edwin. 'Now, what about young Joshua Wilde?'

'Well, obviously he had no part in any of this prior to finding the baby in the stables. That just leaves the problem of moving the baby. Not a minor problem, I agree, but I think we may be able to minimise the impact on Joshua of his actions that evening. What we need now is some good character references. Mr Wilde, senior, has given us some names and addresses. Can I leave that to you, Eleanor?'

'Certainly,' said Eleanor.

'There is one remaining issue to be considered,' said Edwin. 'What do we do about Superintendent Ferguson? Do we need to tell him that Eleanor has identified the mother?'

'What are your thoughts, Talbot?' asked Mr Harriman.

'Well, looking at it from our point of view, all we are doing is identifying a witness who has information relevant to the defence of our client. On the other hand we do have a duty to report a crime, if indeed one has been committed. But what crime is the mother guilty of? If she is telling the truth, it would seem that the baby was still born so there is no crime there. And, at the moment, we have no reason to doubt her story. Also, there is no evidence that she intended to conceal the birth, only that she left the baby temporarily and went back as soon as possible to recover it. And she did not move the body to the Mound.'

Mr Harriman nodded. 'Yes, I think, for the moment at least, there is nothing that we are obliged to report. The only remaining issue is the identity of the baby and Superintendent Ferguson certainly has the means to obtain that. Although he probably lacks Eleanor's ingenuity.'

'It just means it will take him a bit longer,' said Edwin, laughing.

'There is one more thing I'd like to consider though,' said Eleanor. 'I feel like Philip and his piece of Hepplewhite furniture. There is something about Molly's dismissal from the hotel that doesn't seem quite right. I can't point to anything specific but I know I am not going to be happy until I have satisfied myself as to what is causing that sense of something not quite matching. Should we follow that up?'

'I don't recall any suggestion at the time that anything was amiss, but yes, certainly, if you think there is something that needs to be clarified,' said Mr Harriman.

'It's just that Molly was dismissed from the hotel in rather extraordinary circumstances. Mrs Erskine may simply have been punishing Molly because she believed that Mr Erskine was the father of Molly's baby but, as far as we know, she had nothing on which to base that belief. In fact, we don't know whether she actually did believe it. It seems to have been used more as an excuse to dismiss Molly. Mr Erskine's accident happened a couple of weeks after Mrs Erskine found out about Molly's condition, and from what Molly said, during those two weeks Mrs Erskine had not confronted her husband about the baby. Why? If it was really so important. Important enough to dismiss Molly? As Molly pointed out, if Mr Erskine had not died, he would have been able to tell the truth.'

'I suppose it is possible that she did confront her husband and he claimed that it was his,' suggested Edwin. 'Just to annoy his wife.'

'That's perfectly possible, I suppose,' said Eleanor. 'But, if so, why would she not have dismissed Molly at the time, before Mr Erskine died? There is another odd thing, though, when she dismissed Molly, Mrs Erskine seems to have been implying that Molly knew something about Mr Erskine's accident, although Molly says she did not see it. Mrs Erskine knew Molly had seen her in the corridor that leads to the back stairs. Mrs Erskine may have seen something, may even have seen the accident, and, knowing that Molly was also in the corridor, may have feared that Molly had also seen whatever it was she saw. And whatever it was, it was enough for Mrs Erskine to dismiss Molly and threaten her, just in case. Does that all sound too fantastic.'

'It does rather,' said Mr Harriman, 'but, nevertheless, I shall ask James to get the file for me and look at the evidence again just as a precaution.'

0 0 0

It was almost one o'clock, and James was getting ready to close the office. Edwin had stopped at the door of Eleanor's office on his way out just as Mr Harriman came up the stairs.

'Before you go, Talbot, I thought you'd want to see this. The *post mortem* report on the Temple Mound baby. It has just been delivered.'

Mr Harriman gave the report to Edwin, who scanned it.

'Hmmm,' he said, 'Doctor McKenzie has been very cautious.'

'Mainly because of the delay in finding the body, I think,' said Mr Harriman.

'So,' said Edwin, looking at Eleanor, 'Doctor McKenzie gives all the usual details as to weight, length, etc., male, "not full-term, approximately twenty seven weeks' gestation, possibly viable but no evidence of air in the lungs, safe to conclude not a live birth." That does seem to confirm the version given to you by the young person you interviewed yesterday, Eleanor.'

'Yes,' said Eleanor. 'I felt so sorry for her because, although it would have been difficult for her to care for the baby, it would have been better for her if he had lived but at least we can be confident that she is not to blame for his death.'

'And it is a better result for Joshua as well as there seems to be some suspicion as to his role in this affair, in the mind of Superintendent Ferguson, at least.' He handed the document back to Mr Harriman. 'That's excellent news. Right, I'll be off. Enjoy your picnic, Eleanor. Are you on the golf course this afternoon, Harriman?'

'Yes, there's a tournament today.'

0 0 0

Eleanor went to find Mrs Clayton, taking with her that day's edition of the *Buxton Advertiser*. Mrs Clayton had almost finished packing the picnic basket for the trip to Matlock Bath.

'Well, Mrs Clayton, I'm afraid this announcement in the paper answers your question about the Well-Dressings. I'll read you what it says:

> A bird whispers that a committee delegated by the Buxton Borough Council to make arrangements for the Well-Dressings have declined to proceed with their task on the ground that, in themselves, the Well-Dressings would not prove successful in the professed object of attracting people to the town. So it is extremely unlikely that the festival will be revived this year.

Mrs Clayton made her disapproval plain.

Eleanor said: 'I think the next paragraph makes it clear why nothing has been resolved. The report goes on to say:

> We understand that the advocates of attractions subsidiary to the Well-Dressings are conserving their energies for an intensive offensive early next year against the members of the Council antagonistic to the project, and hope that the result will be a "bumper" festival next year.

'Well, isn't that just what I said?' Mrs Clayton stood with hands on hips, the picture of indignation. '*Some people* don't want it revived and the rest of us don't have a say!'

'It does seem as though some people have more influence than others, doesn't it?'

'People in other villages have managed to revive their festivals. And with fewer people and less money than a big town like Buxton. The Council ought to be ashamed.'

'It is disappointing for those most directly concerned. This isn't the official announcement by the committee. I wonder what reasons they will give.'

'I don't agree with that bit about the object being to attract people to the town. Yes, it does attract visitors but that's not the reason it started. It had nothing to do with the visitors. It started because the residents had something to be thankful for. But, it's all about making money these days, isn't it?' Mrs Clayton sighed. 'Oh, well, there's nothing to be done about it. Now, you make sure you enjoy your ride in the new Bentley. Mr Danebridge took my boys out early yesterday morning and they haven't stopped talking about it since.'

Mrs Clayton tucked a few more items into the picnic basket and then said: 'I'll just check my list to make sure I've packed everything. Master Richard has been in several times to make sure I'm doing the job properly. He's anxious to leave on time. He tells me he and his friend are going to navigate for Mr Danebridge.'

'Yes,' said Eleanor, laughing. 'but I am not sure that Mr Danebridge knows what he has let himself in for.'

0 0 0

Buxton Hydro Hotel

Saturday 28th June, 1924

Dear Amelia,

I have just finished lunch at the Hydro and, as I am at leisure and have time to write, I thought this account of my advent-ure on Friday evening would amuse you. You will recall that I had received an invitation to dinner from a Lady Carleton-West. As you advised, I enquired of Mr Lomas, the owner of the Hydro who, of course, knows everyone in town. He cautioned me about her ladyship. She is well-known, locally and, on Friday, everything I had heard about her self-importance proved to be true.

What a baptism of fire and how awkward! The dear lady talked a great deal about her work for the Devonshire Hospital and her acquaintance with the Devonshires. I have never heard them mention the lady so the acquaintance must be slight. I foolishly thought that the purpose of the dinner invitation was to welcome me to Buxton.

Eventually, I realised that she took me for a visitor and had invited me for my title (and, it seems, in the hope of a donation to the hospital) and that she had no idea why I was in Buxton and no idea that you were also here on the day the invitation was sent. By the time I realised this, it was too late to put things right without embarrassing her in public, and at her own dinner table at that! I must say that I admire her effrontery or is it impertinence? I'm not sure she has heard of either of those words. She is rather like one of our battleships whose captain has ordered full steam ahead and then expects all other vessels to accommodate him.

So, I chose not to discuss the purpose for my being here. I thought it wiser. I decided to pay more attention to my dinner companions but they did not contribute much to the conversation, even on the rare occasions when Lady Carleton-West gave them the opportunity. I gathered that many of them were neighbours, with nothing new to say to each other. Probably just there to oblige their hostess and to eat a free dinner. Is that me being perceptive, or as you would say, Amelia, mean spirited?

After dinner there was to be a musical performance and Mr Lomas had warned me about that too. I made my excuses and escaped. I suppose if one is performing, the experience is different but I, very selfishly admit, that I prefer to be in the audience at a professional performance. There will certainly be another encounter with my hostess, probably at her Charity Bazaar which she assured me was the highlight of the Buxton season. I hope by then she will have had time to reflect on the inappropriateness of her conversation with me during dinner. Or, perhaps by then, I shall have had the opportunity to put things right. Better for her to have found out her mistake in the privacy of her own drawing room.

Otherwise, the facts are bound to emerge and there, in public on the day of triumph at her own charitable event, the humiliation would be too much, even for someone of her insensitivity. I admit it would be fun because she is a dreadful snob and frightfully bossy, completely taken up with her own importance but I could not do that to her. I think there is no real harm in her and, as people will insist on saying of busybodies, "she means well."

You will be pleased to know that the evening was not a complete loss! My right-hand neighbour at dinner proved to be a welcome contrast to my hostess and far more interesting than the other guests. Charming manners, intelligent conversation, and gracious. I did not manage to find out very much about her. She will no doubt be at the bazaar. I think you would like her.

Much love,

Hugo

P.S. There is a Sir Marmaduke Carleton-West. He very properly paid a call prior to the dinner party. I observed him at the opposite end of the dining table and I do not believe he uttered a single word during the whole of dinner. Which was quite splendid, by the way. The dinner, I mean, not his silence although it was rather splendid of him to be able to maintain it without any show of embarrassment. H.

CHAPTER EIGHTEEN

At lunch time on Monday, Edwin came into the dining room and began serving himself from the dishes set out by Mrs Clayton on the sideboard. As Eleanor arrived, he said:

'What can I get you, Eleanor? A little of everything?'

'Oh, yes, please.'

As Edwin was handing Eleanor her plate, Mr Harriman came into the dining room. He had asked James to find the file relating to the death of Mr Erskine at the Shakespeare Hotel but, until that morning, had not had chance to look at it. He had now read the medical report and the police statements. He had brought the file with him so as to discuss it with Eleanor and Edwin.

As he served himself from the sideboard, Mr Harriman said:

'After Eleanor expressed her uneasiness about the Erskine case, I thought it wise to have another look at the file in case there was something I had missed and I've had chance to look through it this morning.'

'It would be unlike you to miss something, Harriman,' said Edwin. 'I seem to recall that it was a fairly straightforward case, straightforward enough not to require an inquest.'

'Well, yes,' said Mr Harriman, 'I certainly thought so at the time but it's best to be sure. I am the first to admit that mistakes can be made; however, having looked at the statements again, I am satisfied that Superintendent Johnson did a thorough job with the evidence. Apart from Mrs

Erskine's evidence, there were several other statements. This is a statement made by a Joseph Hallett. He gives an address in Rockingham Street, Sheffield and describes himself as a commercial traveller. The statement was taken three days after the death of Mr Erskine. He was back in Sheffield at the time and Superintendent Johnson had one of the Sheffield police officers prepare the statement. I shall read it to you and you can tell me what you think. This is what he says:

> On the evening of 17 March,1924, I was staying at the Shakespeare Hotel, Spring Gardens, Buxton. I am a commercial traveller and often stay at this hotel in the course of my work. I arrived at about 7 p.m. and went straight up to the room usually allocated to me on the first floor. I had already dined so I remained in my room until about a quarter to nine. I had run out of matches and I knew there would be some available at the reception desk so I went downstairs. The desk was unattended. I found the matches and returned along the passage intending to use the back staircase of the hotel, it being the most direct way up to my room. There is another adjacent staircase which leads down to the basement of the hotel and to the cellars.
>
> I had just reached the foot of the staircase and had taken a couple of steps up when the outside door of the hotel opened and Mr Erskine, the deceased, came into the hotel. I knew him from previous visits to the hotel and wished him good evening. I noticed that he was unsteady on his feet and I thought he had been drinking. He did not return my greeting but instead walked directly to the top of the stairs which lead to the cellars. Just as he was about to step down onto the first step there was a loud bang which startled him. He turned sharply to see what had caused the noise and the sudden movement caused him to overbalance and he fell backwards down the stairs. He was unable to grab the stair rail. I was too far away to be able to prevent

his fall. I called for help and a doctor was summoned by Mrs Erskine.

I later learnt that the noise which had startled Mr Erskine was caused by the rear door of the hotel. It had not been closed properly by Mr Erskine and a sudden gust of wind had caused it to blow shut. Also, it was raining and the soles of his shoes may have been wet and slippery.

And that is the end of his statement.'

'That all seems pretty clear,' said Edwin. 'What about the other statements.'

Mr Harriman said: 'Superintendent Johnson obtained a witness statement from the publican at the Milton's Head hotel who confirmed that Mr Erskine was a regular patron there. On the day Mr Erskine died, he together with his friend, Mr Michael O'Connor, had been at the hotel for most of that afternoon and evening, they both being Irishmen and it being St Patrick's Day. His recollection was that Mr Erskine left at about eight thirty.'

'Did the doctor who was called to the hotel mention alcohol?' asked Eleanor.

'He certainly did. It was Doctor Freeman.' Mr Harriman shuffled the papers in the file and drew out the doctor's report. 'He states: "the patient smelled very strongly of alcohol and there was evidence of alcohol having been spilt on his clothing." Doctor Freeman also noted that the patient was still wearing his overcoat. So that is consistent with Mr Erskine having just come into the hotel from the Milton's Head. Doctor Freeman called an ambulance and he says: "the patient was unconscious when I examined him and remained so during his removal from the hotel to the hospital." Doctor Freeman made a note of the injuries and so did the doctor at the hospital when Mr Erskine was admitted. Mr Erskine died the following day, apparently without regaining consciousness. Doctor Freeman saw him again that second day and signed the death certificate. He was in no doubt as to the cause of death and Superintendent Johnson was satisfied that the fall was an accident, so I saw no need to hold an inquest.'

Edwin said: 'I agree. It does all seem conclusive.'

'What did Mrs Erskine say in her statement?' asked Eleanor.

'Very little,' said Mr Harriman. 'I'll read it to you.

> My husband left the hotel some time during the afternoon, I cannot be sure of the time and I do not know where he went. I was in the dining room which was being prepared for breakfast the next morning, when someone, I don't remember who, called out to me that Mr Erskine had had an accident. Then I saw Mr Hallett, a guest, who told me that Mr Erskine had fallen down the cellar steps and asked me to telephone for a doctor, which I did.

'That is not quite the version that I was given by Molly,' said Eleanor. 'She said Mrs Erskine was in the corridor just before Mr Erskine fell. I know that Molly has every reason to dislike Mrs Erskine and that she might be tempted to make up a story, but why would she? It makes no sense.'

'Mrs Erskine could have just come into the corridor from the dining room, I suppose,' said Edwin.

'Did Superintendent Johnson take a statement from Molly?' asked Eleanor.

'No,' said Mr Harriman.

'I suppose that by the time he was interviewing witnesses, Molly had already left the hotel. She was dismissed straight after Mr Erskine died,' said Eleanor. 'Perhaps he didn't think she would have anything useful to add.'

'Well,' said Mr Harriman, 'there is nothing, at the moment, to cause me to question the evidence provided by Superintendent Johnson. Perhaps we should leave it there, unless anything further emerges and then, of course, I shall certainly consider the case further.'

Eleanor accepted her father's caution regarding the death of Mr Erskine and agreed that taking no further action was the correct approach; however, her curiosity had been piqued. When she had finished lunch, she took Napoleon for his afternoon walk along Broad Walk and mulled over the evidence from the Erskine file. She decided that she needed to know more about this witness, Joseph Hallett, and made a mental note to ask Molly about him.

0   0   0

That evening, Eleanor heard the telephone bell and waited. The office was closed and Eleanor and Mr Harriman were in the sitting room, reading the newspapers with a pre-dinner sherry. Napoleon was snoozing on the hearthrug. The bell stopped ringing so Eleanor knew that Mrs Clayton had answered the telephone and would take a message.

Mrs Clayton came into the sitting room and Napoleon lifted his head to enquire.

Mr Harriman said: 'We heard the telephone bell ring, Mrs Clayton. Nothing important, I hope.'

'It was Doctor Balderstone for Miss Harriman. She asked me to give you a message. I'm to tell you that the person she was expecting today didn't arrive and would you let her know if you want her to make another appointment. She said you would know who she meant.'

'Yes I do know. Thank you, Mrs Clayton.'

'Right, then, dinner's ready to serve. Unless you need anything else, I'll be off.'

Mr Harriman said: 'Ah, thank you Mrs Clayton. No, there's nothing else we need. You get off to those boys of yours. Oh, and would you tell Alf that the papers for Joshua's apprenticeship have been sent to Mr Wilde so he should receive them soon.'

'Will do, Mr Harriman. Good evening, then. Good evening, Miss Harriman.'

When Mrs Clayton had left, Eleanor said: 'I'm disappointed that Molly didn't keep the appointment. I think she really does need help.'

'You and Catherine have probably done all you can. One cannot force the girl to attend if she chooses not to. I think all you can do is make a second appointment.'

0 0 0

DIARY Monday 30th June

Went out very early this morning and walked as far as Bishop's Lane. Glorious weather and that particular spot is splendid. I can see why the Bishop chose it – must check exactly which bishop that was. Noticed the churchyard at Christ Church. Had been informed that this was where all the town patriarchs come to rest in peace, plus their wives and children. Some very elaborate tombstones and statues. Detoured to read the inscriptions. The history of the town seems to be recorded here. Extraordinary sight on leaving. Young woman sitting on ground beside a recent grave. Thought it better not to intrude. Very poetic but also rather sad. Like Niobe, all tears.

CHAPTER NINETEEN

Eleanor was busy with clients all day on Tuesday and did not have time to think about Molly until late in the afternoon. At five o'clock, she asked James to have the motor car brought round from the garage so that she could drive to Fairfield and visit Molly.

As she parked the motor car in the lane near the end of the row of cottages where Molly lived, Eleanor was surprised at how different the area was from her first visit. Whereas previously it had seemed deserted, now everyone was back from work or the fields. There were children playing and making a considerable amount of joyful noise. In the lane, near the end of the row of cottages, three women were standing, chatting. The women eyed the motor car suspiciously and then one of them said something that made the other two women laugh loudly.

Eleanor walked along the path in front of the cottages and knocked on Molly's door. There was no response and no sound of anyone inside. Eleanor knocked again and waited but there was still no response. She walked back to the end of the row and approached the group of women. They fell silent. Eleanor was certain that the women would have known about Molly's baby but she could not be sure that they knew that the baby had been born. She decided to be as vague as possible.

'I wonder if you can help me. I came to visit Molly Brandon but she doesn't seem to be at home.'

'She's not,' said one of the women, who was wearing a floral overall over her dress. 'Not to nosey people, any road,' she added.

Floral Overall was standing at the front of the group, hands on hips, and facing Eleanor. Eleanor judged that she was the self-appointed leader.

'She's not here,' said the woman standing just behind and to the right of Floral Overall. She was wearing a green apron. Floral Overall turned and glared at her.

'Do you know where she has gone?' asked Eleanor, keeping her tone mild so as not to antagonise the group with her questions.

'Who says she's gone anywhere?' said Green Apron.

'What's it to you?' asked Floral Overall.

The third woman remained silent.

'I wanted to help her,' said Eleanor.

'That's what you all say, coming here with your questions,' said Floral Overall.

'She's gone,' said Green Apron.

'Do you know where she is?' asked Eleanor.

'It's nowt to do wi' us,' said Floral Overall.

'Not seen her today,' said Green Apron.

The third woman shook her head.

Eleanor said: 'Molly told me that the friend she is staying with had gone to visit her mother. Do you know if she has returned yet?'

'I do,' said Green Apron.

'Why do you want to know?' asked Floral Overall, crossing her arms in front of her.

'She's gone to join her man fruit-pickin',' said the third woman, earning a glare of disapproval from Floral Overall.

'Who are you anyway? One o' them interfering do-gooders?' asked Floral Overall.

'So-called charity,' added Green Apron.

It suddenly occurred to Eleanor that, as she had come by motor car and was dressed rather formally, she had probably been mistaken for one of those "interfering" ladies from The

Park who came in the name of charity to "administer to the poor." Their intentions were noble but misguided and they could sometimes be insensitive towards people whose way of life was so very different from their own. Their attempts to provide assistance were sometimes viewed with suspicion. She wondered if that was the reason for the women's seeming hostility.

'Not at all,' said Eleanor. 'I'm a solicitor.'

'Oh, aye,' said Floral Overall, in a tone that left no doubt as to her total disbelief.

'I have a client who is in trouble with the police and I am trying to help him.'

Green Apron laughed and said: 'If yer lookin' for someone to help, try Will Fiddler over yonder.'

Floral Overall added: 'Always in trouble.'

The three women looked at each other and laughed loudly, enjoying a private joke.

Eleanor, on hearing the name Will Fiddler, turned to look behind her. Across the road, a young man was sitting on the garden wall in front of one of the pair of single storeyed cottages. It seemed that the women's group solidarity did not extend to all the residents of the lane. He had not been there when Eleanor arrived.

Eleanor turned back to the group. 'Thank you for your time. I'm sorry to have troubled you.'

The three women watched in silence as Eleanor walked across the lane and addressed Will Fiddler.

'Good afternoon, Mr Fiddler. I'm looking for Molly Brandon. Do you know where she is? The ladies across the road thought you might be able to help.'

Will Fiddler remained sitting on the wall and laughed raucously. 'Ladies! Old crones, more like! What do you want wi' Molly?'

'I came here to see her last week and she had an appointment in Buxton yesterday which she didn't keep. I am concerned that she may be ill or in need of help.'

'I wouldn't know nothin' about that.'

'But you do know Molly?'

'Course.'

'Have you seen her recently?'

Will nodded. 'This mornin'. Early.'

'What time was that?'

Will paused, pulled down the corners of his mouth, stuck out his bottom lip and then said: 'Sixish.'

'What was she doing?'

'Walkin' away.'

'Down this lane?'

'Aye.'

'Did she have a bag or anything with her?'

Will shook his head.

'Did you speak to her, at all?'

'Why would I?' He paused. 'That your motor?' he asked, nodding his head in the direction of Eleanor's motor car.

'Yes, it is.'

Will nodded slowly but said nothing.

Eleanor decided it was time to leave.

'Well, thank you for the information. Good-bye,' she said, as she turned and returned to her motor car.

Will Fiddler looked at the motor car enviously as it disappeared down the lane.

As she drove back to Hall Bank, Eleanor thought about Will Fiddler. If he lived at one of the cottages opposite where Molly lived, he must have known about the baby. Did he also know more than he had admitted about the baby being left in the stables? Was he involved in some way? She thought about the events of that Monday morning when Mr Beresford had started work at the Shakespeare Hotel. Was it possible that Will already knew that the baby was in the horse box? Had he made sure that he was in the lane loading the cart when the work reached that last horse box? Had he made sure Joshua found the baby instead? It was his suggestion to move the baby to the Temple Mound, was that more than just a practical joke? Was he intending to make it more difficult to identify the baby?

Eleanor was concerned not only for Molly but also for Joshua. Molly's evidence about the baby was vital for Joshua's case and she had no idea where Molly might be. She tried to think of anything Molly had told her that might provide a clue to her whereabouts. There were too many unanswered questions and Eleanor put them firmly to the back of her mind because she realised that she was not paying attention to the road.

0   0   0

As she was driving down Spring Gardens, Eleanor was reminded of the visit she had made to the Shakespeare Hotel on her way back from seeing Molly for the first time. That afternoon, she had seen a young girl leave the hotel. Eleanor glanced at her watch. It was about the same time now and there was just a chance that, if the girl was leaving at the end of her shift, Eleanor might be able to find her again. If she had worked with Molly, she might know something about her.

Eleanor drove around to Hardwick Mount and parked the motor car there. She walked down the lane towards the rear of the hotel and stood in the lane, hidden from view by the stables and out of sight of the cottages on the land next to the hotel. She was able to see the staff entrance to the hotel. She waited patiently but after five minutes began to wonder if it was a waste of time. After a few more minutes, she glanced at her watch, then told herself to be patient. A couple of minutes later someone came out of the hotel door. Eleanor thought it looked like the same girl that she had seen on her previous visit. The girl headed through the archway and turned left into Spring Gardens. Eleanor walked quickly down the lane and through the archway in pursuit, keeping her quarry well in sight.

The street was busy because a lot of people were leaving work and there was a policeman on duty at the top of Spring Gardens. The girl waited until the policeman had stopped the traffic and then crossed the road. When she reached the foot of The Slopes, she sat down on one of the park benches and looked around her as though she expected to meet someone. That was a complication Eleanor had not planned for and she decided to approach the girl straightaway. She took out from her pocket one of her business cards.

'Good evening,' said Eleanor, 'my name is Miss Eleanor Harriman. May I give you my card?'

The girl looked surprised at being spoken to and reluctantly took the card without looking at it.

'As you will see, I am a solicitor and I am hoping that you may be able to help me with some information. May I join you?'

The girl looked at Eleanor a little uncertainly but nodded. Eleanor sat down beside her.

'I believe that you are employed at the Shakespeare Hotel.' The girl nodded. 'May I ask your name?'

'Mary. Mary Roberts.'

'Miss Roberts, I'm trying to help someone who worked at the hotel until a few months ago. Molly Brandon'

'Is she all right? Has she had the baby?' asked Mary anxiously.

'Yes, she has and that is why I am trying to help her. I spoke to Molly last Friday and when I went to visit her again today, she was not at home although I had expected her to be there. Her neighbours weren't able to help me and I thought perhaps, if you are a friend of hers, you might know where she might have gone. To friends perhaps?'

'I don't know. I know Molly, yes. When you work with

someone you do get to know a bit about them, but you're not exactly friends, if you know what I mean.'

'Yes, I think I understand. You don't see them other than at work. Not like your close friends.'

'Aye, that's it. I like Molly but she didn't say much on account of the fact that she'd lost her fiancé and didn't feel like talking.'

Eleanor could see that this line of enquiry was not going to help her find Molly but she realised that, if she could get Mary's confidence, she could obtain information which would verify what Molly had told her about her time at the hotel.

'I know that Molly was working at The Cosy Corner café as a waitress. Did you see her then?'

'Just once or twice in passing, just to wave through the window, like. Not to stop and talk.'

'I believe Molly stopped working at the hotel in about March this year.'

Mary nodded. 'Just after Mr Erskine died.'

'And is it true that Mrs Erskine told her to leave immediately.'

Mary nodded: ' No notice or nothing.'

'Do you have any idea as to why that was? Had Mrs Erskine complained about her work?'

'Mrs Erskine were always complaining about our work. She were never satisfied with anything we did. But Molly were a good worker. No, it were to punish her.'

Before Eleanor could ask her next question, Mary looked up and smiled. Eleanor, turning round, saw a smartly dressed young man of about the same age as Mary.

'Hello, Mary, you ready? Who's your friend?' he asked, confidently, as he lifted his hat.

'Hello, Frank,' said Mary. She turned back to Eleanor and added: 'Frank and I usually go for a walk together after work.'

'Mary likes to window shop,' said Frank, indulgently. As Mary had not stood up, he hitched himself onto the wall beside the park bench to wait. Then he added: 'We're engaged.'

'This is Miss Harriman, Frank.'

'How do you do, Frank,' said Eleanor. 'And congratulations.'

'Miss Harriman,' said Frank, acknowledging the introduction by touching the brim of his hat. 'Wedding's in two weeks.'

'Then please accept my very best wishes for fine weather on the day and a long and happy life together,' said Eleanor.

Frank said: 'Thank you. We mean it to be, don't we, Mary? Long and happy.'

Mary blushed and looked coy. Then she said: 'Miss Harriman was asking me about Mrs Erskine, Frank.'

'Oh, her!' said Frank, contemptuously.

'Frank doesn't think much of Mrs Erskine.'

'No, nor Mister for that matter,' added Frank. 'No great loss there.'

'So you haven't been very happy working at the hotel?' asked Eleanor.

'No,' said Mary, 'I thought of leaving when Molly left, except it suited me to keep on for a bit. I'm saving to buy things for the house and I knew I wouldn't get another situation not for just the few months before the wedding.'

'That's very sensible of you,' said Eleanor.

'But next week, she'll be giving notice,' said Frank.

Mary nodded. 'I'll not be sorry to be leaving.'

Eleanor nodded and then said: 'Mary, you were going to tell me why Molly left so suddenly.'

'Because of what she knew,' interposed Frank.

'We don't know that for sure, Frank,' said Mary, mildly.

'Course you do. You said so yourself.'

'Well. . . I . . ,' said Mary, doubtfully, but did not continue.

'I believe it was something to do with Mr Erskine,' prompted Eleanor.

'Mr Erskine had had one too many at the pub,' said Frank, 'and he broke his neck falling down the cellar steps.'

'Mr Erskine often had too much to drink,' said Mary. 'As I said to Frank, I think Mrs Erskine were ashamed of him and she regretted marrying him. He were a good bit older than her. Mrs Erskine tried to keep him out of sight but he would insist on sitting in the lounge all day. He'd fall asleep sometimes and snore. She were trying to attract a better class of client and she said it gave the wrong impression. She ran the hotel. He never lifted a finger.'

'Except to bother you girls,' added Frank. 'Following you around, spying on you.'

'That's true,' said Mary.

'She were looking for an excuse to throw him out, if you ask me,' added Frank. 'Glad to be rid of him.'

'That's true, too, although it's not very nice to say so, is it? Him being dead now,' said Mary.

'Were you in the hotel when Mr Erskine had the accident?' asked Eleanor.

'No.' said Mary. 'I'd been poorly and I came back the day after he died.'

'And that was the day Molly left,' said Eleanor.

'Yes. Mrs Erskine got the wrong end of the stick with Molly and whose baby it were,' said Mary. 'She found out about the baby because Molly were sick and she jumped to the wrong conclusion. Molly said Mrs Erskine thought the baby were his.'

'Wouldn't Mr Erskine just have denied it?' asked Eleanor.

'Oh, Mrs Erskine would've ignored anything he said, if it suited her,' said Frank, his voice full of scorn. 'She were looking for an excuse to get rid of him.'

Mary turned to frown at him. 'Now, Frank. . .'

Undeterred Frank continued: 'You said so yourself, Mary

Roberts. And you know what Molly said.'

Eleanor resisted the temptation to ask the obvious question and waited patiently while Mary and Frank sorted themselves out.

Mary frowned and thought for a minute, then she said: 'When she were leaving Molly were upset. She told me Mrs Erskine had said that if anyone asked Molly questions about the hotel or about Mr Erskine she were not to answer. And she said if Molly said anything, Mrs Erskine would make a complaint against her. I couldn't think what Mrs Erskine had to complain about with Molly, she were a good worker, but Molly said she were afraid Mrs Erskine would say she had something to do with Mr Erskine's accident. She made me promise that I wouldn't believe it if anyone said she had because it weren't true. She swore she had nothing to do with it.'

'But had anyone suggested at the time that there was more to Mr Erskine's death than just an accident?' asked Eleanor.

'No,' said Mary, 'although, at the time, we did think . . .' Mary paused.

'We thought it were convenient, his passing,' finished Frank. 'Mr Erskine were no asset, and she had her eye on something better. Everyone knew there were someone willing to take Mr Erskine's place soon as he got the opportunity. Maybe he made the opportunity. He were at the hotel at the time.'

Eleanor remembered something Molly had told her and she decided to probe a little deeper.

'Do you know anything about a commercial traveller who stays at the hotel on a regular basis?'

Mary nodded. 'Yes.'

'Sells photographic supplies,' added Frank. 'Developing fluid, fixer, and such like, that you use to make photographs, and special paper as well.'

'Frank works for Mr Pilkington, in the Market Place, as a

shop assistant,' said Mary, proudly.

'The section of the chemist shop that sells photographic equipment?' asked Eleanor.

'Yes. Frank knows all about photography,' said Mary.

'Well, I don't know about that,' said Frank, modestly, 'but if Mrs Erskine's commercial traveller is in the photographic line of business, I know what sort of things he would sell. And I can make a fair guess at how often his customers are likely to want those things and how often he needs to be in Buxton.'

'There are quite a few photographers and studios in town,' said Eleanor.

'Granted,' said Frank, 'but most people here get what they need from Hunters on Cavendish Circus being as how they're local and have local connections. Mrs Hunter is from Buxton and great friends with Mrs Oram.'

'So what are you suggesting?' asked Eleanor.

'It's not just the sales that bring him here. He's sweet on Mrs Erskine,' said Frank.

'I see. That is very interesting,' said Eleanor. She turned to Mary: 'Does he stay very often?'

'Well, it's not a regular booking. Quite a few of our clients are commercial travellers and some of them have a regular round. They know when they will be next in town so, when they leave, they book for their next visit.' Mary frowned and then thought for a bit. 'But, come to think of it, it's a while since his last visit. Perhaps he's changed his round.'

'Perhaps they've had a falling out,' said Frank. He gave a low whistle 'I've just thought of something.'

Mary and Eleanor both looked at him.

'You don't suppose Mrs Erskine thought the commercial traveller were responsible for Molly's baby?' said Frank.

'You mean that's why she dismissed Molly? Not because of Mr Erskine?' asked Mary. 'No, that's silly.'

'Well, you said yourself, Mary Roberts, that there were

something going on between him and Mrs Erskine. If she thought Molly were getting in her way, well then . . .' Frank folded his arms decisively. 'Maybe she dismissed him as well as Molly.'

Mary smiled, looked at Frank, and shook her head.

'Tell Miss Harriman about Nurse Mackay, then,' said Frank.

'Oh, I couldn't,' said Mary, looking concerned. 'That would be telling tales. I shouldn't be talking about the guests at all. It's not my place. What they do is their own concern.'

'You're too soft, Mary.' Frank looked affectionately at his fiancée. 'Anyway, we'd best be getting on.'

Eleanor was amused by the obvious rapport between the two of them and was sure they would have a happy life together.

'Well, you have both been very helpful. Thank you. I'm sorry to have delayed your walk.'

'Not at all,' said Frank, as he slid off the wall, lifted his hat towards Eleanor, and offered his arm to Mary. Mary stood up and, taking Frank's arm, said goodbye.

Eleanor left them to their window shopping and began walking back to Hardwick Mount to retrieve the motor car. She still had no idea as to where Molly might be but she had learnt a lot more about the Shakespeare Hotel than she had bargained for.

CHAPTER TWENTY

Frank had mentioned a Nurse Mackay and, as Eleanor walked back to Hardwick Mount, she wondered what tale Frank thought the nurse had to tell. She decided to follow that trail, telling herself that it was for the sake of completeness, although it was really more out of curiosity. As she was not far from Catherine's surgery, she decided to call in there and ask. She was sure Catherine would know Nurse Mackay and where to find her.

'Have you come to make another appointment for Molly Brandon?' asked the receptionist.

'No, I went to call on her this afternoon but she wasn't there and I am trying to find her.'

'Catherine's with a patient. I'll let her know.'

'Actually, I came to ask about something else. Do you know a Nurse Mackay?'

'I certainly do,' said the receptionist. 'That will be Moira Mackay, the midwife.'

'Do you happen to have an address for her?' asked Eleanor.

'I do, and she has the telephone connected, for her work of course, so I can give you her number.'

'I just need some information that I think she can help me with. Do you think she would talk to me? I wouldn't want to interrupt her work.'

'I can telephone her now, if you like, and vouch for you.'

'Thank you, that would be most helpful.'

Eleanor waited and listened to a one-sided telephone conversation.

'Nurse Mackay said that she may be called out later this evening and she has appointments all day tomorrow but you could call around in about half an hour, if that is convenient. I shall give you the address.'

0 0 0

Eleanor returned to Hall Bank and, as the office was now closed, she explained to her father where she was going, left Napoleon supervising Mrs Clayton, and walked the short distance to Swan Cottage in Church Lane where Nurse Mackay lived. Eleanor was greeted cheerfully by the midwife, clearly used to putting people at their ease.

When they were settled, Nurse Mackay said:

'Now, my dear, how can I help? What is this information that you need?'

Eleanor noticed the Edinburgh accent immediately, there being many visitors from Scotland in Buxton.

'I'm a solicitor . . .'

'Good for you!' interrupted the midwife. 'There aren't many women in that profession, are there?'

'No, not as yet,' said Eleanor, smiling.

'Sorry, I interrupted you. Please go on.'

'I am trying to find evidence that will help a client, a young man who has been charged with an offence. He has been taken advantage of and is involved through no fault of his own. I am not sure whether anything you can tell me is relevant but I would like to be sure. The offence concerns the Shakespeare Hotel. I met one of the chambermaids, Mary Roberts. I think you may have been a guest there.'

'Yes, I was and I remember Mary. Lovely girl. When I arrived in Buxton, I needed somewhere for a week or two until I could get properly settled.'

'And when would that have been?'

'Erm, let me think, the last two weeks in January. I can

find the exact dates if that is important.'

'I don't think I need to trouble you, not at the moment, thank you. How long did you stay at the hotel?'

'Just two weeks.'

'Were you comfortable there? What sort of hotel is it?'

'A funny sort of place. It was comfortable enough but I wasn't sorry to leave. A very unpleasant landlady.'

'Yes, I have met Mrs Erskine. What was it that you didn't like about her?'

'Plenty of airs and graces. Always beautifully dressed. Quite expensively so, I should guess although I don't know much about clothes. Made up like a film star. She gave the impression that she was dissatisfied with her life, that she thought she deserved better.'

'I rather had that impression as well.'

'But really, well . . . In my profession, Miss Harriman, one learns to assess people and situations. I'm used to sizing up a household quickly and taking control. Who to rely on, who to banish in an emergency. There was an atmosphere in that hotel, hard to describe. Everyone seemed on edge, sensing a brewing storm. You can't afford that sort of thing, not in a hotel. Guests can sense it. I certainly did.'

'There was a young girl working there called Molly Brandon. Do you recall her at all?'

'Yes, I recall Molly. One of the chambermaids, rather timid. She didn't say very much. Not chatty like Mary. Mary was always talking about her fiancé. Frank, I think he was called.' Nurse Mackay laughed. 'She was so very proud of him. Molly was very quiet, not as confident as Mary. She always seemed on the verge of tears, probably because of the unkind way Mrs Erskine treated her staff. She made things particularly difficult for them.'

'In what way difficult?'

'Mrs Erskine never seemed to be satisfied with the girls' work, always hovering around, criticizing, commenting unfavourably, even in front of the guests. And without justification, really. They were efficient enough and very pleasant with the guests but you could see they were always on edge. I think that's partly what contributed to the poor atmosphere. My impression of Mrs Erskine was that she was dissatisfied with her lot and blamed others for it. Mr Erskine included.'

'Mr Erskine must still have been alive when you were staying there,' said Eleanor.

'Yes,' said Miss Mackay, frowning. 'Given to drink, that was obvious, and not much use when it came to running the hotel. In that respect, I think Mrs Erskine was right. She probably *did* deserve better. Mind you, if he was fond of drink, living in a hotel would have left him open to temptation.' Nurse Mackay laughed. 'If you look at it from his wife's point of view, I suppose you can't blame her if she strayed at bit.'

'Strayed?' asked Eleanor.

'Well, my dear, I heard comments along the lines of "no male guest is safe" and she did dress and behave with an audience in mind. She certainly was attentive to the men, and I am not just repeating gossip. I am judging by what I saw and that could lead to only one conclusion as far as I'm concerned.'

'Goodness,' said Eleanor. 'I am intrigued.'

'Let me explain. My profession requires me to be available at all hours, day and night, sometimes at short notice. The hotel is locked between eleven at night and seven in the morning so, when I arrived at the hotel, I arranged to have a key to the staff door so that I could come and go without disturbing anyone. One night, about a week after I had arrived, I'd been out delivering a bairn that was slow in arriving and it was about half past two in the morning when I got back. I don't think Mrs Erskine realised that I was still out, otherwise she might have been more careful. There shouldn't have been anyone around at that time because normally the guests would be in bed. I'd come in through the staff entrance at the back of the hotel and I mistook the way to my room, otherwise I would not have been in that part of the hotel.'

'Is this what I think you mean?' asked Eleanor, frowning.

'What would you think if you saw the landlady coming out of a guest's room in the early hours of the morning?'

Eleanor looked at Nurse Mackay, nodded slowly, and said: 'Ummm. I see what you mean.'

'Still, each to his own, I say. Or rather, her own. I see quite a few things that people prefer to keep hidden and you do learn not to judge.'

'And the guest? Did you know whose room it was? This isn't relevant to my enquiry, I'm just curious.'

'No, but I was able to make a fairly safe guess. See what you make of this. I had a few hours' sleep and then went down to the dining room for breakfast. I counted nine guests: three couples, two women in their late forties each sitting alone at separate tables, and a man, early forties, also at a separate table. It doesn't take Sherlock Holmes to solve that puzzle, does it?'

'Your facts are certainly very persuasive,' said Eleanor, smiling.

'And I was a bit naughty but, like you, my curiosity got the better of me. I went back to my room and waited until Mary came to do my room. I discovered that the lone gentlemen was a regular guest, a commercial traveller, and I suppose they do have more opportunity than most men to conduct liaisons. Mary said he was always given the same room towards the back of the hotel and a bit further away from the other guest rooms. That explained the look of horror on Mrs Erskine's face when she saw me in the corridor. She didn't expect to see anyone there.'

'You must have given Mrs Erskine quite a shock.'

'She gave me an icy stare when she saw me in the dining room that morning.' Miss Mackay laughed.

'And did you see the gentleman at the hotel again?'

'Yes, I did. He was there again the week before I left and I confess to being a busybody. I made a point of introducing myself. Oh, what was his name, now?' Miss Mackay frowned as she concentrated. 'Halford, was it? or Halibut, maybe. No that's a fish.' Miss Mackay shook her head. 'Something like that anyway.'

'And no doubt you heard about Mr Erskine's accident, although that would have been after you left.'

'Oh yes. Falling downstairs. It didn't surprise me. He had trouble even going up the stairs some nights. And sometimes in the mornings he looked terrible. I often saw him sitting in the lounge. Just sitting staring, mind, not even reading a newspaper. I did even wonder if he took drugs of some kind as well as drinking too much.'

'What made you think that?'

'Well, there was a great fuss one evening just before I left. Apparently, Mrs Erskine had a bottle of sleeping tablets and she discovered that it was missing. She accused the girls of stealing it and that did make me wonder. For Mrs Erskine to conduct a liaison with a guest, she must have been able to absent herself from the room she shared with Mr Erskine without him noticing. So, I wondered, you see, if Mr Erskine was very conveniently put soundly to sleep with some sleeping tablets. It would certainly account for his morning stupor. I think the missing bottle turned up some time later and the incident was forgotten.'

'You don't suppose Mr Erskine had found out about the sleeping tablets and hidden the bottle?' said Eleanor.

Nurse Mackay burst out laughing. 'Oh, that is delicious, Miss Harriman! Just imagine! Mrs Erskine reaches for the bottle, planning a night of bliss, and discovers that it is missing. No wonder she was so angry. It would have ruined her plans. I don't remember if the guest was in the hotel that night. Oh, I wish I had thought of your explanation. If I'd known I might have observed the liaising couple's frustration and Mrs Erskine's annoyance.'

'Or Mr Erskine's smugness at having spoilt their evening.'

'What a wonderful piece of theatre you have just conjured up,' said Nurse Mackay, still laughing. 'That would have been a sight.'

'If Mr Erskine had found out what was going on, I wonder what he would have done,' said Eleanor. 'Turned a blind eye or created a scene?

'He owned the hotel, you know, so he could have turned Mrs Erskine out if he'd wanted to.' Nurse Mackay shrugged. 'It's probably just as well he died. He didn't strike me as being strong minded enough to make a decision. I wonder if the liaison has continued after Mr Erskine's death.'

They chatted amicably for a while, Nurse Mackay having been reminded of a couple of other amusing anecdotes about Mrs Erskine and the guests, and then Eleanor left and returned to Hall Bank.

0 0 0

DIARY Tuesday 1ˢᵗ July

Met Grosvenor at Bishop's Lane this morning. Discussed plans for the house. He pronounced the site full of possibilities. – reminiscent of Capability Brown – hope he is not anticipating a grand project on that scale with a fee to match! I have very modest ideas. According to Grosvenor, despite the closeness to the river, the danger of flooding can be avoided. He is to prepare drawings.

CHAPTER TWENTY-ONE

The following morning, Eleanor was on her way to the dining room and paused at the kitchen door. Napoleon had already arrived and taken up his usual post.

'Good morning, Mrs Clayton.'

'Ah, Miss Harriman, good morning. Although I'm not sure what to make of it,' she said, shaking her head. 'I don't know what this town's coming to.'

'Whatever is the matter?' asked Eleanor.

'First the baby and now another body.'

'You don't mean another body has been found?'

'It has, Miss Harriman. Alf was called out last evening to the churchyard at Christ Church.'

'Good heavens!' said Eleanor. Then she added: 'That's where Mr Wilde is sexton, isn't it?'

'It is. He'll be right put out, I should think. He takes good care of that churchyard and there will have been people trampling all over it.'

'And the body. Do you know anything about that?'

'A young lass. That's all Alf knows at the moment. Nothing with her to say who she was. The doctor had gone by the time Alf got there so he wasn't able to hear how she died.'

'That is very disturbing news,' said Eleanor. 'And rather an odd place to be found.'

'Yes, first the Temple Mound and now a churchyard. And Alf said there were flowers scattered about with this one, as well. You don't think there's anything in all that business about pagan worship talked about because of the Well-

Dressings, do you?'

'I was inclined to dismiss it all as nonsense but after this latest news perhaps we should take it a little more seriously.'

Napoleon stood up and moved out of the way as Mr Harriman came down the hall towards the dining room.

'Good morning, Mrs Clayton,' he said.

'Good morning, Mr Harriman. I'll just make the tea and bring it in.'

Eleanor followed Mr Harriman into the dining room and repeated the information about the body in the churchyard.

'My immediate thought was that it might be Molly. When I went to visit her yesterday, she was not at home. She had been seen leaving her house at about six o'clock that morning. And she failed to keep the appointment Catherine made for her.'

'Christ Church is rather a long way from Fairfield, though,' said Mr Harriman. 'What reason would she have to go there? Let's wait until we have a little more information, shall we? Based on what we know so far, it does not seem that Molly was involved in either the death of the baby or the removal of the body so, if she has gone off somewhere, she is perfectly at liberty to do so.'

'Yes, you are right,' said Eleanor, smiling at her father. 'I shall just mind my own business and get on with my work.'

0 0 0

As it was early closing, Eleanor and Philip were due to play tennis at the tennis club that afternoon.

When Philip arrived to collect Eleanor and Napoleon, Eleanor said:

'You are looking very pleased with yourself. What have you been doing?'

'Receiving good news.'

'About what, may one ask?'

'One may. One received a telephone call this morning from the owner of the auction house which commissioned that report I was writing on the Hepplewhite dressing table.'

While Eleanor had been pre-occupied with finding Molly Brandon, Philip had completed his report and, as promised, Edwin had looked over it with him and made some suggestions about presenting the evidence. The report had been sent to the auction house.

Philip continued: 'The report has brought about a peaceful result and the owner of the auction house has now retained me to write other reports in the future.'

'Philip, that is excellent news! Well done. What did you decide about the piece?'

'Most of it was genuine all right, and beautifully made, but I detected an anomaly which was capable of different interpretations. It was either an odd event at the time the piece was made or evidence of a later repair. The anomaly cast doubt which might have been dispelled by taking one of the drawers apart, but both parties, being genuine collectors and respectful of such pieces, agreed that it was better to live with the doubt.'

'So what has the buyer decided to do?'

'To keep the piece and the auction house has negotiated with the seller on his behalf and obtained a reduction in the price.'

'That sounds like a satisfactory result. Tell me about the anomaly.'

'Are you sure? It will require a detailed explanation.'

'Yes, I'm interested.'

'Well, because the undersides of a dressing table and the drawers are not on display, there is no need to create a perfect finish. It is enough to just smooth the wood, and it is on the underside where one usually finds the clues, or in this case, the anomaly. Furniture of this period was made with hand tools so, on the underside of the table and the drawers, one finds the marks left by the hand-held plane used to smooth the wood. As the plane is moved across the wood it leaves very slight, more or less parallel, ridges which can be felt by the fingertips as a sort of ripple effect. When I ran my fingertips over the underside of the table and the drawers, the rippled pattern was there and I could gauge the width of the plane that had been used. On one of the larger drawers, something felt slightly different. I couldn't account for it so I took all of the drawers out and laid them face down so that I could compare them. It was then that I noticed that, on one of the drawers, the ridges were slightly, only very slightly, narrower. I had to measure them to convince myself that I was not imagining things.

'At that period, cabinet makers often had their tools made specially for them and it occurred to me that the odd drawer may have been smoothed using a different plane. Changing tools in mid-construction seemed odd. I decided to look more closely. With a strong light and an even stronger magnifying glass I detected, along one edge of the drawer, a very small slither of wood which was slightly lighter than the rest. Wood changes over time and, originally, this slither would probably not have been visible. Unless you were specifically looking for something odd, as I was, you would not notice it.'

'That is amazing,' said Eleanor.

'Not really. As I said before, it is just the sort of process you go through yourself. Some detail that seems out of place attracts your attention and you have to find an explanation.'

'So what explanation did you come up with?'

'Well, I could explain either the plane marks or the colour difference but not both. I set that out in my report. For instance, imagine the whole piece made in the same workshop at the same time but a different plane used to smooth the underside of the last drawer because the plane used on the rest had been damaged.'

'But that wouldn't explain the difference in colour?'

'Exactly, so, I imagined a shortage of wood to make the base of the last drawer and a different piece of wood being substituted and then, after the drawer had been constructed, being stained to match.'

'But that wouldn't explain the difference in the marks of the plane.'

'That's right. Then I started imagining all sorts of convoluted explanations. I even imagined someone cutting the drawer bottom to the wrong size, his horror at realising what he had done, and the lengths he might go to in order to create a substitute panel to hide his mistake.'

'That is very amusing. You are developing as wild an imagination as mine.'

'Yes, but, as you have taught me, the simplest explanation is often the correct one. I suspect that, at some time in the past, the drawer had been very skilfully repaired. The fact that the marks were made by a hand plane of an unusual width, probably not now available, suggests that the repair may have been done very early in the life of the dressing table. Whoever made the repair could not get wood of the same colour, hence the stain. Then, over the years the wood had contracted which exposed a very small slither of unstained wood.'

'And I suppose that, whereas a modern repair made using a machine might seem cold and invasive and reduce the value of the item, a repair made at a more contemporary period using the same methods and tools, might add a warmth and a certain charm to the piece.'

'Careful, old thing!' said Philip, laughing. 'You are in danger of becoming as sensitive to pieces of furniture as I am.'

Eleanor also laughed. 'I think I have a long way to go yet. But, congratulations. That is an excellent result. For you at least if not for the buyer. I imagine that every time anyone admires that dressing table, the poor man will feel obliged to explain.'

'I'm sure you are right,' said Philip. 'When I had finished the report, I was tempted to inspect all my own pieces of furniture again just in case I had overlooked something when I bought them.'

'Are you going to inspect them?'

'Probably not. I suspect this is one situation in which ignorance definitely is bliss.'

0 0 0

DIARY Wednesday 2nd July

Inspected the work on my rooms. Brocklehurst almost finished. Must say he is a good worker and has done an excellent job. Toured the Hospital this morning. Very impressed with the quality of the facilities and the high standard of care provided. Hartington was unstinting with his praise for the Hospital when he first proposed the consultancy and I can see that he was not exaggerating.

This afternoon met my two young friends for some more batting practice at the nets. They are both quick at understanding and are showing great improvement. Very satisfying.

CHAPTER TWENTY-TWO

Unfortunately for the editor of the *Buxton Herald*, published on Wednesday mornings, news of the finding of a body in the churchyard at Burbage came in too late to meet the paper's deadline. A report appeared in the next day's edition of the Sheffield *Evening Telegraph*.

> BUXTON. Wednesday 2nd July. The body of a young woman was found in the churchyard of Christ Church, Burbage, just after five o'clock on Tuesday evening. Mr Walter Hobson, a bell-ringer at Christ Church, was making his way to the church for the purpose of helping to repair one of the bell ropes prior to the bell-ringers' regular practice. Mr Hobson was taking a short cut through the churchyard from Bridge Farm, where he is employed, when he noticed a large piece of flowered material. His first impression was that it was perhaps a curtain, draped across one of the newer graves on the lower section of the churchyard.
>
> As he approached, he realised that the flowered material was, in fact, a woman's dress and that there was a woman lying across the grave. Flowers had been scattered about around her. Mr Hobson said: "I thought she were visiting to put the flowers on the grave and had been taken poorly so I went to see if I could help. When I got closer though, I saw there were nothing I could do for the young lassie."

> Mr Hobson had previously arranged to meet Mr Wilde, the sexton of Christ Church and the tower captain, at the door of the church. When Mr Wilde arrived, Mr Hobson apprised the sexton of the situation and the two men went back to Bridge Farm and telephoned to the authorities. It is understood that the preliminary opinion of the doctor who examined the body is that the presence of bruising to the neck and throat was consistent with strangulation. The identity of the young woman has not yet been ascertained. The police are continuing their enquiries. The young woman is reported to be about 18 years of age, blonde and blue eyed, and approximately five feet tall.

Eleanor stared at the newspaper, letting her eyes go out of focus, as she summoned up a picture of Molly Brandon, and compared that picture with the description in the newspaper. Then she tried to imagine the scene in the churchyard.

It was lunchtime and, as she was thinking about Molly, Mr Harriman and Edwin came into the dining room.

Mr Harriman said: 'I see you have the newspaper report, Eleanor. I received the notification from Superintendent Ferguson about ten minutes ago. I am beginning to think that your fears about Molly may turn out to be well-founded. Doctor McKenzie has done a preliminary examination. There is evidence of strangulation but he is being cautious. He is not willing to reach any conclusion as to the cause of death until after the *post mortem* examination. He did not elaborate further. He did confirm though that the girl had recently given birth. Very recently.'

'To the baby on the Temple Mound?' suggested Edwin.

'It's a possible link,' said Mr Harriman, cautiously.

'The police now have an unidentified baby with no mother and an unidentified mother with no baby,' said

Edwin. 'That seems to be a link.'

'Particularly as the mother of the baby has disappeared and may, therefore, be the girl in the churchyard,' said Eleanor. 'The description given in this newspaper report does seem to fit Molly.'

'I agree that the evidence does seem to point that way,' said Mr Harriman, 'to us at least because, don't forget, thanks to Eleanor, we have more information than the police have. That is something we shall now have to address.'

'And, if the young woman in the churchyard is the mother, that doesn't help young Joshua much,' said Edwin. 'She would have been able to give evidence as to how the baby came to be in the stables. That would have removed any doubt as to the extent of Joshua's involvement and certainly would have been helpful given Superintendent Ferguson's current position.'

'But if the young woman in the churchyard is the baby's mother, would it help Joshua if she is identified or is it better for him if she remains unidentified?' asked Eleanor. 'What I mean is, the natural tendency of people, including the police, to speculate might lead to them making a connection between the two deaths when in fact there may be none.'

'Yes, despite the *post mortem* report on the baby, Superintendent Ferguson is just as likely to arrest Joshua for the death of the young woman as well,' said Edwin. 'But, seriously, I understand the point you are making, Eleanor.'

'If the young woman is identified and her identity publicised, other information about her might come to light and any new information might be helpful to Joshua's case,' said Mr Harriman.

'Perhaps it might move things further forward if Superintendent Ferguson were to ask either Mrs Erskine or the tea shop owner, Miss Swinscoe, to view the body of the girl in the churchyard.' said Eleanor

'And how do we persuade Superintendent Ferguson to do

that?' asked Mr Harriman.

'It might not be easy,' said Edwin. 'If, as we have been told, he prides himself on his ability as a detective, he is unlikely to appreciate suggestions from people who have no experience of police work.'

'There is another alternative,' said Eleanor. 'Could you arrange for me to view the body of the young woman? We would then know if it is Molly.'

'Well,' said Mr Harriman, 'as it would not be done through official channels it would not be acceptable as formal identification and, if it is not Molly, it would merely eliminate her without establishing identification.'

'Establishing the identity of the mother and the absence of any link between her and Joshua is a legitimate enquiry and an essential part of our preparation of his defence,' said Eleanor. 'If an unofficial identification turns out to be useful, Superintendent Ferguson can always arrange an official one himself.'

'That's true,' said Mr Harriman. 'I shall make the necessary arrangements. Of course, we may be opening a can of worms. If the young woman was strangled, Superintendent Ferguson will be looking for a suspect and, as you pointed out Talbot, that might put Joshua in the limelight.'

'But,' said Edwin, 'it is in Joshua's interests for the mother to be alive and able to give evidence and that might suggest a lack of motive on his part.'

0 0 0

Later that afternoon, Eleanor went along to the morgue and when she returned to Hall Bank, Edwin was in Mr Harriman's office. It was time for Edwin to go home but he had been waiting for Eleanor's return. Napoleon, lying in the entrance hall, was also waiting for her. He greeted her and they both went into Mr Harriman's office. Edwin and

Mr Harriman looked at her expectantly and saw by her face that the news was not good.

'Well?' said Mr Harriman.

Eleanor slumped down on a chair and Napoleon, sensitive as ever to everyone's mood, rested his chin on her knee. She stroked his ears, absentmindedly.

'I was right,' said Eleanor. 'It is Molly. I'm finding it a little difficult to take in. My suggestion that it *might* be her seemed very remote from the reality of seeing that it is her. I can't believe that I sat talking to her in the cottage at Fairfield only a few days ago and now there she is, lying in the morgue, dead. She was so very upset at losing the baby. I arranged for her to see Catherine in the hope that she would be all right given time. I must tell Catherine. She was puzzled as to why Molly didn't keep her appointment. I was worried that Molly might do herself some harm but I never thought for one moment that she was in any danger of being killed by someone else.'

'I don't think any of us could have predicted what has happened,' said Edwin.

'Certainly not,' said Mr Harriman.

'But who could possibly have wanted Molly dead?' said Eleanor. 'And for what reason? Who could possibly benefit from her death?'

'Well,' said Mr Harriman, 'at the moment, all we can do is speculate. We shall have to wait until we have more of the facts.'

0 0 0

'Right, that was a successful morning's work and one problem resolved satisfactorily,' said Edwin, as he came into the dining room at lunchtime on Friday, took a plate, and served himself from the various dishes prepared by Mrs Clayton and set out on the sideboard.

Mr Harriman and Eleanor were already in the dining room and had begun their meal.

'Sorry I'm late,' said Edwin. 'I've been with Superintendent Ferguson.'

'Joshua Wilde?' asked Mr Harriman, putting down his fork and turning to look at Edwin.

'Yes, but it's good news this time. I've managed to persuade Ferguson not to proceed with the charge against Joshua.'

'Oh, well done,' said Eleanor. 'That is good news.'

'It is indeed,' said Mr Harriman. 'You must have been very persuasive.'

Edwin sat down at the table. 'I'm afraid I played on the Superintendent's vanity. I was chatting to the clerk at Court last week and he pointed out that the charge against Joshua in relation to the Temple Mound would be the first charge before the Court since the arrival of the Superintendent in town. He commented that it was not much of a case with which to start building a reputation and thought the Superintendent could have done better than that.'

'And in that regard, he has to compete with Superintendent Johnson's reputation. He was held in high regard, as all of his farewell dinners will testify,' said Eleanor.

'Precisely,' said Edwin. 'I hadn't realised that Joshua's was his first case and that set me thinking. Superintendent Ferguson has a murder enquiry to deal with now and he will want everyone to remember that as his first success, not some obscure offence that most people probably have never even heard of, especially if it is thrown out of Court.'

'And that is a real possibility he has to consider,' said Mr Harriman.

'I thought that he would probably be losing interest in the Temple Mound case, particularly if I could persuade him that Joshua had nothing to do with Molly's murder. Mrs Clayton happened to mention to me yesterday that Joshua has been helping her brother in his workshop until his apprenticeship starts. I checked with Alf and Joshua was with him all day on Tuesday. He arrived at nine o'clock and only went home when Alf was called out to the churchyard after Molly was found. So, I went to see the Superintendent this morning and gave him that information so that he could dismiss Joshua from his thoughts in relation to his murder case. Then I said that, in view of the facts that I now had, it was very likely that, at the first opportunity, I would be making an application for the charge against Joshua to be dismissed. I reminded him of the law of master and servant and the responsibility, liability even, of a master for the acts of his servants. I emphasised the fact that Mr Beresford, in his capacity as master, had ordered Joshua to move the baby and that Joshua, being his servant and also of such a young age, had been obliged to obey. Superintendent Ferguson then said that he was pleased I had mentioned that because he had been considering the matter and come to the conclusion that the charge should be withdrawn. He hinted that the Inspector had not been able to gather much evidence in the interviews that he conducted with Joshua. So the charge against Joshua now has been withdrawn.'

'And now, Joshua can concentrate on learning his trade with Alf. What a wonderful birthday present for him,' said Eleanor

'Yes,' said Edwin, 'I've spoken to Mr Wilde and, of course, he is delighted and very thankful for our assistance. He sends his regards to you both.'

CHAPTER TWENTY-THREE

After lunch, Eleanor went to Chillingham & Baynard's bank to do a completion of the sale of a property for one of Mr Harriman's clients. When she returned to Hall Bank, she was greeted by Napoleon who had been keeping James company.

'Ah, Miss Eleanor,' said James. 'A Mrs Wilks telephoned while you were out. She asked you to telephone her when convenient. She did not refer to any current matter and she left no message.'

'Thank you, James. No, she is not a client. She is the new Mrs Wilks, a recent arrival in Buxton and a new member of Lady Carleton-West's committee. I expect it's something to do with the Charity Bazaar.'

'Very likely,' said James.

'I shall telephone now if you would put the call through.'

'Certainly,' said James.

Eleanor went upstairs to her office, took off her hat, coat, and gloves and settled down at her desk. Napoleon went to his observation post at the bay window. The telephone rang. Eleanor picked up the desk stand and put the earpiece to her ear.

She heard James say "Mrs Wilks" and then she said: 'Good afternoon, Mrs Wilks. It's Miss Harriman speaking.'

'Oh, Miss Harriman. Thank you. I'm not sure if . . . .'

The new Mrs Wilks sounded flustered and there was a pause while she collected her thoughts. Eleanor waited patiently.

The new Mrs Wilks began again, timidly: 'I'm very sorry

to trouble you when you are working and I'm sure you are busy and it may be nothing important at all . . . . '

There was another pause and Eleanor said: 'How can I help you, Mrs Wilks?'

'Oh, I'm so sorry, Miss Harriman. I'm not making myself very clear. I do not need help.'

Eleanor waited.

'This is about the girl who was found in the churchyard at Burbage.'

'I see,' said Eleanor. 'Have you heard something about that?'

'Well,' said Mrs Wilks, 'yes, but it might not be very important.'

'Even the smallest piece of information can sometimes be useful,' said Eleanor, trying to sound encouraging.

'I felt I ought to tell someone, just in case. One is always conscious of the need to do one's duty as a good citizen and . . .'

There was a pause and Eleanor said: 'Mrs Wilks, if you think you know something that might help the police . . .'

There was a hasty interruption from Mrs Wilks, who sounded alarmed and offended:

'Oh no, Miss Harriman, goodness, no! It is not I. I know nothing whatever about the matter! I just happened to mention it to Lady Carleton-West at bridge this afternoon and Lady Carleton-West advised me not to take heed of servants' gossip.'

Mrs Wilks sounded contrite and, perhaps even a little wistful. Eleanor imagined that the new Mrs Wilks, alone in a large house, without company of her own age, and a long way from her family and her own friends, would find a conversation with her parlour maid a welcome distraction. Eleanor also imagined the manner in which Lady Carleton-West would have dealt with Mrs Wilks. Although Mrs Wilks had mentioned advice, Eleanor knew that Lady Carleton-

West gave orders not advice.

'Perhaps you could tell me what it is you mentioned to Lady Carleton-West and then I shall know how best to advise you,' said Eleanor, patiently.

'Lady Carleton-West said that it was of no importance, but that if I thought it absolutely necessary to tell someone I should telephone to you. She said that as you are known to the police you would deal with it.'

Eleanor almost laughed out loud at this piece of impertinence from Lady Carleton-West. She was well aware of Lady Carleton-West's opinion of her choice of profession and she found it amusing rather than offensive.

'So what is it that you have heard, Mrs Wilks, that you think the police ought to know about?'

'I didn't hear anything, Miss Harriman. It's Alice, my parlour maid, she knows the parlour maid in the employ of a Mrs Mostyn-Davies.'

'I see,' said Eleanor. She frowned, still unable to see a connection with the death of Molly. 'So, it is Mrs Mostyn-Davies' parlour maid who may know something about the girl who was found in the graveyard of Christ Church, is that correct?'

'Yes.'

'Then perhaps you could ask Mrs Mostyn-Davies to notify the police that her parlour maid may have information of use to them.'

'Oh, I couldn't do that. I don't know Mrs Mostyn-Davies. She lives on Green Lane.'

Eleanor smiled at this. Having grown up in The Park, Eleanor was well versed in the importance accorded to a person's rank on the social scale. So when Eleanor heard Mrs Wilks' last statement, she was amused but understood its meaning. For the residents of The Park, anywhere beyond its boundary was foreign territory. Mrs Mostyn-Davies was unlikely to be on Mrs Wilks' list of morning calls.

'Besides, one wouldn't want to place another person, even someone one does not know, in such a very awkward situation.'

'I don't understand the difficulty, Mrs Wilks.'

'But, Miss Harriman, the police might want to go to her house asking questions. What might the neighbours think?'

'Mrs Wilks, I don't know Mrs Mostyn-Davies but I could telephone her and enquire if you think that will be useful.'

'Oh, would you, Miss Harriman? That's very kind. That is such a relief. Thank you.'

'Not at all, Mrs Wilks.'

Eleanor said goodbye and replaced the telephone stand on her desk. She had no idea as to whether this information, whatever it was, would be in any way relevant to her own enquiries and she was reluctant to be burdened with trivial information which she would feel obliged to pass on to the police. Although there was always the chance that the information might be useful it did seem unlikely and she decided to think about it later on when she had dealt with the files on her desk. She pulled towards her the file on the top of the pile and began work. A few minutes later, she was interrupted by the telephone.

James said, in an appropriately ominous tone of voice: 'Lady Carleton-West, Miss Eleanor.'

'Thank you,' said Eleanor, raising her eyebrows. She waited while the call was put through.

'Lady Carleton-West, good afternoon.'

'Ah, Miss Harriman, good afternoon.'

Lady Carleton-West, in her usual authoritative way, began talking very rapidly, without giving Eleanor a chance to speak further.

'The new Mrs Wilks consulted me this afternoon at bridge. You met her at the last committee meeting. Apparently, Mrs Wilks has heard via one of her own servants that a servant of Mrs Mostyn-Davies knows something about the girl who was found in the churchyard at Christ Church.'

'Yes, I have just been sp . . .'

Eleanor was unable to finish the sentence.

Lady Carleton-West said: 'Mrs Wilks was quite concerned about this information, whatever it is, and it may just be servants' tittle tattle. The new Mrs Wilks is very young and needs guidance. I have cautioned her against paying too much attention to her servants. Mrs Mostyn-Davies is known to me.' Lady Carleton-West paused for breath. 'She is the Secretary of the Chrysanthemum Society.'

Eleanor wondered if this was intended as a recommendation or a matter for reproach.

Lady Carleton-West continued: 'We all have our civic duty but it is not appropriate for Mrs Mostyn-Davies to call at the police station. I know that you think nothing of dealing with the police and will contact them if you consider it necessary. I shall leave it to you to decide. I telephoned to Mrs Mostyn-Davies myself and explained the position. Mrs Mostyn-Davies will have her parlour maid delivered to your office at four thirty this afternoon.'

Eleanor was tempted to point out that the parlour maid was not a parcel but she held her tongue. She also knew better than to protest that this arrangement had been made without consulting her convenience.

'What is the name of the parlour maid, please?' she asked.

'I have no idea.'

Eleanor duly thanked Lady Carleton-West for her assistance and hoped that her words sounded sincere. She knew from past experience that it would never have occurred to Lady Carleton-West that other people saw her as interfering, bossy, and overbearing. Instead, she would expect to be congratulated on her ingenuity, and thanked for resolving this difficulty over the parlour maid.

Eleanor telephoned to James to explain about the parlour maid. Then she looked at her watch, decided that there was enough time to get some work done before the parlour maid arrived. She settled down with the file which she had open on her desk.

0 0 0

Just after four thirty, James brought the parlour maid up to Eleanor's office. She was in her late twenties, very neatly dressed, and she stood timidly in the doorway, looking around her apprehensively.

'Miss Annie Ramsden, Miss Eleanor,' said James.

'Thank you, James. Miss Ramsden, thank you for coming to see me. Please, do sit down.'

Eleanor had not banished Napoleon as she usually did when she was seeing clients because she had observed on previous occasions that people not used to solicitor's offices found his presence reassuring. He had turned from his post at the window and was observing Miss Ramsden with interest as he waited to be introduced.

'I hope you don't mind dogs, Miss Ramsden. This is Napoleon.'

Annie smiled and extended her hand towards Napoleon. He sniffed the hand by way of greeting and then sat down beside Annie's chair.

'I understand that you are employed by Mrs Mostyn-Davies.'

'Yes, Miss Harriman,' said Annie. 'I'm Mrs Mostyn-Davies' maid. Parlour maid, that is.'

'And where do you live, Miss Ramsden?'

'At Highwood. On Green Lane, Miss Harriman.'

'At Mrs Mostyn-Davies' house?'

'Yes, Miss Harriman.'

'I see,' said Eleanor. 'I don't know whether Mrs Mostyn-Davies explained to you why you were asked to come here but I understand that you might have some information about the girl who was found in the churchyard at Christ Church last Tuesday. Is that correct?'

'Well, I don't know as it's information, Miss Harriman. I only know what I heard.'

'All right. Perhaps if you begin by telling me where you were when you heard whatever it was. And, Annie,' Eleanor smiled, 'you're not in any kind of trouble, so please don't be anxious.'

Annie nodded. 'At the War Memorial.'

'On The Slopes?' asked Eleanor, gesturing towards the direction of the Buxton War Memorial nearby.

'No, at Burbage.'

'Oh, I see.'

The War Memorial in Buxton is located on The Slopes and surrounded by parkland and trees. By contrast, the War Memorial at Burbage is located at the side of a busy road junction. This choice of location was due to a typical English compromise: a decision reached by a committee that offended no-one but, at the same time, suited no-one. The proposal for a separate War Memorial for Burbage began with a sermon preached at Christ Church by the Vicar in December 1918. Some of the fifty or so soldiers who had been killed were parishioners of Christ Church and their relatives favoured a memorial in the church itself. However, many of the soldiers had belonged to the local non-conformist Chapel so a memorial in the church or in the churchyard would not have been appropriate for them. It was agreed that the names of all the soldiers should be listed both in the church and on the War Memorial, but then a suitable location had to be found. Many Burbage residents wanted a park setting for their Memorial but others wanted it in the centre of the village in full view not hidden away in a park. Eventually, in 1920, a site was chosen close to both the public hall, the Chapel, and the Church: a dusty, noisy, island at the junction of five roads.

Eleanor asked: 'And when did you visit the Memorial?'

'Last Tuesday afternoon.'

'Can you be certain of the date?'

'Oh, yes, Miss Harriman. That were the day my husband were killed.'

'Oh, I see. I'm sorry. That is why you were at the War Memorial that afternoon?' asked Eleanor, gently.

'Yes, I wanted to lay some flowers for him. His name's on the Memorial at home and I couldn't get there so I went to Burbage.'

'And where is home?'

'Sheffield. We used to live there but, after he were killed, I had to find work.'

'I understand. So you came to work for Mrs Mostyn-Davies and she let you have time off to go to the Memorial?'

'Yes, she said she understood that I'd want to go, having lost her own son in France. She let me have some flowers from the garden.'

'That was good of her. So you put the flowers on the Memorial and then what did you do?'

'I just stood for a bit looking at the Memorial and reading the names and thinking about Jimmy. I wondered if any of them were buried near Jimmy. They told me the name of the place where he is but I don't rightly know where that is. It had a foreign name and they're hard to remember.'

'Perhaps one day you might be able to go there. I believe that it is now possible to visit the cemeteries.'

'P'raps, but I expect it costs a lot to go there.'

'Yes,' agreed Eleanor, 'I suppose so. Perhaps Mrs Mostyn-Davies might go and, if it were possible, she might take a photograph for you.'

'She might. She's been very kind to me.'

'I suppose, having lost her son, she understands what it is like for you.' Annie nodded but did not respond. 'Do you know what time it was when you arrived at the War Memorial?'

'About a quarter past twelve. Mrs Mostyn-Davies said I could go out during my dinner time. She was going to be out so I weren't needed.'

'And you mentioned that you heard something. Where were you then?'

'Just getting to the Memorial.'

'From the end of Green Lane?

Annie nodded.

'And the noise, can you describe it for me?'

'Well, a sort of yell, angry like. I thought as how it might be someone being set upon but then when I thought about it later on, it weren't a scream or anything, like you'd expect.'

'And where was the noise coming from, do you think?'

'From the churchyard, I think.'

'And was it a man or a woman?'

'I'm not really sure.'

'Was there very much traffic?'

'Not much because it were dinnertime.'

'Had you noticed anyone going into the churchyard.'

'No.'

'And you stayed at the War Memorial for a little while. Did you see anyone leave the churchyard after you had heard the noise?'

'No.'

'Did you see anyone at all while you were at the Memorial?'

'Only the man with the cart.'

'Tell me about him.'

'He stopped his cart and came over to speak to me. He asked who the flowers were for 'cos he knew some of the men whose names are on the Memorial. He thought the flowers might be for one of them and so I had to explain. Then I told him about the noise. I asked if he thought he should go and see, just in case. So, he said yes and he tied up the horse and went over to the church to see.'

'And did he see anyone in the churchyard?'

'No, he said he couldn't see anyone.'

'So I suppose whoever it was had gone by the time he got there. Do you know this man's name or where we might find him?'

'No, only that he came from the Buxton Lime Firms. That's what it said on the cart.' She paused and then added. 'Oh, and his horse's name is Durbar. He laughed when he told me that. He thought it were funny but I couldn't see the joke.'

'It is an odd name for a carthorse and I think the carter has a lively sense of humour, Miss Ramsden. Durbar was a thoroughbred racehorse. He won the Derby in 1914.'

Annie laughed, appreciating the joke. 'His horse were no racehorse. His Durbar didn't look like he'd even be bothered to trot.'

'Well, thank you very much for coming to see me, Miss Ramsden. Every piece of information, however small, is always useful and it is important to have passed it on as you have done.'

CHAPTER TWENTY-FOUR

Before Edwin left for home that afternoon, there was a discussion about what to do, if anything, about the information they now had regarding the death of Molly Brandon. Eleanor had passed on the information she had received from Annie Ramsden.

'Let's see if we can tease out the facts that we have so far, see what we can make of them, and then decide what else we need to know,' said Edwin.

'Well,' said Eleanor, 'if the newspaper report is to be believed, the cause of death is strangulation. Therefore death was not accidental and not self-inflicted. Molly must have been attacked. Annie Ramsden's yell may be evidence of that. But why was she attacked? There are a lot of possible answers to that question, not all relevant, I'm sure, but they do need to be considered, just in case, and then, if necessary, discarded.'

'Such as?' asked Edwin.

'Well, a random attack, that's the first option,' said Eleanor, 'although then there would be no real motive.'

'If we assume for the moment that this is not about Molly personally, is there anyone else who has been affected by the death of the baby?' said Edwin.

'Such as someone who knew about the baby and knew Molly was unmarried,' suggested Eleanor.

'Some high minded self-appointed guardian of public morals outraged at children being born out of wedlock?' suggested Edwin.

'Something like that,' said Eleanor, smiling. 'but as far as we know, only one or two people knew that Molly had had the baby.'

'It could possibly be someone who linked her to the Temple Mound incident and feared the revival of pagan practices that we have heard so much about with the Well-Dressings. Revenge by a person who thought she had killed her baby?' suggested Edwin.

'But who had enough information to connect Molly with the Temple Mound incident?' said Eleanor. 'Some people know about Molly, and others know about the baby on the Temple Mound but who knew both facts, apart from us?'

'I don't think there is anyone who would make that connection. Not even the police,' said Edwin.

'It's a bit like Philip's report on the Hepplewhite furniture, isn't it? He had two pieces of information that didn't fit. He could explain each one separately but not together.'

'Yes,' laughed Edwin. 'He did very well with that report, didn't he? He's putting us to shame. We'd better pull our socks up. What do we know about the father? A father might blame Molly for the baby being born dead or might even have thought Molly killed the baby because she didn't want it.'

'True,' said Eleanor, 'but the father is dead.'

'Are we certain of that?' asked Edwin.

'I think so, although I admit, I do only have Molly's word for it. She told me he was killed in an accident and I must try to find out more about that.'

'What about the girl's mother or father? Unmarried mothers are often regarded as bringing shame on the family.'

'Her mother is dead,' said Eleanor, 'and Molly wasn't living at home. She lived-in at the Shakespeare Hotel, so I'm not sure how much her father knew about the baby.'

'The parents of the father, then?' suggested Edwin.

Eleanor thought back to her interview with Molly. 'No,' she said. 'Molly told me that the father didn't know about the baby so he couldn't have told his parents. He died before she could tell him.'

'Who knew that the baby had been born?' asked Edwin.

'Not many people because it was not full-term. Mary Roberts, the chambermaid, didn't know. Miss Swinscoe at The Cosy Corner might have guessed because Molly suddenly stopped going to work at the café but I can't see any reason why it would be of concern to her. Will Fiddler must have known. Molly's other neighbours at the cottages as well. Mrs Erskine made no reference to a connection between Molly and the baby in the stables so I don't know whether she knew that it had been born, although she may have guessed and remained silent if she really did suspect that Mr Erskine was the father.'

'But with Mr Erskine dead and the baby dead, why would that give her a motive to kill Molly?' asked Edwin. 'We seem to have a lot of loose threads here, do we not?'

Eleanor sighed. She said: 'The only people who have been affected in any way by the baby being left in the stables and then on the Temple Mound are Joshua, Mrs Erskine, and Mr Beresford. Mrs Erskine and Mr Beresford have suffered the mild inconvenience of having work on the conversion of the stables held up for a day but that is hardly a motive for killing Molly.'

'It is rather difficult to see how Molly's death would change anything for either of them,' said Edwin. 'And Joshua had more to gain by Molly being alive to give evidence regarding the baby.'

'When I spoke to Mrs Erskine,' said Eleanor, 'she was cross about having the police there at the hotel. I thought it was just because a police presence was bad for business but perhaps there was more to it than that. If she believed that Mr Erskine was the father of Molly's baby she would not have wanted that story to be made public. She had warned Molly never to gossip or answer questions about the hotel, so she might not have wanted the police to question her staff in case that story came out.'

'It's possible, I suppose,' said Edwin, slowly. 'But surely killing Molly would be an extreme measure for such a small risk. Would her reputation or that of the hotel really be affected if the story came out?'

'It's unlikely, isn't it?' said Eleanor. 'And anyway, Mrs Erskine might have suspected that the baby in the stables was Molly's but she couldn't have been sure. There is no evidence that she made the connection.'

'Well, the only other person I can think of is Will Fiddler?'

'Why him? Was there a connection of some kind?'

'Yes, I think so,' said Eleanor. 'He knew Molly. He lives in a cottage opposite the ones where Molly was staying. I met him the second time I went there. I am not sure what his connection with Molly was and it may be only that they were neighbours but he must have known about the baby. And he probably knew Molly worked at the Shakespeare Hotel. There are no secrets in that clannish community where Molly was living. They're just as bad as the residents of The Park when it comes to monitoring everyone's behaviour and making sure they come up to standard. Also, he told me that he had seen Molly leave the cottages early on Tuesday morning. He could have followed her to the churchyard. There may be other things about him that we don't know. The women I met at the cottages hinted that he had been in trouble with the police.'

'Did he have any reason to want Molly dead?' asked Edwin.

'I can't think of one at the moment,' said Eleanor.

'He was the one who suggested leaving the baby on the Temple Mound, wasn't he?' said Edwin.

'Yes, and that makes him the only person who could have made the connection between the baby at the Temple Mound and the girl in the churchyard,' said Eleanor.

'Perhaps on that Monday morning, he already knew, or guessed, that the baby was in the stables and made sure Joshua was the one who found it.'

'It did seem odd that Joshua was the one who found the baby and had been left alone at the time. It might have been planned rather than chance. If Will Fiddler knew that Molly had left the baby in the stables, and if he thought Molly had killed it, he might also have thought that by leaving it on the Temple Mound, he would be diverting suspicion from her.' Eleanor paused. 'Or is that too fanciful an explanation?'

'Well no, but then there would be no obvious reason why he would then want to go on and kill Molly?' said Edwin, frowning. 'If he had been the father and thought that Molly had killed the baby, that might have made sense but, according to Molly, he was not the father.'

'Where does that leave us? asked Eleanor.

'In relation to the question "why," we are no further forward, I think,' said Edwin. 'Let's look at the other facts. Why was Molly in the churchyard?'

'I think I can probably answer that. I suspect that the father of the baby is buried there and it was probably his grave where she was found,' said Eleanor.

'So, why would she have been visiting his grave?' asked Edwin.

'She told me that, when the baby was born, she went to the churchyard to tell the father. She didn't say which churchyard. Perhaps she was there again for the same reason. To be with the father.'

'Why on that particular day? Was it for the same reason as Annie Ramsden?' suggested Edwin.

'No, it wasn't the anniversary of his death,' said Eleanor. 'He was killed last February. Mr Wilde was at the churchyard when Molly was found so he will know which grave it was. He will be able to provide a name and other details. I shall telephone to him first thing tomorrow.'

'That's a good idea,' said Edwin. 'That will give us one step forward at least. What else can we do?'

'We need to talk to the Buxton Lime Firms' carter,' said Eleanor.

Edwin laughed: 'A man with a carthorse called Durbar should be easy to identify. Let's deal with that tomorrow.'

CHAPTER TWENTY-FIVE

'I have some information for you, Eleanor,' said Mr Harriman, as he came into Eleanor's office on Saturday morning. 'The Buxton Lime Firms' carter who stopped to talk to Annie Ramsden is Percy Alcock. He lives on Grin Low Road at Harpur Hill. I wrote down the directions that I was given. Mr Alcock's cottage is, and I quote "just down from the Parks Inn, and fourth from the end, counting from the lane." I hope when you get there all will become clear. If not, I'm sure that someone will be able to direct you. Mr Alcock will see you at six thirty on Monday. No choice of time was offered so I hope that will be all right.'

'Yes, of course.'

'Is Philip going with you?'

'I haven't asked him yet but I am sure he will,' said Eleanor. 'I have a piece of information, too. I asked Mr Wilde whose grave it was where Molly was found. Arthur Saunders, aged nineteen, buried on the twenty-second of February this year. That is certainly the baby's father. Molly said he died in February and that she intended to call the baby Arthur after his father. That explains why, when she left the baby in the stables, she was away for such a long time. She said she had gone to tell the father and she must have walked all the way to Christ Church and back to the Shakespeare Hotel.'

'One can't help but feel for her,' said Mr Harriman, 'with no-one to turn to.'

'Yes, it's a shame.' Eleanor sighed. 'The only thing we can do for her now is find out who killed her.'

'Let's hope that Mr Percy Alcock will have something useful to tell you.'

0 0 0

Eleanor went up to the office of the *Buxton Advertiser* on Eagle Parade and asked for access to the archived newspapers. She wanted to find the report of the death of Arthur Saunders and now that she had a name and a date it did not take long to find it. He was employed at the Hoffman kiln and, just after midday on the fifteenth of February, he was going home for his dinner. To get there he usually followed a track which led down the steep slope from the quarry to the end of the lane where his home was. This was a short cut that the workers were not supposed to use because to reach it they had to cross a railway line which ran along the edge of the quarry site and then down to Ladmanlow. Arthur Saunders was about to cross the line to reach the beginning of the track when his attention was distracted by someone, lower down on the slope, calling his name. He turned to see who it was and did not see the railway wagons being shunted on the line. An enquiry as to the circumstances of the accident had been conducted by the Inspector of Mines and Quarries.

The large quarry produced limestone which was processed in a huge kiln, known as the Hoffman Kiln. Most of the residents of Harpur Hill were employed there in one capacity or another. It was a small tight-knit community, as mining and quarrying towns often are, and Arthur's death would have affected them all. The newspaper also reported that Arthur Saunders' mother was a widow, her husband having died in 1919 in the influenza epidemic, and Arthur was her only child.

Having made a note of the relevant details, Eleanor walked slowly back to Hall Bank thinking about Arthur's mother. Some women had to cope with loss many times in their lives and she wondered how they found the strength. She also thought about Molly and her feeling of guilt at causing Arthur Saunders' death. She must have been the one who called to him and distracted his attention from the approaching railway wagon.

0   0   0

At eleven o'clock, Mrs Clayton was doing her morning tea round. Napoleon looked up from his snooze, as Mrs Clayton came into Eleanor's office.

'Ah, Mrs Clayton, you are a welcome sight. It's warm today.'

'It certainly is, and such a pleasant change after the weather we've had. Let's hope it stays this way for a bit.'

Mrs Clayton put the cup and saucer on Eleanor's desk.

'The sunshine has certainly brought everyone out. I was up at the *Advertiser* office this morning and the market was very busy,' said Eleanor as she picked up the cup and saucer.

'That's good. The stall-holders will be pleased. It's not much fun for them up there when the weather is bad,' said Mrs Clayton, as she tucked the empty tea tray under her arm and turned to leave.

'Oh, Mrs Clayton, before you go, you might be able to help me with some information.'

Mrs Clayton turned back towards Eleanor.

'I was at the *Advertiser* looking for a report of an accident up at the Harpur Hill quarry last February. Father and I were in London when it happened so I didn't read about it at the time. Do you recall the accident, at all? A young man called Arthur Saunders was killed.'

'Oh, yes. Terrible that was. Doesn't bear thinking about. It was an accident and, of course, he shouldn't have been crossing the line. But they all do it, taking a short cut home.

It affected people badly. Specially Old Walter.'

Eleanor looked surprised. 'You mean Walter Clough, the man you were telling me about?'

'As owned the land at Bishop's Lane you were puzzling about. Yes, Miss Harriman.' Mrs Clayton nodded.

'Oh, I see. I remember that you said some people thought the shock of his grandson's death had caused Old Walter's death. Arthur Saunders was his grandson?'

'Yes. Walter died just after. A matter of days. He's buried next to his grandson.'

'And it was the grandson he was saving the land for?'

'That's right.'

'Do you know anything about Walter's family?'

'Not much. He had a daughter, Arthur's mother, but no other children as far as I know, not living anyway, and I believe Arthur was his only grandchild. The daughter's husband died some time back and he's in the churchyard at Christ Church too. Some families don't have much luck, do they, and maybe that's what made Old Walter so cantankerous.'

'Yes, it sounds as though he had every right to be,' said Eleanor. 'It was a terrible way to lose his grandson.'

0 0 0

Philip, Eleanor, and Napoleon were due on the golf course that afternoon. They were members of the Burbage Ladies Golf Club and, accompanied by Napoleon, had spent many happy hours on the nine hole course laid out on Devonshire land between Macclesfield Road and Green Lane. The golf course was due to close shortly because the Duke of Devonshire, who was keen on golf, had decided to replace the nine hole course with a new eighteen hole course to be named the Cavendish. Work had begun early the previous year and it was nearing completion. The members of the

Burbage Ladies Golf Club were hoping to be invited to transfer their membership to the new club but, in the meantime, the old nine hole course continued to serve them.

It was a perfect summer's day and, earlier that morning, Cecily had telephoned to suggest a picnic lunch and Eleanor and Philip had agreed to meet her and Richard in the Gardens before going to the golf club. When they were all relaxing comfortably having almost finished lunch, Philip said:

'You've had a rather gloomy week, Lella. If you need cheering up, I thought we might all go to the Opera House tonight to see the current play. What do you think?'

'I don't know. Last week's offering sounded pretty gloomy. Is this one any better?' asked Eleanor.

'Well, I've read the review in the *Advertiser*. It purports to be a comedy. It's called *The Piccadilly Puritan*.'

'Puritan? When did that lend itself to comedy?' asked Eleanor.

'Yes, one does wonder.'

'What's it about?' asked Eleanor.

'Boy, rich, meets Girl, Girl is pretending to be poor in order to capture Boy, Chaperon fond of drink and poor morals provides the comic element, Boy's rival, rich with title, is the villain, Boy and Girl involved in several scenes of confusion and deception but, by the end of the play, manage to pass the character test successfully, and reach happy ending. According to the review, the play is poorly written but the acting is good.'

'Let's hope the acting saves it then. Why are so many plays based on this same boy meets girl theme, do you suppose?' asked Eleanor.

'Perhaps to encourage us to be optimistic about relationships,' said Philip, laughing. 'Despite the evidence that, in real life, so many of them do not have a happy ending.'

'Or to warn us that we are all destined to enter them in

the hope that they will be perfect,' suggested Eleanor.

'And be disappointed,' added Philip. 'Yes, the happy ending of the play is really only a happy beginning, isn't it? The author cleverly leaves us with the illusion that all is well and very kindly shields us from reality which must inevitably follow.'

Eleanor laughed. 'If the girl in this play is pretending to be poor in order to capture the boy, the relationship is based on deception from the start. It does not auger well for the future.'

'Never mind, even a silly play will provide a welcome distraction,' said Philip.

'You're right,' said Eleanor, smiling. 'Let's risk it.'

'What do you think, Cecily?' asked Philip, offering Napoleon the last piece of his ham sandwich.

'I think both of you must have had a very unsatisfactory week,' said Cecily, smiling. 'You sound very discouraged and pessimistic. Not all relationships are unhappy. Yours isn't.' Philip winked at Eleanor. 'Anyway,' continued Cecily, her tone becoming serious. 'I think you are wrong. Real relationships can have a happy ending even if, at the beginning, there is a misunderstanding.'

Eleanor surreptitiously gave Philip a questioning look. Cecily did not usually express her opinion so firmly.

Cecily continued: 'Going to see a frivolous play will do you both good. I'd like to come but I can't. Thomas is coming to stay with Richard this evening. His parents are going to a charity ball.'

The mention of Thomas reminded Philip of the kite flying episode.

'Aunt Lella told me that you've been enjoying flying your kite, Richard,' said Philip.

Richard nodded enthusiastically. 'Oh, yes. It's going really well now. Someone showed us. He likes kites too.'

'And I heard that when you first met this person, Thomas

nearly knocked him over,' said Philip.

'Yes, it was very funny,' said Richard, giggling, 'but he was awfully good about it.'

'And what is the name of your kite expert?' asked Eleanor, recalling the tall gentleman she had seen in the Gardens demonstrating his skill.

'Me and Thomas . . .' began Richard.

'Thomas and I,' said Cecily, quietly.

'*We*,' said Richard, with emphasis, glancing sideways at his mother and ignoring the correction, 'we call him Mr Kite.' He saw Cecily frown and added, in defence of himself and his friend: 'He said we could!'

'And what does he do, this Mr Kite?' asked Eleanor.

'He's really wizard at cricket as well as kites. He played for Oxford. You should see him bowl! And he's teaching us to bat properly. We've been at the nets lots of times. And he's going to show us how to make a better kite for when it gets really windy again.'

'Is he here for the Season, then?' asked Eleanor.

'Oh no, he's coming here to live,' said Richard, confidently.

'Does anyone want this last sandwich?' asked Cecily. 'There is cake.'

Richard said: 'Aunt Lella, can Napoleon have it if no-one wants it?'

'Yes,' said Eleanor.

Cecily said: 'But take Napoleon a bit further away, please, or he'll drop crumbs all over the rug.'

Richard and Napoleon moved away and Richard broke the sandwich into pieces and then asked Napoleon to offer his paw in exchange for each piece. Napoleon knew the drill and was paw perfect.

As they watched this scene, Philip said: 'This Mr Kite seems a remarkably accommodating fellow.'

Eleanor said: 'From what I saw of him in the Gardens on

the day he met Richard and Thomas, he seemed to be enjoying himself immensely. Glad of the excuse to be a boy again, I'd say. He was with a very elegantly dressed lady and he certainly seemed to be a gentleman.'

'Oh, I can assure you that he is,' said Cecily.

'So you've met him?' asked Eleanor, surprised by this news. She turned to look at Cecily.

'Oh, yes,' said Cecily, casually. 'Richard wanted to show him Wilfred's medals. Do have some cake. Susan made it especially this morning.'

As Cecily concentrated on taking the lid off the cake tin, Eleanor and Philip exchanged glances. Philip raised his eyebrows and Eleanor shrugged and gave him a puzzled frown in return. The cake tin was passed around and Cecily quickly moved the conversation on to Lady Carleton-West's charity bazaar.

When the cake had been eaten, it was time for Eleanor, Philip, and Napoleon to head for the golf course so there was no more talk of Mr Kite.

CHAPTER TWENTY-SIX

When Eleanor and Philip returned to Hall Bank from the Opera House that evening, Mr Harriman was reading that day's edition of the *Buxton Advertiser* and Napoleon was snoozing at his feet. There were greetings all round and offers of a whisky or sherry nightcap.

When they were settled, Eleanor said to Mr Harriman: 'I notice that you were reading the *Advertiser*. Have you seen the paragraph about the Well-Dressings?'

'Yes,' said Mr Harriman, 'The Council has finally had the courage to announce that the event has been abandoned.'

Philip said: 'Abandoned probably is exactly how the townspeople are feeling.'

'Mrs Clayton certainly shares that view. She is very disappointed.'

'I thought the reasons given were quite spurious,' said Mr Harriman. 'The lateness of the season, the difficulty of obtaining suitable flowers, and the very poor response to the appeal for assistance in dressing the wells.'

'Yes,' said Eleanor, 'I accept that we had some very poor weather during the earlier part of this year and that the summer was late in arriving but that has been more than made up for recently and there is now an abundance of flowers. And, as Mrs Clayton pointed out, other villages have managed to overcome these problems and arrange their well dressing festivals.'

'And as to the poor response, what can the committee expect,' said Philip. 'There was no notice of any intended date so people could not plan ahead. One can understand the reluctance of the townspeople to commit to giving their assistance at the busiest time of the year. How can they be sure to be available if they are not given a date?'

'Yes,' said Eleanor, 'according to Mrs Clayton there is support for the revival but the people who usually organise the event have received very little encouragement from the Town Hall.'

'It is hard to know where the truth or rather where the blame lies and it seems that little has changed,' said Mr Harriman, referring to his newspaper. 'In his usual column headed "Buxton 50 years ago," the Editor, very cleverly, has included today an extract from the *Advertiser* regarding the 1874 Well-Dressings, fifty years ago almost to the day, on Saturday 4th July. According to the editor writing the report in 1874, there was no question on which Buxton people were more divided. The same expressions of support and opposition appear to have been raised then as now. That year, at the very last minute, a few people hastily improvised and, apparently, worked wonders so that the ceremony could proceed.'

'It does sound awfully familiar,' said Philip.

'Yes,' said Mr Harriman. 'The strongest faction held that the ceremony had lost its meaning and become too secular. Their focus was not really the Well-Dressings themselves but the additional fair-ground type of entertainment that they attracted. I suspect that what the critics really meant is that it attracted the wrong sort of people who were too rowdy for the gentlefolk. Instead of saying so, they blamed the ceremony for reviving pagan customs. No doubt the authorities, then as now, saw this opposition as an opportunity to avoid incurring the expense of the event.'

'And yet,' said Eleanor, 'there are plenty of photographs of the Well-Dressings from last century which show ladies in flounced gowns and bonnet and gentlemen in top hats standing around enjoying the Maypole dance and it all looks very peaceful. It really all comes down to how well the event is controlled and it is the Council who have the power to do that. The truth is they are not prepared to incur the expense. Sadly, this year, unlike 1874, it is already too late for anyone to rescue the situation, no matter how willing they are to try.'

'Co-incidentally, when you came in,' said Mr Harriman, 'I was reading a letter to the editor sent by a visitor, complaining of the lack of entertainment provided for visitors and warning of the effect that will have on the town.'

'Unfortunately, I think the visitor is right,' said Eleanor. 'Even in the days when the purpose of coming to Buxton was to take the waters, the visitors still expected to be entertained. And when they began coming just for pleasure, there was certainly a great choice of activities.'

'I agree that we do need to bring visitors back into the town if we are to survive,' said Philip, 'and we must provide them with a reason for them to come. But it is more than that. Reviving the Well-Dressings is one more step towards returning to the life we enjoyed before the War.'

'Yes,' said Eleanor, 'The War drained our energy and our belief in the future. We need to revive that optimism.'

'In my view, the problem is the lack of strong leadership,' said Philip. 'There will always be factions with competing opinions and preferences. A leader has to understand that, and be clever enough and resourceful enough to find a middle course.'

'And also be confident enough to lead people forward to believe in that middle course,' agreed Eleanor.

'I couldn't agree more,' said Mr Harriman. 'We have experienced this before. You're too young to remember the old Market Hall. It was built in 1857 and burnt down before you were born. It would have been 1885, I think. Then, for two years, there was a great deal of heated argument but no decision as to what to do with the site. You see, the Market Hall had been built on the initiative of the town's traders using private funds. Fortunately, there was an insurance policy in place. Naturally, those who had contributed the money to build the Market Hall wanted to use the insurance money to re-build it. But by then, thirty years had passed, and control of the town was in the hands of a very different group of people. They had their own vision as to what the town needed. Their ambition was to have a Town Hall and, to them, the empty Market Hall site together with the insurance money presented the ideal opportunity for them to achieve their goal.'

'I imagine that opinion was bitterly divided,' said Eleanor.

'Oh, equal amounts of dissatisfaction on both sides,' said Mr Harriman, smiling. 'Both urging people to support their view. And there were some rather rowdy meetings as well. I realised that the civic leaders were right in wanting to improve the image and status of the town but I had a certain amount of sympathy for the market traders whose hard earned money was being used to achieve that purpose. Eventually, after two years of heated argument, a compromise was reached in favour of the building we now have: a Town Hall for civic purposes together with facilities for the market traders. I believe that the basement of the old Market Hall is still under the Town Hall.'

'It must have caused quite a bit of resentment,' said Philip, 'even after the compromise was offered as a solution.'

'Yes,' said Mr Harriman, 'when any change is proposed, there will always be opposition. It's human nature. But, as you rightly said, resolution can only be achieved through strong objective leadership, not too partisan and not too self-interested. Sadly, that is what we are lacking at the moment. The strength is in the factions rather than in the leaders.'

'The Editor of the *Advertiser* must have been inundated with strongly worded letters about the proposal to build the Town Hall,' said Philip. 'I wonder what Lady Carleton-West would have written.'

'Oh she would certainly have been on the side of the civic leaders and not the traders,' said Eleanor, laughing. 'There may well be, somewhere in the archives at the Council, strongly worded letters from her informing the Council as to what action she expected them to take.'

'I'm sure there are,' said Mr Harriman, smiling. 'I wonder what people will make of them in a hundred years from now. But, in a way, the Well-Dressings is a repetition of the Market Hall episode. The impetus for the first Well-Dressings came from the people of Buxton themselves and, although the event does attract visitors, it really is their day. They provide most of the initiative and supply most of the labour free of charge. Planning the event and taking part in it draws the community together and provides a great deal of enjoyment. It is the people and not the Council who will be most affected by the abandonment again this year. But let us not end on that dispiriting note, tell me about the play. The visitor who wrote to the *Advertiser* complaining about the lack of entertainment was most dissatisfied with the offerings at the Opera House. According to him, one very seldom sees a company worth paying anything to see. Was he right?'

The evening ended with much laughter as Eleanor and Philip reviewed the performance of *The Piccadilly Puritan* for Mr Harriman's benefit.

0 0 0

DIARY Saturday 5th July

Furniture, new and old, and my boxes delivered yesterday to my rooms. Spent whole day sorting out papers, books, etc. Rooms look almost respectable. Ready to begin work on Monday. At last!

CHAPTER TWENTY-SEVEN

After lunch on Sunday, Eleanor and Mr Harriman were in the sitting room reading when the front door bell sounded. Napoleon was immediately on his feet looking towards the door. Eleanor looked at her watch as she stood up.

'That will be Catherine,' she said to Mr Harriman.

'Enjoy your walk,' he said, as he turned over a page of *Punch*.

Eleanor opened the sitting room door and Napoleon raced down the stairs. He waited in the hall ready to welcome their guest as soon as Eleanor opened the front door. Then, having greeted Catherine, he began to pace up and down the hall, eager to begin their walk. Eleanor told him to wait and he stood still, although he could not help shuffling his large front paws up and down on the spot in anticipation. Eleanor put on her hat, coat, and walking boots, took Napoleon's lead off its peg and announced that she was ready.

'Where to?' asked Catherine. 'It's your turn to choose, I think.'

'Bishop's Lane,' said Eleanor. 'Up to Edgemoor, across to Watford and when we get to Manchester Road we can decide how much further we want to go. Does that suit you?'

'Excellent. Any particular reason for that choice?'

'Yes, actually. I recently sorted out a boundary on a parcel of land on Bishop's Lane and I thought it would be worth having a look at it. I haven't had a chance so far.'

They walked down Hall Bank towards The Square. Ahead of them, a tall gentleman emerged from the arcade at the corner of The Square, paused on the pavement to check for traffic, and hurried across the road to reach the entrance to the Gardens. Eleanor thought she recognised him but was not sure why.

She frowned and then, as they were passing the Opera House, she said: 'Oh, of course! It's Mr Kite. That's why he looked familiar but I don't really know him at all.'

'Who or what is Mr Kite?'

Catherine turned around to look but saw only a crowd waiting to enter the Pavilion Gardens.

'He just crossed the road ahead of us. I couldn't place him at first. It isn't someone I actually know. Just someone I have seen in the Gardens.'

They turned into St John's Road and, as they walked, Eleanor told Catherine the story of the kite flying episode with Richard and Thomas. After they reached the end of Park Road, there were only scattered houses so Napoleon was allowed off the lead and he bounded joyfully ahead.

'So, what sort of week have you had? asked Eleanor. 'Any better than last week?'

'Mixed,' said Catherine. 'What about you?'

'Same,' said Eleanor. 'What did your mixture involve?'

'Quite a bit of good news, patients happy to be told that they are expecting babies, patients cured, patients not receiving the diagnosis they were expecting, but then two elderly patients dying although not unexpectedly. The really mixed bit, though, is the frustration of not being able to do anything at all for some patients.'

'Such as?'

'Mothers who lost their sons in the War. I'm sure you saw all the In Memoriam notices for the Somme this week. But one of my patients is a mother whose son would be better off dead. She has never said that, of course, but I am sure she has thought it. Sent back to her, one arm and part of his jaw missing, brain severely damaged, not able to look after himself. No assistance from the government despite all the promises and, of course, she doesn't have the means to employ a nurse. The father left home unable to accept what had happened. Mother exhausted from trying to cope alone.'

'Yes, I can see that would be very frustrating. What can you possibly do to help?'

'Well, I did discover a charitable organisation which arranges holidays for these ex-soldiers and their families. I'm going to try to interest Lady Carleton-West in the idea of raising funds for them. It has some suitably aristocratic patrons, as well as Princess Mary, so I shall mention that to her ladyship as an incentive.'

'That should do the trick,' said Eleanor, laughing.

'I've managed to get the mother on their waiting list and, at least that will give her something to look forward to, but it is all I can do, I'm afraid.'

'I'm sure she is thankful though.' Eleanor was silent for a moment or two and then sighed. 'Although I miss Alistair and Edgar and all our friends awfully, at least they have been spared any further suffering. We just imagined that they would all come home from the War and continue their lives as before but that may not have been the case. They might have come home badly injured like that poor woman's son and we would have had to watch them every day struggling to carry on living with damaged minds or bodies.'

'That's true,' agreed Catherine. 'Philip hasn't any obvious injuries but there are some things he can no longer do.'

'Yes. He makes light of that fact and he counts himself lucky compared with others.'

'And it could have been the same for Cecily. Wilfred could have come home badly injured. At least she has been able to make a new life for herself and provide for their son.'

'Yes, having Richard to look after has been a great help, I'm sure,' said Eleanor.

'I suppose with this year being the tenth anniversary of

the beginning of the War it has prompted people to mark it in various ways. I've seen quite a lot of advertisements for what are being called Battlefields Tours. It's a form of organised tour, I gather, and more affordable than private travel. Only wealthy people could arrange tours in the early days.'

'Wilfred's parents are planning to go to France in September to visit Wilfred's grave,' said Eleanor, 'although they are going privately, of course. They've invited Cecily to join them and Wilfred's mother is particularly keen for Cecily to go.'

'Have you thought of going? You have two graves to visit.'

Eleanor shook her head. 'No,' she said. 'I feel no need to go to France and I am sure I would derive no benefit from doing so. On the contrary, I think it would revive all the anger that I felt but could not express at the time.'

'I know exactly how you feel. During the War, we were expected to contain our emotions and look on their deaths as a sacrifice they made willingly for their country. And our own sense of loss really did seem unimportant against their loss of life but, nevertheless, our loss was painfully felt.'

'Doubly so, I think, from not being able to be expressed.'

They walked on in silence until they reached the corner of Bishop's Lane, and Catherine pointed in the direction of Christ Church.

'Has there been any progress in relation to Molly?'

'On the part of the police, I couldn't say, but unofficially, yes, some progress. I know why Molly was found in the churchyard. There is an official record of all the graves in the churchyard and I know the person who keeps the record.'

'What it is to have contacts!' Catherine laughed. 'You know the strangest people.'

'Just one of the benefits of my chosen profession,' said Eleanor, smiling. 'The baby's father is buried in the grave where Molly was found.'

'That explains the location, at least. It is quite a way from Fairfield though. Do you know why she was in the churchyard?'

'Yes, she told me that after the baby was born she went to the grave to tell the father about the baby and I doubt that that visit was the first. The father was killed in an accident a few months ago and Molly blamed herself. I don't think she had fully accepted the fact of his death. On the day of her death she was probably visiting his grave again.'

'I wish she had kept her appointment. I might have been able to help her.'

'Yes, I wish that too. I am sure you could have helped.'

They had now reached the point where Nursery Lane joins Bishop's Lane and Eleanor stopped.

'I haven't had a chance to look at where Molly was found. Do you mind if we go back and detour through the churchyard?'

'Not at all,' said Catherine.

They turned back up Nursery Lane and when they reached the entrance to the churchyard, Eleanor called Napoleon to heel. He trotted obediently towards her, waited while she put him on his lead, and then walked beside her as they went through the gate.

Eleanor said: 'To the right, I think. That is where the newer graves will be.'

They walked down the slope and then turned left along a path which ran parallel to the church but was well below the ridge on which the church stood. Halfway along the path, a narrow foot track led off to the left. It climbed a steep, grassy bank, and over the years of use, a series of steps had been formed in the earth by the boots of those who had used the track to get from the lower level up to the church.

Eleanor stopped and looked at the track and Napoleon sat beside her and waited. She looked towards St John's Road where the main entrance to the church was. She thought back to what Annie Ramsden had told her. The church was on the same level as St John's Road but the part of the churchyard in which they were standing was considerably lower. The Buxton Lime Firms' carter standing at the corner of the church would perhaps not have been able to see this part of the churchyard.

Eleanor turned and looked out over the fields towards Burbage Edge.

'The bell-ringer who found Molly came from Bridge Farm. I suppose he came over the fields and then intended to take this track up to the church.' Eleanor turned and pointed to the track which went up to the higher level.

'That would be the most direct way,' agreed Catherine.

'So he must have come past the graves in this area of the churchyard. Molly must have been on one of those graves there,' said Eleanor, pointing to four graves which, as yet, had no headstone. 'The one nearest the steep bank is completely grassed over, the next two have only patchy grass. This one closest to the path, still has bare earth and the earth has been trampled recently. The flowers are wilted but they have clearly been disturbed.'

Catherine said: 'Yes, perhaps those who found Molly trampled on that one in order to reach the grave where Molly was.'

'The soil on the next one has been trampled as well but not as much so perhaps that is where Molly was.'

'I think it is likely to be this one,' agreed Catherine. 'I'll leave you to your deliberations.'

Catherine wandered away to read a nearby headstone, and Eleanor contemplated the scene. Napoleon sat patiently watching. There were a few petals scattered in the long grass at the edge of the grave which had not been so badly trampled. Eleanor imagined that Molly had probably brought some flowers to put on the grave and, if so, the flowers had probably been cleared away after Molly's body was moved. Eleanor crouched down to look more closely at the petals. She picked one up and Napoleon, always curious, sniffed at it. Eleanor saw that it came from a lily. She could not imagine Molly being able to afford lilies nor could she imagine her choosing them. If Molly had brought flowers, they would most likely have been wild flowers. The petals had been crushed but they were not wilted like the ones on the newer grave closest to the path. She stood for a while looking down at the grave and trying to imagine the scene found by the bell-ringer.

Catherine returned. 'Have you seen enough?' she asked.

'Yes, I think so,' said Eleanor.

Napoleon had been sniffing at the ground where the petals were and was now pawing at the long grass between the graves, trying to dislodge an object that he had found. Eleanor turned to see what he was doing and, as she did so, a glint of light caught her eye. She crouched down to see what Napoleon had found. Hidden in the long grass was a small brown bottle. She picked it up and looked at the label, which was partly torn away.

'*Veronal*,' she said, as she handed the bottle to Catherine.

'Indeed it is,' said Catherine. 'This reminds me of our recent conversation about how readily available *Veronal* used to be. The label is damaged. I can just read the last part of the chemist's name, something ending with the letters R-S-O-N. The address is in Sheffield. West Street. Not a local chemist.'

'Hmm,' said Eleanor. 'Possibly nothing to do with Molly then. Perhaps a visitor dropped it. I'll keep it anyway, just in case.' Eleanor took the bottle back from Catherine and put it in her pocket. 'Thank you for the detour. We can get back onto Bishop's Lane from here.'

They walked down the hill and then followed the track which the bell-ringer had taken. It brought them to the bridge on Bishop's Lane. Napoleon flopped down on the cool grass of the verge.

'That's the boundary I was sorting out,' said Eleanor, waving her arm in the direction of the Wye river which flowed towards the road and then under the bridge. 'It's quite a big plot. I believe the purchaser intends to have a house built here and the agent mentioned a tennis court as well.'

'It's certainly a big enough plot. Who's bought it, do you know?' asked Catherine.

'Unfortunately, no. Our client was the agent of the vendor not the purchaser and we did not act on the sale.'

'Well,' said Catherine, as she looked at the land and imagined the future mansion. 'I wouldn't mind having a house here.' She sighed. 'But it's not for the likes of us, Eleanor.'

Eleanor laughed. 'No, but I have no regrets. We both know from our own parents' and grandparents' experience, how many servants are required to run a large house properly and we also know how difficult it is to get even a decent parlour maid these days. It's the main topic of conversation at one of Lady C's events.'

'Must you always be so practical! You've just burst my bubble.' Catherine pretended to pout. 'Couldn't you just leave me with the dream of a mansion once in a while?'

'Dream? I'm rescuing you from a nightmare.'

'There's no cure for you,' said Catherine, laughing and shaking her head. 'You will be content with Hall Bank and your dusty old files forever. Don't you sometimes regret leaving that beautiful house your family had in The Park? You were all so happy there and I have such fond memories of it.'

'No, those days disappeared with Edgar's and my mother's deaths, I'm afraid. I'm much happier with my dusty old files. Besides, they provide the perfect excuse for not having to attend all those dreary social occasions that I used to loath.'

Catherine said: 'Yes. I have to admit that your working life at Hall Bank suits you far better than being idle in a mansion in The Park. Anyway, how do you know that the person planning to build this house hasn't got pots of money, enough to pay very attractive wages and employ good staff.'

'In these difficult financial times? More daydreaming. Come on, we have a hill to climb.'

Catherine laughed and shook her head. Napoleon stood up ready to go and, as they were going through farm land, Eleanor kept him on his lead and the trio resumed their walk.

0   0   0

Buxton Hydro Hotel

Sunday 6th July 1924

Dear Amelia,

You will be amused by my adventure last Thursday afternoon, although, as you are the mother of two adventurous boys, you must not be alarmed because I assure you the tale has a happy ending.

On Tuesday last, I went with Grosvenor to discuss plans for the land at Bishop's Lane. Grosvenor is keen to proceed and I received a letter from him on Thursday morning sending notes and with preliminary sketches, so I went back to Bishop's Lane that afternoon to consider his suggestions. As I was standing in the lane contemplating the scene, I noticed my two kite flying enthusiasts, Richard and Thomas, further up the lane. I learnt later that they had been at one of the farms further up, visiting a school-friend of Thomas's.

A horse and rider coming from Edgemoor was in the

lane a little way behind them when a loud noise – an explosion of some kind – startled the horse and it bolted. The rider called out to warn Richard and Thomas and they only just had time to leap out of the way. Richard, who was on the side closest to the edge of the road, fell awkwardly against the stone wall of the farm boundary and I feared that he had bumped his head. Thomas sustained a nasty graze to his leg and one hand. Fortunately, I had taken my motor car instead of walking as I usually do and I was able to take the two boys home. We met the horse and rider at the end of the lane, both unharmed and, on the part of the rider, full of apologies.

  I drove the boys back to the address Richard gave me and found Richard's mother at home. She turned out to be my fellow guest at Lady Carleton-West's dinner party! She was the neighbour on my right that I mentioned in my previous letter. Fate has brought us together! She proved to be as charming as I imagined. Very sensible and capable. Saw immediately that her son was not injured, made sure Thomas was in no danger, returned with the medicine chest and very efficiently handed me the things I needed to treat Thomas's wounds. We then all had tea, Richard showed me his father's medals, and then I delivered Thomas home to his mother.

  I arranged to see Richard again the next day ostensibly to check on him, but really it was an excuse to re-visit Oxford House. I shall introduce you when you return to Buxton. You did promise to come for the Bazaar remember. You will recall Mr Lomas, the owner of the Hydro. He has proven to be a most entertaining host and full of amusing stories. He told me of a rumour that Lady Carleton-West had seen your name in the list of visitors next to mine but dismissed it, not realising the connection between us. She was, apparently, mortified when she realised that the dinner party invitation ought to have been extended to you as well. Although Mr Lomas, who knows the lady only too well, suggested that her grief was probably more for the loss of another titled person at her dinner table than for the breach of etiquette. So, you must come to the Bazaar and meet her ladyship to show that there are no hard feelings.

Love to you all,

HUGO

CHAPTER TWENTY-EIGHT

At a quarter past six on Monday evening, Philip arrived at Hall Bank, as arranged, to accompany Eleanor to Harpur Hill for the meeting with Percy Alcock. They didn't want to attract attention to their visit to Mr Alcock so they had decided not to take the Bentley.

On Grin Low Road, following Mr Harriman's directions, Eleanor parked the motor car at the end of a row of "two up two down" cottages built to house the quarry workers. The cottages were well-cared for: walls limewashed, windows recently cleaned, doors painted, one or two with pots of geraniums beside them. A group of children playing a game of hopscotch stopped to stare at the arrival of a motor car.

'It's the fourth from this end,' said Philip.

'The one with the front door open. It looks as though Mr Alcock is expecting us.'

As Philip approached, a man appeared in the doorway.

'Mr Alcock?'

'Aye, it is. Percy Alcock. That's me,' he said confidently. 'You'd best come in.'

Mr Alcock was a stockily built man of about fifty, hair done, and very neatly dressed. He looked like a man who enjoyed life. Eleanor couldn't imagine him going to this trouble for an interview and wondered if he were intending to go out for the evening. Philip introduced himself and then introduced Eleanor.

The front door opened directly into a living room, beyond which was the kitchen. The staircase to the upper floor occupied one wall of the living room. Everything was very neat and well cared for. Mr Alcock offered Eleanor and Philip the two armchairs which were pulled up on opposite sides of the fireplace and returned to sit at the table in the centre of the room, at which he had been reading the sporting pages of the newspaper.

'Nar then, what's all this about,' said Mr Alcock, folding up the newspaper and addressing Philip. 'The boss said someone wanted to ask me questions.'

'It's nothing to worry about, Mr Alcock,' said Philip. 'You may be able to help us with some information that's all. You have no doubt heard that a young girl was found dead in the churchyard at Burbage last week.'

'I did,' said Mr Alcock, slowly and cautiously.

'That was last Tuesday. Miss Harriman has spoken to a young woman who was at the War Memorial at Burbage that afternoon laying flowers. The young woman recalled that you stopped to speak to her.'

'That's right. I did.' Mr Alcock, nodded decisively. 'A bonny lass, too.'

'She told Miss Harriman that, prior to your arrival, she had heard a noise coming from the direction of the churchyard.'

'Aye, I recall she mentioned that. Asked me to go and see if something were amiss,' said Mr Alcock, guardedly. 'What's this about? Something to do the young lassie as died there?'

'Possibly. At the moment, we are not sure.'

'I hope's as you're not suggesting I had anything to do wi' it?'

Percy Alcock crossed his arms in front of his chest and leaned back in his chair.

'No, not at all. Miss Harriman is trying to help a client and just needs to clarify some information she has been given, particularly about the time. The young woman at the Memorial wasn't able to provide very much detail and it is possible that you, being more observant, might be able to fill in some of the gaps for her.'

'Ah,' said Mr Alcock, unfolding his arms and resting them on the table, reassured. 'Ask your questions, then.'

'Thank you, Mr Alcock. We really appreciate your help. Perhaps you could describe, as best you can remember, what happened that afternoon. How did you come to be passing the War Memorial?'

Eleanor was impressed by the way Philip was handling the conversation. Mr Alcock had barely noticed her and was looking directly at Philip as he launched into his narrative. Eleanor sensed that he would not have been so comfortable talking to a woman.

'Well, I were on me way to deliver some lime to one of the allotments on Macclesfield Road when I sees the lassie standing at the Memorial. O' course, I knew it were the anniversary of the start of the Somme.'

'Yes,' said Philip. 'There were quite a few notices in the In Memoriam column of the *Advertiser*.'

'We lost fifteen of our lads in the War. It's a while ago since they went but I remember 'em all like as if I only saw 'em yesterday. Anyroad, I thought as how it might've been someone I knew.'

'The young woman might have been there to remember someone whose name was on the Memorial?'

'Aye.'

'And did you know the young woman?'

'No. I pulls Durbar oop and gets down from the cart to talk to the lassie, thinkin' as I'd know 'er, only she weren't local, like. 'er man were killed at the Somme right enough, that's why she were there but he were from Sheffield so 'is name's on a different Memorial. She couldn't get to Sheffield because she's in service 'ere now. Anyways, we stood chatting for a bit wi' me pointing out the names of our lads, and then she mentioned the noise she'd heard.'

Percy Alcock stopped his narrative there, folded his arms across his chest, and sat back in his chair. He seemed to think he had reached the end.

'Yes, apparently the young woman was a bit worried and asked you to have a look.'

'Aye. She did. She weren't sure what sort o' noise it were. So, I thought I'd best go and see, just in case. I told Durbar to stand and went into the churchyard. And that's all I can tell you.'

'There was no-one there?'

'No. No sign of anyone.'

'How far into the churchyard did you go?'

'Just as far as the big angel. You can see a good bit from there.'

'And then you went back to talk to the young woman?'

'For a minute or two.'

'And then what did you do?'

'I gets back on the cart and goes down the Macclesfield road to the allotments.'

'Do you recall what time that was?'

'I might, as it happens, 'cos I remember glancing up at the church clock as I went by.' Percy Alcock frowned, blew out his cheeks, and looked up at the ceiling. He looked back at Philip. 'It were twenty five minutes past twelve.'

'From there you would have been able to see down St John's Road. Did you notice anyone walking along that road near the church?'

Percy Alcock shook his head.

'And on Macclesfield Road? I think you can see the entrance to the churchyard from there.'

'Aye, you can see directly down to Nursery Lane, past the Duke of York. Bert's cart were there, as usual of course. Usually is at that time o' day.'

'Bert?'

'Works for Westman's the wine and spirit people. Drops

in at the Duke for a pint at lunchtime.'

'He must have a very understanding employer.'

Percy laughed out loud. 'Understanding? That's a good-un. Bert only keeps that job because his sister's married to the boss's son.'

'Oh, I see,' said Philip, laughing along with Percy.

'So you completed your delivery to the allotments and did you go on from there or back past Christ Church?'

'Back the way I'd come but there were no-one about. Bert's cart were gone.'

Philip paused at this point and sat back in his chair. Thinking that perhaps he was going to stop there, Eleanor had to restrain herself from interrupting with a question she was anxious to ask. Then, to her relief, Philip continued.

'Can you think back to the time before you got to the Memorial, you said you were on your way to deliver lime to the allotments. Where had you been coming from? Which road were you on?'

'I were coming down from the yard at Ladmanlow.'

'As you were coming down that road, I don't suppose you saw anyone going into the churchyard?'

There was a pause while Mr Alcock considered this question. He scratched his head.

'Well,' he said, slowly, 'not as you might say, going in. I know how you lawyers like to be precise.' Percy glanced at Eleanor and grinned. 'But I know someone who might have been going in.'

Philip looked at Eleanor and then looked back at Percy Alcock. Eleanor held her breath.

'How did that come about?'

'Ah, well,' said Mr Alcock, 'it's a bit awk'ard. I'm not supposed to have anyone on the cart with me, you see, and I don't usually. And I might get into bother if this comes out.'

'I see,' said Philip, smiling. 'A bit ticklish, eh?'

'Aye, you could say so,' agreed Mr Alcock, frowning.

'I don't suppose there will be any need to mention this to your employer and, in any event, it may be of no interest to Miss Harriman's enquiry. It's just to try to get the facts straight, you see. Do you think this person on the cart was intending to go to the churchyard at Christ Church?'

'Well, she might 'ave been intending to. But if you ask me to be precise and lawyer like, well, she didn't *say* she were going there and I didn't ask. I just saw her on the road, she's a neighbour, you see, that's why I made an exception. Doesn't talk much so I knew she wouldn't let on.'

'And where did you meet her?'

'As I were going down this road.' He waved his arm in the direction of Grin Low Road at the front of the cottages. 'On the way to Ladmanlow.'

'And what made you think she was intending to go to the churchyard at Christ Church?'

'Well, you wouldn't be on this road if you didn't want to go to Burbage 'cos there's nowhere much else to go. If you wanted to be in Buxton you'd go t'other way. She had some flowers with her, the ones that smell, so I thought p'raps she were going to the churchyard. Couldn't think of any other reason. There's nowt you can buy in Burbage that you can't buy in Harpur.'

'So you took her as far as the churchyard?'

Percy Alcock shook his head, vigorously. 'I dropped her off just before Ladmanlow. I had to stop off at our yard there to make a delivery so she had to get down before I got there. Didn't want to be seen with someone on the cart.'

'No, of course not. About how long were you at the Ladmanlow yard?'

Mr Alcock frowned and pursed his lips as he considered this question. 'Ten minutes? Not more than fifteen.'

'And did you see your passenger again while you were on your way towards Macclesfield Road?'

'No. She would've got to the churchyard by then, I

reckon. If that's where she were goin', of course.'

'And there was no one else?'

'Not a soul.' Percy paused. 'It were dinner time,' he added, as though the absence of people at that time of day should have been obvious enough not to have been stated.

'And did you see your passenger again when you were on your way back to Harpur Hill?

Mr Alcock shook his head.

'And your passenger, she lives locally?' asked Philip, casually.

'Aye, just around the corner.' Mr Alcock gestured in the direction of the lane next to the row of cottages. 'Last house at the end.'

Mr Alcock looked at the clock on the chimney piece and said: 'Now, if that's all, I hope you'll excuse me. I've got a darts match to go to at the Parks Inn and I'm due there in a few minutes.' He stood up.

Philip looked at Eleanor. She stood up and Philip followed suit.

Eleanor said: 'Please don't let us keep you, Mr Alcock. It was very good of you to see us and what you have told us is very helpful. Thank you.'

'Good evening, Mr Alcock, and thank you for your help. Good luck at the match,' added Philip.

They returned to the motor car and as Eleanor got in she said: 'Do you mind if we continue on this road and take the route Mr Alcock took in his cart?'

'Not at all,' said Philip. 'Do you think it is worth speaking to the woman he mentioned?'

'Yes, I do because she might have seen someone in the churchyard or heard the noise Annie heard.'

'It was stupid of me not to have asked Mr Alcock for her name,' said Philip.

'No, not at all.' said Eleanor, firmly. 'Mr Alcock was clearly anxious to get to his darts match and, anyway, I don't want it to look as though I'm conducting an inquisition, especially as he was doing something he shouldn't have. He did say where she lived so that's enough. And I shall be able to find her. No, I congratulate you, Philip. You handled that interview superbly, much better than I would have done.'

'One does one's best, old thing. Coming from you though, that is praise indeed,' teased Philip.

'No, really. You asked all the questions I needed answered and you used just the right tone of voice and pace to get Mr Alcock comfortable about being questioned. I don't think he would have responded as well to me. And he probably wouldn't have owned up to me about allowing someone on his cart against the regulations.'

Philip laughed. 'You mean he would expect a man to understand about breaking the rules and refrain from asking awkward questions.'

'Absolutely,' said Eleanor, smiling. 'Men always stick together in a situation like that.'

'Because women will persist in asking awkward questions. Serves you right.'

Eleanor pulled a face at Philip and then concentrated on the road. They reached the end of Grin Low Road and the turning at Ladmanlow.

Eleanor said: 'This must be where Mr Alcock stopped to let the woman off. She must have walked from here to the churchyard. I shall have to work out how long it would have taken her.' Eleanor paused: 'I wonder what sort of flowers she was carrying. Mr Alcock said they smelled.'

'Lilies perhaps' said Philip. 'What about this Bert fellow that Mr Alcock mentioned? He seems to have been near the churchyard at the time. If he is usually there at lunchtime, he should be easy to find. Perhaps we should go there tomorrow.'

'Yes. Definitely. If you are free. He might have seen or heard something.'

CHAPTER TWENTY-NINE

The following day, at lunch time, Eleanor and Philip sought out Bert. They drove along St John's Road, this time in the Bentley, and as they turned into Nursery Lane, Philip said:

'That looks promising.'

Parked at the side entrance to the Christ Church churchyard was a delivery cart bearing the name Westman's Wine and Spirit Merchants.

Philip parked the motor car and looked at his watch. 'We shouldn't have to wait too long.'

They got out and strolled in the churchyard while they waited. The Duke of York public house was just across St John's Road. After a short while, they saw a man cross the road and walk towards the delivery cart.

'Is the cart in the way of your motor?' said the man, as he approached.

'Hello,' said Philip. 'No, not at all, thank you. Are you by any chance, Bert?'

'I am,' said the man, squinting at Philip cautiously.

'Then I wonder if you might be able to help me with some information.'

'That depends.'

'I understand that it is your custom to leave your delivery cart here around about this time of day while you visit the Duke of York.'

'Well, your honour, whoever said that were telling the truth. This here cart is heavy and lugging it about, it gives rise to a powerful thirst, that it does. And it just so happens that the thirst comes on gradual like and takes me terrible bad just as I get to this point on me round. So I just pops across to the Duke and has a quick one. It does no harm but Mister Westman doesn't agree with me, see.' Bert emphasised the word Mister in a sarcastic way indicating contempt. 'Someone, an interfering sort of person I suspect, saw me coming out of the Duke one day and Mister Westman, he says to me: "Bert, it doesn't look right. You goin' into the public house when you're in the middle of doing your round. What impression does that give the customers?" Now, I ask you, is that a reasonable attitude to take to one as is doing his best with the deliveries?'

'I understand your difficulty,' said Philip, nodding sympathetically.

'I can't see the 'arm in it meself and I tried to explain but he weren't having any. I mean, think on 't, your honour. If I see no harm in having a drop, it reassures the customers that there's no 'arm in it to them either, no matter what they tea total lot sez to the con'try. It shows the customers they have no cause to worry. It'd be different if he'd caught me handing out a tract against strong drink with every bottle I deliver. He'd be quite within his rights to ask his question then. He would have cause for complaint, I grant you. But not when I'm endorsing the very product that he's selling. I do admit to overdoing it a bit on the King's birthday last month but that were the fault of the publican, I can assure you. He offered me a dram to drink the 'ealth of His Majesty and, bein' a patriotic soul, as I am, I couldn't refuse. That wouldn't be right, your honour, now would it?'

'Absolutely not,' said Philip, patiently. 'I wonder if you could cast your mind back to last Tuesday, that was the first of July. You might have heard that a young girl was found dead in the churchyard. It is possible that you might have been visiting the Duke of York that day.'

'I hopes you're not accusing me of anything,' said Bert

indignantly.

'Not at all, of course not,' said Philip, mildly. 'No, I merely wondered whether you might have seen or heard something that might help to explain what happened.'

'Well, you're right there. I did wonder to meself if I'd 'eard and seen summut. But I don't rightly recollect what that were, not just at the moment, like. If you get my meaning.'

Bert put his hand into his trouser pocket, then drew his hand out again, empty, and looked at it forlornly.

'Ah,' said Philip, nodding slowly. 'I understand your meaning perfectly.' He paused. 'What if I were to offer you the funds for another toast to His Majesty, would that be likely to improve your memory?'

'That's very understanding of your honour. Very likely it would.'

Eleanor watched in amazement as Philip took out his wallet. Bert smiled. She admired Philip's perceptiveness.

'Now, you just reminded me. I did 'ear something. A yelling. Well, I say yelling but . . .'

Philip nonchalantly slid a banknote out of his wallet.

'Could you explain what sort of yelling. Was it words, or perhaps a call for help, or a yell of surprise.'

'Now, you've got me there. I couldn't rightly say except it were a woman.'

'And where were you when you heard the yell.'

'I were just about 'ere. Standin' beside the cart thinkin' on where I had to go next.'

'You didn't go to investigate?'

Bert shrugged. 'It weren't 'owt to do wi' me.'

'And I think you mentioned that you might have seen something as well.'

Philip moved the banknote slightly so that the denomination was visible. Bert's eyes went to the banknote and his tongue moved slowly across his top lip in anticipation.

'Well, your honour.' Bert lowered his voice. 'This is just between you and me. I were standing beside that tree over there.' Bert pointed to a tree in the churchyard just inside the gate. 'A call o' nature, as you might say.'

'And you saw something or someone?'

Bert stroked his chin. 'Aye, rushing along the path down yonder and out the gate.'

'And what did you do?'

'Waited for it to go quiet and went back to the cart.'

'And the person rushing along the path. Man or woman?'

'Woman.'

'Could you describe her?'

''Ow d'yer mean?'

'Well, what was she wearing, for instance?'

'Couldn't rightly say. Only caught a glimpse, bein' a bit occupied wi' me own affairs.'

'When the woman reached the gate down there which way did she go?'

'Down the lane. Not this way.'

'Do you have any idea what time it was when you saw this woman?'

'Now you're asking.' Bert screwed up his eyes as he considered the problem. 'Maybe half past twelve?'

'Well, thank you very much for your help,' said Philip, as he handed the banknote to Bert. 'Here's to the health of His Majesty.'

Bert took the bank note, looked at it, folded it carefully, and put it in his pocket.

Then he said: 'Oh, and I recollect now, your honour, the yelling were sort of a screech. The noise women make when something riles them. Now, I'll bid you good day and get on wi' me round.' He touched his cap.

'Good afternoon,' said Philip, raising his hat. 'And thank you again.'

He watched as Bert and the cart moved off and then

turned to Eleanor. She was shaking her head in disbelief.

'That was a superb performance,' she said, smiling broadly. 'Better acting than anything we saw at the Opera House on Saturday. How did you know he needed inducement.'

'Instinct, old thing, that's all. He was jolly useful and worth the money, I think.'

'Certainly. I shall ask James to open the petty cash tin when we get back to Hall Bank.'

'What are you going to write on the chit: bribing a witness, maybe?' asked Philip.

'It certainly was an inducement to talk. However, given Bert's close relationship with the Duke of York, I'm not sure one would want to rely on his evidence in Court. He's more of a loveable rogue than a reliable witness, I think.'

Philip laughed. 'I suspect him of acting a part of a drunken fool just to annoy Mister Wiseman.'

'You're probably right. Nevertheless what he told us was interesting and we can certainly make use of it.'

0   0   0

'I've done a plan of the area around the churchyard and I've noted some times on the plan as I've been trying to work out the sequence of the events we have been told about on the day Molly died.'

Eleanor was sitting in Edwin's office after lunch and she handed over her sketch map of the area around Christ Church.

'Let's have a look,' said Edwin.

'We don't have much to go on,' said Eleanor. 'The difficulty is that, apart from Percy Alcock who looked at the church clock, all of the times have been estimated. The first fact we have is from Annie Ramsden. She walked along Green Lane from Mrs Mostyn-Davies' house to get to the

Burbage War Memorial and reached the main road at about a quarter past twelve. Fact number two. As Annie reached the Memorial, she heard what she described as a yell. She thought it came from the churchyard. There was no-one else around at the time and she hadn't seen anyone going into the churchyard.'

'So, if the noise did come from the churchyard and, if it has got anything to do with Molly, whoever made the noise, Molly or her attacker, must have been in the churchyard already when Annie arrived at the end of Green Lane.'

Eleanor nodded. 'No-one else was around and probably most people in the vicinity would have been having their dinner. Fact number three. On his way to Ladmanlow, Mr Percy Alcock met a neighbour who may have been intending to visit the churchyard. He left her at Ladmanlow to walk the rest of the way to Burbage. I estimate that it would have taken her about ten or so minutes to walk from there to Burbage and Mr Alcock did not see her on his way down from Ladmanlow to the War Memorial.'

Edwin added: 'So if she did go to the churchyard she must have arrived there before he passed the Memorial on his way to the allotments.'

'Fact number four. Mr Alcock went into the churchyard as he put it "as far as the big angel" and he said he could see most of the churchyard from there. He saw no-one. Fact number five. When Mr Alcock left the War Memorial after talking to Annie, he looked at the church clock and it was twenty five past twelve. He didn't see anyone on St John's Road so it seems there was no-one going into or leaving the churchyard at that time. By either entrance. He drove his cart down Macclesfield Road, noting as he passed the Duke of York, that Bert's cart was in Nursery Lane. He made his delivery to the allotments and, as he passed by the church on his return journey, he didn't see anyone enter or leave the churchyard.'

'So the person who attacked Molly may still have been in the churchyard or have already left during the time Mr Alcock was carrying out his delivery on Macclesfield Road,' said Edwin.

'And he didn't see his passenger again on his way back to Harpur Hill. She may not have been sure what time Mr Alcock would be returning or might not have wanted to presume, it being against the rules.'

'In which case,' said Edwin, 'she may have walked into Buxton or taken a 'bus and gone the long way round back to Harpur Hill. She would not have wanted to face the long climb back up Grin Low Road.'

'So, facts number six and seven,' said Eleanor. 'At least I hope they are facts because it is Bert's story of hearing what he described as a screech. He also said he saw a woman leave the churchyard in a hurry via Nursery Lane. That was at about twelve thirty and just after the screech. Mr Alcock would have been at the allotments by then and would not have seen anyone leaving the churchyard. The noise that Annie heard was about fifteen minutes earlier than Bert's screech.'

'How do we reconcile these facts?' asked Edwin. 'Do we, perhaps, have two noises? An angry yell at twelve fifteen and a screech just before twelve thirty? If so, what happened between twelve fifteen and twelve thirty? And the woman fleeing from the churchyard at twelve thirty, when did she enter the churchyard? Is she connected with the yell or the screech or both?'

'Or none?' added Eleanor. 'Bert is fond of having a drink at lunchtime at the Duke of York so he may not be an altogether reliable witness, especially concerning the timing.'

'It could have been Mr Alcock's passenger, of course, but why would she be running out of the churchyard?' asked Edwin.

'Or leaving the churchyard via Nursery Lane?' said

Eleanor.

And if the running woman wasn't Mr Alcock's passenger, where was she? Had she already left the churchyard? If, in fact, she ever went into it.'

'And what, if any, connection did the passenger have with Molly?' said Eleanor.

'So many questions! said Edwin. 'If Molly was in the churchyard when Annie heard the noise that she reported, Molly must have arrived there before twelve fifteen.'

'Annie and Mr Alcock had both left the War Memorial by about twenty five past twelve, so someone could have entered the churchyard after that. That leaves five minutes in which to attack Molly,' said Eleanor.

'And have caused the noise Bert heard, and then left again by twelve thirty. That's possible, I suppose,' said Edwin.

'Actually,' said Eleanor, 'anyone could have entered the churchyard any time before twenty five past twelve without being seen if he or she went in via the entrance in Nursery Lane. That entrance is about a hundred and fifty yards further away from the main entrance and well out of sight of the War Memorial where Annie and Mr Alcock were standing. But to do that they would have to have got to Nursery Lane from St John's Road. So if that was Molly's attacker, that would suggest someone coming from Buxton. St John's Road is the most likely route to take from there.'

'Well, that could be true of Molly also. Molly would have been coming from Fairfield so on the way in she would have come along St John's Road,' said Eleanor. 'But, obviously, it wasn't Molly who was rushing out of the churchyard into Nursery Lane.'

'Perhaps we were wrong in assuming that Molly was in the churchyard when Annie arrived at the War Memorial. She could have arrived via Nursery Lane after Annie left and the noise Annie heard may have nothing to do with Molly's death.'

'Yes,' said Eleanor. 'I have been basing all of this on an assumption that there is a connection between the noise Annie or Bert heard and Molly's death which would put the time of death between about twelve fifteen and twelve thirty. But we don't have the *post mortem* report yet, do we? So, the time of death may be earlier or later than that. She may have entered the churchyard after any of our witnesses had gone away.' Eleanor sighed. 'Oh, dear, their evidence may have nothing at all to do with Molly's death.'

'It may still be worth talking to Mr Alcock's passenger, I suppose. If she was actually visiting a grave, she may have wanted to stay in the churchyard for a while.'

'She may just have seen or heard something so I shall go and see her as soon as I can.'

'How are you going to find her? There are a lot of graves in the churchyard that she could have been visiting.'

'Yes, but she is a neighbour of Mr Alcock's and he told us where her house is.'

'I see. Then, yes, it would be useful to interview her.' Edwin thought for a second or two. 'And there is another assumption that we have been making. Strangulation does require a certain amount of force and that means that the killer is more likely to have been a man than a woman. For that reason alone, it is likely that the woman running down Nursery Lane had nothing to do with Molly's death.'

Eleanor thought for a moment. 'What about this then? Someone strangled Molly, a man. Some time later, someone came into the churchyard from Nursery Lane, the woman Bert saw, for instance, saw Molly's body, screamed, and ran out of the churchyard from fear, or horror.'

Edwin nodded. 'That is plausible, I suppose. That would very neatly explain Bert's screech and the running woman.'

'But, we still have no evidence that there was a man or anyone else near the churchyard before twelve fifteen, so when did the killer arrive and leave? It would have to be before twelve fifteen.'

'He could still have been in the churchyard with the body. That would give the running woman even more incentive to scream.'

Eleanor said: 'Yes, and that might mean that the first noise, the yell, came from Molly.'

Edwin smiled and shook his head. 'We're just speculating, aren't we? We need more facts.'

'Yes,' said Eleanor, pulling a face. 'All the information that I have so far been treating as facts may just be a shoal of red herrings.'

'Army,' said Edwin.

Eleanor frowned. 'What is?'

'A group of herring,' said Edwin. 'I believe it's called an army. According to a pedantic schoolmaster I once had. At least, if it's the ordinary sort.'

'A Red Army, then.'

CHAPTER THIRTY

As James was closing the office for the day, Eleanor, Napoleon, and Edwin were in Mr Harriman's office.

'That bottle of *Veronal* that you found in the churchyard, Eleanor, has an interesting provenance. I was curious about it so I made a few enquiries. I found the pharmacist in West Street, Sheffield whose name ended with the letters R-S-O-N. His name is Pearson. I looked at a map of Sheffield and noticed that Rockingham Street runs off to the south of West Street.'

'That name rings a bell,' said Edwin.

'So it should,' said Mr Harriman. 'It is the address that Joseph Hallet gave in his statement in relation to Mr Erskine's death.'

Eleanor and Edwin's eyebrows went up in unison.

'I spoke to Mr Pearson by telephone this afternoon. I explained that I was trying to obtain information in my official capacity as coroner and that a bottle of *Veronal* tablets, apparently supplied by him, had been found in Buxton. I assured him that I did not want him to divulge any information about his customers but I suggested that if I were to ask him a series of questions based on what I already knew he would not be breaching any confidences. He agreed and I asked if he had customers who had prescriptions for *Veronal*. He confirmed that he did. I suggested that his delivery boy might be in the habit of delivering a parcel to an address in Rockingham Street and asked if he would check his register. He said that he did not need to do so because he only had two customers for *Veronal* and, yes, that was the delivery address for one of them. I then asked if the name of the client was Hallett and he said yes. "Would that be Mr Joseph Hallett," I asked. "No," Mr Pearson said. Then he added, "I am sure that, as coroner, you have encountered nervous housewives who seek the support of products from their pharmacist. You may draw your own conclusion from that, Mr Harriman." Which, of course, I did. So, I leave you to draw your own conclusion as to how that bottle found its way from Sheffield to Buxton.'

'Well!' said Eleanor.

'Eleanor's methods are rubbing off on you, Harriman,' joked Edwin.

'I couldn't have managed it better myself,' said Eleanor, laughing.

'I am above flattery,' said Mr Harriman, solemnly, keeping a straight face. 'So, what do we make of this new information?'

'If that bottle I found in the churchyard was supplied to Joseph Hallett's wife, it must have been taken by him and brought to Buxton,' said Eleanor.

'It would seem so. And why would he do that?' asked Mr Harriman.

'What about that story you got from Nurse Mackay, Eleanor?' asked Edwin.

'Yes,' said Eleanor, slowly, as she reviewed that conversation. 'Nurse Mackay said Mrs Erskine made a fuss because a bottle of sleeping tablets went missing. Nurse Mackay didn't say that the sleeping tablets were *Veronal* but she suggested that Mrs Erskine was using the tablets to drug Mr Erskine so she could spend part of the night with the hotel guest. Nurse Mackay only half-remembered the guest's name but I am pretty sure she meant Hallett.'

'So perhaps the bottle was taken by someone at the hotel,' said Mr Harriman.

'No,' said Eleanor, 'I am certain that Nurse Mackay said

the missing bottle had been found at the hotel later on. I remember us laughing about the incident.'

'So if either Mrs Erskine or Mr Hallett still had that bottle, how did it get to the churchyard? Should we assume that it was dropped accidentally? If so, by which one of them?' asked Edwin.

'Perhaps Hallett strangled Molly,' said Eleanor. 'If there was something suspicious about Mr Erskine's death, he may have had just as much to hide as Mrs Erskine and, he may have thought that Molly knew something about it. Surely that gives him a motive.'

'We certainly need a little more information about Mr Joseph Hallett,' said Mr Harriman. 'In the evidence obtained by Superintendent Johnson, there was no suggestion of any connection between Joseph Hallett and the Erskines, other than that he was a regular guest at the hotel. He had stayed at the hotel previously in the course of his work as a commercial traveller and, I suppose because of that, the information he gave about himself was just accepted. The information you obtained from Nurse Mackay, Eleanor, which suggested an association between Mrs Erskine and Joseph Hallett piqued my curiosity and it seems the *Veronal* bottle may be evidence of that link. Another piece of information you provided was also relevant. The fiancé of your chambermaid, Mary Roberts, said that he couldn't understand why Joseph Hallett bothered to come to Buxton because most local people got their supplies from R.F. Hunter's shop at Cavendish Circus. I wonder, therefore, if he is a commercial traveller at all, or just comes to Buxton to see Mrs Erskine.'

'Or, perhaps Hallett really is a commercial traveller but supplies something far less glamorous than photographic equipment and didn't want to admit it,' suggested Edwin.

'What did you have in mind?' asked Eleanor. 'Flea powder, mouse traps, fly papers, perhaps?'

'Medical trusses? There's no glamour there,' said Edwin, laughing. 'People generally avoid all mention of them.'

'Well, whatever it is he sells, his customers don't need a regular supply,' said Eleanor, 'because Mary Roberts told me that, unlike their other guests who are commercial travellers, Mr Hallett does not have a regular booking.'

'Well,' said Mr Harriman, 'I have been concerned about the enquiry into the death of Mr Erskine. On the basis of the evidence presented to me by Superintendent Johnson, I decided that an inquest was not necessary. The circumstances of Mr Erskine's fall were adequately explained by the evidence provided by Joseph Hallett. I accepted that evidence in the belief that Joseph Hallett was an independent witness, merely a guest at the hotel. He was the only person present when Mr Erskine fell. I have been bothered by the information you have uncovered, Eleanor, and I have been wondering at the soundness of my decision and considering whether or not there was something that I overlooked, something more to be uncovered. At the time, there appeared to be nothing to suggest that the witness, Joseph Hallett, was not telling the truth. Now it seems that he may have had reason to lie, and even have wanted Mr Erskine out of the way. The dismissal of Molly Brandon immediately after the accident was also not something that came to the attention of Superintendent Johnson.

'I was troubled by the fact that I had been lied to, so I went back over the statements looking for evidence that Mr Erskine's fall might not have been an accident. The *post mortem* report was not very detailed but it concluded that the cause of death was trauma to the deceased's head as it struck the steps in the course of the fall. And it occurred to me that I know someone who could possibly enlighten us further. You may remember, Eleanor, that when we went up to London in February this year, I visited the Middle Temple and I met up with an old friend from my days at Oxford. I introduced you to him.'

'Yes, I do remember. Professor Fergus Ballantyne.'

'That's right. He's at the University of Edinburgh in the Department of Pathology but he was in London giving evidence at a murder trial. He told me that, two years ago, he had been asked to advise on a couple of suspicious deaths involving falls and he felt that there was insufficient evidence to reach a conclusion. Since then, together with one of his doctoral students, he has been undertaking research hoping to be able to identify evidence that will allow them to distinguish more confidently between an accidental fall and one that was not. We had a very interesting conversation about that research. I wondered if there was anything he could tell us about Mr Erskine's fall so I sent him a copy of the medical evidence and asked for his opinion. I had a telegram from him yesterday which said: "Interesting case for our research. Thank you. Notes in post." So, I should receive those notes shortly. Now, in the meantime, is there any other action that we ought to take in relation to Molly Brandon's death?'

'I am proposing to visit the passenger on Mr Alcock's cart. She may have seen or heard something useful when she was in the churchyard.'

'Excellent,' said Mr Harriman.

'Another thing that it might be useful to know,' said Edwin, 'is whether or not Mr Joseph Hallett has been back to the Shakespeare Hotel since Mr Erskine died.'

'I think I can find out about that,' said Eleanor.

'And perhaps also, whether or not he was in Buxton on the day Molly died,' added Edwin.

0 0 0

Tuesday 8th July

Too preoccupied to write yesterday. Was asked to see a very interesting and unusual chest case at the Hospital and to give an opinion. Suggested a course of treatment and have agreed to take on this case. I think it will also help my research into this malady. My clinical notes will provide a good outline for an article for The Lancet at least. Ended up assisting in the operating theatre. Pneumothorax, emergency and very tricky, patient with existing chest condition. Touch and go at one point, but managed to patch him up. Good assistance from resident surgeon and theatre staff. Very promising. Saw patient again today, stable, with good prospects of recovery. Good to be back in harness.

CHAPTER THIRTY-ONE

Early on Wednesday morning, before the office opened, Eleanor drove up to Harpur Hill and parked the motor car outside the cottages on Grin Low Road where Mr Alcock lived. At right angles to that row of cottages, there was a lane with another row of cottages along its left hand side. At the end of the lane was a footpath leading up the slope towards the quarry.

Eleanor knocked on the door of the last cottage in the row. She waited.

The door was opened, cautiously, by a woman. She was wearing a floral pinafore over a house dress and her hair was untidy. It was hard to judge her age because her face looked drawn and there were dark circles under her eyes. Eleanor thought she looked careworn.

'Yes?' said the woman, in a tired, toneless voice.

'Good morning,' said Eleanor. 'My name is Eleanor Harriman. May I give you my card?'

Eleanor held out her card but the woman made no attempt to take it.

'May I ask your name?'

The woman made no reply. Her eyes were staring at Eleanor but she had a faraway look, as though she were not seeing her.

'I wanted to ask you about something you did last Tuesday. I believe that you went to Burbage.'

There was no response.

'To the churchyard at Christ Church, perhaps.'

'What of it?' she said, curtly.

She narrowed her eyes, daring Eleanor to challenge her.

'I wondered if you had seen anyone else in the churchyard while you were there?'

'No.'

The woman was about to close the front door when a man walked past the row of cottages heading for the track that led up to the quarry.

Seeing the door open, he called out cheerily, as he passed: 'Morning, Mrs Saunders.'

As Eleanor heard the name, she began rapidly processing the information in her head. Quickly putting together the facts she had, she realised that this was Arthur Saunders' mother and it made complete sense that she should have been visiting the churchyard.

'You were visiting your son's grave, I suppose?'

'Can't a mother visit her son on his birthday?' she said, and then added: 'There's no law against it.'

'I believe your son died in an accident at the quarry here.'

'Accident?' said Mrs Saunders. She sneered. 'She killed him.'

'What do you mean?'

'She had no business to be there. She'd lived in Harpur all her life, she knew better. Even her own father said so. He were that ashamed of her. Turned her out of his house when he found out what she had done.'

Eleanor's first impression had been of a careworn woman but now she saw a woman filled with bitterness.

'At the time, she wasn't thinking very clearly.'

'Thinking. She only ever thought about herself.'

Eleanor remembered how Molly had said that Arthur's mother had not thought she was good enough for her son.

'Distracting Arthur like that. What was so important it couldn't wait.'

This was a statement not a question. Mrs Saunders was becoming angry. She had grabbed the lower part of her pinafore and was twisting it agitatedly. She was glaring at Eleanor but her words were meant for Molly.

'Mrs Saunders, I believe that Molly's intention in going to the quarry was to tell your son about the baby she was expecting.'

Mrs Saunders looked stunned. 'Baby!' she said sharply, her eyes wide with shock.

'His baby.'

'Never! Never!' she repeated. 'If that's what she said, she's worse than I thought.' Mrs Saunder's face was distorted with emotion. 'She killed him, the hussy. And now blackening his character as well. And him not here to defend himself.'

'That is what she told me,' said Eleanor, calmly.

'Trollop, that's what she was. It's a filthy lie. I won't hear a word against my son. Get out!'

Mrs Saunders stepped back, grabbed the door handle, and slammed the door shut.

Eleanor stepped back quickly in surprise and then stood still for a moment, wondering what to do next. From Mrs Saunders' reaction, Eleanor was quite sure that the existence of a baby was news to her. She considered knocking at the door again and trying to talk to Mrs Saunders but then she realised that, as Mrs Saunders was clearly both shocked and outraged by this news, there was probably no point in trying to talk to her until she had had time to get used to the idea and calm down. Eleanor turned away and then, realising that she was still holding her card which Mrs Saunders had refused to take, she tucked it between the door and the door jamb, just in case Mrs Saunders changed her mind. Then she walked back to her motor car.

0   0   0

When Eleanor returned to Hall Bank, she found Napoleon

keeping James company.

'I've left the motor car outside, James. I shan't need it again today. Would you have the garage collect it please.'

'Certainly, Miss Eleanor. And Mr Talbot has just joined Mr Harriman in his office. The post from Edinburgh has arrived. I thought you might be interested.' James smiled.

'Ah, yes, Very interested. Thank you, James.'

Eleanor took off her hat and coat and she and Napoleon went into Mr Harriman's office and he and Edwin looked at her enquiringly.

Eleanor said: 'Well, I had the door slammed in my face. But my visit was not wasted. The woman I went to see turned out to be Arthur Saunders' mother. And, yes, she was the woman that Percy Alcock took on the cart to Ladmanlow and she did go to the churchyard. I didn't have chance to ask her anything about that, except that she did say that she didn't see anyone in the churchyard when she was there. I mentioned Molly's baby and I am pretty certain that she knew nothing at all about it. She was obviously shocked by what I said and that is why she slammed the door shut. I might go back when she has had time to calm down.'

'Well, success or not in relation to Molly's death, you have timed your return well,' said Mr Harriman. 'We now have Professor Ballantyne's response. It came in this morning's post.'

'Yes, James told me.'

'Well, now,' said Mr Harriman, 'I sent Professor Ballantyne the report from Doctor Freeman who was called to the hotel when the accident happened and the notes made by the doctor in the hospital where Mr Erskine died. You will recall that, after falling down the stairs, Mr Erskine did not die immediately. He died in hospital the following day. By that time, the evidence of the witness as to the fall, Joseph Hallett, was common knowledge. Ballantyne suggests that Doctor Freeman, who later provided the medical evidence for Superintendent Johnson's report, may have been, albeit subconsciously, influenced by the lay evidence. He may have made only a cursory examination at the scene, realised Mr Erskine was still alive, and arranged for him to be taken to the hospital as quickly as possible. There would have been no opportunity for a detailed examination and Mr Erskine was fully clothed, including an overcoat. Doctor Freeman appears to have relied on what he was told, that Mr Erskine had fallen down the stairs, he had died the next day, and the two facts were clearly connected. In his statement he concluded that the fall was the cause of death. And that is quite true, as far as it goes.

'Professor Ballantyne refers to the description of the wounds which were recorded by the second doctor who examined Mr Erskine after he had been admitted to the hospital. His examination was more thorough and, by this time, Mr Erskine's clothing had been removed. The doctor's description of the location of the wounds is quite precise and Ballantyne was particularly interested in the position on the skull of the wound caused by contact with the edge of the stair tread. Ballantyne has included in his letter, a brief note as to the nature of the research being carried out in his department. He urges caution and he emphasises that their research is only at a preliminary stage, but what he suggests is that, from the position of the wound as recorded by the hospital doctor, it is possible that Mr Erskine's journey down the stairs involved a slightly greater momentum than is consistent with an accidental fall and he wonders if force may have been involved.'

'Phew!' said Edwin, with a long, low whistle. Napoleon immediately sat up and looked at Edwin in surprise and then at Eleanor for reassurance. She stroked his shoulder.

'Exactly,' said Mr Harriman. 'Ballantyne did add, though, that if force had been applied in the form of a push or a punch one, would usually expect to find some evidence of that, such as bruising or marks on the chest, but nothing of that nature was recorded in the report. However, he did suggest that it might have been overlooked or considered irrelevant if the doctors concerned thought they were dealing with an accidental fall. Alternatively, he suggests that, given Mr Erskine's consumption of alcohol and the, apparently, awkward way he was standing on the stairs, very little force may have been required, in which case, bruising would not have occurred.'

'So,' said Edwin, 'if someone helped Mr Erskine to fall down the stairs, who was available for that task? Joseph Hallett's own evidence puts him close to the top of the stairs.'

'And,' said Eleanor, 'from what Molly told me, Mrs Erskine was not far away, despite what she says in her statement.'

Mr Harriman pulled out the statement, scanned it, and said: 'She was tidying up in the dining room when there was a call for help.'

'But Molly said that she had seen Mrs Erskine in the corridor that leads to the rear entrance. It must have been just before Mr Erskine fell because Molly heard a commotion just after she had seen Mrs Erskine. She didn't mention Joseph Hallett though, but I suppose she couldn't see the rear entrance from where she was. And I remember now, Mrs Erskine sent Molly up to her room and told her not to come down even though, as Molly said, she had not finished her work. It's possible that Mrs Erskine dismissed Molly because she thought Mr Erskine was the father of Molly's baby and she was either punishing Molly or trying to avoid a scandal but it seems more likely that it was to deter Molly from mentioning that she had seen Mrs Erskine in the corridor. She didn't mention seeing Joseph Hallett but, Mrs Erskine probably told him that Molly had been in the corridor at the time.'

'So,' said Mr Harriman, 'if Joseph Hallett was next to the rear stairs and saw Mr Erskine fall, as he says, and he didn't push Mr Erskine, Mrs Erskine must have pushed him, witnessed by Joseph Hallett. If Joseph Hallett pushed Mr Erskine, Mrs Erskine may not have seen that happen if she was in the corridor and not the dining room, but she would have got to the stairs before anyone else and in time to ask what had happened. Either way, knowing that Molly had been in the corridor nearby Joseph Hallett and Mrs Erskine may have assumed that Molly either saw or guessed what had happened. Joseph Hallett and Mrs Erskine might both have had reason to fear Molly,' said Edwin.

'Reason enough to kill her?' asked Mr Harriman.

'I've just remembered that Mary told me she was not at work that night because she was poorly so she would not have seen or heard anything. There must have been something Molly knew about that night that Joseph Hallett and Mrs Erskine didn't want revealed.

There was silence for a moment and then Edwin said: 'We need to know where both Mrs Erskine and Joseph Hallett were on Tuesday.'

'I can't help with Joseph Hallett but I can find out about Mrs Erskine,' said Eleanor. 'I also need time to think about this new suggestion of a non-accidental fall.'

'I think we all do,' said Mr Harriman. 'It does put things in a rather different light.'

0   0   0

Eleanor and Napoleon went upstairs to Eleanor's office. Eleanor sat down at her desk to think and Napoleon sprawled on the floor beside it to snooze. Eleanor spent some time staring into space and then an equal amount of time making some notes. Then she wrote a list of the questions to which she needed answers. She had written the questions at random as they occurred to her so she went back and numbered them and made a note of how she was to find answers. There were six questions.

To find the answer to her first question, she asked James to telephone to Pilkington's Chemist on the Market Place and ask if Miss Pilkington was available. The owner of the shop was Mr William Pilkington, a pharmaceutical chemist and the employer of Mary Roberts' fiancé, Frank. For many years, Mr Pilkington had also been the Borough Meteorologist and was now assisted by his daughter, Miss Edith Pilkington. She was destined, in just over twelve months, to take over from her father and make headlines across the world as the first female appointed as an official meteorologist and also for her quirky and amusing weather reports.

When the call came through, Eleanor picked up the stand, put the earpiece to her ear and said:

'Miss Pilkington, I'm very sorry to bother you but I wonder if you could do me a favour. I need some information about the weather and my enquiry is connected to an investigation that I am undertaking for a client. . . .Yes. Oh, thank you. That is very kind of you. This is what I should like to know. . . '

Then Eleanor took a sheet of paper and on it she wrote four of her six questions, folded the sheet of paper, and put it in an envelope.

She then turned her attention to her other files and worked solidly for the rest of the morning.

0 0 0

At a quarter to one, Eleanor left Napoleon with Mrs Clayton, supervising the preparation of lunch, put on her hat, gloves, and coat, picked up the envelope from her desk, and left the office. She crossed the Market Place and then waited at the corner of Market Street, a little way away from the entrance to Mr Pilkington's shop and, after a few minutes, Mary Robert's fiancé, Frank, left the shop by the side door.

Eleanor stepped forward and said: 'Hello, Frank, had a busy morning?'

Frank turned in surprise then, recognising Eleanor, lifted his hat and said, cheerfully: 'Ay oop, Miss Harriman.'

'Frank, this isn't a chance meeting. I came to find you because I need Mary to find out some information for me and I didn't want to bother her at the hotel.'

'Ah,' said Frank, conspiratorially, 'understood. What is it you want to know? It won't get Mary into trouble will it?'

'No, not at all. It's information which she probably already has so there will be no need for her to ask questions.'

'Right you are then. Ask away.'

'There are four questions. I've noted them down for you to give to her. And perhaps, when Mary has read the questions, you had better keep this piece of paper with you. I wouldn't like it to get lost.'

'Or find its way to the hotel, eh, Miss Harriman?'

'Frank, you are very perceptive,' said Eleanor, laughing. 'You will go far.'

'I intend to, Miss Harriman.' Frank smiled and then looked at the questions. He nodded and then he said: 'I see where this is going. I've read them stories in the papers about hotels in Brighton where people go because they want a divorce. The chambermaids are asked to say what they know. Two people sharing a room or being there together in the morning when the tea's taken up. That sort of thing. How shall I get the answers to you?'

'Would you write me a note and drop it off at my office on Hall Bank on your way to work. Would that be convenient?'

'I'll call round to Mary this evening and see she gets the questions and I'll let you have your answers as soon as I can.'

'Thank you, Frank. Here is my card with the address of the office. I am very pleased that you are able to help and I know I can trust you not to mention this to anyone other than Mary.'

CHAPTER THIRTY-TWO

When Eleanor returned to the office, James said: 'Miss Pilkington called while you were out, Miss Eleanor. She left you a message.' James looked at his note and continued: 'I'm to tell you that despite the date, Saint Patrick passed a very dry night and experienced no wind at all. Miss Pilkington said she was also adding her own observation. Around nine o'clock, sky clear, still air, slight frost next morning, no rain in gauge.'

'Thank you, James. That is most curious but interesting, nevertheless.'

'Very good, Miss Eleanor. Miss Pilkington certainly knows how to make the weather more interesting.'

As it was early closing, James was in the process of closing the office and Edwin was in Mr Harriman's office, about to return home for lunch with his wife and their two boys.

Eleanor joined them and said: 'Earlier this morning, I asked Miss Pilkington about the weather on the night Mr Erskine fell down the stairs and I've just received her message. There was no wind.'

Edwin and Mr Harriman both looked at Eleanor in surprise.

'Then,' said Edwin, 'where did the gust of wind come from that banged the door shut and startled Mr Erskine into falling down the stairs?'

'I suppose the door could have banged of its own accord and Hallett just assumed that it was the wind?' said Mr Harriman.

Eleanor and Edwin gave him a look of disbelief.

'Just playing devil's advocate,' he added, in justification.

'It's possible,' said Edwin, 'but didn't Hallett also claim that it had been raining?'

'He did,' said Eleanor. 'There was no rain that night. I have asked a few other questions as well and I am hoping to have some answers by tomorrow.'

'Excellent,' said Mr Harriman, 'and speaking of answers, Doctor McKenzie has just sent me a copy of the *post mortem* report on Molly Brandon. I'll summarise and you can each read it later. Doctor McKenzie states that in many cases of asphyxiation following strangulation there has been a preceding argument with the victim or rage on the part of the attacker. Therefore, the act of strangulation is done on the spur of the moment and takes the victim by surprise without the victim being fully prepared to resist. He also notes that a certain amount of force is required to bring about asphyxiation and, at the same time, the attacker must be strong enough to hold the victim still. There are also usually marks of a struggle and an attempt on the part of the victim to free him or herself. In the case of Molly, he states:

> Examination of the body at the site revealed bruising indicative of manual strangulation together with regional venous obstruction to the neck, suggestive of considerable pressure having been applied. However, there was an absence of fingernail marks on the deceased's neck normally present and suggestive of a struggle. *Post mortem* examination confirmed that there was limited injury to the neck. No contusion haemorrhage was found in either the super-ficial or deep musculature, the hyoid bone was intact and there was no cartilage fracture. The degree of force applied would have been sufficient to cause the deceased to lose consciousness but may not have been sufficient to cause death.

'That puzzled Doctor McKenzie and, as he is very thorough, he ordered an analysis of the stomach contents and the blood. He says that a quantity of barbiturates was found in the system sufficient to have caused death. He suggests that, at the time of the attempted strangulation, the effect of the barbiturates may have been advanced enough to have prevented the deceased from resisting. This would explain the absence of evidence of a struggle. Doctor McKenzie has concluded, therefore, that the cause of death was barbiturate poisoning.'

'And if the barbiturate was *Veronal*, that might explain the bottle found at the graveside,' said Eleanor.

'And we know where that bottle came from,' said Mr Harriman.

'That means that, without the drugs, Molly might have been able to fend off the attack and she could have survived,' said Edwin. He paused and then said: 'I'm just canvassing possibilities here. Should we assume that Molly took the tablets? Or did her attacker force her to take them before attacking her to make doubly sure of her death? But how could one force another person to swallow a sufficient number of tablets to cause death? Assuming the barbiturates were in the form of tablets and came from that bottle. That sounds a bit far-fetched, doesn't it?'

'Just a bit,' said Eleanor. 'In fact, unsatisfactory because, after forcing the person to take the tablets, one would then have to wait while they took effect, giving the victim time to escape.'

'You're quite right, Eleanor,' said Edwin.

'Surely taking the tablets must have happened before the attacker arrived, otherwise if the attacker had seen her taking them, he or she would have realised that Molly was trying to kill herself and would not have gone to the trouble of strangling her,' said Eleanor. She paused and then added: 'Although only if the attacker was satisfied that enough tablets had been taken.'

'If Molly took the barbiturates voluntarily and before the attacker arrived, he or she would have been unaware that Molly was going to die anyway,' said Edwin.

'But,' said Eleanor, 'Doctor McKenzie says that the degree of force used was sufficient to cause unconsciousness but not sufficient to cause death. He doesn't say for how long that unconsciousness would have lasted. Could this be a possible explanation? The attacker thought that he or she had killed Molly by strangling her and left the scene. Molly then recovered consciousness and took the barbiturates.'

'It's possible, I suppose, but it doesn't alter the cause of death,' said Mr Harriman.

'Agreed. And we do know that Molly had access to *Veronal*. That bottle that I found in the churchyard could have been taken from Mrs Erskine's room by Molly at any time while she worked at the hotel,' said Eleanor. 'We know that while Nurse Mackay was staying at the Shakespeare, a bottle of *Veronal* disappeared and was later found. That might have been how Molly discovered that Mrs Erskine had *Veronal*. The episode Nurse Mackay told me about happened before Arthur Saunders died. Later on, after he died, Molly may have taken that same bottle or a different one supplied by Mr Pearson, and considered using it.'

'Well, with a really good defence counsel, whoever it was who attacked Molly should be able to avoid the death penalty,' said Edwin. 'Despite the apparent intention to cause death, which no doubt the prosecution will argue for, the medical evidence suggests that asphyxiation caused by strangulation was not the cause of that death. Which leaves attempted murder, or possibly just assault if intention to kill is not made out.'

'So, given this new evidence, what can we make of the evidence of the witnesses you found, Eleanor, and the time scale you drew up?' asked Mr Harriman. 'There is one other piece of information which might help with the timing of the attack. Doctor McKenzie estimates that, given the level of barbiturates detected, Molly's death could have occurred as quickly as twenty minutes after ingestion but almost certainly within sixty minutes. He estimates that she had been dead for about four or five hours when she was discovered.'

'I'm not sure whether that helps or not,' said Eleanor. 'We have so few facts from the witnesses and they seem to be contradictory. Although if Molly had been dead for four or five hours that does fit with her being attacked around the time the witnesses were near the churchyard. If she was walking from Fairfield it would have taken Molly forty five minutes to get to Christ Church, possibly longer. So, it's safe to assume that Molly didn't take the barbiturates until she arrived in the churchyard. Will Fiddler said that Molly left Fairfield at about six o'clock, so she could even have reached the churchyard as early as seven and been at Arthur Saunders' grave most of the morning trying to decide what to do. If so, Annie Ramsden would not have seen her enter the churchyard. But if the noise Annie heard was connected with Molly's death, she must have taken the tablets not long before that for them to have made it difficult to resist the attack but not yet have killed her. I am not sure how the two noises fit into that though.'

'The two witnesses could easily have been mistaken as to the time, especially this Bert character.' said Edwin. 'It must have been a reasonably loud noise to have been heard by the witnesses as they were not very close to the grave where Molly was found. If Molly was already affected by the barbiturates when she was attacked, it is unlikely that Molly made the noise. Therefore, if the yell or screech is connected with Molly's death, it must have been made by the attacker not Molly.'

'What about Percy Alcock? If Molly was already dead

when he arrived, why did he not see her body when Annie Ramsden asked him to go into the churchyard? asked Mr Harriman.

'When I was at the churchyard, last Sunday, I thought about that. He only went as far as Mellor's angel and if, at that time, Molly had been lying on the grave where she was found, he would not have been able to see her.'

'So Molly could have been attacked at the time when Annie Ramsden heard the noise. Who could have attacked her? It's going to be a process of elimination then. We have suggested that the only motive is linked to the Shakespeare Hotel. I think we need to know where Mrs Erskine and Joseph Hallett were at that time,' said Edwin.

'Yes,' said Eleanor. 'I expect to have that information fairly soon.'

'Excellent,' said Mr Harriman.

'Well done.' said Edwin. 'Right, if you will excuse me, I'm off home.'

'And, after lunch, I'm due to meet Philip for tennis.'

0 0 0

Wednesday 9th July

Met my two rascals for cricket practice at the nets this afternoon. A welcome distraction after such intensive work at the hospital. Both improving. Thomas was as entertaining as ever. Escorted them home and shared afternoon tea with them and Richard's mother. Heard all about the new Bentley of a family friend and the excursion they made to Matlock Bath recently to try it out. They seem a really delightful family. I look forward to meeting the rest of them and introducing Amelia.

CHAPTER THIRTY-THREE

On Thursday morning, Eleanor and Napoleon were just completing their morning walk and had ended up on The Slopes at the high point just past the War Memorial from which it is possible to see all of that part of the town which focusses on Spring Gardens. In the days before Buxton existed, anyone standing at this point would have been at the edge of a steep cliff looking down on the River Wye as it emerged from the sacred grove of trees and flowed north alongside an ancient trackway which would later become Spring Gardens. Now, the trees were gone and the whole area was covered by buildings, pavements, and roads.

At this time in the morning, being the main route into Buxton from the north, Spring Gardens was busy with motor cars, horse-drawn carts, hand carts, and pedestrians. At its southern end, it intersected with other roads bringing traffic in from the west, via Manchester Road and The Quadrant, and from the east, via High Street and Terrace Road. Additional traffic was also fed in from The Crescent and round the Turner Memorial. Anxious railway passengers, running late for their train and dashing across the road to reach Station Approach added to the confusion by weaving their way through the traffic. Thus, at the top of Spring Gardens, during busy periods of the day, there was a policeman on point duty regulating the traffic flow, ordering pedestrians to wait, or allowing them to cross. Eleanor and Napoleon, both being inveterate people watchers, stopped and looked down at the policeman who, using hand signals, was skilfully controlling the flow of road users. From here,

Eleanor could see the long curve of Spring Gardens and the wall of the Shakespeare Hotel that jutted out from the neighbouring buildings.

Watching other people work is always restful and, as Eleanor looked down on the scene, she let her mind drift idly from one idea to another, aware of, but not paying attention to, the movement below. Images and words flowed through her mind as well, although she didn't pay particular attention to them either. Then, from somewhere at the back of her brain an idea began to form. Creditors flowing along, someone controlling that flow, ordering them to wait, allowing others to pass. Then her attention was caught by a scene outside the Grove Hotel, one of the oldest hotels in Buxton and a former coaching inn. Two guests had emerged from the main entrance, a woman looking at her wristwatch and a man, struggling with luggage and searching about in his pocket, apparently trying to reassure himself that he had the train tickets. Looking at the Grove Hotel reminded Eleanor that it had once had a neighbour called the Angel, also a coaching inn, but that hotel no longer existed. Then a sentence came into her head, one she had heard a few days ago: "he wanted to sell the hotel." Another idea floated into her brain: something that Mrs Clayton had told her. Her brain began to focus on her thoughts. Her eyes re-focussed on the scene below. This was the way to answer the last of her six questions. She looked at Napoleon.

'Come on, Leon. I've just realised something important. We've got work to do.'

As they walked back across The Slopes to Hall Bank, Eleanor was considering how to obtain the information she needed. Mr Harriman was still in the dining room, drinking tea and reading the paper. Eleanor explained to him her idea.

He looked thoughtful and then said: 'That does seem plausible.' He nodded and then added: 'It would provide a very strong motive. I think the sooner we can establish the facts the better. How do you propose to do that.'

'I shall have to go to the library so I'll go straightaway. We have the date of death so the search shouldn't take too long. That will give us the name of the solicitor who is undertaking the Probate application. He will have all the information we need and, as Coroner, you should be able to persuade him to give you the facts.'

'I'll do my best,' said Mr Harriman, smiling.

0 0 0

Just after a quarter past nine, Eleanor left Napoleon to his post-walk, post-breakfast snooze and went up to the Town Hall and into the library. When a deceased estate was being administered, it was customary, for the benefit of creditors and other people having a claim on the estate, to publish details of the address to which a claim should be sent. The notices were published in the *Government Gazette* and in a newspaper circulating in the local area. They were usually placed by the solicitor acting for the executor and Eleanor was looking for the notice published in relation to Mr Erskine's estate in order to find the name of the solicitor who was acting. As there would most likely have been a delay of several weeks between the date of death and the date of the notice, Eleanor decided to work backwards. After about thirty minutes, she found what she was looking for, made a note of the details, and returned to Hall Bank. She gave the information to Mr Harriman and went upstairs to her office.

Eleanor unlocked one of the drawers in her office desk and took out the files she intended to work on that morning. She arranged them in the correct order on her desk and settled down to work. Napoleon was now awake and standing at the bay window, his nose to the glass pane, evidently curious about something going on in the street below.

Two minutes later, James came upstairs to Eleanor's office and said: 'Miss Eleanor, are you expecting to see anyone this morning?'

'Oh dear, have I forgotten an appointment?'

'No, you have no appointments this morning that I am aware of. That's the difficulty. A lady has just arrived asking to see you. She would not say what it is about and I suggested that she make an appointment but she insists that she must speak to you immediately. I'm a little concerned about her because she looks, well, I'm not sure how to put this, very anxious but also rather wild looking. I noticed her pacing up and down outside the front door for several minutes before she rang the bell.'

'Ah, that explains what Leon was doing. A few moments ago, he was looking out of the window at something. I had better see what this person wants. Did she give her name?'

'Mrs Saunders.'

'Oh!' said Eleanor, surprised. 'I wonder why she is here. This is connected with the death in the churchyard at Christ Church. She may have information we need. I went to see her yesterday and she slammed the door in my face. Yes, I shall see her. Would you take Napoleon upstairs for me, please.'

'Certainly, Miss Eleanor, but . . .' James hesitated. 'I know that it's not my place to comment on clients, but are you sure you should see her? The lady does look a little . . . well, not in her right mind.'

'I see,' said Eleanor, frowning. 'I definitely do need to speak to her. Is Mr Talbot available? Perhaps, we should both see her.'

'I think that might be advisable. I'll go and enquire.'

While she waited for James to return, Eleanor took out the timeline she had made as to everyone's movements on the day that Molly died and glanced at it so as to remind herself of the questions she wanted to ask Mrs Saunders.

James came back into Eleanor's office.

'Mr Talbot thinks it would be best if you both see the lady.'

'Right. I'll leave Napoleon here then and go into Mr Talbot's office. Thank you, James.'

Eleanor closed the door of her office and went into Edwin's office. She looked at him apprehensively and said:

'I'm sorry to disturb you, but James thought it best.'

'That's quite all right. James is a good judge of character. I hope Mrs Saunders will be able to add a little more information about the churchyard on the morning of Molly's death.'

James brought Mrs Saunders into Edwin's office and went back downstairs.

Eleanor was shocked at the change that had taken place in Mrs Saunders' appearance. It had only been about twenty-four hours since she first saw her. Then Mrs Saunders had seemed careworn and then angry. Now, she seemed possessed with an energy, a determination, that was quite disturbing and, as James had noted, her eyes were wild.

Edwin had stood up when Mrs Saunders arrived and indicating a chair said:

'Mrs Saunders, I'm Mr Talbot. Please, do sit down.'

Mrs Saunders ignored Edwin and remained standing. Before he could finish speaking, she looked directly at Eleanor and said: 'I've come for the baby.'

'I'm sorry, Mrs Saunders. I don't understand,' said Edwin.

'She knows,' said Mrs Saunders, still looking at Eleanor. 'My grandchild. I want my grandchild.'

Eleanor was confused and slightly alarmed. 'Do you mean Molly Brandon's baby?' she asked.

'My son's baby.' Mrs Saunders emphasised the word "son." 'Arthur's baby. Not hers. She took my son. I want his child. My grandchild.'

'But when I saw you yesterday, you . . .'

Mrs Saunders did not let Eleanor finish. 'Is it a boy or a girl?' she demanded.

'A boy,' said Eleanor. 'Molly called him Arthur.'

'How dare she! Where is he?' Mrs Saunders looked wildly from Eleanor to Edwin and back again.

Edwin said, calmly: 'Mrs Saunders, please do sit down so that we can explain.'

'What have you done with him?' she almost shrieked. 'You have no right to keep him!'

'Mrs Saunders, please do sit down and try to be calm,' said Edwin. He raised his voice slightly and looked directly at Mrs Saunders.

'Where is my grandson?' Mrs Saunders hissed, staring at Edwin. 'Tell me!'

'I am sorry. The baby died,' said Edwin, softly.

Mrs Saunders went white in the face, staring blankly at Edwin. Edwin thinking she was about to faint, steered her to the chair he had offered her. She collapsed into the chair, her head in her hands, and there was a long, keening noise.

'Can I get you some water? Or tea, perhaps?' asked Eleanor, helplessly.

Mrs Saunders did not respond. She looked up and stared straight at Edwin, her face contorted as if she were in pain.

'She killed him as well!' Mrs Saunders spat the words out. Her body was rigid with hatred. 'She bewitched my son and then she killed him. Now she's killed my grandson. She was evil. Evil!'

'Mrs Saunders, nobody killed your grandson,' said Edwin. 'The baby was still born. He was born early and was not strong enough to live. Let me assure you. There can be no doubt on that point. I have seen the doctor's report.'

Mrs Saunders stared at Edwin but whereas before she had seemed to look through him, her eyes now began to focus on him. As his words began to sink in, the rigidity slowly left her body. She began to collapse inwardly and shrink down, like a balloon when it loses air. Then, her eyes lost focus again and she looked down at the floor. Eleanor and Edwin waited in silence.

'She didn't deserve to be alive, not with my son dead and lying in his grave.'

Edwin glanced at Eleanor, raised his eyebrows questioningly. Eleanor made a small gesture to indicate that she was not sure. Edwin sat down and they waited in silence.

Eleanor thought back to her visit to Mrs Saunders. She had been so angry when Eleanor had mentioned that there was a baby and had denied that it was possible. Eleanor imagined Mrs Saunders, after she had slammed the door in Eleanor's face, sitting brooding on what Eleanor had told her. She may have gradually, grudgingly, accepted the fact of the baby because it accounted for Molly's presence on the footpath near the quarry when her son was killed. She had not known about the baby at the time and probably no-one had been able to explain why Molly had distracted her son. Then, no doubt, she had convinced herself that the baby would replace her dead son. Now, she had been deprived even of that.

Mrs Saunders started speaking, her head bowed, occasionally shaking her head, and twisting one of the buttons on her coat.

'She came between us. She took him away from me.'

Eleanor glanced at Edwin and he nodded.

Eleanor said: 'Mrs Saunders, I know you went to visit your son's grave last Tuesday. In the churchyard at Christ Church. You took him some lilies, I believe.'

'They were for my son.'

'And did you meet anyone else in the churchyard?'

'She shouldn't have been there . . . . Not on that day. Not his birthday . . . . He was my son.'

Eleanor mentally ran through the timetable she had drawn up for that day and she imagined the scene in the churchyard.

'When you reached your son's grave, Molly was there already, wasn't she?'

There was a long pause while the button twisting continued.

'At his grave. Coming between us again . . . . pretending she cared, pretending to be sorry. . . .she never cared about him as much as I did. She wasn't good enough for him. But he wouldn't listen to me. She bewitched him.'

'Did she speak to you?'

Mrs Saunders sat up straight and looked at Eleanor, eyes flashing. 'She said my son loved her and she loved him. How dare she! You don't kill people you love!'

Mrs Saunders slumped forward slightly, looked down at the floor again, and seemed lost in her own thoughts. The button twisting stopped.

Eleanor imagined the scene at the grave. Both women there to visit Arthur on his birthday. Rivals for his love. Both out of their minds with grief. Mrs Saunders suddenly confronted with the sight of the woman she blamed for her son's death. She had probably not seen Molly since the accident. All the anger and the other conflicting emotions that had built up over the months since her son's death suddenly finding a focal point, a target. Rage overtaking reason.

Edwin waited until he was sure Mrs Saunders' brief burst of anger was over and then said, very quietly: 'Mrs Saunders, on the day you visited the churchyard, Molly was found dead beside your son's grave. The doctor who went to the graveyard and examined Molly's body said that there were marks on Molly's throat. He thought that someone had grasped her very violently around the neck. Do you understand what I mean?'

Mrs Saunders looked up and met Edwin's eyes. 'If she died, it were her own fault. Because of what she had done,' she said, coldly. 'I'm not sorry.' She looked down at the floor again.

'Was anyone else in the churchyard apart from you and Molly?' asked Edwin.

Mrs Saunders shook her head without looking up.

'And then you left Molly,' said Edwin.

'Lying there. On his grave and she had no right to be there. I couldn't bear the sight of it.'

'And then you left her there and went out of the churchyard. Did you leave the same way that you went in?'

Mrs Saunders frowned as though trying to remember.

'I don't know. I ran from her as far away as I could.'

'Mrs Saunders, I don't understand exactly what happened in the churchyard and now is not the time for me to ask any further questions but you do understand that I have to advise you to go to the police and tell them that you were in the churchyard on Tuesday,' said Edwin. 'They will want to talk to you about what happened to Molly. Do you understand?'

Mrs Saunders looked up at Edwin. 'Nothing matters now. I've got no-one left.' She let out a long sigh. 'I'm ready to join my son.'

'You are not alone and I am going to arrange for someone to help you. I'm just going to make a telephone call.'

Edwin picked up the telephone stand and, when James responded, asked him to put the call through to another solicitor who was a friend of his. 'Good morning, Gerald. . . .Yes, I do need your help. . . . . *Pro bono?* Yes . . . .I have someone who needs to give a statement to the police in connection with a death . . . . I'm afraid so . . . . Are you, by any chance, available? . . . . Yes, here with me now . . . . Preferably, yes . . . . The new Superintendent . . . . I know . . . . Yes, I agree . . . .thanks awfully, Gerald.'

Edwin replaced the telephone stand on his desk and stood up.

'Mrs Saunders, if you would like to come downstairs with me and wait in the hall, I have arranged for someone to help you. He will be here in a few minutes.'

Mrs Saunders looked at Edwin but said nothing. She stood up slowly.

'This way then, please,' said Edwin, guiding her to the door.

When they had gone, Eleanor went back to her own office and was greeted enthusiastically by Napoleon. She sat on one of the visitors' chairs and Napoleon sat beside her, his chin on her lap. He could always read her mood. She fondled his ears as she reflected on the scene she had just witnessed. She pictured Mrs Saunders going to visit her son's grave on the day of his birthday. She remembered the petals from the lilies she had seen there. Percy Alcock had noticed that the flowers his passenger was carrying had a scent. Eleanor remembered what Mrs Clayton had told her about Old Walter and realised that not only was Mrs Saunders' son buried in the churchyard but her father, Walter Clough, was there too, buried not long after Arthur. She wondered if the newer grave next to where Molly had been found was Old Walter's grave. And somewhere else in that churchyard, Mrs Saunders husband had been buried five years before. After her husband died, she had probably carried on with her life, stoically, as so many women did, pushing resentment or self-pity to the back of her mind, and living only for her son. But the strength to carry on had vanished on the death of that son.

When she arrived at the churchyard and saw Molly there, young and still alive, that must have released all the resentment and unhappiness that had filled her life since her son's death. Then, Eleanor wondered how Molly had reacted at the sight of Mrs Saunders, knowing that Mrs Saunders did not approve of her. And if Molly's son had lived, would she have been as protective of him as Mrs Saunders was of Arthur? Would she have allowed Mrs Saunders to see him? Eleanor thought about the relationship between mothers and sons. What was it that could turn women into tigresses when any young female showed an interest in their son. Then she wondered why women were usually compared with tigresses and not with some other species of animal. Eleanor thought of her brother, Edgar, and remembered her mother's fondness for him, her only son and favourite child. She remembered too her mother's grief when Edgar was killed in France. If Edgar had survived the War, would her mother have fended off any woman that Edgar showed an interest in. Eleanor sighed. Napoleon sighed. He looked at her with his big, brown eyes.

Eleanor sighed again and said: 'Human relationships are far too complicated for me, Leon. Come on, let's go for a walk. And you needn't think that I was fooled by that sigh. It was not in sympathy with me. It was because you were getting bored.'

Napoleon was not listening. He was already half-way down the stairs.

CHAPTER THIRTY-FOUR

When Eleanor and Napoleon came back from their walk, Edwin was in the hall talking to James.

'Ah, have you been out walking to clear your mind?' asked Edwin.

'Exactly,' said Eleanor. 'I think you handled that interview awfully well.'

'Thank you, Eleanor. It was a difficult one, certainly. And a sad case.'

Eleanor turned to James. 'And thank you for your caution and your suggestion about the interview. I'm pleased you dissuaded me from seeing Mrs Saunders alone. It needed two people to hear that evidence.'

James nodded his appreciation of the compliment.

'One can't help feeling for someone in that position,' said Edwin. 'Losing one's family members like that. It must upset one's balance.'

'People can be rather possessive though, can't they?' said Eleanor.

'Yes,' agreed Edwin. 'That is often what causes people to be violent. You have certainly uncovered evidence of that in the past.'

'We'd best let Father know.'

They all went into Mr Harriman's office and, after they had described to Mr Harriman the interview with Mrs Saunders, Edwin said:

'From what Mrs Saunders said I have the impression that she thought she had killed Molly. Whether she intended to or not, I don't know. And I am not sure whether she will be relieved or disappointed to find that she did not. It was not appropriate for me to question her and I thought it best to leave that part of the proceedings until she has someone to advise her. Gerald Hislop, runs a pro bono service and has agreed to interview her and then advise her. If she goes to the police voluntarily it will count in her favour.'

Mr Harriman nodded. 'And as we said before, there appears to be no doubt as to the cause of death. With a decent defence council, she would certainly avoid the death penalty.'

'I doubt if she would care,' said Eleanor, 'and that is the saddest thing. She seems to have just given up and, really, who can blame her.'

'She may have given up,' said Mr Harriman, 'but others may be willing to save her. This case may prove to be very interesting from a legal point of view. I can think of several defence counsel of my acquaintance in chambers in London who would be quite eager to be briefed by Gerald Hislop, even appearing pro bono. It would afford them an excellent opportunity to display their skills as clever advocates and demonstrate their knowledge of the law, not to mention bringing them to the attention of the profession.'

'This visit from Mrs Saunders somewhat changes our perspective on both Molly's death and the Erskine matter,' said Edwin. 'There did seem to be a motive for either Mrs Erskine or Joseph Hallett in relation to the death of Molly but from what Mrs Saunders said she was the only one in the churchyard apart from Molly and she was most likely the person Bert saw running out of the Nursery Lane entrance.'

'That may be true,' said Mr Harriman, 'but Eleanor is not prepared to let go of the incident at the Shakespeare Hotel just yet. She has been gathering other information about those two individuals.'

◊ ◊ ◊

Eleanor was already in the dining room when Mr Harriman came in at lunch time.

'Ah, Eleanor, I have been meaning to tell you and it slipped my mind with all this investigating going on. I was at the Club last evening and someone mentioned that Berkeley-Trent chap. You remember, Cecily met him at Lady Carleton-West's.

'Yes, I remember. He was the guest of honour and Cecily was sitting next to him.'

'He's coming to live in Buxton. His family is friendly with the Devonshires and, of course, the Marquis of Hartington is on the board of the Devonshire Hospital. He's a doctor, well, a surgeon actually. Interested in chest complaints, and quite well-regarded, apparently. He's setting up in private practice in the Square but he's also providing his services to the Devonshire Hospital as a consultant.'

Eleanor began to laugh.

'What is so amusing?'

'I was just remembering Cecily's story of the conversation with Lady C. She'd said something that nearly made the guest of honour choke trying not to laugh. Cecily thought he was a visitor and Lady C was trying to enlist him as a donor to the Hospital Fund. Lady C obviously didn't realise that he was to be a consultant at the Hospital. She was no doubt so dazzled by the title that she didn't bother to enquire further.'

'Oh, I see what you mean.' Mr Harriman grinned. 'It probably didn't occur to her that a gentleman with a title would be a doctor. And I gather he's a fourth son, so he's probably had to make his own way in the world. His uncle is a doctor, in Harley Street. The chap I was talking to at the Club said Berkeley-Trent volunteered in 1915, only recently qualified, worked as a surgeon and ended up as a decorated hero. A DSO, no less. He risked his own life for the sake of his patients when the field hospital was under attack. There were other exploits as well.'

'Catherine told me there was to be a new consultant at the Hospital, but she didn't know his name. She didn't know much about him other than that he was a war hero. I didn't realise that she was talking about Hugo Berkeley-Trent, the dinner guest.'

'I was told he had quite a reputation both for bravery not just in the field but for ordering Generals about when he wanted medical supplies. I suspect he will be more than a match for Lady C.'

'I look forward to that contest,' said Eleanor, laughing. 'And Lady C will be determined to have Mrs Berkeley-Trent on her Hospital fund raising committee.'

'I'm afraid she's going to be disappointed there. There isn't one, as far as I know. There was, but she died at Etaples in 1918 in the influenza epidemic. She was a VAD and nursing at the hospital there. That's where they met and they hadn't been married very long.'

'Oh, that's terrible,' said Eleanor.

'Yes. Yet another casualty of that awful War. I intend to call on Berkeley-Trent and make him welcome. He's staying at the Hydro. He may wish to join the Club and will need a proposer.'

Edwin arrived and they served themselves with lunch. Halfway through their meal, James appeared at the door of the dining room. As far as he was concerned, the lunch hour was sacrosanct and, other than fire breaking out, he did not consider any reason sufficient to warrant interrupting his employers during their meal.

'James!' Mr Harriman looked at him in surprise and concern. 'Is there a problem?'

'I'm sorry to intrude, Mr Harriman, but a young man named Frank was most insistent. He said he had information which Miss Eleanor had asked to be obtained and delivered at the earliest possible moment. He requested that I give this letter to her immediately. I thought it best to deliver it.'

Eleanor said: 'Thank you, James. That was Frank who works for Mr Pilkington. He is a very capable and very energetic person. I did ask him to provide the information as soon as possible and he has taken me at my word.'

James looked much relieved and handed over the letter. He bowed and retreated.

Eleanor opened the letter and found the answers to her four questions. She said:

'These are answers to questions that I put to Mary Roberts. It occurred to me that Molly had not mentioned Joseph Hallett in relation to Mr Erskine's fall and I wondered why. Mary was not working at the hotel that day. She was away ill so she would not have known. So, I asked her to check the register. I'll just read what she has to say.

Question: Was Joseph Hallett a guest at the hotel on the 17th of March this year?

Answer: No. His name is not in the register'

'Well, that question was certainly worth asking.' said Edwin smiling.

Mr Harriman was frowning, somewhat thunderously.

Eleanor said: "I'll read the rest of the note.

Question: What was the date of his previous stay at the hotel immediately prior to the 17th of March?

Answer: He signed the register on the 16th of March. Stayed for that night only.

Question: Has Joseph Hallett stayed at the hotel since

the 17th of March?

Answer: No. His name is not in the register and I do not remember seeing him at all.

Question: Was Mrs Erskine in the hotel between twelve noon and five o'clock on Tuesday last, 1st July? If not, do you know when she left, when she returned, or where she went?

Answer: In the hotel for serving lunch, supervising. Lunch is between twelve and one o'clock. She had an appointment for two o'clock at Madam Annette's the hairdressers in Spring Gardens to get her waves re-done and I know she went there. You can always tell by the smell of the stuff they use to make the waves. She came back just before five. They take ages to set.'

When I saw Mrs Erskine, her hair was very carefully waved.' Eleanor smiled. 'I can't imagine "no nonsense" Mary being attracted by that sort of thing. There's a P.S. at the bottom. It says:

In case you have more questions, please be advised I have given notice. Tomorrow is my last day.

Mary is about to get married. I'm glad I managed to get this information in time.'

Edwin said: 'So, Mrs Erskine was nowhere near the churchyard on Tuesday when Molly died. It seems that it must have been Mrs Saunders that Bert saw running away.'

Mr Harriman frowned. 'But, going back to the Erskine matter. It's just as we thought. Joseph Hallett's witness statement is a pack of lies. He was not at the Shakespeare Hotel on the night Mr Erskine died. He cannot be accused of being directly involved in the death of Mr Erskine but his false statement leaves him open to other very serious charges.'

'Yes,' said Edwin. 'Superintendent Ferguson will have a choice of several offences, starting with being an accessory, and going down in severity from there. Mr Hallett will probably be facing a prison sentence.'

'And Mrs Erskine?'

'There will have to be an inquest,' said Mr Harriman, firmly. 'Eleanor may have uncovered a possible motive for Mr Erskine's death.'

'Well,' said Eleanor. 'We did consider whether or not Mrs Erskine might have been motivated by anger if she thought that Mr Erskine was responsible for Molly's baby. But then there was the other possible motive that I heard of from Nurse Mackay. She told me about the relationship between Joseph Hallett and Mrs Erskine. I thought perhaps that Mrs Erskine might have wanted to be free of Mr Erskine so that she could take up with Joseph Hallett. But then we discovered that there was a Mrs Hallett, which presented rather an obstacle. Also, Nurse Mackay told me that no male guest at the hotel was safe and it seems that Mrs Erskine may have used sleeping tablets to keep Mr Erskine in ignorance of her liaisons. If so, she really had no need to remove him in order to do as she pleased. Then I remembered that Molly had mentioned that Mr Erskine wanted to sell the hotel but Mrs Erskine didn't agree with that. She was trying to improve the hotel and attract a better class of guests. With Mr Erskine out of the way, Mrs Erskine was free to keep the hotel and make improvements, such as turning the old stables into garages. Money suggested a far stronger reason than love for getting rid of Mr Erskine.'

Mr Harriman turned to Edwin and said: 'Eleanor

suggested looking into the question of Mr Erskine's estate and searched for the relevant details. At the moment, I am waiting for the solicitor to telephone me. I want to discuss Mr Erskine's Will. When I telephoned this morning, I was told that Mr Dickenson was not available but would telephone me at two o'clock.'

They turned their attention back to the food on their plates, eating in silence, and mulling over the facts they now had.

Then Edwin said: 'You know, Hallett's witness statement may not be a complete pack of lies. There may be some grains of truth in there.'

'Such as?' said Mr Harriman, grudgingly, not disposed to believe that any part of it was true. 'Apart, that is, from the name and address, which I have verified myself via Mr Pearson the chemist.'

'Well, if Hallett was not at the hotel, we can discount the first part of his statement. It sounded convincing but he may be because he was just describing what he had done when looking for matches on a previous visit to the hotel. It is simple to fabricate a statement in that way and give it the ring of truth. It's an old trick used for concocting a false alibi. The second part of the statement deals with Mr Erskine's return to the hotel. Hallett's statement as to Erskine's sobriety matches the evidence of the landlord of the Milton's Head and Mr Erskine's drinking companion, so that part is true. Hallett then describes Mr Erskine's entry into the hotel. Most of that part of Hallett's statement could also be based on something he witnessed on a previous visit or even on several visits. Mr Erskine is known to be fond of drink and is a regular customer at the Milton's Head. Mr Erskine may well have been in the habit of returning to the hotel, pausing at the top of the cellar steps, intending to go down and fetch more drink. Mr Hallett may have seen him do that before. That may even be an accurate description of what happened on the seventeenth of March, it is just that Hallett didn't actually witness it.

'Mr Erskine would have been unsteady on his feet. The landlord of the Milton's Head testifies to that. Mr Erskine may have been startled by a noise, turned around, and lost his balance. Thanks to Eleanor, we know that there was no wind that night. That seems to be the only information in Hallett's statement that relates to that specific night. Some other noise or movement may have caused Mr Erskine to turn and lose his balance. Or, there may have been no noise and Mr Erskine may have been helped by a push and fell with more than natural force and suffered a more serious injury than might otherwise have been the case. Unlike Mr Erskine, people do fall downstairs and live to tell the tale. That whole sequence may actually be the truth, except for the push. The noise was simply inserted so as to hide the push, which was the real cause of the fall. If Mr Erskine had already started to lose his balance, it would have required very little force to cause the fall to be fatal and that may not have caused bruising on his chest.'

Mr Harriman nodded slowly. 'You may have a point there, Talbot. If Mrs Erskine persuaded Hallett to make that statement, she could have described to him what actually happened, just adding the banging door and omitting the push.'

'It is even possible that Hallett believed that Mrs Erskine's account was the truth,' added Edwin, 'and, in his statement, simply repeated what she had told him.'

'Yes,' agreed Eleanor, 'As far as he was concerned, he may have thought that in the second part of his statement he was describing Mr Erskine's accident truthfully. If so, he may not have considered it wrong to lie in the first part of the statement about being at the hotel.'

'In which case, he may even now still believe, that Mr Erskine's death was an accident,' added Edwin.

'But what could have persuaded him to lie and pretend that he was at the hotel?' asked Mr Harriman.

'And if he believes that Mr Erskine's death was an accident, why has he not returned to the hotel since,' said Edwin. 'Does that suggest that he came to suspect Mrs Erskine?'

'Mrs Erskine might have told him the truth and pleaded with him to save her,' suggested Eleanor. 'But why would he agree to do that unless there was some benefit to him? What has he gained by providing a false statement? His affair with Mrs Erskine must be over. Surely he would have returned to the hotel otherwise. It's been nearly four months.'

'What about this?' said Edwin. 'When he gave his statement to the police, he believed Mrs Erskine's version and then later found out something that caused him to change his mind and stay away from the hotel.'

'We noticed one discrepancy in the evidence,' said Eleanor. 'Mrs Erskine said she was in the dining room when Mr Erskine fell down the stairs. Joseph Hallett was in no position to know where she was and Mrs Erskine would have realised that and could say what suited her. However, Molly saw Mrs Erskine in the corridor which leads to the back door, she then heard a commotion, presumably Mr Erskine falling downstairs. Mrs Erskine reappeared and sent Molly to her room out of the way. Molly did not provide a statement so that information didn't become public knowledge. Presumably, Molly wasn't questioned and Mrs Erskine obviously saw to that.'

'And if Joseph Hallett didn't return to the hotel after the fall, he would not have known of Molly's version but that does not explain how he would come to doubt the version Mrs Erskine had given him,' said Edwin.

'He must have known that Mrs Erskine had big plans for the hotel. He was a regular guest,' said Eleanor. 'That was common knowledge amongst her staff. Perhaps he did believe, at first, that Mr Erskine's death was an accident, and saw an opportunity to better himself. Mrs Erskine was about to inherit the hotel, he could divorce himself from Mrs Hallett and her *Veronal* tablets, and become a landlord instead of a commercial traveller. Certainly a more settled occupation and probably more lucrative.'

'That is a plausible explanation,' said Edwin. 'And perhaps when he tried to discuss that idea with Mrs Erskine, he came to realise that his ambition would be thwarted by Mrs Erskine not taking kindly to the idea of being under the thumb of a second husband.'

'And feared that he might suffer the same fate as Mr Erskine!' said Eleanor.

'Maybe the explanation is less complicated than that,' said Edwin. 'He had put himself in a precarious position by giving his statement and he had no idea where it might lead. Maybe he realised what a fool he had been and that cured him of Mrs Erskine. Perhaps he decided that a quiet life was preferable and went home to Sheffield and his long-suffering wife.'

'I suppose it is possible that once Mrs Erskine had achieved her goal of owning the hotel, she may have tired of him and threatened to tell the police that his statement was all true and that he had pushed Mr Erskine down the stairs,' said Eleanor.

'But he would just have denied being at the hotel,' said Edwin.

'True,' said Eleanor. 'She could have altered the hotel register.' Eleanor paused for a moment, then added: 'In fact, why didn't she think to do that anyway. If she had put his name in the register, we would not have discovered that he was not in the hotel that night.'

'There is always one little mistake that gives the criminal away,' said Edwin.

'So,' said Eleanor, 'if Molly's version was correct and Mrs

Erskine was in the corridor near the back stairs and not the dining room as she claimed, and most of the second part of Joseph Hallett's statement is correct, Mr Erskine came through the back door of the hotel, unsteady on his feet from having spent several hours in the Milton's Head, and he headed for the cellar stairs to get yet more alcohol. The sight of him must have annoyed Mrs Erskine. Her sudden and unexpected appearance may have been what startled Mr Erskine and caused him to turn awkwardly. As he was beginning to lose his balance, he was pushed backwards by Mrs Erskine, in a fit of pique.'

'That sounds plausible,' said Edwin.

'All I know is that I intend to get to the bottom of this,' said Mr Harriman. 'Both Mrs Erskine and Joseph Hallett are going to tell the truth.'

'I shall be interested to hear what the solicitor acting for Mr Erskine's estate has to say,' said Edwin.

CHAPTER THIRTY-FIVE

At three o'clock, Edwin and Eleanor were sitting in Mr Harriman's office waiting to hear the result of Mr Harriman's phone call. Mrs Clayton, followed by Napoleon, brought in tea and biscuits. Mrs Clayton left and Napoleon stayed and considered the biscuits.

Mr Harriman said: 'Well, Eleanor, that was a stroke of genius on your part suggesting that we find the solicitor acting for the Erskine estate. These last couple of weeks have been full of surprises and reverses and I thought there could be no more left but I was wrong. It seems that we are now dealing with a comedy of errors. Mr Dickenson, to whom I spoke, practises in Manchester. He confirmed that he is now acting for the executor, a Mr Hillier who is a former business partner of Mr Erskine. Mr Hillier emigrated to the United States in 1914 and has been living in California for the last ten years. He had lost touch with Mr Erskine and did not hear of his death. Mr Erskine's Will was executed in 1913, after his marriage to Mrs Erskine. The Will had been drawn up by Mr Dickenson and the original was left in safe custody with him. That was the last time that Mr Dickenson had any dealings with Mr Erskine. He also was not aware that Mr Erskine had died.

'Apparently Mrs Erskine believed that the Will had been made in her favour but did not know where it was. She consulted a solicitor and he placed the usual advertisement seeking information. Mr Dickenson did not see the advertisement. He had just appointed a locum and gone on holiday. He spent two months travelling in Europe. By the time he had returned to Manchester, the other solicitor, having received no response to his advertisement, placed it again and, this time, Mr Dickenson saw the notice. He notified Mrs Erskine's solicitor and, realising that Mr Erskine had died, set about finding Mr Hillier, the executor. He also informed Mrs Erskine's solicitor that the Will was, indeed, made in favour of Mrs Erskine. Mr Dickenson was retained by Mr Hillier and began identifying the assets and liabilities of Mr Erskine's estate. When I explained to Mr Dickenson my interest in this matter, he very kindly provided me with some information about the hotel.

'It is at this point that the comedy of errors turns to tragedy. The only significant asset is the hotel, which is leasehold, of course, not freehold. Mr Dickenson held the document in safe custody. When he looked at it, he discovered that the lease was only a sub-lease and was about to expire.'

'That would explain why Mr Erskine resisted spending any money on improvements and vetoed the conversion of the old stables into garages,' said Eleanor.

'Which suggests,' said Mr Harriman, 'that he was aware that the sub-lease was about to expire.'

'But apparently he talked of selling the hotel.' said Eleanor. 'That would have given Mrs Erskine the impression that he owned the hotel.'

'Perhaps Mr Erskine deliberately misled his wife,' said Edwin.

'Then perhaps he was less of a docile drunkard than we have been led to believe,' said Eleanor.

'If so, he is certainly having his revenge,' said Mr Harriman.

Eleanor was shaking her head. 'And Mrs Erskine is unaware of any of this.'

'At the moment, yes,' said Mr Harriman. 'Mr Dickenson intends to inform her solicitors of the situation but I have no doubt that, very soon, she will also receive a notice informing her that the sub-lease will expire in October this year.'

'And the sub-lease for the hotel? Can it not be renewed?'

Mr Harriman shook his head. 'No. Another fact which he appears to have omitted to mention to Mrs Erskine is the other company which has the head lease. Mr Dickenson has explained to me the history of the site which is very interesting. The original lease for the hotel site was due to expire in 1914 and a new lease was granted to a company called F. W. Woolworth & Co. That company intended to close the hotel and develop the site as a shop, some kind of American style fancy goods store apparently. But, in September 1914 when news of the War broke, the company decided to postpone the new venture and allow the hotel to continue operating. They granted a ten year sub-lease to Mr Erskine. Mr Dickenson has contacted the solicitors acting for F.W. Woolworth & Co. and has been told that the conversion of the site is to go ahead and development plans have already been drawn up.'

'So if Mr Erskine was pushed down the cellar stairs, it was all for nothing.' said Eleanor.

'Yes,' said Mr Harriman. 'Apparently there is little else in the estate for her to inherit.'

0　0　0

The rest of Friday afternoon was devoted to tidying up loose ends. There was an exchange of information in Mr Harriman's office before closing time.

Mr Harriman said: 'I have spoken to Superintendent Ferguson about the Erskine inquest and the one for Molly. Dates have been fixed for both. I've authorised the release of Molly's body and the baby's body has also been released. Superintendent Ferguson is sending someone to speak to Mr

Brandon. We know he lives in Harpur Hill and works at the quarry so it should be easy to find him. I suppose he is aware of his daughter's death. Her name was mentioned in the newspaper report after she had been identified. If he really has disowned Molly he may not want to take responsibility for a funeral. If so, do you have any thoughts, Eleanor?'

'I think the most fitting thing would be to bury Molly and the baby together in the churchyard with Arthur Saunders,' said Eleanor. 'I am sure that is what Molly would have wanted. And, fortunately, suicides are no longer banned from burial in a churchyard. I have thought of a way to make is possible without Mrs Saunders knowing because I know she would not approve but I need help.'

'Help from whom?' asked Mr Harriman.

'As to the cost, either Molly's father or the Council. As to the burial, Mr Wilde. If Mr Brandon refuses to meet the cost of a burial, Mrs Clayton says Alf will deal with getting the Council to pay for a pauper's funeral and he will sort out the paperwork.'

'And where does Mr Wilde come in?' asked Mr Harriman.

'Well, it occurred to me that if there was a cremation instead of a burial, Mr Wilde, as sexton, might agree to bury the ashes of Molly and the baby in Arthur Saunders' grave and no-one would be any the wiser, including Mrs Saunders. Mrs Clayton says the nearest crematorium is at Sheffield.'

'That is clever but devious,' said Edwin, smiling. 'Mr Wilde is very appreciative of the way we have been able to protect Joshua and he is greatly indebted to Alf for taking Joshua on as an apprentice. I have found Mr Wilde to be a very compassionate man and he just might agree to that. I will approach him.'

'There's just one more, small thing to tidy up. I thought a wedding gift for Mary and Frank. They are a lovely couple, very well suited, and they have been very helpful,' said Eleanor. 'Unless, that is, Mary would need to be a witness at the Erskine inquest. I wouldn't want it to look like a bribe.'

Mr Harriman reflected for a moment. 'I think we are unlikely to need her. Order something suitable from Hargreaves. I'm sure Mrs Clayton will know what to suggest.'

0   0   0

Friday 10th June

Grosvenor has come back to me with plans. His work is excellent and there is very little that I would amend. Will write to ask him to proceed. Amelia arrives tomorrow.

CHAPTER THIRTY-SIX

By Saturday morning, Hall Bank had almost returned to normal and a great deal of work was done on both neglected files and the remaining loose ends. Notes were compared as James was preparing to close the office.

'Talbot, you were going to enquire from Mr Wilde whether or not Molly's ashes could be buried in the churchyard.'

'Yes, I have spoken to him. He said that he had never had such a request before, cremation being a relatively recent thing. He was concerned that if the ashes were to be buried, he would need the permission of Mrs Saunders and would also have to record the burial. However, he says that he can see no reason why they should not be scattered on the grave privately.'

'That seems a satisfactory compromise,' said Mr Harriman. 'Superintendent Ferguson telephoned a few moments ago to report that he had sent a man to interview Molly's father. He was aware of her death and has definitely disowned her. He refuses to pay a penny.'

'That does seem harsh,' said Eleanor.

'The Council will probably pay for a burial in Buxton but perhaps not a cremation as it will have to be Sheffield,' said Mr Harriman.

'They might,' said Edwin, 'I suspect the cost of cremation will be the cheaper alternative.'

'I am sure that Alf will be able to sort something out,' said Eleanor. 'He knows all the right people.'

○ ○ ○

At Top Trees that morning, preparation was underway for the Charity Bazaar. The marquee had been erected in the grounds, the gardener and the chauffeur had put up the bunting and the flags. Large potted palms had been delivered and, at the direction of Lady Carleton-West, had been positioned at various places at the entrance to the marquee and around its interior, been re-positioned, put back in their original places, swapped about, and, to the relief of the gardener and the chauffeur, had finally come to rest in what Lady Carleton-West was satisfied was a tasteful arrangement. The merchandise had been set out on the stalls, in enticing displays, supervised by Lady Carleton-West, whose advice was largely ignored. The caterers had begun arriving and Lady Carleton-West had now turned her attention to directing them instead.

At The Grange there appeared to be no sign of activity on the part of Lady Carleton-West's rivals. They had been undeterred by the threat of competition from the Top Trees Bazaar and still intended to hold their American Tea. Such an event being an altogether more relaxed affair did not require such a formidable amount of effort and the organisers were still taking tea and reading their morning newspapers.

By half past two, Richard and Thomas were sitting on the front doorstep of Oxford House awaiting the arrival of the Bentley. They were all going to the Top Trees Bazaar and Richard and Thomas were counting their money and discussing the sweets they intended to buy. Philip was in the process of collecting Eleanor from Hall Bank. They were leaving Napoleon at Hall Bank and then, after the Bazaar, intended to collect him and go on to play a round of golf at Burbage. Mr Harriman, not being fond of Bazaars, had sent a donation and was already on the High Peak golf course at

Fairfield.

Philip guided the Bentley slowly down the slope of the carriage drive beside Oxford House and brought it to a halt at the front door. There was then confusion as Richard and Thomas rushed forward to greet Philip and Eleanor and ask permission to sit in the motor car while they waited for Cecily.

Cecily came out of the front door, greeted Eleanor and Philip, and then, she saw a tall gentleman, accompanied by a lady, walking along Broad Walk. She went down the steps onto Broad Walk and walked towards them. Philip looked at Eleanor and made a questioning gesture. Eleanor shrugged.

Then Thomas spotted the tall gentleman. He nudged Richard and said: 'Look. And he's with the lady!' The two boys clambered out of the motor car and raced out onto Broad Walk to join the group.

'It looks as though introductions are being made,' said Philip. 'Perhaps we'd best get down, old thing, and join the queue.'

Eleanor laughed. 'I think I know to whom we are about to be introduced.'

The group had now reached the Bentley.

Cecily smiled at Eleanor and said: 'Eleanor, may I present . . .' but did not finish the sentence.

Thomas said proudly: 'Mr Kite!'

Mr Kite laughed, raised his hat, and made a small bow: 'Hugo Berkeley-Trent. How do you do.'

'How do you do,' said Eleanor, extending her hand and smiling.

'May I present my sister, Lady Amelia Anneresley.'

Hugo turned to the lady beside him. Eleanor recognised immediately the elegant lady she had seen in the Gardens when Richard and Thomas were flying their kite unsuccessfully.

Cecily turned to Philip and said: 'And may I present our very good friend, Mr Philip Danebridge.'

When these introductions were completed, Hugo smiled at Richard and Thomas and said: 'And Amelia and I needed no introduction to these two scamps. We're old friends, aren't we?'

'Rather!' said Richard. Thomas nodded enthusiastically.

Cecily said to Eleanor and Philip: 'Mr Berkeley-Trent has taken rooms in The Square and has been appointed as a consultant at the Devonshire Hospital.'

Eleanor said: 'Then, welcome to Buxton. I do hope you will be very happy here.'

'Thank you. With the welcome I have had so far, I am sure that I shall be,' said Hugo.

Cecily said: 'Lady Amelia lives in Cheshire but I am hoping to persuade her to spend some of The Season here.'

'Yes,' said Lady Amelia, 'Unfortunately, I must return home tomorrow. My husband, Rupert, and my two boys are coming to collect me but I shall bring the boys back for a few weeks later in The Season. I know they will enjoy it here. And, of course, we shall be regular visitors once Hugo gets settled and his new house is finished.'

'Mr Berkeley-Trent has bought some land on Bishop's Lane,' said Cecily. 'Near the bridge.'

'Next to the river?' asked Eleanor, hiding her surprise.

'Yes,' said Hugo. 'There was a difficulty about the boundary but that has all been sorted out. Apparently, there was some long-standing family dispute which the vendor's agent was aware of. No-one had ever managed to get to the bottom of it. He engaged a local solicitor who was able to uncover an obscure reference in an old document which, my solicitor informed me, settled the issue beyond doubt. My solicitor said it was a brilliant piece of detection on the part of the other solicitor, whoever he was.'

Eleanor smiled and said nothing. Philip grinned at Eleanor

and winked. Before she could decide whether or not it would be appropriate to disclose her role in the land at Bishop's Lane, Hugo turned towards Cecily and said:

'We were hoping to persuade you to walk with us to Bishop's Lane. Amelia hasn't seen the plot yet.'

'Oh,' said Cecily. 'That is a shame. We were intending to leave shortly to go to Top Trees for Lady Carleton-West's Charity Bazaar. We are duty bound to go I'm afraid.'

'Ah, yes, the famous Bazaar,' said Hugo. 'I have explained to Amelia about Lady Carleton-West and her dinner party *faux pas*. I did promise to attend this famous Bazaar and I should really honour that promise. I didn't realise that it was today. Perhaps we could all look in at the Bazaar. What say you, Amelia?'

'Yes, I think the Bazaar sounds like fun and I really should meet this formidable lady,' said Lady Amelia.

Eleanor thought back to Cecily's account of the dinner party and wondered what Lady Carleton-West would make of them all turning up to Top Trees together.

Hugo turned to Philip and said: 'Lady Carleton-West invited me to dinner just after I arrived. I had not heard of her and she had no idea that I was coming as a consultant to the Hospital. She took me for a potential wealthy benefactor, told me in great detail about her charity work raising funds for the Hospital, and tried to touch me for a donation. It was all rather embarrassing really.'

'Knowing Lady Carleton-West, she was probably just attracted by your title,' said Eleanor.

'Yes,' said Cecily. 'Mr Berkeley-Trent and I have laughed about that dinner party. Lady Amelia should really have been invited as well. It was rather a breach of etiquette.'

'Lady Carleton-West would be mortified if she knew,' said Philip. 'She's quite a stickler for the rules.'

'Would there still be time to go to Bishop's Lane after the Bazaar,' said Amelia.

'That is an excellent idea,' said Hugo. 'That way, we can mix duty with pleasure.' Turning to Philip, he asked: 'Is this the new 3 litre?'

'Yes,' said Philip 'I took delivery of it a couple of weeks ago.'

'I heard about your excursion to Matlock Bath from these two chaps,' said Hugo.

'They navigated for me,' said Philip.

'May one inspect it?' said Hugo.

'Please do,' said Philip.

Eleanor, Cecily, and Amelia looked at each other and slowly shook their heads.

'We have plenty of time before the Bazaar opens,' said Cecily. 'Shall we go inside and sit down while we wait for the motoring enthusiasts to finish. Tell us about your boys, Lady Amelia. What are their interests?'

The two mothers became absorbed in the conversation about their offspring, Philip and Hugo were absorbed in discussing the Bentley's engine, having raised the bonnet to facilitate a thorough inspection, and Richard and Thomas were listening eagerly to the conversation.

Eleanor said: 'I shall go and ask Susan to make some tea.'

She recognised an ideal opportunity to cross-examine Cecily's maid on the subject of Mr Kite.

CHAPTER THIRTY-SEVEN

Hugo had walked the short distance back to the Hydro and collected his own motor car and he, Amelia, Cecily, Richard, and Thomas all went to Top Trees together.

'Well,' said Philip, when he and Eleanor were settled in the Bentley. 'What about that, then?'

'I'm not sure what to make of it?'

'I like Hugo.'

'Because he admired your motor car?' teased Eleanor. 'Yes, I like him too.'

'Should you like him as a brother-in-law?'

'Goodness, do you think that it will come to that? Cecily has only known him a couple of weeks.'

'I shouldn't be surprised. He's clearly very impressed with Cecily and they seem to have quite a bit in common.'

'Do you remember when we were having our picnic lunch last week, Richard mentioned Mr Kite and I thought Cecily was hiding something. I have to confess that I have been so involved with Molly's death and the Erskine case over the last couple of weeks that I haven't seen Cecily as much as usual.'

'I wonder if she would have said anything, if you had seen her,' said Philip.

'Yes, when we were little, she used to keep things to herself.'

'She might have been worried about what you thought.'

'Well, I agree that Hugo seems the right sort of person for Cecily. But it's not what I think, it's what Wilfred's mother will think.'

'Yes. Has Cecily decided whether or not to go on the battlefields visit?'

'I'm not sure. If she is serious about Hugo, she might feel she ought to go.'

'To square it with Wilfred?'

'Exactly.'

'I have absolutely no desire to go back to that hell hole but I would be happy to accompany you if you wanted to go, if you thought it would be helpful.'

'I'm not sure it would be,' said Eleanor. She paused. 'No, but thank you for offering.'

'It's difficult to believe that it has been nearly ten years since the beginning of the War. There is already quite a bit planned to mark the anniversary.'

'In some ways it seems longer and in other ways is seems only yesterday. I remember those days so vividly. The lists of casualties in the newspaper. The dread of receiving a telegram. So many young men killed. It was hard to comprehend. And every time someone was killed, people turned away from the news and said: "Life must go on." It was all they could do. There didn't seem to be any alternative. But life didn't go on, did it? That was just not possible, not for a long time.'

'Not without those who were missing,' said Philip.

'And those who were left could not continue to live: they could only exist. That was all. Now, though, life has started to return. Gradually, and perhaps without us noticing. There will always be a special place in my heart for Edgar and for Alistair but I have moved forward. I feel as though I have left them behind.'

'I understand exactly how you feel,' said Philip. 'I miss being able to share things with Alistair the way we always did as boys when we were growing up and at school. In his own way, Alistair is still here, part of our shared past and visiting his grave would not change that.'

They sat for a minute in silent contemplation.

'Right, Lella,' said Philip, as he started the engine. 'To the Bazaar!'

'Oh, bother the Bazaar!' said Eleanor, crossly. Then she sighed. 'No, we must go, but let's just do our duty and then slip away as soon as we can. The others are intending to walk to Bishop's Lane afterwards so Hugo will bring them all back here in his motor car.'

'Excellent idea. We'll still have time for that round of golf. You've had a very trying week. Would hitting a small ball about help to counterbalance that?'

'I think it probably would,' said Eleanor, smiling. 'But wouldn't you prefer to take your motor car for another run?'

'We can still do both. What about the Cat and Fiddle road? I wouldn't mind trying her out on the curves.'

0   0   0

As Eleanor and Philip approached the front door of Top Trees, they exchanged greetings with Ash. He looked appreciatively at the Bentley and gave Philip a conspiratorial smile and said:

'There is no need to move your motor car, Mr Danebridge. I don't think her ladyship will have any objection to having such a fine vehicle displayed on the carriage way during the Bazaar.'

'Thank you, Ash,' said Philip.

'Although her ladyship's chauffeur will be disappointed at not having the opportunity to move it.'

'Another time, perhaps,' said Philip, smiling at Ash. 'We shan't be very long.'

'Very good, Mr Danebridge.'

They crossed the entrance hall, and went through the conservatory to the garden. As they reached the entrance to the marquee, they were accosted by the Pymble twins.

'Oh, Miss Harriman, good afternoon, and Mr Danebridge, too. How delightful.'

'How very nice to see you both,' added Miss Felicity.

Miss Pymble's bony hand gripped Eleanor's wrist. She said: 'Do you see the tall gentleman talking to Lady Carleton-West? He seems to be with the lady in the blue hat.'

'We saw him arrive earlier,' said Miss Felicity. 'Do you know who they are?'

Philip, who was standing behind the twins, looked at Eleanor and grinned.

'Yes, I do know who he is,' said Eleanor. 'He's the new consultant at the Devonshire Hospital.'

'So, he's not just visiting,' said Miss Pymble, eagerly.

Eleanor smiled as she remembered Catherine saying that all her female patients were likely to desert her on account of the new arrival.

'No, he is setting up practice here.'

'Oh, how wonderful,' said Miss Pymble.

'He's very handsome,' said Miss Felicity.

Eleanor said: 'He is The Honourable Hugo Berkeley-Trent and the lady is his sister, Lady Amelia Anneresely. Their father is the Earl of Milborough.'

'Oooh!' said the Pymble twins in chorus, eyes wide.

'They are friends of my sister. Would you like me to introduce you?' asked Eleanor.

'Could you really?' asked Miss Pymble.

'Oh, how thrilling,' twittered Miss Felicity.

Philip was afraid that the two ladies would swoon with excitement and he put out a steadying hand in case.

'I'm sure they would be delighted to meet you,' said Eleanor.

Eleanor steered a way through the crowd and Philip went to browse along the stalls and chat to people he knew. As soon as she could, Eleanor returned to Philip and they purchased quite a few items of which they had no real need.

'Really, it would be simpler to just make a donation,' whispered Eleanor.

'Must keep up appearances, old thing,' said Philip. 'Have we done our duty yet, do you think?'

'I think so. Golf?'

'What about Cecily?' asked Philip.

'I checked. Her new friends are taking her home. Let's go and collect Leon on the way.'

0 0 0

As Eleanor and Philip made their way around the golf course, Napoleon sat obediently at each tee and each green and, in between holes, meandered his way along investigating scents. They decided to dispense with the services of a caddy so that they could dawdle around at their leisure, although Philip paid the fee just the same.

When they had completed the eighth hole, Philip said:

'Feeling a bit better, old thing?'

'Yes, fully restored, thank you,' said Eleanor. 'A round of golf was an excellent cure.'

They played to the next hole and Eleanor stopped at the edge of the green, Napoleon beside her. It was Philip's turn to putt.

'I've been thinking,' said Eleanor, as she walked to the centre of the green and removed the flag.

'I thought so. You have been unusually silent for the last couple of holes.'

'I know we've decided that we don't need to go to the battlefields, but there is always Le Mans.'

Philip putted the ball and missed the hole. He turned to look at Eleanor in surprise.

'You mean the race?'

'Well, if this new Bentley is as good as you say . . .'

Philip nudged the ball into the hole. Eleanor handed him

the flag and walked to where her ball was. She putted the ball successfully.

'My round, I think.'

Philip picked up Eleanor's ball and replaced the flag. Eleanor completed the score card.

'And there's plenty of time to prepare for the next race,' said Eleanor.

Philip thought about the suggestion. 'No,' he said slowly. 'Tempting, very tempting. But not this Bentley. I don't want it to end up like the last one.'

The trio began walking back towards the club house.

'I wouldn't mind driving around the course though, just to see what it feels like.'

'And to see how quickly you could get round it?'

'Of course. That's the whole point,' said Philip.

As they walked towards the motor car, Philip gave Eleanor a sideways glance.

'You are serious, aren't you, old thing?' he said, doubting but hopeful. 'About Le Mans, I mean.'

'Absolutely serious.'

Eleanor and Napoleon got into the motor car as Philip stowed the golf bags. Philip walked around to the passenger side of the motor car and Eleanor turned to look at him. Napoleon was standing in the well between the front and back seats and he rested his chin on the side of the motor car. Philip reached out to scratch the favourite spot behind his ear.

'What about this then? We could go across with Cecily and Wilfred's parents and while they visit the battlefields, we could go on to Le Mans and do the circuit. My parents should be back in France by then as well.'

'That's a brilliant idea,' said Eleanor. She thought for a minute and said: 'You would want to do the circuit at a reasonable pace, I suppose.'

'Well, at a proper speed for a Bentley, yes.'

'And, at a proper speed for a Bentley, how long would it take to do the circuit?'

Philip considered the question. 'Three straight stretches and three tricky corners, they slow things up a bit. This year's fastest was just over nine minutes. But that wasn't a Bentley.'

'I think I can hold my breath for that long. What about Leon?'

'I'm sure he can.'

Eleanor rolled her eyes. 'I meant, would there be room for him?'

Philip looked at Napoleon, affectionately. 'Always. Our tour would be incomplete otherwise.'

0   0   0

The ashes of Molly and her baby, together with petals and leaves, were scattered on Arthur Saunders' grave at sunset one evening by Joshua Wilde and his grandfather.

Joseph Hallett was called to give evidence at the inquest held by Mr Harriman into the death of Mr Erskine and, when asked about his statement to the police, immediately confessed that he had not told the truth and admitted that he had been a fool. Mr Harriman was inclined to agree with him but asked for an explanation. Joseph Hallett admitted that he had not been at the hotel on the night Mr Erskine died and that he had merely repeated word for word Mrs Erskine's description of the incident which she had given him in a telephone conversation the day after Mr Erskine died. When asked why he had acceded to this request, he explained that Mrs Erskine was very upset and had told him that she was afraid she would be blamed for Mr Erskine's death because the handrail on the stairs was loose. She had been meaning to have it repaired and Mr Erskine might have grabbed at the loose rail and lost his balance. Both Mr

Harriman and Superintendent Ferguson failed to see the logic in this. Joseph Hallett was charged with and convicted of perverting the course of justice.

Superintendent Ferguson considered various charges against Mrs Saunders and eventually she was brought to trial. There appeared to be no evidence that she intended to kill Molly. Because of the *Veranol*, the medical evidence was inconclusive as to the cause of Molly losing consciousness. The injuries to Molly's neck were minor and not sufficient to amount to strangulation and, after much legal argument in the absence of the jury, who were convinced that something of importance was being kept from them, and after careful direction by the trial judge, Mrs Saunders was convicted of the lesser offence of common assault for which she served two months' imprisonment. As Mr Harriman had predicted, she was represented at the trial by a clever and ambitious defence counsel who went on to become a QC and eventually a judge.

Mrs Erskine had her last starring role at the Old Bailey in a trial for murder where she played to a jury of twelve men and a packed courtroom, and received daily reviews by the press. She chose to portray the role of aggrieved but forbearing wife. Professor Ballantyne came down from Edinburgh to explain the medical evidence and he impressed the jury with his performance although they did not pretend to understand his description of the mechanics of falling down a staircase. The jury did not find Mrs Erskine's performance convincing. It was their considered opinion that she had pushed her husband down the stairs in a fit of pique. She was found guilty. The trial judge donned his black cap to pronounce the sentence.

Lady Amelia Anneresley kept her promise and brought her two boys to Buxton for three weeks in August and they stayed at Oxford House, where they were visited more frequently by Hugo Berkeley-Trent than was strictly necessary even for the most doting of uncles. The Anneresley boys became firm friends with Richard and Thomas, being of a similar age and having similar interests. Batting practice continued and two new kites were built. Thomas went on to become one of the most popular and best loved radio personalities of his day.

At the shooting party in August, Lady Carleton-West made sure that her fellow guests were in no doubt as to the names of two titled persons who formed part of her social circle in Buxton but when Sir Marmaduke was asked what he thought of Berkeley-Trent, he looked puzzled and said: 'Eh? Never heard of the fella!'

In September, Cecily visited the battlefields with Wilfred's parents, feeling that it was the honourable thing to do, and then had the difficult task of explaining to Wilfred's mother that she would be changing her name from Sherringham to Berkeley-Trent. Everyone at Hall Bank was delighted with this news and Mr Harriman gave the happy couple his blessing.

Old Walter approved of the resolution of the boundary dispute, the sale of his plot of land, and the new house on Bishop's Lane. It was built to Grosvenor's plans without incident and completed in time for the wedding.

Mary and Frank lived happily ever after.

Philip and the Bentley completed the 10·7 mile circuit at Le Mans in just under nine minutes. Both Eleanor and Napoleon had their eyes shut.